COLLECTION

January 2015   February 2015   March 2015

April 2015   May 2015   June 2015

Gla
Lii
na

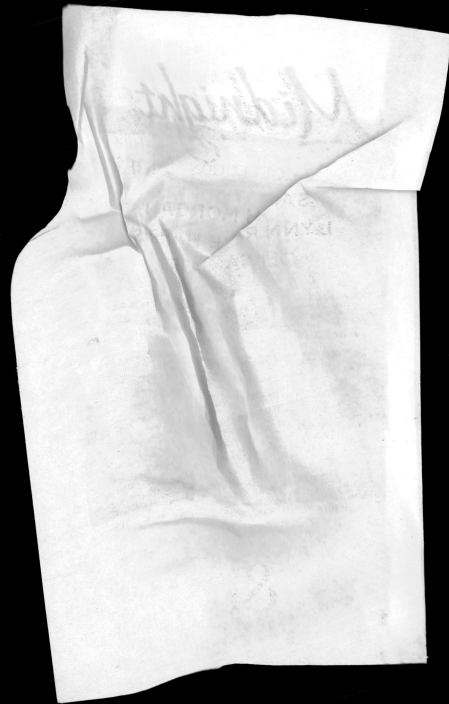

Midnight
under the
Stars

SARAH MORGAN

LYNN RAYE HARRIS

OLIVIA GATES

Published in Great Britain 2015
by Mills & Boon, an imprint of Harlequin (UK) Limited,
Eton House, 18-24 Paradise Road, Richmond, Surrey, TW9 1SR

MIDNIGHT UNDER THE STARS © 2015 Harlequin Books S.A.

Woman in a Sheikh's World © 2012 Sarah Morgan
Marriage Behind the Façade © 2012 Lynn Raye Harris
A Secret Birthright © 2012 Olivia Gates

ISBN: 978-0-263-25360-3

024-0615

Harlequin (UK) Limited's policy is to use papers that are natural, renewable and recyclable products and made from wood grown in sustainable forests. The logging and manufacturing processes conform to the legal environmental regulations of the country of origin.

Printed and bound in Spain
by CPI, Barcelona

Woman in a
Sheikh's World

SARAH MORGAN

USA TODAY bestselling author **Sarah Morgan** writes lively, sexy stories for both Mills & Boon® Modern™ and Medical Romance™. As a child Sarah dreamed of being a writer and, although she took a few interesting detours on the way, she is now living that dream. With her writing career she has successfully combined business with pleasure and she firmly believes that reading romance is one of the most satisfying and fat-free escapist pleasures available. Her stories are unashamedly optimistic and she is always pleased when she receives letters from readers saying that her books have helped them through hard times.

Sarah lives near London with her husband and two children, who innocently provide an endless supply of authentic dialogue. When she isn't writing or reading Sarah enjoys music, movies and any activity that takes her outdoors. Readers can find out more about Sarah and her books from her website: www.sarahmorgan.com. She can also be found on Facebook and Twitter.

CHAPTER ONE

S<small>HE</small> dreamed of the desert.

She dreamed of dunes turning red gold under the burning fire of the sun and of the clear blue waters of the Persian Gulf lapping beaches of soft white sand. She dreamed of savage mountains and palm-shaded pools. And she dreamed of a Prince—a Prince with eyes all shades of the night and the power to command armies.

'Avery!' He was calling her name but she carried on walking without looking back. The ground crumbled beneath her feet and she was falling, falling…

'Avery, wake up!'

She rose through clouds of sleep, the voice jarring with the image in her head. It was wrong. *His* voice was rich, deep and everything male. *This* voice was female and amused. 'Mmm?'

The delicious aroma of fresh coffee teased her and she lifted her head and stared at the mug that had been placed next to her on the table. With a groan, she sat up and reached for it, half blind from sleep. 'What time is it?'

'Seven. You were moaning. That must have been some dream.'

Avery pushed her hand through her hair and tried to wake herself up. She had the same dream every night. Thankfully when she woke it was to find herself in

London, not the desert. The discordant blare of taxi horns announced the start of the morning rush hour. No mountains and no shaded oasis—just Jenny, her best friend and business partner, pressing the button on her desk to raise the blinds.

Sunshine poured into the spectacular glass-clad office from all directions and Avery felt a sudden rush of relief to be awake and realise that the ground hadn't crumbled beneath her feet. She hadn't lost everything. This was *hers* and she'd built it from sheer hard work.

'I need to take a quick shower before our meeting.'

'When you ordered this couch for your office, I didn't realise the intention was to sleep on it.' Jenny put her coffee down on Avery's desk and slipped off her shoes. 'Just in case you don't actually know this, I feel it's my duty to point out that normal human beings go home at the end of the working day.'

The disturbing dream clung to Avery's mind like a cobweb and she tried to brush it off, irritated by how much it could affect her. That wasn't her life. *This* was.

Barefoot, she strolled across her office and took a look at her reality.

Through the floor to ceiling windows, the city sparkled in the early morning sunshine, mist wrapping the River Thames in an ethereal cloak as delicate as a bride's veil. Familiar landmarks rose through the milky haze and down on the streets below tiny figures hurried along pavements and cars were already jammed together on the web of roads that criss-crossed beneath her office. Her eyes stung from lack of sleep but she was used to the feeling by now. It had been her close companion for months, along with the empty feeling in her chest that nothing could fill.

Jenny was looking at her. 'Do you want to talk about it?'

'Nothing to talk about.' Avery turned away from the

window and sat down at her desk. *Work,* she thought. Work had been everything until her world had been disturbed. She needed to get that feeling back. 'The good news is that in my extended insomnia moment last night I finished the proposal for the launch in Hong Kong. I've emailed it to you. I think I've excelled myself this time. Everyone is going to be talking about this party.'

'Everyone always talks about your parties.'

The phone she'd left charging overnight buzzed. Back in business mode, Avery reached for it and then saw the name on the screen. Her hand froze in mid-air. *Again?* It was at least the fifth time he'd called.

She couldn't do this now. Not so close to the dream.

Her hand diverted and she switched on her computer instead, her heart thundering like a stampeding herd of wild horses. And layered under the panic was pain. Pain that he could intentionally hurt her like this.

'That's your private number. Why aren't you answering it?' Jenny peered at the screen of the phone and her head jerked up. 'Mal? The Prince is calling you?'

'Apparently.' Avery opened the spreadsheet she'd been working on and noticed with a flash of irritation that her hand wasn't quite steady. 'I should have changed my number.' He had no right to call her private line. She should have cut all ties. Should have made sure he wasn't able to call her except through the office.

'Over' should have meant just that except that he'd made sure that couldn't happen.

'All right, enough. I've ignored what's going on for too long.' Jenny plonked herself down in the chair opposite. 'I'm officially worried about you.'

'Don't be. I'm fine.' The words had been repeated so often they fell out of her mouth on their own. But they didn't convince Jenny.

'The man you loved is marrying another woman. How can you be fine? In your position I'd be screaming, sobbing, eating too much and drinking too much. You're not doing any of those things.'

'Because I didn't love him. We had an affair, that's all. An affair that ended. It happens to people all the time. Shall we get to work now?'

'It was so much more than an affair, Avery. You were in love.'

'Good sex doesn't have to mean love; I don't know why people always think that.' Did she sound calm? *Did she sound as if she didn't care?* Would anyone guess that the numbers on her screen were nonsense? She knew that people were watching her, wondering how she was reacting as the wedding of the Crown Prince drew closer. There were times when she felt like an exhibit in a zoo. It seemed that the whole world was waiting for her to drop to her knees and start sobbing.

And that, she thought, was a shame for them because they were going to be waiting a long time. She'd throw out her stilettos before she'd sob over a man. Especially a man like Mal, who would take such a display of weakness as a sign of another successful conquest. His ego didn't need the boost.

The ringing stopped and then immediately the phone on her desk rang.

Jenny looked at the phone as if it were an enraged scorpion. 'Do you want me to—?'

'No.'

'He's very insistent.'

'He's a Prince—' Avery muted her phone '—he can't help insisting. Mal only has two settings, Prince and General. Either way, he's commanding someone.' No wonder they'd clashed, she thought numbly. No relationship could have two bosses.

There was an urgent tap on the door and Chloe, the new receptionist, virtually fell into the room in her excitement. 'Avery, you'll never guess who is on the phone!' She paused for dramatic effect. 'The Crown Prince of Zubran.' Clearly she expected her announcement to have more impact than it did and when neither of them reacted she repeated herself. 'Did you hear me? *The Crown Prince of Zubran!* I tried to put him through but you weren't picking up.'

'Insistent and persistent,' Jenny murmured. 'You're going to have to answer it.'

'Not right now. Chloe, please tell him I'm unavailable.'

'But it's the Prince himself. Not his assistant or his adviser or anything, but *him*. In person. Complete with melting dark voice and a very cultured accent.'

'Give him my sincere apologies. Tell him I'll call back as soon as I can.' As soon as she'd worked out her strategy. As soon as she was confident she wasn't going to say, or do, something she'd later regret. A conversation like that had to be carefully planned.

Chloe gaped at her. 'You sound so relaxed, like it's normal to have someone like him just calling on the phone. I can't believe you know him. I'd be dropping his name into every conversation. He is so gorgeous,' she confessed in a breathy voice. 'Not just in the obvious way, although I wouldn't object if he wanted to take his shirt off and chop wood in front of me or something, but because he's just such a *man* if you know what I mean. He's tough in a way men aren't allowed to be any more because it's not considered politically correct. You just know he is not the sort to ask permission before he kisses you.'

Avery looked at their newly appointed receptionist and realised with surprise that the girl didn't know. Chloe was one of the few people not to know that Avery Scott had once had a wild and very public affair with Crown Prince Malik of Zubran.

She thought about the first time he'd kissed her. No, he hadn't asked permission. The Prince didn't ask permission for anything. For a while she'd found it exhilarating to be with a man who wasn't intimidated by her confidence and success. Then she'd realised that two such strong people in a relationship was a recipe for disaster. The Prince thought he knew what was best for everyone. Including her.

Jenny tapped her foot impatiently. 'Chloe, go to the bathroom and stick your head under cold running water. If that doesn't work, try your whole body. Whatever it takes because the Prince is not going to be kissing you any time soon, with or without permission, so you can forget that. Now go and talk to him before he assumes you've passed out or died.'

Chloe looked confused. 'But what if it's something really urgent that can't wait? You *are* arranging his wedding.'

Wedding.

The word sliced into Avery like a blade through soft flesh, the pain taking her by surprise. 'I'm not arranging his wedding.' The words almost choked her and she didn't understand why. She'd ended their relationship. Her choice. Her decision, freely made. So why did she feel pain that he was marrying another woman? In every way, it was the best possible outcome. 'I'm arranging the evening party and I sincerely doubt that he is calling about that. A Prince does not call to discuss minor details. He won't even know what's in the canapés until he puts them in his mouth. He has staff to deal with details. A Prince has staff to do everything. Someone to drive his car, cook his meals, run his shower—'

'—someone to scrub his back while he's in the shower—' Jenny took over the conversation '—and the reason Avery can't talk to him now is because I need to talk to her urgently about the Senator's party.'

'Oh. The Senator—' Visibly impressed by all the famous names flying around the office, Chloe backed towards the door, her legs endless in skinny jeans, bangles jangling at her wrists. 'Right. But I suspect His Royal Highness is not a man who is good at waiting or being told "no".'

'Then let's give him more practise.' Avery pushed aside memories of the other occasions he'd refused to wait. Like the time he'd stripped her naked with the tip of his ceremonial sword because he couldn't be bothered to unbutton her dress. Or the time he'd…

No, she *definitely* wasn't going to think about *that* one.

As the door closed behind the receptionist, Avery groped for her coffee. 'She's sweet. I like her. Once we've given her some confidence, she'll be lovely. The clients will adore her.'

'She was tactless. I'll speak to her.'

'Don't.'

'Why the hell are you doing this to yourself, Avery?'

'Employing inexperienced graduates? Because everyone deserves a chance. Chloe has lots of raw potential and—'

'I'm not talking about your employment policy, I'm talking about this whole thing with the Prince. What possessed you to agree to arrange your ex's wedding? It is killing you.'

'Not at all. It's not as if I wanted to marry him and anyway I'm not arranging the actual wedding. Why does everyone keep saying I'm arranging his wedding?' A picture of the desert at dawn appeared on her computer and she made a mental note to change her screen saver. Perhaps it was the cause of her recurring dreams. 'I'm responsible for the evening party, that's all.'

'*All*? It has the most influential guest list of any party in the last decade.'

'Which is why everything must be perfect. And I don't find it remotely stressful to plan parties. How could I? Parties are happy events populated by happy people.'

'So you really don't care?' Jenny flexed her toes. 'You and the hot Prince were together for a year. And you haven't been out with a man since.'

'Because I've been busy building my business. And it wasn't a year. None of my relationships have lasted a year.'

'Avery, it was a year. Twelve whole months.'

'Oh.' Her heart lurched. A *year*? 'OK, if you say so. Twelve whole months of lust.' It helped her to diminish it. To label it neatly. 'We're both physical people and it was nothing more than sex. I wish people wouldn't romanticize that. It's why so many marriages end in divorce.'

'If it was so incredibly amazing, why did you break up?'

Avery felt her chest tighten. She didn't want to think about it. 'He wants to get married. I don't want to get married. I ended it because it had no future.' *And because he'd been arrogant and manipulative.* 'I'm not interested in marriage.'

'So these dreams you're having don't have anything to do with you imagining him with his virgin princess?'

'Of course not.' Avery reached into her bag and pulled out a packet of indigestion tablets. There were just two left. She needed to buy more.

'You wouldn't need those if you drank less coffee.'

'You're starting to sound like my mother.'

'No, I'm not. No offence intended, but your mother would be saying something like "I can't believe you've got yourself in this state over a man, Avery. This is exactly the sort of thing I warned you about when I taught you at the age of five that you are responsible for every aspect of your life, including your own orgasm.""

'I was older than five when she taught me that bit.' She chewed the tablet, the ache in her jaw telling her that she'd been grinding her teeth at night again. *Stress.* 'You want to know why I said yes to this piece of business? Because of my pride. Because when Mal called, I was so taken aback that he was getting married so quickly after we broke up, I couldn't think straight.' And she'd been hurt. Horribly, hideously hurt in a way she'd never been hurt before. There was a tight, panicky feeling in her chest that refused to go away. 'He asked if it would feel awkward to arrange the party and I opened my mouth to say *yes, you insensitive bastard, of course it would feel awkward* but my pride spoke instead and under its direction my mouth said no, no of course it won't feel awkward.'

'You need to re-programme your mouth. I've often thought so.'

'Thanks. And then I realised he was probably doing it to punish me because—'

Jenny lifted an eyebrow. 'Because—?'

'Never mind.' Avery, who never blushed, felt herself blushing. 'The truth is, our company is the obvious and right choice for an event like that. If I'd refused, everyone would have been saying, "Of course Avery Scott isn't organising the party because she and the Prince were involved and she just can't handle it."' And he would have known. He would have known how much he'd hurt her.

But of course he already knew. And it depressed her to think that their relationship had sunk that low.

'You need to delegate this one, Avery.' Jenny slid her shoes back on. 'You're the toughest, most impressive

woman I've ever met but organising the wedding of a man
you were once in love with—'

'Was in lust with—'

'Fine, call it whatever you like, but it's making you ill.
I've known you since we were both five years old. We've
worked together for six years but if you carry on like this
I'm going to have to ask you to fire me for the good of my
health. The tension is killing me.'

'Sorry.' Out of the corner of her eye Avery noticed that
her screen saver was back again. With a rush of irritation
she swiftly replaced the desert with a stock picture of the
Arctic. 'Talk to me about work. And then I'm going to take
a shower and get ready for the day.'

'Ah, work. Senator's golden wedding party. Fussiest client we've ever had—' Jenny flipped open her book and
checked through her notes while Avery cupped her mug
and took comfort from the warmth.

'Why do you insist on using that book of yours when I
provide you with all the latest technology?'

'I like my book. I can doodle and turn clients into car-
toons.' Jenny scanned her list. 'He's insisting on fifty
swans as a surprise for his wife. Apparently they repre-
sent fidelity.'

Avery lowered the mug. 'The guy has had at least three
extramarital affairs, one of them extremely public. I don't
think this party should be celebrating his "fidelity", do
you?'

'No, but I couldn't think of a tactful way to say that
when he called me. I'm not you.'

'Then think of one and think of it fast because if he
mentions "fidelity" to his wife on the big day we'll have
a battlefield, not a party. No swans. Apart from the fidelity connotations they have very uncertain tempers. What
else?'

'You want more?' With a sigh, Jenny went back to her notes. 'He wants to release a balloon for each year of their marriage.'

Avery dropped her head onto her desk. 'Kill me now.'

'No, because then I'll have to deal with the Senator alone.'

Reluctantly, Avery lifted her head. 'I don't do balloon releases. And, quite apart from the fact that mass balloon releases are banned in lots of places, isn't our Senator working with some environmental group at the moment? The last thing he needs is publicity like that. Suggest doves. Doves are environmentally friendly and the guests can release them and have a warm, fuzzy eco feeling.' She sat back in her chair, trying to concentrate. 'But not fifty, *obviously*. Two will be fine or the guests will be covered in bird droppings.'

'Two doves.' Jenny made a note in the margin and tapped her pen on the pad. 'He is going to ask me what two doves signify.'

'A lot less mess than fifty swans—OK, sorry, I know you can't say that—let me think—' Avery sipped her coffee. 'Tell him they signify peace and tranquillity. Actually, no, don't tell him that, either. There is no peace and tranquillity in their relationship. Tell him—' She paused, grappling for the right word. *She knew nothing about long-term relationships.* 'Partnership. Yes, that's it. Partnership. The doves signify their life journey together.'

Jenny grinned. 'Which has been full of—'

'Exactly.' With her free hand, Avery closed down the spreadsheet on her computer before she could insert any more errors. 'Take Chloe to help at the Senator's party. We need to cure her of being star-stuck. It will be good experience for her to mingle with celebrities and she can help out if the doves become incontinent.'

'Why don't you let us do the Zubran wedding without you?'

'Because then everyone will say that I can't cope and, worse than that—' she bit her lip '—Mal will think I can't cope.'

Was he still angry with her? He'd been furious, those hooded black eyes as moody as a sky threatening a terrible storm. And she'd been equally angry with him. It had been a clash from which neither of them had pulled back.

Jenny looked at her. 'You miss him, don't you?'

Yes. 'I miss the sex. And the rows.'

'You miss the *rows*?'

Avery caught Jenny's disbelieving glance and shrugged. 'They were mentally stimulating. Mal is super-bright. Some people do crosswords to keep their minds alert. I like a good argument. Comes of having a mother who is a lawyer. We didn't talk at the dinner table, we debated.'

'I know. I still remember the one time you invited me for tea.' Jenny shuddered. 'It was a terrifying experience. But it does explain why you can't admit that you cared for the Prince. Your mother dedicated her life to ending marriages.'

'They were already broken when she got involved.'

Jenny closed her book. 'So this wedding is fine with you? Pride is going to finish you off, you know that, don't you? That and your overachieving personality—another thing I blame your mother for.'

'I *thank* my mother. She made me the woman I am.'

'A raving perfectionist who is truly messed up about men?'

'I won't apologise for wanting to do a job properly and I am not messed up about men. Just because I'm the child of a strong single parent—'

'Avery, I love you, but you're messed up. That one time

I came for tea, your mum was arguing the case for doing away with men altogether. Did she ever even tell you the identity of your father? Did she?'

The feelings came from nowhere. Suddenly she was back in the playground again, surrounded by children who asked too many questions.

Yes, she knew who her father was. And she remembered the night her mother had told her the truth as vividly as if it had happened just yesterday. Remembered the way the strength had oozed from her limbs and the sickness rose in her stomach.

She didn't look at Jenny. 'My father has never been part of my life.'

'Presumably because your mother didn't want him interfering! She scared him away, didn't she?' Jenny was still in full flow. 'The woman is bright as the sun and mad as a bunch of bananas. And don't kid yourself that you had to say yes to this party. You did the launch party for the Zubran Ferrara Spa Resort. That was enough to prove that you're not losing sleep over the Prince.'

The knot in Avery's stomach tightened but part of her was just relieved that the conversation had moved away from the topic of her father. 'There was no reason to say no. I wish Mal nothing but happiness with his virgin princess.' There was a buzzing sound in her head. She *had* to stop talking about Mal. It was doing awful things to her insides. Now she had hearing problems. 'I'm doing the wedding party and then that will be it.' Then everyone would stop speculating that she was broken hearted because of a man. 'You call him, Jen. Tell him I'm out of the country or something. Find out what he wants and sort it out.'

'Does his bride really have to be a virgin?' Jenny sounded curious and Avery felt something twist in her stomach.

'I think she does. Pure. Untouched by human hand. Obedient in all things. His to command.'

Jenny laughed. 'How on earth did you and the Prince ever sustain a relationship?'

'It was…fiery. I'm better at being the commander than the commanded.' The buzzing sound grew louder and she suddenly realised that it wasn't coming from her head, but from outside. 'Someone is using the helipad. We don't have a client flying in today, do we?'

As Jenny shook her head, Avery turned to look, but the helicopter was out of view, landing above her. 'It must be someone visiting one of the other businesses in our building.'

Flanked by armed bodyguards, Mal strode from the helicopter. 'Which floor?'

'Top floor, sir. Executive suite, but—'

'I'll go alone. Wait here for me.'

'But, Your Highness, you can't—'

'It's a party planning company,' Mal drawled, wondering why they couldn't see the irony. 'Who, exactly, is going to threaten my safety in a party planning company? Will I be the victim of a balloon assault? Drowned in champagne? Rest assured, if I encounter danger in the stairwell, I'll deal with it.' Without giving his security guards an opportunity to respond he strode into the building.

Avery had done well for herself since they'd parted company, he thought, and the dull ache that was always with him grew just a little bit more intense as did the anger. She'd chosen this, her business, over their relationship.

But he couldn't allow himself to think about that. He'd long since recognised the gulf between personal wishes and duty. After years pursuing the first, he was now committed to the second. Which was why this visit was professional, not personal.

If he knew Avery as well as he thought he did, then pride would prevent her from throwing him out of her office or slapping his face. He was banking on it. Or maybe she no longer cared enough to do either.

Maybe she'd never cared enough and that was just another thing he'd been wrong about.

Mal passed no one in the stairwell and emerged onto the top floor, through a set of glass doors that guarded the corporate headquarters of Avery Scott's highly successful events planning company, Dance and Dine.

This was the hub of her operation. The nerve centre of an organisation devoted to pleasure but run with military precision. From here, Avery Scott organised parties for the rich and famous. She'd built her business on hard work and sheer nerve, turning down business that wasn't consistent with her vision for her company. As a result of making herself exclusive, her services were so much in demand that a party organized by Avery Scott was often booked years in advance, a status symbol among those able to afford her.

It was the first time he'd visited her offices and he could see instantly that the surroundings reflected the woman. Sleek, contemporary and elegant. A statement of a successful, confident high achiever.

A woman who needed no one.

His mouth tightened.

She certainly hadn't needed him.

The foyer was a glass atrium at the top of the building and light flooded through the glass onto exotic plants and shimmered on low contemporary sofas. A pretty girl sat behind the elegantly curved reception desk, answering the phones as they rang.

For this visit he'd chosen to wear a suit rather than the

more traditional robes but apparently that did nothing to conceal his identity because the moment the receptionist saw him she shot to her feet, panicked and star struck in equal measure.

'Your Highness! You're…ohmigod—'

'*Not* God,' Mal said and then frowned as the colour faded from her cheeks. 'Are you all right?'

'No. I don't think so. I've never met a Prince in the flesh before.' She pressed her hand to her chest and then fanned herself. 'I feel a bit—' She swayed and Mal moved quickly, catching her before she hit the ground.

Torn between exasperation and amusement, he sat her in her chair and pushed her head gently downwards. 'Lean forward. Now breathe. That's it. You'll soon feel better. Can I get you a glass of water?'

'No.' She squeaked the word. 'Thank you for catching me. You're obviously every bit as strong as you look. Hope you didn't put your back out.'

Mal felt a flash of amusement. 'My back is fine.'

'This is seriously embarrassing. I should be curtseying or something, not fainting at your feet.' She lifted her head. 'I presume you're here to see Miss Scott. I don't suppose there is any chance you could not mention this? I'm supposed to be cool with celebrities and famous people. As you can see, it's still a work in progress.'

'My lips are sealed.' Smiling, Mal straightened. 'Sit there and recover. I'll find her myself.' At least the receptionist hadn't pretended her boss wasn't in the building, which was good because his extremely efficient security team had already confirmed that she was here. The fact that she'd refused to pick up the phone had added another couple of coals to his already burning temper but he wasn't about to take that out on this girl. He only fought with people as strong as him and he rarely met anyone who fitted that description.

Fortunately Avery Scott was more than capable of handling anything he dished out. She was the strongest woman he'd ever met. Nothing shook that icy composure. Apparently not even the fact that he was marrying another woman.

Temper held rigidly in control, he strode away from the reception desk and towards the offices and meeting rooms.

Deciding that Avery would choose a corner office with a view, he swiftly calculated the direction of the Thames. There was a large door at the end of the glass atrium and he thrust it open and there, seated behind a large glass desk and talking to another woman was Avery, immaculate as ever, that sheet of shiny blonde hair sliding over a pearl coloured silk shirt.

In those few seconds before she saw him, a tightness gripped his chest.

He felt something he only ever felt around this woman.

As always, the image she presented to the world was impeccable. She projected glamour, efficiency and capability. No one meeting Avery Scott could ever doubt that she would get the job done and that it would be done perfectly. She had an address book that would have made an ambitious socialite sob with envy but few knew the woman beneath the surface.

She'd shut him out. The closer he'd tried to get, the more she'd blocked him.

He almost laughed at the irony. He'd spent his life preventing women from getting too close. With Avery that tactic had proved unnecessary. *She* was the one who'd erected the barriers. And when he'd pushed up against those barriers too hard, she'd simply walked away.

They'd been lovers for a year, friends for longer, but

still there had been days when he'd felt he didn't know her. But there were some things he *did* know. Like the way a tiny dimple always appeared in the corner of her mouth when she smiled, and the fact that her mouth was addictive. Remembering that taste stirred up a response he'd thought he had under control.

The first time he'd met her he'd been attracted by her confidence and by the way she squeezed every drop of opportunity from life. He'd admired her drive, her success and her utter belief in herself. But the same qualities that had attracted him were the reasons they'd parted. Avery Scott was fiercely independent and terrified of anything she believed threatened that independence.

And he'd threatened it.

What they'd shared had threatened it. And so she'd ended it. Crushed what they had until there was nothing left but the pain.

People assumed that a man of his position had everything.

They had no idea how wrong they were.

Mal stood for a moment, tasting the unpalatable combination of regret and anger and at that moment she looked up and saw him.

He searched for some evidence that his unexpected appearance affected her, but there was nothing. Outwardly composed, she rose to her feet, elegant and in control and displaying the same unflappable calm she demonstrated even in a crisis. 'This is a surprise. How can I help you, Mal?' Cool. Professional. No hint that they'd once been as close as it was possible for two people to be, apart from the fact that she'd called him Mal.

His name had slipped from those glossy lips without thought and yet only a handful of close friends ever called him that. And Avery had once been in that hallowed circle. She knew his closest friends because she'd been one of them; one of the few people indifferent to his wealth or his status. One of the few people who'd treated him like a man and not like the next ruler of Zubran. For a while, when he'd been with her, he'd forgotten about duty and responsibility.

Mal thrust that thought aside along with the others. Those days were gone. Today's visit was all about duty and responsibility. He wasn't going to make this personal. He couldn't.

He was about to marry another woman.

'You didn't pick up your phone.' He dispensed with formal greetings or pleasantries, considering them unnecessary.

'I was in a meeting. You, a world leader who is generally considered an expert in the art of diplomacy, will surely understand that I couldn't interrupt a client.' She spoke in the same neutral tone he'd heard her use with difficult clients.

Somewhere deep inside him he felt his nerve endings spark and fire and he remembered that their verbal sparring matches had been their second favourite way of passing the time they spent together.

As for the first...

His libido roared to life and Mal turned to the other woman in the room, because privacy was essential for the conversation he was about to have. 'Leave us, please.'

Responding to that command without question, the woman rose. As the door closed behind her Avery turned on him, blue eyes ice-cold.

'You just can't help it, can you? You just can't help telling people what to do.'

'This is not a conversation I intend to conduct in public.'

'This is my office. My business. You are not in charge here. Whatever your reason for being here, nothing justifies you walking in without knocking and breaking up my meeting. I wouldn't do it to you. I don't expect you to do it to me.'

It was as if a high-voltage electrical current had suddenly been diverted through the room. It crackled, sizzled and threatened to leave them both singed, and it aggravated him as much as he knew it irritated her.

'Why wouldn't you take my calls?'

Two streaks of colour darkened her cheeks. 'You called at inconvenient moments.'

'And does ignoring your clients' phone calls generally work well for you? I'd always assumed that customer service is everything in your business.'

'You weren't calling about business.'

'And you weren't thinking about business when you refused to take my calls so let's stop pretending we don't know what's going on here.' Deeply unsettled by the strength of his own feelings, Mal strode to the huge glass windows that enveloped her office and reminded himself that his reason for being here had nothing to do with his past relationship with this woman. That was irrelevant. It *had* to be irrelevant. 'Nice views. You've done extraordinarily well for yourself. Your business is booming while others fold.'

'Why do you find it extraordinary? I work hard and I understand my market.'

Her reply made him smile but he kept that smile to himself. 'Less than five minutes together and already you're picking a fight.'

'You're the one who landed a helicopter on my roof and barged into my office. I would say you were the one picking the fight, Mal.'

For the first time in weeks he felt the energy flow through him. Not to anyone would he have admitted how good it felt to have someone speak without restraint. To argue with him. *To challenge—*

'I was merely congratulating you on the astonishing growth of your business in a difficult economic climate.'

'You could have done that in an email. I have absolutely no idea why you're here or why you've been phoning me every two minutes but I'm assuming you don't want to talk about guest lists or colour schemes.'

'I am not remotely interested in the details of the party. That is your job.'

'For once we're in agreement. And now I'd be grateful if you'd leave so that I can do that job.'

Sufficiently energized, he turned. 'No one but you would dare speak to me like that.'

'So fire me, Mal. Go on. Do it. Take your business elsewhere.' Those eyes locked on his and he wondered why she would be encouraging him to back out of what must be for her a prime piece of business. Under the perfectly applied make-up, she looked tired. His gaze slid to her hands and he saw her fiddling nervously with the pen she was holding.

Avery never fiddled. Avery was never nervous.

His attention caught, he watched her for a moment, trying to read her. 'I'm not firing you.'

'Then at least get to the point. Why are you here?'

'I'm here because at the moment the party cannot go ahead. Something crucial is missing.'

The mere suggestion that something might be less than perfect had her bristling defensively as she always did if anyone so much as questioned her competence. That beautifully shod foot tapped the floor. Those eyes narrowed as she mentally scrolled through the checklist she kept permanently updated in her head. 'I can assure you that nothing is "missing", Mal. I have been over the plans meticulously

and checked every last detail personally. It will all be absolutely as planned.'

She had complete confidence in her own ability and
that confidence was justified because Avery Scott never
overlooked anything. Nothing escaped her. Her attention
to detail drove her team mad. It had driven *him* mad, and
yet at the same time he'd admired it because she'd built
herself a successful business on the back of nothing but
her own hard work. This woman had never freeloaded in
her life. Nor had she ever asked anyone for anything. She
was the first woman he'd met who wasn't interested in
anything he had to offer.

For a moment he felt a pang of regret, but regret was
a sentiment he couldn't afford and he moved on quickly.

'You misunderstand me. I'm sure that everything your
company has planned is perfect, as ever.'

'So if that is the case, what can possibly be missing?'

Mal paused, hesitating because he was about to trust
her with information that he hadn't entrusted to another
living soul. Even now he was wondering whether coming
here had been a mistake.

'What am I missing? The most important thing of all,'
he drawled softly. 'I'm missing my bride.'

CHAPTER TWO

'YOUR *bride*?' The word clung to her dry mouth. Oh God, she was cracking up. The effort of holding it together was just too much. It was bad enough that he was here in person, but the fact that he was here to talk about his bride was a double blow. Did he have no tact? No sensitivity at all?

Shock cut through the sickness she felt at seeing him. She needed to think, but that was impossible with him dominating her office in that sleek dark suit that emphasised the width of those shoulders and the muscular strength of his powerful frame. It bothered her that she noticed his body. It bothered her even more to feel the answering response in her own. This office was her personal space. Having it invaded by him felt difficult and she hated the fact that it felt difficult because she so badly wanted to feel nothing. She was used to being in control of herself at all times. Wanted it most of all at *this* time.

But as that control slipped from her, she felt a buzz of panic. Over the past year she'd turned off news coverage about economic and political stability in his country. Even though her company was responsible for the evening party to follow his wedding, she'd averted her eyes from stories about that event. If she didn't need to read it, she didn't read it. When their paths crossed at events she was organizing or attending as a guest, she restricted their contact to a brief nod across a crowded room even though the only man in the room she ever saw was him. She'd avoided it all in an attempt to regain control of her life and her feelings. Everything she did, she did to protect herself. Mal had hurt her. And he'd hurt her so badly that seeing him now brought her right back to the edge.

What frightened her most wasn't the sense of power and authority that could subdue a room full of people, nor was it his spectacular looks, even though the lethal combination of dark masculinity and perfect musculature was sufficient to make happily married women contemplate infidelity. No, what frightened her—*what made her truly vulnerable*—was the sensual gleam in those dangerous black eyes.

He was the most sexual man she'd ever met. Or maybe it was just their history that made her think that about him.

The look he gave her was reserved for her and her alone. It was a look that blatantly acknowledged a past she would rather have forgotten. It made every interaction deeply personal and the last thing she wanted was personal. She wanted to forget every intimacy they'd ever shared.

He was marrying another woman.

Remembering that, she kept her tone neutral and refused to let herself respond to that velvety dark gaze that threatened to strip away every defence she'd constructed between them. This wasn't about her. It was about his bride.

'Kalila is missing?' Despite her own tangled emotions and natural instinct for self-preservation, she felt a rush of concern. She'd met Kalila on a few occasions and had found her friendly, if rather shy. The girl had seemed more than a little overwhelmed by the Prince even though they'd reportedly known one another for years. 'Are you saying she's been kidnapped or something?'

'No, not kidnapped.'

'But if she's missing, how can you be so sure she hasn't

been kidnapped? I mean, she is a princess. I suppose there are people who—'

'A note was delivered to me.'

'A note?' Her brain wasn't working properly. All she could think about was him. 'But—'

'Not a ransom note. A note from her.'

'I don't understand.' It was a struggle to concentrate. Looking at him sent images chasing into her head. Images that usually only haunted her when she slept.

'She has run away—' The words were offered up with obvious reluctance and Avery stared at him in silence. And that silence stretched so long that in the end he broke it with an impatient gesture. 'Her reasons are irrelevant.'

'Irrelevant?' She shook her head to clear it of all the thoughts she shouldn't be having. What would have driven the shy, compliant Kalila to do something so radical? 'How can her reasons possibly be irrelevant? How can you dismiss her views like that?'

'I'm not dismissing her views. But what matters is not the reasons she left, but getting her back.'

'And you don't think the two of those things might be linked? Why did she leave? For someone like Kalila to do something so dramatic, she must have had a really good reason.'

'She doesn't want this marriage.' He spoke through his teeth and Avery wondered if the tension she heard in his tone reflected his irritation at the disruption of his plans or his sentiments towards his bride-to-be.

Mal was a man who was relentlessly sure of himself, a skilled negotiator, composed and in control and she knew from personal experience that he didn't react well to anything that disrupted his plans.

'Oh dear.' It was a pathetic commentary on the situation but the best she could come up with. 'That *is* inconvenient. Hard to get married without a bride, I do see that.'

'It is far more than "inconvenient". This wedding *must* go ahead.'

'Because it is what her father wants?'

'Because it is what *I* want. I need to reassure her that our marriage can work. I need her to know I am nothing like her father. I can protect her.'

Avery stared at him numbly.

Had he ever been this protective of her? No. Of course not. And she wouldn't have wanted him to be. She didn't *need* protecting, did she? She never had. What hurt was the fact that he could move from one woman to another with such ease. 'So you're about to leap onto horseback wielding your sword to protect her. Good. That's…good. I'm sure she'll appreciate the gesture.' All this time she'd been telling herself that this marriage was no more than a political union. That he didn't have feelings for Kalila.

Clearly she'd been wrong about that, too.

He had *strong* feelings. Why else would he be so determined to go through with this?

Her throat felt thick. There was a burning sensation behind her eyes.

Fortunately he didn't notice. 'She is extremely vulnerable. Not that I'd expect you to understand that. You don't do "vulnerable", do you?'

He had no idea. 'I understand that you want to slay her dragons.'

'Whereas you would rather a man gave you a dragon so that you could slay it yourself.'

'I'm an animal lover. If you'd bought me a dragon I would have kept it as a pet.'

Once, an exchange like that would have ended in laughter. He would have challenged her. She would have challenged him right back and eventually the clash would have led where it always led—to the bedroom, or any other place that could afford them the privacy they craved.

'I simply think it would be wiser if she learned to protect herself.'

'Not every woman is like you.' There was a dark bitterness in his tone that stung wounds still not healed. She'd started to despair they ever would be.

Her stress levels soared skyward. Her jaw ached from clenching her teeth. Her insides were churning and suddenly she wished she hadn't drunk the coffee on an empty stomach. 'I do see your problem. It's hard to get married without a bride. However, while I sympathise with your dilemma and applaud your macho protective streak, which I'm sure your bride will find extremely touching, I really don't understand my role in this. I carry spares of most things, but not brides I'm afraid.'

'Kalila liked you. She admired you. She considered you her friend. Or as close to a friend as someone with her life could ever have.' His wide shoulders shifted slightly as if he were trying to ease tension and she realised that he was every bit as stressed as she was. There was a glint in those eyes, a simmering tension in that powerful frame that told her he was feeling what she was feeling. 'I'm asking for your help.'

'*My* help?' She wondered why he made her feel vulnerable. She was tall, but his height and build overpowered her. 'I don't understand how I can possibly help.' Looking at him now, she wondered how they'd ever sustained their relationship for so long. He was so autocratic. Very much the Crown Prince, a man of breathtaking power and influence. There was no sign of the man who had laughed with her and enjoyed philosophical arguments long into the night. *This* man was austere and, yes, intimidating.

Those eyes looked straight through to her mind, seeing things she didn't want him to see. He'd once told her that he could judge a person's reaction more accurately from what they did than what they said. It was a skill that had stood him in good stead in handling diplomatic tensions between neighbouring countries.

Remembering that, she stood still and did nothing. She didn't allow her gaze to slide from his. If her body language wasn't silent, then at least it was muted. 'I cannot imagine what help I can possibly offer. I organize parties. I have it on good authority that I lead a life of unimpeded frivolity.'

The glance he sent her told her that he remembered that bitter exchange as well as she did. Her business had been just one more point of contention between them.

'You are a resourceful and independent woman and you knew her. She talked to you—' he ignored her reference to their past '—I wondered if you had any idea where she might have gone. Think back to your conversations. Did she ever say anything that might be of use? Anything at all.'

She'd been trying to forget those conversations. She'd been trying to forget Kalila altogether because whenever she imagined her, she imagined her entwined with Mal and the image was so painful to view she wanted to close her eyes and scream.

Feeling her hands start to shake again, Avery clasped them behind her back. 'I honestly don't—'

'Come on, Avery, *think*! What did you talk about?' His voice was harsh. 'Several times you talked to her at parties. You helped her choose a dress when she hosted that charity dinner. You put her in touch with her wedding dress designer. She idolized you. You were her role model. She longed to be like you.'

'Really?' A small laugh escaped. Afraid that she sounded

hysterical, she clamped her mouth shut. 'Well, that's ironic. I'm sure you talked her out of that fast enough.'

His only response to that oblique reference to their shared past was a slight tightening of his beautiful mouth. 'Did she say anything?'

'No.' *Leave, why don't you? Just leave,* she thought. But of course he didn't because the Prince didn't leave until he had what he wanted. 'I honestly don't know where she would have gone.' And worry slowly uncurled itself inside her because Kalila *was* vulnerable and Avery didn't like to think of any woman being vulnerable. As soon as Mal left, she'd call her. Not that there were any guarantees that she'd pick up the phone but at least she would have tried.

'Did she mention a particular place to you?' Those ebony eyes locked on hers, his intention no doubt to increase the impact of his words. Instead he succeeded only in increasing the intimacy and the chemistry between them. His response to that was to frown. Hers was to back away, hit by such a powerful need to touch him that retreat seemed like the only option. And of course he noticed that step backwards, because he was a man who noticed everything.

The tension snapped tight between them. Heat poured through her body and into her pelvis and still he looked at her and she looked right back at him because to look away was something her pride wouldn't allow. Or maybe it was just because she couldn't. The look connected them in a way far deeper than any verbal exchange and Avery felt her stomach plunge.

'You're the one with a high-tech security team just a phone call away.' Somehow her voice sounded normal. 'Can't they track her down?'

'Not so far. We think she might have adopted a disguise, but I can't question people without raising suspicions and I want to solve this as discreetly as possible.'

'Have you talked to her friends?'

'She wasn't allowed friends. She was raised in a very protected environment.'

Avery remembered her saying as much when they'd spoken. Remembered thinking how odd it must be to live like that, a prisoner of luxury, locked away from reality.

'You're the one marrying her. You should be the one who knows where she is.'

'We've spent very little time together.' The admission was dragged from him with obvious reluctance and he paced over to the window, leaving her only with a view of his back. 'I admit that was a failing on my part. I made assumptions.'

'You always do. You always know what's best for everyone.'

The tension in his shoulders increased but he chose not to respond to that. 'That is not important right now. What is important is finding her. If this marriage does not go ahead there will be serious diplomatic consequences.'

'Diplomatic consequences?' Avery rolled her eyes in exasperation at his priorities. 'No wonder Kalila left—it's not very romantic, is it?'

'I'm surprised you're even able to recognise a romantic.' He stood like a conqueror, powerful legs spread apart as he stared down at the view.

'Why? Because I'm not romantic myself? We're not talking about me.' Reflecting on the fact that men could be truly clueless when it came to women, she tried to control her emotions. 'She really gave you no clue that she felt this way? The two of you have known each other for years.'

'We've barely spoken five words to each other.'

Avery hid her surprise. 'Oh.' *So if he didn't love Kalila, why had he been in such a hurry to marry her?* Only one explanation presented itself. They'd broken up. He was angry. He'd done it to hurt her.

'On the few occasions she spoke to me, she usually just agreed with whatever I was saying.'

Numb, Avery thought about all the lively debates they'd shared on every topic from economics to human rights and wondered how a man like Mal could be happy with a wife whose sole purpose in life was to agree with him.

He'd be bored rigid.

And it would serve him right if he were consigned to a life of misery for taking this enormous step just to score points against her.

'If she's that obedient maybe you should have just ordered her to "sit" and "stay".'

'This is *not* the time for sarcasm. I came to see if you could shed any light on her whereabouts.'

'I can't. And truly I cannot imagine why you would ask me.' And now she was just desperate for him to leave, not just because of the way he made her feel but because she wanted to call Kalila and make a few enquiries of her own.

It wasn't right that Kalila should be used as a pawn in their fight.

'You and I were friends once—' He turned his head to look at her and just for a moment she saw the past in his eyes. 'Good friends.'

What he'd introduced into the room was more frightening than any dragon. 'Mal—'

'I'm asking you as a friend. There are few enough people I can trust in my life but, despite everything, I do trust you. Whatever happened between us, I still trust you and I realise that this situation is potentially awkward—' His dark gaze fastened on her like some sort of high-tech imaging device designed to penetrate flesh and bone in the search for truth. 'If you still had feelings for me I would never have involved you. You ended our relationship so I assumed that wasn't the case. If I was wrong about that then tell me now.'

Tell him what? That she dreamed about him every night? That she found it hard to focus and that it took her twice as long to accomplish simple tasks because she was preoccupied? That in the months following their break-up she'd barely recognised the woman she'd become?

Even now, she sometimes looked in the mirror and saw a stranger staring back at her.

Avery's mouth was dry. Her heart was bumping against her chest so hard she was surprised he couldn't see it. *'If you still had feelings for me—'* No mention of *his* feelings. Which shouldn't have surprised her and certainly shouldn't have hurt. If he'd had feelings for her he wouldn't have been able to move with such ease from one woman to another.

'I don't have feelings.' She adopted the chilly tone she used when men tried to get too close to her at functions. 'My inability to help you has nothing to do with our history, but the fact that I have no useful information.'

'What did you talk about when you were together?'

'I can't remember—' she didn't *want* to remember because talking to his bride had been like sticking knives into herself '—shoes, dresses and education for women. She never talked about running away.' Or had she? The ghost of a memory flitted into her head. Avery gave a tiny frown and Mal spotted the change in her instantly, pouncing like a lion on a gazelle.

'What?'

'Nothing.' She shook her head. 'I—'

'"Nothing" is all I have to go on right now.'

'Is there a chance she might have gone into the desert?'

Mal's expression changed. His eyes were shuttered. 'Definitely not. Kalila hates the desert.'

'I know.' And she'd always thought it really odd that a girl raised in that landscape could loathe it. Even more strange that she'd agreed to marry a man whose love for the desert was widely known. 'She told me how much it scared her—' She broke off, an uncomfortable memory pricking her conscience.

His eyes narrowed as he registered the guilt in her face. 'And what advice did you offer on that topic?'

Avery felt her cheeks heat. 'We might have had a conversation about facing our fears,' she muttered. 'Just a short one.'

His mouth tightened ominously. 'And?'

'And nothing. I just said that the best way to get over being afraid of something is to just do it, which actually is very sound advice, but *obviously* that comment wasn't directed specifically at her.' But what if she'd taken it that way? Avery shifted uncomfortably, her guilt trebling as she watched the colour drain from his handsome face.

'You told her that she should go into the desert alone?'

'No, of course not!' But Avery felt a stab of panic as she realised how her words could have been interpreted. 'I just suggested that sometimes it's empowering to do something that scares you. That you learn you can cope with it and you come out stronger.'

'Or you come out dead. Do you realise how dangerous the desert is for someone with no experience or expertise in desert survival?'

'Yes! And I don't know why you're blaming me!' Her voice rose. 'I did *not* tell her to go into the desert alone.'

'Then let's hope that isn't what she's done. She would last five minutes.' Anxiety stamped into his features, Mal pulled out his phone and made a call, talking rapidly to his security team while Avery stood there, an agonized witness to his obvious worry and feeling hideously responsible for the part she'd possibly played.

What if Kalila really had taken her literally and gone into the desert alone?

Surely she wouldn't have done anything so foolish. *Would she?*

Her brain argued it back and forth and eventually she pressed her fingers to her forehead as if by doing so she might be able to shut down her thoughts. 'Look, maybe I can—'

'You've done enough. Thank you for your help. You've told me all I need to know.' He was chillingly formal. There was a hardness to him that she didn't remember ever seeing before. He was tough, yes, and she knew that most people found him intimidating, but she never had. And he hadn't found her intimidating either. Unlike many men, he hadn't been daunted by her success and that had been so refreshing.

'This is *not* my fault.' But her voice lacked conviction because deep down she was afraid that it was at least partially her fault. Had she unwittingly put the idea in Kalila's head? 'And if that is what she's done, then maybe it isn't such a bad thing. Maybe this will build her confidence in herself. I think it was very brave of her to go into the desert if that is what she's done…' Her voice tailed off as he turned on her savagely.

'Brave?' Contempt dripped from him. 'Will you think she's "brave" when she's been bitten by a scorpion? Caught in a sandstorm? Drowned in a flash flood?'

Guilt ignited her own temper. 'Maybe she'll surprise you. And maybe the experience will be the making of her. Maybe it will give her the courage to stand up for herself and tell you what she wants. And whether it does or doesn't, you should ask yourself why she finds the prospect of those things less scary than marriage. She's run into the desert to get away from you, Mal!'

The truth earned her a fierce look. 'You are assuming that her disappearance is some sort of statement about our relationship.'

'Well, that's how it looks from where I'm standing.'

'She agreed to this. She wanted this marriage.'

'How would you know? Did you even ask her? Or did you "assume" like you always assume. Maybe she didn't want this marriage and she was afraid to tell you.' Avery knew she should stop talking. Stop now, before something was said that couldn't be unsaid, but she couldn't help herself. 'Maybe marriage was the last thing she wanted.'

'Not every woman sees marriage as captivity to be avoided at all costs.' His eyes clashed with hers and her heart started to race because suddenly they weren't talking about Kalila.

They were sparring, as they'd always sparred. The only difference was that this encounter wasn't going to end with their mouths and bodies locked together. And he was clearly thinking along the same lines because a tiny frown appeared between those bold black eyebrows and his eyes darkened dangerously.

The air was stifling.

Avery wondered how the conversation had shifted from safe territory to unsafe territory. Had that been her fault or his?

'We were talking about Kalila.' She snapped the words and then hated herself for appearing anything other than calm in his presence.

'Yes. Kalila.' His voice was thick and it was clear he wasn't faring any better than she was with the direction the conversation had taken.

'All I'm saying is that maybe she expressed her opinion in the only way she was able. She voted with her feet. I don't know anything about the politics of this situation, nor do I want to, but you asked me what I thought and—'

'No, I didn't. I already know your position on marriage so I would never ask. Our opinions on that subject are in direct opposition, as we both know.'

Why did he keep bringing the subject back to her when it should have been his bride-to-be that they were discussing?

'As you rightly point out, I am unlikely to have the faintest clue what Kalila is feeling. But it's obvious she's panicking about the wedding.' And now perhaps she was lying in the desert, gasping with thirst or worse… Perhaps she was already unconscious, her frail body being pecked by giant birds.

Crap.

'What is obvious to me is that she has indeed followed your advice and gone into the desert. It would explain why we can find no trace of her in the city.' Anger shone in his eyes. 'I suppose it's too much to ask to expect you to know exactly where she went? Was there a particular place that you recommended as perfect for her to "face her fears"?'

Avery squirmed. 'No! But maybe I could—'

'You've already done more than enough.' He strode towards the door. 'Thank you for your time. I know how precious it is, so feel free to bill me.'

So that was it. He was leaving.

The pressure in her throat increased. 'Mal—'

'I have to go. I do not want to leave this innocent girl out there at the mercy of the desert and the capricious whims of the man who she is unfortunate enough to have as a father. She is extremely vulnerable.'

Avery felt something twist inside her. She felt an irrational spurt of jealousy for the woman who had dragged such tender feelings out of a man known for his lack of sentimentality. Mal was tough. A soldier and a skilled diplomat, used to dealing with the toughest of adversaries. She'd never seen him reveal any soft, sensitive feelings before. The fact that he was doing so now for another woman made her insides ache.

Whatever his reasons for marrying Kalila, it seemed he *did* care for her.

Any tension between them had been burned away by that exchange and now he was chillingly detached. 'I will let you know if the wedding party is likely to proceed. In the meantime you can put your arrangements on hold and invoice me for any costs incurred to date.'

'For goodness' sake, stop talking about money! I don't care about the money. I'm worried about Kalila, too. Wait!'

'I have a desert to search.'

'Then I'll search it with you.' The words came tumbling out of her mouth and she didn't know which one of them was the more surprised. He turned to face her, incredulity lighting his eyes.

'I beg your pardon?'

Avery took a step backwards but the words were out there now and they couldn't be withdrawn. She couldn't believe she'd actually said it. A moment ago she hadn't been able to wait for him to leave and now she was suggesting travelling into the desert with him? What the hell was she doing? When their relationship had crashed she'd almost lost everything. Everything she'd worked so hard to build. What they'd shared had been so intense, so powerful, and here she was volunteering to risk exposing those raw tender feelings again, and all so that she could help him marry another woman.

Avery wanted to pull the words back but her conscience

wouldn't let her. 'If Kalila had thought she could talk to
you, then she would have talked to you. If you do find
her—'

'*When* I find her—' His eyes promised all sorts of dire
punishments if that didn't happen and Avery swallowed.

'Of course, that's what I meant. *When* you find her,
you'll need to have a proper conversation, but what if she
won't talk to you? She's never managed to talk to you before, has she? Why would she talk to you now? She's more
likely to talk to me.'

There was a long, throbbing silence.

'Let me get this straight—' dark lashes shielded the expression in those ebony eyes '—you're offering to help find
my bride and then talk her into marrying me?'

'Absolutely.' Avery forced the words out and he stared
at her for a long moment as if he were trying to peel away
the layers and see beneath the façade she presented to the
world. 'Why not?'

Her question was greeted by prolonged silence and
then he straightened his shoulders. 'I thought maybe—'
his voice was rough '—it might be difficult for you to see
me marrying another woman.'

'Difficult?' She hoped her laugh sounded more convincing to him than it did to her. 'Why would you think
that? Our relationship is in the past, Mal. No one is more
enthusiastic to see you married than I am. How else am I
going to organize an after-wedding-party and bill you for
shedloads of money? Let's get this done.'

CHAPTER THREE

'You said *what*? OK, now I know for sure you're mad. You're going into the desert to find a wimpy princess who doesn't have the courage to speak her own mind so that she can marry the man you were in love with?' Jenny lay sprawled on the bed in Avery's apartment, watching as her friend packed. 'It's like something out of a really bad soap opera. Scratch that—no one could make this stuff up. It is going to end in tears. And those are going to be *your* tears, by the way.'

'I've never cried over a man in my life. And stop saying I was in love with him.' A skilled packer, Avery rolled a couple of shirts to prevent them creasing. 'And Kalila isn't wimpy. It's not her fault if she's been bullied into submission all her life by her father. I feel sorry for her. Better not to have a father around than have a bad one.'

'Let's leave your father issues out of this. There's enough going on without that.'

'I do not have father issues.'

Jenny rearranged the pillows and cushions on the bed and slumped against them. 'What I don't understand is why the Prince would even ask you to do this. That must have taken some nerve.'

'He didn't ask. I offered. Without a bride he can't get married and I want him married.'

'You *want* him married?'

'Of course.' Avery added two pairs of trousers to her packing. Once he was married there would be no going back. If nothing else could kill her feelings for Mal, then surely marriage would. It would bring the finality she'd been looking for. 'And I want the party to go ahead. It's bad for business if a party is cancelled.'

'So you're doing this for the business?'

'I'm doing it because I'm worried about Kalila. You should have seen the way he looked at me when I told him what I'd said to her. As if I'd pushed her into the lion's cage and locked the door from the outside. I like her.'

'Really? She sounds like a wimp to me.'

'I think she's a victim of her circumstances. She's sweet. And yes, I feel responsible.' Avery sorted through her make-up, picking out the bare minimum she needed in order to not look like a train wreck. 'And guilty. That is the last time I ever tell anyone to face their fears.'

Jenny picked up a lipgloss and tried it on the back of her hand. 'You're not responsible for the fact she clearly has appalling judgement and did something rash and stupid. Nice colour, by the way.'

'Maybe I am responsible.' Avery rescued the lipgloss and added it to her bag. 'I was the one who put the idea in her head. Without me, she wouldn't even have thought of doing something so radical.' She packed carefully, referring to the list on her phone, knowing that the right clothing might be all that stood between her and an unpleasant experience in the desert. She picked items designed to cover her, not just because of concessions towards modesty or even protection against the sun, but because she wanted to do nothing that might be remotely described as provocative. The last thing she needed was Mal thinking she was trying to attract his attention.

'This is ridiculous. You're running a business, Avery. You don't have time to gallivant off after some woman you barely know with a guy you used to date. You should have—what are those—?' Jenny stared in alarm as Avery packed her sturdy hiking boots.

'"Those" are going to save me from snake bites and scorpion stings.'

Jenny recoiled. 'OK, forget my last sentence. No wonder the Princess ran away. She isn't wimpy, she's sensible. She's thinking long-term. Better a brief stint in the desert now than a lifetime of the place. If I had to wear boots like that I wouldn't marry the Prince either. It was meant to be a glass slipper, honey, not a hiking boot.'

'The desert is beautiful. Wild and stunning.'

'This from a woman who never likes to be more than ten minutes from a spa?'

'Actually I did stay in a spa while I was there, but I also stayed in a Bedouin camp and I enjoyed that as much. It's a really romantic place.'

'You're not romantic.' Jenny shook her head slowly. 'You're in trouble; you know that, don't you?'

Yes, she knew that. 'I'm not in trouble. I know what I'm doing. I'm in control.'

Jenny flopped back against the cushions. 'So I guess this means I'll have to call the Senator myself and break the news about the swans and the balloons.'

'Yes. Just speak with authority. And if there are problems you can call me. I'll have my phone. What I might not have is a signal. But Mal will have a satellite phone so I can use that to call you. You're not to tell anyone where we are. We're going to rescue her and then make up some story to cover her absence.'

'What sort of story?'

'I don't know. The spa idea is a good one. Maybe she

and I went into the desert for a girly break or something. I just need you to be vague. If anyone asks, tell them I'm with a friend. I'll be gone two days. Three at the most.' Avery caught Jenny's expression. 'What? Why are you looking at me like that?'

'You're assuming she's going to want to come back with you, marry Mal and live happily ever after. What if it doesn't happen like that?'

'It will.'

'She ran away from him.'

'They just need to start communicating with each other. It will be fine.' *She was going to make sure it was fine.*

'I hope you're right.' Jenny handed her a bottle of sunscreen that had fallen out of her bag. 'In the meantime, you don't even know where to start looking.'

'We've got a few ideas. I've already spoken to Kalila's sister. She thinks she's probably hiding out in a desert community she was sent to when she was a teenager so we're going to start there.'

'Like a summer camp?'

'That sort of thing.' Avery found her passport and dropped it into her bag. 'It's a find-yourself, Zen type of place.'

'Camp with scorpions. Thank goodness my parents didn't send me to that one.' Jenny shuddered but Avery didn't smile because she knew her problem wasn't going to be the desert wildlife or even the inhospitable terrain.

It was Mal. Or, more specifically, her feelings about Mal.

'The scorpions aren't a problem as long as you remember to shake your boots out in the morning before you put them on and you're careful about moving rocks and things.'

Jenny curled her legs under her. 'You are the woman

who knows everything there is to know about throwing a good party. When did you learn about scorpions?'

'I spent time in the desert with Mal.' And she didn't want to think about that now. Didn't dare think about it, but of course having heard that comment Jenny wasn't about to let it go.

'He's the Crown Prince. I assumed that when he went into the desert he had jewel-encrusted tents and hundreds of people to wait on him. Surely scorpions aren't allowed in the royal presence?'

'His father sent him to spend a year with a desert tribe to understand how they lived. And he spent a couple of years in the Zubrani military after Cambridge. He knows the desert, although this is different because we're travelling into Arhmor, which is where his princess comes from. Which hat?' Avery held two of them up and when Jenny pointed she dropped it into her bag. 'Apparently we're pretending to be tourists.'

'Won't he be recognised? For that matter, won't *you* be recognised? With your blonde hair and your blue eyes, you're going to stand out like a pair of red shoes at a white wedding.'

'That's why I'm packing the hat.' Avery added a silk wrap to her packing. 'And anyway, no one will expect to see the Crown Prince of Zubran slumming it in a four-by-four, and because they don't expect to see him, they won't see him. But you make a good point. I don't think travelling in disguise is his thing. Can you grab me a baseball hat with "I love London" on it or something?'

Jenny shuddered. 'If I have to. But are you absolutely sure you're fine with travelling alone through the desert with a man you were once in love with?'

'I wasn't in love with him. I've told you that a thousand times.'

'Maybe after another thousand times I might actually believe you.' Jenny slid off the bed. 'I'm just worried this is going to be so hard for you.'

'It's not. It's going to cure me.' Avery snapped her case shut. 'Five minutes alone with Mal in the desert and he'll be driving me mad. I'll be doing everything I can to make sure he marries someone else. In fact I'll probably push her up the aisle myself.'

She was driving him mad.

Five minutes alone in her company and already Mal was asking himself how they'd ever survived a year together. No other woman had this effect on him. Certainly not the woman he was supposed to be marrying. His mouth tightened as he contemplated Kalila's obvious change of heart. Could he really blame her for running? They had no relationship and never had. He hadn't lied when he'd told Avery they'd barely spoken. What *had* been a lie was the implication that their lack of communication had been driven by Kalila's strict upbringing. In fact even when the opportunity had arisen, they'd had nothing to say to each other.

The marriage was about duty, nothing more. The deal was clearly as distasteful to Kalila as it was to him, but he'd made his choice and he'd thought she had too. And if there had been a moment in his life when he'd thought that duty and desire just might coincide, then that was in the past.

Except that the 'past' was hoisting a bag off her shoulder and glaring at him as if he were personally responsible for global warming and the economic crisis.

He was a fool to have allowed her to come. *To have put himself in this position.*

'I'll drive.' She slung her bag into the back of the four-by-four, slim and elegant in linen trousers and a long-sleeved shirt that shielded her slender arms from the sun.

That shiny blond fall of hair was restrained in a tight plait that fell between her narrow shoulder blades.

Mal dragged his eyes from the lean lines of her body and focused on her face. As always, her skin was flawless and her make-up perfect. There were no signs that she was finding the situation stressful. And why would she? She'd ended their relationship, hadn't she? And since that day—*that day now forged in his memory*—she'd shown no regrets about that decision.

'I'm driving.' He wanted to give himself something to focus on other than her. 'It will attract less attention.'

'The driver attracts more attention than the passenger. I will drive.'

'Are we going to argue every point?'

'That's up to you.' Her blue eyes were cool. 'If you're a tourist then you need to look like a tourist. Good job I brought you a gift from London.' She tossed a baseball hat at him and he caught it and read the words on the front.

'"*I love London*"?'

'I tried to get a matching T-shirt but no luck. They only had small or medium. At least you look slightly closer to "tourist" than you did five minutes ago.' Her eyes skimmed his shoulders. It was such a brief look that to an outsider it wouldn't have seemed significant but he was looking for other signs and this time he found them. The slight change in her breathing. The way she was careful to step away from him. 'Now all you have to do is stop ordering me around.'

'I have never ordered you around. You have always done exactly as you wanted to do.' Because he was still watching, he saw her expression flicker.

For a moment he thought she was going to say something personal. Possibly even admit that travelling alone together like this was far more difficult than she'd imagined it would be. But then she gave a careless smile.

'Good. So in that case you won't mind if I drive.' Breaking the connection, she opened the driver's door and was about to jump inside when he caught her arm and pulled her back to him. The contact was minimal but that was all it took, the attraction so deep, so fierce that he released her instantly. But it was too late because his body had already recognised her. This close, her perfume seeped into his senses and the scent of it was so evocative it acted like a brake to his thinking. He couldn't remember what he'd been about to say. He couldn't think about anything except how much he wanted her.

Her mouth was so close to his that he could feel the tiny shallow breaths that were her attempts to draw air into her lungs. He knew that mouth. *He wanted that mouth.*

Her eyes lifted to his and for one unguarded moment he saw something there he'd never seen before. Not pain. It was so much more than pain. Misery? Heartbreak? *Fear?* Even as he was struggling to name what he saw, it was gone—as if someone had closed a blind on a window, leaving him wondering if he'd imagined that brief glimpse into someone's strictly guarded privacy.

She was the one who looked away first. 'Fine, you drive if it bothers you so much.' There were many shades of emotion in her voice, but not the one he was looking for. He heard bored. He heard amused. He didn't hear heartbreak or pain and he assumed he'd conjured that from his own brain.

'Avery—'

Ignoring him, she strode round to the passenger side and dragged open the door. 'If you need to reinforce your masculinity behind the wheel, you go right ahead. Maybe you can spear us an antelope for lunch, or strangle us a rattlesnake with your bare hands. Whisk us up a tasty scorpion soup?' She sprang inside, lithe and athletic, the plait of her hair swinging across her back like a shiny golden rope. 'But drive at a decent pace, will you? Nothing makes me madder than tentative male drivers and you don't want to be trapped with me when I'm mad.'

Mal ground his teeth.

He didn't want to be trapped with her at all. It was already driving him mad.

Only the knowledge that she'd be useful once they found Kalila prevented him from making the decision to leave her behind.

He slid into the driver's seat. 'We will check the desert camp first. We should arrive there tomorrow morning.'

If she was unsettled at the thought of a night in the desert with him then she didn't let it show. 'You could just fly there in your helicopter.'

'Which would alert everyone to the fact that my bride has run away.' He snapped on his seat belt and eased the vehicle onto the dusty road. 'For obvious reasons I'm trying to avoid that. I'm trying to protect Kalila. If possible, I don't want her father to find out. Since my helicopter is emblazoned with the colours of the Royal Flight, using it would hardly help me stay under the radar.'

'Yes, it's not great publicity, I can see that. *The Prince and his Runaway Bride* isn't the best headline. Your PR team are going to have fun spinning that one.' As the vehicle hit a bump she gripped her seat. 'Any time you want me to drive, just let me know.'

'We have barely been moving for five minutes. You are a terrible passenger.'

'I like to be the one in control. If I'm going to die, I want to choose when and where. And generally, who with, but beggars can't be choosers.'

His mouth twitched. 'I'm an exceptionally good driver.'

'To be exceptionally good at something requires practice and you were virtually born in a chauffeur-driven armoured limousine.'

'I frequently drive myself unless I have work to do. I fly myself, too. And you know it.' He gave her a sideways glance and met her glare.

'Keep your eyes on the road. You need to be in one piece when you meet up with your little virgin princess.'

'As a matter of interest, is your objection to the fact she is a virgin or a princess?'

'I don't have any objections. It was just a descriptive phrase.'

'Interesting choice of words. You don't like Kalila?'

'I like her very much.' She leaned forward and fished in her bag for a pair of sunglasses. She slid them on, protecting her eyes from the harsh glare of the desert sun. 'I happen to think she's perfect for you.'

'Meaning?'

'She won't ever disagree with you. Whatever you do or say, you'll always be the one in charge and sweet Kalila will admire you and never question whether you're right or not because it wouldn't enter her head that you wouldn't be.'

'That could be because I *am* right.' He saw the smile curve her soft lips and felt a rush of irritation. 'Kalila is a sweet-natured, compliant young woman.'

'As I said—' she adjusted her glasses with a perfectly manicured finger '—perfect for you. Oh look! Are those gazelle?'

Dragging his eyes from those slim fingers, he followed the direction of her gaze and watched as a small herd of slender gazelle sprinted away. From this distance they appeared to be floating on the sand. 'Yes. You think I am afraid to be challenged?'

'You hate to be challenged, Mal. And it happens so rarely you're unlikely to have the opportunity to get used to it. Which is why you always assume you're right. Isn't it unusual to see herds of gazelle here? What type are they?' She reached into her bag for her phone so that she could take a photograph. 'They're *gorgeous*. So graceful.'

'They are sand gazelle—the word gazelle comes from the Arabic *ġazāl*. We support numerous conservation projects. Protecting wildlife and preserving their natural habitat is important to us. Killing and capture of all wildlife is illegal in Zubran. And you should stop changing the subject.'

'I love the colour of their coats. So pale.'

'Typical of you to comment on their appearance.' His gaze flickered briefly to the plait of blonde hair that gleamed like gold in the sunlight. 'The sand gazelle has adapted for life in the desert. The coat reflects the sun's rays instead of absorbing them and of course it provides camouflage. And, by the way, I have no objection at all to being challenged.' He knew she was trying to rile him and wondered why she would feel the need when the atmosphere in the car was already heavy with tension. 'My wife will be my equal.'

Her laughter was spontaneous and genuine and she was still laughing as she slipped her phone back into her bag. 'Sorry, but you have to admit that's funny.'

'*What* is funny?'

'You thinking that your wife will be your equal. In which universe, Mal?'

It was a struggle to hang onto his temper. 'She *will* be my equal.'

'As long as she agrees with you.' Laughter gone, she was cool and suddenly he wanted to shake that cool.

'So the thought of me marrying her doesn't upset you?'

'Why would I be upset?' The sunglasses were back on her nose, obscuring her expression. 'You are free to marry whomever you choose. It's none of my business, although I'm wishing now I'd made it my business. I should have called Kalila and given her the chance for girl talk. Poor thing.'

'Poor thing? You and I were together for over a year.'

'It felt much, much longer, don't you think? And now we're not together, which is a big relief for both of us. If you're asking me if news of your wedding was a shock, then the answer is no. I always knew you'd get married. You're the marrying kind, Mal.' Her answer was just a little too swift. A little too glib.

'And what is "the marrying kind"?'

'Someone who wants to get married, obviously. People get married for different reasons. Sometimes it's because they need financial security. Sometimes it's because they're too maladjusted to live by themselves—' she suppressed a yawn '—increasingly it's because they see divorce as a lucrative option. In your case it's because you have a sense of responsibility towards your father and your country. You feel a duty to produce children and for that you need a wife because you wouldn't contemplate any other alternative.'

Mal had forgotten just how cynical she was about marriage.

He assumed her extreme reaction was somehow linked with her own background but, apart from telling him her mother had raised her alone, she'd given him no details. They'd spent their time in the present, never revisiting the past.

Would things have been different, he wondered, if he'd questioned her more? Would it have helped if he'd gained more insight into the workings of her mind?

'You think those are the only reasons for marriage?' He drove fast, speeding along one of the wide roads that crossed the desert, wishing they'd never started this conversation. Truthfully, he didn't want to talk about his impending marriage. He didn't want to *think* about it until the moment came to make his vows. He'd delayed for as long as he could and now it was oppressively close, reality pressing in on him like dark clouds.

It was true that he'd proposed marriage to Kalila within weeks of his relationship with Avery breaking down, but there were reasons for that. Reasons he hadn't shared with her and didn't intend to share with her.

What was the point?

Her phone rang and she took the call. Already this morning she'd been on the phone to the office at least four times, addressing problems.

'Doves?' Mal failed to keep the sarcasm out of his voice as she ended yet another call. 'You really do deal with the big issues, don't you?'

'If you're implying that my business has no value then I feel obliged to point out that the success of the launch party I arranged for the opening of the new hotel in Zubran has resulted in such effective publicity that the place is now running at one hundred per cent occupancy, thus offering a considerable boost to your local economy both in terms of employment and increased tourism, which has additional benefits for the surrounding area.' Without looking up, she scrolled through her emails. 'But it's true that as well as the proven commercial benefits of employing my company, there are less tangible ones. I create memories for people. Memories that will last for ever. I am often privileged to be present at the happiest moments of people's lives. Anniversaries, engagements, weddings—moments that would undoubtedly always be special, but which I can make unforgettable. By recommending those doves that you consider to be of so little importance, I have probably saved his marriage. It's ironic, don't you think, that I, a self-confessed cynic about marriage, should be working to preserve one while you, a staunch supporter, mock my efforts.'

'I wasn't mocking you.'

'You mocked my business, Mal. You never took my business seriously.' There was a snap in her voice and she leaned her head back against the seat and closed her eyes. 'Sorry. This is history. I don't know why we're talking about it except that it passes the time.'

'I apologise,' he breathed. 'No one could fail to admire what you've achieved with your company.'

'Is it the "frivolous" nature of my business that disturbs you most, or the fact that I work like a man?'

'I don't know what you're talking about.' But he did know what she was talking about and his hands gripped the wheel just a little bit tighter.

'Oh come on, Mal! You like to think of yourself as progressive, but you're not comfortable with a woman who is as passionate about her work as a man would be. You don't think I should fly around the world, live out of suitcases and occasionally sleep in my office. That's what men do, isn't it? You believe that work is what a woman does until she finds a man, marries and has a family. It would be quaint if it weren't so exasperating.'

'I have no problems with your work ethic. I admire it.'

'From a distance. Even now, you can't admit the truth.'

'And what is "the truth"? Enlighten me.' They were snapping at each other, releasing the almost intolerable energy they created together in the only way open to them.

'You want a woman barefoot and pregnant in the kitchen. No opinions. No life of her own. That is why you are marrying Kalila.'

He was marrying Kalila because it was the only option left to him.

'This is a pointless conversation.'

Her glossy mouth curved into a smile. 'Men always say that when they've lost. Never "you're right" or "I screwed up", just "this is a pointless conversation". Do they give speeding tickets out here? Because if they do then you're going to get one. You seem angry. Are you angry?' She was pushing him and he realised just how easy he made that for her. It was doubly frustrating because normally the desert relaxed him.

'I'm concerned about Kalila. It's important that we make the edge of the mountains by dusk.' He slowed the speed fractionally, exasperated with himself for allowing her to wind him up. 'I know a good place to camp, but I want to set up while there is still some light.' That observation was greeted by silence.

'So no chance of reaching your bride tonight then?'

'If she is where her sister suspects she is, then no. We will have to stop for one night.' A night alone in the desert with this woman. He was greeting that prospect with almost as much enthusiasm as his impending wedding.

'So if her sister knew where she was going, why didn't she stop her?'

'She didn't know. Kalila sent her the same note she sent me. Jasmina was afraid of her father's reaction, so she contacted me instead. Which was fortunate because at least we have more to go on than we did before. She is covering for her sister. At the moment the Sheikh does not even know his daughter is not in her rooms.'

'Her father sounds like a real treasure. Better to not have one than have one who induces fear.'

It was the first time he'd ever heard her mention her father.

Mal turned his head and glanced at her, but she was looking forwards, a tiny frown between her eyes as she focused on the sand dunes that rose either side of them. 'I love how they change colour with the light. And the way the pattern changes—it's fascinating.'

'It's the combination of wind and sun.' He'd watched her fall in love with the exotic, mysterious dunes the first time round and he could still remember the delight on her face when she'd witnessed her first desert sunset. Another irony, he thought, that this woman who had been raised in a Western city should feel an affinity for the place of his birth while Kalila, with her desert heritage, found the place nothing short of repellent. 'Your father wasn't around when you were young?'

'Are we playing psychotherapy next?' She met question with question and he sighed, wondering what it took to get her to open up.

'In all the time I've known you, you've never talked about your father.'

'That's because there is nothing to say.' Her cool tone was like a wind blown straight from the Arctic, her words designed to freeze that line of questioning in mid-flow.

Mal refused to be deflected even though part of him was wondering why he was choosing to ask these questions now, when it was too late for them. 'Did he leave when you were young?' It was a personal question, and probably unadvised given his vow to avoid the personal, but nevertheless he asked it. He'd always assumed that her father was somehow responsible for her aversion to marriage but she'd never given him any detail.

'Why the sudden interest in my father? We were talking about Kalila's situation, not mine.'

'I'm just thinking it must have been hard for you growing up without a man in your life.'

'You're doing it again—assuming that a woman needs a man to survive.'

Mal breathed deeply, refusing to rise. 'That is *not* what I assume. Why are you deliberately misinterpreting my words?'

'I'm not. I just know you, Mal.'

'Maybe you don't.' He wondered how he could have been so blinkered. *She was afraid*. Why hadn't he seen that before?

'We both know you have very traditional views on the role of women.'

'Do not assume to know what I am thinking.'

'It's not hard to guess. You're marrying a woman you barely know so that you can have a traditional set-up and breed children.'

'Is it so wrong to think a child benefits from being raised in a traditional family unit?'

'I wasn't raised in a traditional family unit and I'm fine.'

No, he thought. *You're not fine.* 'I'm not saying that a child can't be fine with one parent. But family offers security.'

'You're talking rubbish. Take Kalila's father—would she be better off with a mother who teaches her to be strong and independent or a father who bullies her?' She spoke just a little too quickly. Was a little too anxious to move the conversation away from her own situation.

Mal thought of his own father. Strict, yes, and often busy, of course. But never too busy to spend time with his son. 'Your mother didn't remarry?'

'I don't know why you're going on about fathers. Kalila's has frightened her into running away and yours has pressured you to marry a woman you barely know.'

She hadn't answered his question. 'He didn't pressure me.' This was the point where he should tell her the truth about his union with Kalila but something held him back. 'We are well suited.'

'Because you give out the orders and she says yes? That's not a relationship, Mal. That's servitude. You've barely had a conversation with her. You know nothing about her likes and dislikes and you have no idea why she's run away or where she could be heading. None of that suggests an unbreakable bond.'

Their conversations had always been lively, but never before today had she been so openly antagonistic. It was as if she were trying to goad him.

'I have a great deal of respect for Kalila and I value her opinion.'

'When has she ever expressed an opinion? When has she ever actually voiced a thought that isn't yours?'

'Perhaps we think alike.'

Her beautiful mouth twisted into a wry smile. 'More likely she's afraid to tell you what she really thinks. Or perhaps she doesn't even *know* what she really thinks because she's never been allowed to find out. You need to do something about that, Your Highness. Not only is it politically incorrect to want a passive wife, it's going to bore you in five minutes.' The car bumped into a pothole and she winced. 'And while you're ruling the world, you really do need to do something about the state of your roads.'

And the state of his nerves. He was tense. On edge. *Angry.* 'This road is not my responsibility. We left Zubran half an hour ago. You are now in Arhmor and infrastructure has never been a high priority for the Sheikh.' The scenery had changed. They were approaching mountains and the road was rougher. Everything about Arhmor was rougher. 'Let's hope we don't blow a tyre. This is not somewhere to break down.'

'So instead of mending his roads, the Sheikh tries to

build his empire. I suppose that's what this marriage is about, is it? You are the wealthier state. I assume he's hoping that if you marry his daughter, you'll fix his roads for him.'

'It's true that this marriage will bring political advantages—' Mal turned the wheel to avoid another deep rut in the road '—but that is not the only reason for the marriage. Kalila is a princess with an impeccable bloodline.'

'You make her sound like breeding stock. On the other hand, I suppose that's what she is. A brood mare to produce lots of little Sultans for the future.' Her tone flippant, she turned her head and looked over her shoulder. 'Are you sure you're taking the right route? Because according to the sat nav you should have turned left back there. You should have let me drive. Everyone knows a man can't do two things at once.'

She was definitely goading him.

What he didn't understand was why. Why would she want to make this journey more difficult and unpleasant than it already was?

Mal breathed deeply, transferred his gaze to the screen and cursed softly. She was right. He'd missed an important turning. Not because he couldn't do two things at once, but because he'd been so distracted by Avery and by his impending marriage that he hadn't been concentrating. Slamming the vehicle into reverse, he took the correct route. Around them, the landscape grew steadily more bleak and barren. 'Say one word and I'll dump you by the side of the road.'

'I wouldn't dream of making a sound.' It was clear from her voice that she was enjoying his mistake and he tightened his grip on the wheel.

'You're infuriating, you know that, don't you?'

'Because I pointed out you were going the wrong way?'

'I'm perfectly capable of driving. If you want to pick a fight, you're going to have to choose a different battleground.'

'This is why our relationship ended. Because we can't be civil to each other for five minutes. The only thing we were ever really good at as a couple was fighting.'

So that was it. That was the game she was playing.

She was snapping because she was terrified of what they'd once shared. She was terrified that if she stopped snapping, something else would happen. Something far, far more dangerous.

Wondering how he could have been so dense, Mal slammed his foot on the brake and the car stopped suddenly.

Anger throbbing inside him, he turned to look at her. 'That is *not* why our relationship ended.' His voice thickened with emotion and he wondered what it was about this woman that triggered such extreme feelings. 'And we were good at a great deal more than fighting.' He saw the change in her. Saw her spine grow rigid and her breathing grow shallow.

'No, we weren't.'

'We both know *exactly* why our relationship ended, Avery, and it had nothing to do with the arguments.'

Her skin was flawless, smooth and very, very pale. Her mouth was a tight line in her beautiful face. 'There is nothing to be gained by talking about this.'

'Maybe not, but we're talking about it anyway.'

'Mal—'

'Our relationship ended because I asked you to marry me,' he said harshly. 'And you said no. *That's* why it ended.'

CHAPTER FOUR

'STOP the car!' For a fleeting second she'd tried telling herself that it wasn't worth going over this, but her emotions were too raw for that. She was so angry that all of her was shaking. Her knees. Her hands… 'Stop the damn car, *right now*.' She was out of the door before the vehicle came to a standstill and Mal was right behind her, the slam of the door breaking the stillness of the burning air.

Theirs was the only vehicle in sight. They were alone in the spectacular open space of the desert, surrounded by shimmering dunes and the soaring mountains.

'You intend to walk from here?'

'Is that really your recollection of events? You truly believe that you "asked" me to marry you?' Her hair swung across her back as she turned to confront him. Her heart was racing and she felt the heat of the sun beating down on her head. She realised that she'd left her hat in the car, but it was too late to care about that now. 'We must be existing in a parallel universe or something because I remember it *very* differently.' Right now her anger was hotter than anything produced by nature but underneath that pulsing anger were layers of different emotions. Pain. Desire. Sexual awareness. Feelings. *Feelings she didn't want to feel.* And he clearly didn't either if his expression was anything to go by. He was watching her with the same cautiousness he would give an enraged scorpion.

'Avery—'

'And when you think about it, that's not surprising because you never *ask* anyone anything, do you? You command. You order. You instruct.' She ticked them off on her fingers while he watched with a dangerous glint in those dark eyes.

'Are you finished?'

'I've barely started. You're so arrogant you never involve anyone else in your decisions. No wonder your virgin bride has run into the desert.'

His eyes flared dark. '*Stop* calling her that.'

'Tell me something.' Still shaking, Avery put her hands on her hips. 'Did you actually *ask* her to marry you, Mal? Or did you just book the wedding and then mention it to her in passing? Perhaps that's what's wrong here. Perhaps no one remembered to tell her she was supposed to be getting married. Did you miss her off the invitation list?'

A muscle flickered in his bronzed cheek. 'I'm the first to admit that my proposal to you went awry, but there were circumstances—'

'*Awry?* It didn't go "awry", Mal. It didn't happen. There was no proposal. There was just assumption. Lots of arrogant assumption.' All the anger and humiliation came piling back on top of her. And the terror. She'd almost lost everything. All of it. Everything she'd worked for. 'You assumed I was a sure thing. That of course I'd say yes to you because who wouldn't? You were so sure of yourself you didn't even pause to think about *my* needs, and you were so sure of me you didn't even bother to ask my opinion on the topic. And there are no circumstances that can explain or excuse your arrogance!'

'And if there were, you wouldn't listen to them.'

'The first I knew of your "proposal" was *not* when you and I had a private moment during which you asked me if I'd consider marrying you, but when one of my biggest clients rang to cancel his contract with me because he'd heard that I was no longer going to be running my company. When I asked him where that rumour had originated, he told me that he'd heard it from you. That you'd told him that once you married me I would no longer be taking on more business. Because of you, I lost clients. I could have lost the whole business. *My* business. The business I built from nothing.' The thought of how close she'd come to losing everything that mattered to her sent her spiralling into panic. 'That is what our "romance" did for me. And you wonder why I'm not romantic?'

There were lines of strain visible around his sensual mouth. 'That is not what I said to him.'

'Then what *did* you say to him because he was pretty sure of his facts when he took his business elsewhere. Important business, I might add. Business that would have led to more business. Instead I found myself explaining to some very confused people why I wasn't getting married.'

His eyes were a dark, dangerous black. 'And in doing so you humiliated me.'

'No, *you* humiliated *me*, Mal! You made me look like some brainless, witless woman who was just waiting for a rich, handsome Prince to come along and rescue her from her sad life. All those times you said you loved me for who I was. You said you loved my independence and my strength. And then you cut me off at the knees. Did you really think I'd just give up my business and marry you?'

'I thought you'd trust me. We'd been together for a year,' he said in a thickened tone. 'We were happy together.'

'We were happy until you tried to take over my life.

*"Once we're married she won't have time to run your par-
ties."* Wasn't that what you said to him?'

There was a tense silence. 'Yes. But there were reasons—'

'Yes, and we both know what those reasons were. You
have to be in control. You've been giving orders since you
were old enough to put two words together and you don't
know any different. The problem is, I'm not great at taking orders, Mal. I like to run my own life. In fact, I insist
on it. Damn it, why are we even having this conversation?'
Furious to feel her eyes stinging, she stomped back to the
car but as she touched the door handle his hand covered
hers. 'Get away from me. It's my turn to drive.'

'This conversation isn't finished.'

'It is as far as I'm concerned.'

'What happened with Richard Kingston was a mis-
judgement on my part, I admit it. But there were circumstances—'

'There isn't a single circumstance that would successfully excuse a man discussing his marital intentions with
everyone before the woman he intended to marry.' She
felt the warmth of his hand, the strength of those fingers
as they stayed in contact with hers and forced herself to
pull away.

'Are you crying?'

'Don't be ridiculous. I've got sand in my eyes. This is
a very sandy place.'

'You're wearing sunglasses.'

'Well, clearly they're not very efficient.' Furious and
miserable, Avery pulled open the door and slid inside. Her
heart was pounding, her control shredded and her emotions
raw. Why on earth had she decided to put herself through
this? And in the desert. A place so closely entwined with

her relationship with Mal that she wasn't even able to look at a picture of it without feeling sad.

On her first visit to Zubran she'd fallen in love. Twice. First with the country; with the contrast between stunning beaches and the wild beauty of the ever-changing dunes. Second, with the man. And somehow the two had become inextricably linked so that she couldn't imagine one without the other. He was part of this wild place and part of the place existed within him, had bred the strength and resilience that formed that steel core of his personality.

Her feelings for him had terrified her and they terrified her still. And yes, that was why she'd done nothing but snap at him from the moment she'd got into the vehicle. The alternative was allowing that dangerous chemistry to take hold and she couldn't do that. She *wouldn't* do that.

Avery tightened her fingers on the wheel as she drove, every tiny part of her alive with awareness despite all her efforts.

Next to her in the passenger seat, Mal sat sprawled, beautiful eyes narrowed behind sunglasses as he stared ahead.

She was silent and so was he, but that silence did nothing to defuse the tension.

An hour passed.

And another hour.

Neither of them spoke a word. And she was relieved to be driving. Relieved to have something to focus on other than him. Except that it didn't work like that, of course, because no matter how much she focused on the road, she was still aware of him, right there beside her. Within touching distance, except that she wasn't allowed to touch. And awareness grew and grew until the air was almost too thick to breathe. Until the desire to touch him was almost overwhelming and she had to grip the wheel until her knuckles were white with the pressure.

This was why she wanted his marriage to go ahead, she thought savagely. Because only then would he be out of her head and out of her heart. She wasn't the sort of woman who could hold onto feelings for a married man. That would be it. She could get back to a normal life.

After what felt like hours of silence, he finally spoke. 'We'll camp by those rocks up ahead.' His tone was neutral. Devoid of emotion. 'They should offer some protection from the elements.'

She didn't need protecting from the elements. She needed protection from *him*. Or was it herself? She was no longer sure.

Confused and jittery, Avery parked and sprang from the vehicle. 'You can camp by that rock and I'll camp by the other.' Distance, she thought. She needed distance. They needn't even see each other until morning. She'd zip her tent up and she'd keep it zipped.

'There is just one tent, Avery.'

'What?' His words blew out the foundations of her fledgling plan and answered any remaining questions she had about her feelings for him. 'Just one? Why?'

'Why does that matter?' He seemed unusually interested in her reaction and she pushed away disturbing images of his muscle-packed length stretched next to hers.

'Well, for a start, it isn't exactly the done thing for a man to sleep with one woman when he is engaged to marry another. And then there's always the chance that I'll kill you in my sleep.' *If* she slept. Which seemed unlikely.

'I don't intend to sleep with you.' He leaned in and pulled a bag from the vehicle. 'Just share a tent with you. It isn't as if we haven't done it before.'

But the last time they'd been lovers. Intimate in every

way. They were both hot-tempered and stubborn and those traits had simply intensified the sexual connection between them.

Avery watched as he hauled the tent and the gear from the vehicle. 'Why didn't you bring two tents?'

'I wasn't expecting company. If you recall, you were the one who insisted on coming. Having already spread the word that I wanted a couple of nights in the desert alone, I could hardly articulate the need for a second tent.' He focused his attention on creating their camp and she forced herself to help, even though doing so brought her into close proximity with him. She tried to subdue the choking, panicky feeling in her chest at the thought of sharing that confined space with him.

He'd be sleeping with his head next to hers. His body within touching distance.

She looked at his shoulders and immediately looked away again.

What if she had one of her nightmares? What if she reached for him in her sleep?

Making a mental note to lie on her hands and stay awake until he was asleep, she helped secure the tent, working without speaking. And it was exasperating to discover that he was as competent at this as he was at everything else.

Avery gritted her teeth. She wasn't looking for things to admire about him. She didn't *want* to admire him. Not when they were about to spend a night crammed into a relatively small space.

At least it wasn't cold. She'd stay outside until the last possible moment before going into the tent. With luck, he'd be asleep by the time she joined him.

'Nice to know you can function without staff.' She watched as he lit a fire and proceeded to cook their supper. He'd thrown a rug on the ground and she knelt on it, watching as the flames flickered to life. 'So we should reach the oasis tomorrow? What if she isn't there?'

'I think she will be.'

'You could have just asked your security team to check it out.'

'If I'd done that it would have been impossible to keep this situation contained. I want to keep this as quiet as possible.'

'To protect your ego.'

'To protect my bride, at least until I've decided how best to sort this out.' He cooked without fuss, lamb with spices chargrilled over the open flame and served with rice. And because she was trying hard to make the whole experience less intimate she insisted on cooking her own, even though she did nowhere near as good a job as he did.

She burned the edges but still it tasted good and Avery ate hungrily until she caught him looking at her. Immediately her appetite vanished, as if someone had flicked a switch.

'What? It's delicious.'

'It's hardly gourmet. You eat in five star restaurants all the time and fly in celebrity chefs to cater for your parties.'

'Yes, but that's my work. This is different. There's something about food eaten outdoors in the desert. I've always loved it here.' Immediately she regretted saying it out loud because everything she'd loved about the desert was entwined with everything she loved about him. *Not* love. She corrected herself quickly. Felt. Everything she loved about the desert was entwined with everything she *felt* about him.

Because she knew he was looking at her, she kept her eyes on the view and that was no hardship because she could have stared for hours at the desert landscape that altered minute by minute under the fading light. The area he'd picked for camping was rocky, but they were still on the border with Zubran and dunes rose ahead of her, dark gold under the setting sun, the beauty of it holding her captivated until the sun dipped behind a mound and darkness quickly spread over the desert.

Grateful for that darkness, she lifted her eyes to the sky and picked a neutral topic. 'Why do the stars always seem so much brighter out here?'

'Less pollution.' His tone short, he rose to his feet, doused the fire and gestured to the tent. 'We need to get some rest. I'd like to leave at dawn.'

So he didn't want to linger any more than she did. Didn't want to prolong the time they spent together. The knowledge should have brought a feeling of relief but instead she just felt hollow and numb.

'Dawn is fine with me.' Anything that meant less time in the tent with him had to be good.

She wiped her bowl clean, nibbled on one of the dates he'd left out on a plate and tried not to think about their first trip into the desert together. It had been at the beginning of their relationship, during those heady first months when they'd been consumed by their feelings for each other. He'd been so frustrated by the unrelenting demands on his time and privacy that he'd arranged a secret trip. They'd joked that he'd kidnapped her, but really they'd stolen time away, as normal couples did all the time. He'd dismissed his security team. She'd left her phone behind. It was the first time they'd really been on their own, away from the craziness of his existence and the craziness of hers.

It had been the happiest week of her life.

Thinking about it now brought a lump to her throat. The ache in her chest felt like a solid lump and she sneaked a glance towards him, only to find him watching her, that dark gaze fiercely intense.

'Say it.'

'Say what?'

'Say what you are thinking.'

Avery swallowed. 'What am I thinking?'

'You are thinking of that week we spent together. Just the two of us.' His voice was rough and suddenly she couldn't breathe and the panic pressed down on her because that was *exactly* what she'd been thinking.

'Actually I was thinking how bleak it is here.'

His expression told her that he didn't believe her but he didn't push her. Instead he turned away, leaving her feeling more vulnerable than she ever had before.

Now what?

Not speaking about her feelings didn't change the fact they existed. And the thought of going into that tent—of being so close to him—kept her sitting outside long after she should have gone inside. She postponed the moment as long as possible. Postponed the moment when they'd be forced together in that cramped, confined space that was designed to force intimacy even between two people who were avoiding it.

Would she have insisted on joining him if she'd known about the sleeping arrangements? No, probably not. Self-preservation would have outweighed the guilt she felt towards Kalila.

Kalila. *He was going to marry Kalila.*

She had no idea how long she sat there. Time blurred. Misery deepened. Fatigue, the mortal enemy of optimism, caught up with her.

'Avery? You need to come inside the tent now. It's dark.' His voice was deep and sexy and she squeezed her eyes closed and tried to block out the images created by that voice.

'I'm not afraid of the dark.'

'No, you are afraid of intimacy, but intimacy is not on offer so you are perfectly safe in this tent with me.'

'I'm not afraid of intimacy.'

'Good. In that case, get in this tent before you become a tasty snack for a desert creature. Unless you'd rather I pick you up and put you here myself?'

That would be the worst of all options. She didn't want him to touch her but she knew he would make good on his threat if she didn't move, so she put her hand down on the rug to lever herself up and felt a sharp pain. 'Ow.' She snatched her hand away and there was a scuttling sound. 'What—? Ugh, Mal, something just bit me. And it rattles.'

He was by her side in an instant. The torch flashed and a scorpion scuttled under the rug.

'Not a rattlesnake—a scorpion. Good.'

'*Good?* Why is it good? From where I'm sitting it's seriously creepy. If we were playing "marry, kiss or push off a cliff", the scorpion would be the one off the cliff, I can tell you that.' Her voice rose and she hugged her hand to her chest. 'Are there any more out here?'

'Hundreds, probably. They come out at night.'

'*Hundreds?*' Horrified, she sprang at him, clinging like a monkey. 'Don't put me down.'

'Avery—'

'Whatever you do, don't put me down. I'm never touching the floor again. Do you seriously mean hundreds? Please tell me you're kidding.'

She'd forgotten how strong he was. His arms closed around her, strong, protective. She thought he might have been laughing but told herself he wouldn't dare laugh at her.

'I thought you were fine with desert wildlife.'

'I'm fine with the theory. Not so good with the reality

when it closes its jaws on me. And if you dare laugh I will kill you, Your Highness. Just a warning.'

'I'm not laughing. But I'm not going to let you forget this in a hurry.'

'I just bet you're not.' She buried her face in his neck, wondering why he had to smell so good.

'It's worth savouring. The moment Avery Scott became a damsel in distress.'

'No one will ever believe you and I will deny it until my dying breath, which may be soon if there are truly hundreds of those things out there. I'm not distressed. More freaked out. I can tell you this is the first time in my life I've jumped on a man.'

'I'm flattered you chose me,' he drawled. 'As a matter of interest, are you going to let go?'

'Are they still out there?'

'Yes.'

'Then I'm not letting go. You threatened to carry me to the tent. Go ahead.' She tightened her grip and he gave a soft curse.

'You're choking me.'

'I don't care.'

'If I die, you fall to the ground and they'll swarm all over you.'

'You have a sick sense of humour.' But she loosened her grip. 'Move, Mal! I want to be in the tent.'

'Damsels in distress don't usually give the orders. And I *was* in the tent. You were the one who chose scorpions over my company. Are you telling me that you're rethinking that choice?'

'Don't be flattered. All it means is that you're better than a scorpion. Don't make me beg.' She clung, her hands pressed to those solid shoulders. '*Are* you laughing?'

'No.'

'Good, because if you were laughing, I'd have to punch you with my good hand. My other hand hurts. Am I going to die?'

'It is rare for scorpion bites to cause fatalities.'

'Rare? So that means that sometimes people die, right?'

His hesitation was brief. 'Yes, but it's usually only in the very young or in people with health issues and you don't fall into either category.'

'That's not very reassuring. You're supposed to say, *"No, Avery, of course you're not going to die."* Why don't men ever know the right thing to say at the right moment?'

'If men said the right thing at the right moment, we'd be women.' He ducked inside the tent, lowered her onto a sleeping roll he'd laid out for himself and gently detached himself from her grip. The movement brought their faces very close together. She could feel his breath on her cheek. All she had to do was turn her head and their mouths would meet. And she didn't have to wonder how that would feel because she *knew*. And he knew, too.

Their eyes met and she saw the heat in his and knew he would see the same in hers because the chemistry was there, as powerful as ever. It sucked at her stomach and brushed over her skin, making her crave the impossible. She hadn't kissed a man since him and she missed him terribly.

It was a dangerous moment and it felt as if it lasted for ever. In reality it was less than a couple of seconds and she was about to push him away when he turned away from her, suddenly brisk and efficient.

'Do you normally react to bee stings or wasp stings?'

The only thing she reacted to was him.

Her mouth was so dry it felt as if she'd fallen face down in the desert. 'I have no idea. I've never been stung by either before.' The chemistry between them had shaken her almost as much as the scorpion bite. She felt vulnerable, and she hated feeling vulnerable. The last time she'd felt like this was when they'd split up.

'How are you feeling?'

'My hand throbs.' She squinted down at it and he hesitated for a moment and then slid back the sleeve of her shirt and studied it under the light. His fingers were strong and firm and she had to concentrate on keeping still. On not responding.

He wasn't hers any more. And she wasn't his.

Avery stared at his bent head; at the glossy dark hair that flopped over his forehead. She knew exactly how it would feel if she sank her hands into it because she'd done that. She'd trailed her mouth over his skin and tasted him. Everywhere.

As if feeling her thoughts, he lifted his head and she jerked back slightly, feeling guilty even though all she'd done was look.

The man was marrying Kalila. The fact that they seemed to barely know each other wasn't her business. The fact that Kalila had run away wasn't her business.

Studying her hand, he muttered something under his breath. 'I should have used the ultraviolet torch out there.'

'And how would that have helped?'

'There is a compound in the exoskeleton of the scorpion that causes it to glow in UV light.' He adjusted the light to get a better look. 'It means that we can see where they are. They show up as a ghostly green colour.'

Avery looked away so that she couldn't see his hand touching hers. Bronze against creamy white. Male against female. 'That is *disgusting*. How do you even know these things?'

'This is my country. It is my business to know.'

'Ghostly green scorpions.' She shuddered. 'I'm almost glad I couldn't see them. Remind me why I came?'

'Because you wanted to help Kalila. Tell me how badly it hurts.'

'I don't know—worse than a headache, better than the time I bounced off the trampoline and smashed my head on the floor of the school gym. Do you mind not frowning? Frowning means you're worried or that there is something seriously wrong. By the way, my hand feels as if it's on fire. Is that OK?'

Mal's mouth tightened. 'I should have made you come into the tent sooner.'

'I didn't want to do that.'

'And we both know why.'

There it was again. The chemistry that neither of them wanted.

'Let's not go there.'

'No.' There was a ripple of exasperation in his voice. 'But from now on you are by my side the whole time, no matter how uncomfortable that makes you feel. Stay there a moment and don't move. I'll be back soon.'

'You're leaving?' Without thinking, she reached out and grabbed his arm. 'Where are you going?' Realising what she'd just done, she let her hand drop. God, what was the matter with her? She was having a complete character transformation.

'To the car to get some ice.' He watched her, his expression revealing that he was every bit as surprised as she was. Reaching down, he closed his hand over her shoulder. 'You will be fine, *habibti*.'

Habibti.

Shock held her still because the last time he'd called her that, they'd been in bed together. Naked. Her legs tangled with his. His mouth hard on hers.

And he must have been experiencing the same memory because his eyes darkened and his gaze slid slowly to her mouth and then back to her eyes. Their whole past was in that one look.

This time she was the one to look away first.

'You're right. Of course I'll be fine,' she said quickly. 'I was just—' Clinging. Like a desperate female. She, who had never clung to anyone or anything before in her life, had clung. She didn't even want to think about what that would do to his macho ego. And she certainly didn't want to think about what it did for her reputation.

Horribly embarrassed, Avery shifted back as far as she could. 'Go and get the ice. Make sure you bring a bottle of Bollinger with it. And tell the scorpions to dine elsewhere. I'm no longer on the menu.'

'Are you sure you'll be all right? Only a moment ago you were clinging to me.'

'Clinging?' Her attempt at light-hearted laughter was relatively convincing. 'I was just trying to avoid being bitten by another scorpion. I'd rather they bit you than me.'

'Thanks.'

'If there had been a boulder handy, I would have stood on that. Anything to get above ground level. Don't take it personally. Now go. I'm thirsty.'

It was the first time he'd seen her lower her guard, even briefly.

And he'd lowered his guard too and called her *habibti* and that single word had shifted the atmosphere. He didn't know whether to be amused or offended that she considered him a bigger threat to her well-being than the scorpion.

Relieved, he thought grimly as he remembered the way he'd felt when she'd wrapped her arms around his neck. Unlocking the door, he removed ice and the first aid kit he carried everywhere, trying to block out the way it had felt to hold her. She was slender, leggy...*and she'd lost weight.*

Was that because of him?

No. That would mean she cared and he knew she didn't care.

He stood for a moment, listening to the sounds of the desert and the disturbing notes of his own thoughts. Then he cursed softly and slammed the door.

Inside the tent, she was sitting quietly. She looked shaken and a little pale but he had no way of knowing whether her reaction was a result of the scorpion bite or the pressure of being in such close contact with him.

Trying to concentrate on the scorpion bite and nothing else, Mal pressed ice to her burning hand and she flinched.

'Only you can produce ice in a desert.'

'I have a freezer unit in the vehicle.' And right at that moment he was working out ways to sit in it. Anything to cool himself down.

'Of course you do,' she murmured, 'because a Prince cannot be without life's little luxuries, even in this inhospitable terrain.'

'I suppose I should be relieved that you're feeling well enough to aggravate me.'

'I really don't need ice. You're hot, Your Highness, but not *that* hot.' But despite her flippant tone her cheeks were flushed. Was it the effects of the bite?

'Tell me how you are feeling.' And suddenly he realised just how bad this could be. They were miles from civilization. Even if he called a helicopter, it wouldn't arrive within an hour. He told himself that she was fit and healthy and not in any of the high-risk groups, but still anxiety gnawed at him because he knew that for some people the bite of the scorpion could be deadly. 'I don't carry anti-venom.'

'Well, thank goodness for small mercies because there

is no *way* I'd let you jab me with a needle and inject me with more poison.' She flinched as he moved the ice. 'That is freezing. Are you trying to give me frostbite?'

'I'm trying to stop the venom spreading. Does it hurt?'

'Not at all. I can't even feel it.' It was obvious that she was lying and he threw her a look.

'You are the most exasperating, infuriating woman I've ever met.'

'Thank you.' She smiled and that smile snagged his attention.

'What makes you think it was a compliment?'

'I take everything as a compliment unless I'm told otherwise. Am I going to die?'

'No.' Hiding his concern, he put his hand on her forehead. 'We need to get your clothes off.'

Her eyes flew open. 'You're warped, do you know that?'

'This isn't seduction. This is first aid.' And he didn't want to think about seduction. He didn't dare. His hands were firm as they stripped off her clothes and she made a feeble attempt to stop him.

'I can't let you see me naked.'

'I've already seen you naked on many occasions.' Too many occasions. She was the hottest, most beautiful woman he'd ever met and he didn't need to be in this position to be reminded of that fact.

'That was different. You weren't about to marry another woman. I don't get naked with almost married men.' She snatched at the sleeping bag and he let her cover herself but not before he'd caught a tantalizing glimpse of creamy skin. A glimpse that tested his self-control more than it had ever been tested before.

It was a struggle to focus on what he was doing. 'I have to cool you down and you need to stop snuggling inside that sleeping bag because you're overheating.' He poured cool water on a cloth and held it against her head. 'Females tend to have a more severe reaction because of their body mass.'

There was a dangerous gleam in her eyes. 'Are you calling me fat?'

'Did I mention the word fat?'

'You said "mass". Don't use the word "mass" in relation to my body.'

'Even if I tell you it's because you have a smaller body mass?' He didn't want to be amused. He didn't want to feel anything for this woman. 'Be silent. You need to rest.'

'I can't rest with you this close.'

He rubbed his fingers over his forehead, exhausted by the drain on his self control. It was fortunate that both of them were too principled to give in to it.

'I'm watching you for any adverse reaction.'

'Well, stop watching me. It feels creepy.' She rolled onto her side, but a moan escaped her. 'How long am I going to feel like this, Mal?' The tremor in her voice concerned him more than anything because he knew how tough she was.

'You feel bad?'

'No, I feel great.' Her words were muffled by the pillow. 'I just want to know how long this great feeling is going to last so that I can make the most of it. How long?'

'Hours, *habibti*.' He hesitated for a moment and then allowed himself to stroke her hair away from her face, telling himself that touching her was all about comfort and nothing else. 'Possibly a bit longer.'

'I was stupid. You must be furious with me.'

If only. 'I'm not furious.'

'Then try harder. It would make it easier if you were furious.'

Mal gave a cynical smile because right at that moment he doubted anything would make it easier. He placed his fingers on her wrist. 'Your pulse is very fast.'

'Well, that's nothing to do with you, so don't go flatter- ing yourself. Scorpions always get me going.'

'It's the venom. You need to tell me how you're feel- ing. If necessary I'll call the helicopter and have us air- lifted out of here.'

'No way. We need to find your virgin bride.'

Mal cursed under his breath and reached into his first aid kit for a bandage. '*Stop* calling her that.'

'Sorry.' She turned slightly, opened one eye and peeped at him. 'Are you angry yet?'

'No, but I'm getting there. Keep it up.'

She grinned weakly. 'I bet the scorpion is angry, too. I flung him across the ground. Horrible creature.'

'Actually they play a critical role in the ecosystem, con- suming other arthropods and even mice and snakes.'

'Too much information.'

'They can control how much poison they inject into you. I think you got away lightly.'

'So does that mean he liked me or he didn't like me? Ow—*now* what are you doing?'

'I'm bandaging the bite and lifting your arm. I want to slow the spread of the venom. If this doesn't work, I'll have to call the helicopter.'

'Could we stop calling it venom? And honestly, Mal, it's fine. Stop fussing. Can we take the ice off now? It's cold.'

'That's the idea.'

'Scorpions don't like their food chilled?'

But she didn't feel cold to touch. She was boiling-hot and her arm was burning. 'Have you ever suffered an al- lergic reaction to anything in the past?'

'No, nothing. I'm as healthy as a horse.'

Mal felt a rush of exasperation that they hadn't avoided this situation. 'Why didn't you come into the tent sooner?'

'Because then we would have killed each other.' Her

response was glib, but her smile faltered. 'Sorry. And this time I really am apologising.'

'Apologising for what? For being aggravating? That is nothing new and you've never felt the need to apologise before.'

'For messing everything up,' she muttered. 'For making things harder for you. I shouldn't have come on this trip. I was worried about Kalila and I thought I could help but I haven't helped and it was all my fault anyway.' Her apology was as sweet as it was unexpected and he felt something squeeze inside his chest.

'I am touched that you cared enough to come,' he breathed. 'And you will be able to talk to Kalila and persuade her to confide in you, which is important given that I have failed so miserably to deliver in that area.' And he blamed himself for that. For being unapproachable, for assuming that just because his bride to be hadn't said anything, it meant that everything was fine.

They had no relationship, he thought bleakly, and it was impossible not to compare that with the feelings he and Avery shared.

'You'll make a perfect couple. I'm sure you'll be very happy. And I mean that. I'm not being sarcastic. She's very sweet and she won't drive you crazy. That's always good in a marriage.' Her voice was barely audible and she turned her head, the movement dislodging her hair from the plait. It poured over her shoulders like honey and he stared down at the silken mass, fighting the urge to sink his hands into it. Once, he'd had the right to do that. And he'd done it. All the time. It had been the most physical relationship of his life.

'Right now I am not thinking of Kalila.'

'Don't, Mal.' Her voice was muffled. 'Don't do this.'

Was this the moment to be honest? He hesitated,

wrenched apart by the conflict between duty and his
own needs. And honesty would just worsen the situation,
wouldn't it? 'This marriage with Kalila—'

'Will be good. If she's having second thoughts then
it's because you haven't tried hard enough. You can be
charming when you want to be. Of course the rest of the
time you're aggravating and arrogant, but don't show her
that side of you for a while and it will be fine.' Her eyes
were closed, her eyelashes long and thick against her pale
cheeks.

Mal stared down at her, unable to think of a single time
when he'd seen Avery vulnerable. It just wasn't a word he
associated with her. But tonight—yes, tonight she was vulnerable. He wanted to hold her but he didn't dare take the
risk. He wasn't convinced he'd let her go.

Instead he settled for sitting close to her. 'Tell me why
you avoided my calls.' Still worried about the bite, he tightened the bandage as much as he dared.

'I was super-busy.'

'You are the most efficient woman I know. If you'd
wanted to answer my calls, you could have done. When we
parted company I thought we would remain friends.' He
should have been thinking about his bride-to-be, but all he
could think about was the relationship he'd lost.

'I'm too busy for friends. About this scorpion—' as always when a subject became uncomfortable, she shifted
direction '—he only bit me once. Should I be offended?
Does that mean he didn't like the way I tasted? Or am I like
expensive caviar—better consumed in small amounts?'

He didn't want to think about the way she tasted.
Couldn't allow himself to. Frustration made his voice
rougher than he intended. 'I am going to give you a couple
of tablets and then you're going to rest.' *And stop talking.*

'I don't take tablets. I'm a drug-free zone.'

'You'll take these. And if the rash on your arm hasn't calmed down in an hour or so, I'm going to fly you out of here.' And maybe that would be the best thing for both of them. Reaching into his bag, he found the tablets in the supplies he carried and handed them to her with a drink of water, relieved when she swallowed the pills without question or argument but at the same time concerned because it was so unlike her not to question and argue. 'If you feel bad, I can call the helicopter now.'

'No.' Her eyes drifted shut again. 'I want to stay. I need to be with you.'

The atmosphere snapped tight. Mal felt a weight on his chest. How many times had he waited for her to say those words? And she said them now, when his life was already set on a different course. Was that why she'd picked this moment? Because she knew he couldn't act on the emotion that simmered between them? *I need to be with you.* From any other woman those words would have felt oppressive. From Avery they felt like victory. A victory that was too little, too late. 'You need to be with me? You are telling me this now?'

'Yes.' Her voice was barely audible. 'I need to be there when you find her. I need to talk Kalila into marrying you. It's the best thing for all of us.'

CHAPTER FIVE

SHE dreamed of the desert. Only this time when she dreamed of the Prince he was holding her and she couldn't walk away because he held her close, refusing to let her go.

Trapped.

She struggled slightly but she was held in a strong grip.

'Shh. It's just a dream. Go back to sleep.'

The deep male voice lifted her from sleep to semi-wakefulness and she realised that Mal was holding her. It was still dark and she didn't know which frightened her more—the realisation that she felt truly terrible, or the feeling that came from being held by him. Her head was on his chest and she could feel the slow, steady thud of his heart. She knew she should pull away, but she didn't.

She'd planned to sleep in the furthest corner of the tent but here he was, lying next to her, holding her. And it felt good.

Too good.

She could feel the brush of his leg against hers and the warmth of his body as he held her in the curve of his arm. The faint glow of light from the torch simply increased the feeling of intimacy.

'For God's sake Mal, move over,' she muttered, 'you're in my personal space.'

'I'm worried about you.'

Her stomach flipped because no one had ever worried about her in her life before. 'Don't be. I don't like the idea you're waiting for me to drop dead. And you certainly don't need to hold me.'

'You're the one holding me.' He kept his eyes closed, those dark lashes inky black against his cheek. 'You did it in your sleep, because you just can't accept help when you're awake.'

'That's because I don't need help when I'm awake.'

'Right. And I suppose you didn't "need help" last night when you used me as a climbing frame?'

'That was different. We were invaded by scorpions and if it's all right with you I'd like to forget about last night.' She wanted to forget all of it, especially this. She wondered why he was still holding her when the safe and sensible thing to do would have been to let her go.

'How long have you been having bad dreams?'

'I don't have bad dreams.'

'You had a bad dream. That's how you ended up clinging to me.'

Embarrassment washed over her like burning liquid. 'If I had a bad dream last night then it must have been a scorpion-venom-induced nightmare.' She tried to pull away but he was stronger than she was and he held her tightly.

'It wasn't scorpions you were talking about in your sleep.'

She'd been talking in her sleep? Could this get any worse? She wanted to ask if she'd spoken his name, but didn't want to hear the answer and anyway it was impossible to concentrate with him holding her. It felt dangerously familiar.

'That's another scorpion venom thing—' Her cheek was still against his chest and she could feel hard muscle through the softness of his T-shirt. 'Check out Wikipedia.

I bet it will say something about nightmares. And I'm well and truly awake now, so you can let me go.'

He didn't. 'Go back to sleep.'

He expected her to sleep while he was holding her? She could have pulled away, of course, but she didn't. *Couldn't.* This was the way she wanted to sleep. Holding each other. Not wanting to be parted even in sleep. And she'd longed for it so much over the long, barren months they'd been apart. This was the last time they'd ever hold each other and she didn't want it to end. Without warning, her eyes started to sting. 'I don't need you to fuss over me.'

'You never need anything, do you, Avery Scott?' His voice was soft in the darkness and she squeezed her eyes tightly so that the tears didn't fall. She couldn't believe she was actually crying. She could just imagine what her mother would say to that.

'Sometimes I pretend to need someone, just to stroke a masculine ego.'

'I doubt you have ever stroked a man's ego in your life. Knifed it, possibly.'

She smiled against his chest, safe in the knowledge that he couldn't see her. 'Good job yours is robust.'

'Are you smiling?'

'No. What is there to smile about? I'm scorpion chow.' And she was a mess. The pain in her hand was nothing compared to the pain in her heart and he must have sensed her feelings because she felt his hand stroke her hair. Just the slight brush of his fingers, but it was enough to make her tense and he must have felt that too because he stilled, as if aware he'd crossed a line.

'Go back to sleep, Avery. And, just this once, don't fight me. A woman doesn't have to be in charge one hundred per cent of the time.' His soft voice melted everything hard inside her.

When they'd parted it had almost broken her. Being with him had threatened everything she'd built. She should be pulling away from him, but what she wanted to do was bury her face in his neck, touch her mouth to his skin and use her tongue and her lips to drive him wild.

Picturing Kalila in her head, she eased away from him and this time he let her go.

'I'm still in charge,' she whispered back. 'I just let you hold me because it feeds your manly ego.'

'You're all heart.'

Well, that was true, she thought bleakly as she turned on her side with her back to him. It was a good description because, right now, it was the only part of herself of which she was aware and it was filled to the brim with her feelings for him.

Even with her back to him, she could feel him watching her and she squeezed her eyes shut and refused to let herself turn and look at him.

Gritting her teeth, she resigned herself to a night without sleep.

She was alone in the tent when she woke.

Outside she could hear noises. Mal was up and dismantling their camp.

Avery lay for a moment, staring up at the canvas, remembering the night before in excruciating detail.

Muttering a soft curse, she sat upright. The bite on her hand had calmed down overnight and was now nothing more than a red mark. If only all her other feelings had faded so easily. She didn't want to think about the way he'd held her. She definitely didn't want to think about what she might have said when she'd talked in her sleep.

Grabbing her bag, she cleansed her face with one of the wipes she always carried, applied suncream and minimal make-up and scooped her hair into a ponytail. Then she tugged a fresh shirt out of her bag and changed quickly.

That was the easy part. The hard part was leaving the tent.

Facing him, after what had happened the night before.

'Coffee—' Mal handed her a small cup of strong coffee and she took it with a murmur of thanks, avoiding eye contact as she sipped.

'So you're ready to move out?'

'Whenever you are. How are you feeling?'

'Fine! Never better.' And never more embarrassed. She couldn't decide whether to pretend it hadn't happened or talk it down.

'Let me see.' He took her hand in his and somehow she resisted the impulse to snatch it away.

'It's settled down.' Which was more than could be said for her pulse rate. Could he feel it? *Could he feel what he was doing to her?* 'How's the scorpion feeling this morning? Perky?'

His mouth flickered at the corners. 'Deprived, I should think. He only got to take a single bite. I'm sure it was nowhere near enough.'

Her eyes skidded to his and then away again. 'Well, that's all he's getting.' She tugged her hand away from his and finished her coffee. 'I'll take the tent down.'

'No. I want you to rest your hand. I'll do it.' He strode away from her and Avery breathed out slowly. She felt weird and she didn't know if it was the after-effects of the scorpion bite or the after-effects of a night spent close to Mal.

He had the tent down in record time and the site cleared while Avery stood, eyeing the ground for more scorpions and wondering whether or not to say something. 'Listen—' she watched as he threw the tent into the trunk, distracted

as the powerful muscles in his shoulders rippled and flexed
'—about last night—'

'Which part of last night?'

'The part when I—' She cleared her throat. 'The part
when I wasn't quite myself.'

'Was that the moment when you clung to me, or the moment you begged me not to leave you?'

'I didn't beg. And I didn't cling.' She emptied the dregs
of her coffee onto the ground. 'Not exactly.'

'You needed me. But I can understand that it's hard for
you to admit to needing anyone.' There was an edge to his
voice that she didn't understand because surely they were
way past this in their relationship.

'I didn't need you, but if it suits you to believe that then
fine. I wish I'd never mentioned it. How long until we find
your bride?' The sooner the better as far as she was concerned. Suddenly she wished she hadn't allowed her conscience to push her into this trip. No matter what she'd said
to Kalila, if the girl had chosen to leg it into the desert that
was ultimately her responsibility, wasn't it? Nothing was
worth this additional stress.

'It is about a two-hour drive from here.' He slung the
rest of their gear into the vehicle and sprang into the driver's seat.

Two hours and that would be it, she thought numbly.
He'd find his bride. They'd sort things out. Mal would
marry her. And all she'd ever be to him was a past he
wanted to forget.

They'd see each other at the occasional high profile
party. They'd be polite and friendly and formal. And in
time the pain would fade.

She rubbed her hand over her chest.

He caught the movement and frowned slightly but Avery

ignored his quizzical look and walked round to the passenger side.

This time, instead of arguing, they made the journey in silence but it didn't seem to make a difference. She was painfully conscious of him, her eyes drawn to every tiny movement. The flex of his thigh as he drove, the strength of his hands on the wheel. The atmosphere was so tense and loaded that when they finally pulled in to the camp Avery was the first out of the car. She wanted to get this done. She *had* to get this done.

'Stay there. I'll ask a few questions and try to find out where she is. You'll draw too much attention to yourself.' Without waiting for his response, she walked towards the tent that doubled as 'reception' but, before she reached it, she noticed the slim figure of a girl hurrying, head down, into a tent at the far side of the camp.

Kalila?

Sure it was her, Avery walked straight towards the tent where she'd seen the girl disappear.

'Have you seen her?' Mal was right behind her and she scowled at him.

'I don't know. I think so, but presumably she doesn't want to see you or she would have gone to you in the first place. I think you should wait in the car.'

'Am I so fearsome?' Those ebony eyes glittered down at her and just for a moment she felt the connection, powerful and unsettling. *Yes, he was fearsome.* Because of him she'd almost lost everything she'd worked to build.

'I have no idea what she thinks about you. And I'm not going to find out if you're standing there scowling. Go and take a stroll in the desert for a few minutes.' Pulling aside the flap of the tent, she stepped inside. And stared in dismay because there, in the centre of the tent was Kalila.

And wrapped around her was a man. A man who was most certainly *not* her bridegroom to be.

Avery absorbed the undeniable evidence that yet another relationship had crashed and burned. Despite her own unshakeable cynicism, this time she was shocked. Of all the scenarios that had played around in her head, this had not been among them. Or maybe she hadn't allowed herself to think that the marriage might not go ahead. It had to go ahead. It *had* to.

Panic rippled through her and this time she didn't know if it was for herself or Kalila.

Maybe if Mal didn't see—if she could just talk to Kalila—do *something*—

She tried to back out of the tent before the couple noticed her and almost tripped over Mal, who was right behind her. Her retreat blocked by his powerful body, she tried to thrust him back. 'It's not her. My mistake.'

He stood firm, refusing to budge, his handsome face blank of expression as he contemplated the scene in front of him. There was no visible sign of emotion, but it wasn't hard to guess his feelings and her heart squeezed.

Damn. It wasn't even as if she believed in happy endings. But to have the ending before the beginning was particularly harsh. Whatever his reasons, he'd wanted this marriage to work.

She wanted to cover his eyes, to push him away, to catch his illusions in her bare hands before they hit the ground and shattered. But it was already too late for that.

In the circumstances, his control surprised her. There was no cursing or explosion of possessive temper. Instead he just stood, legs braced apart as he watched in silence. Everything about him screamed power and Avery felt her breath catch because most of the time she thought of him as a man first and Prince second but right now he was very much the Prince.

Clearly Kalila thought so too because as she caught sight of him she dragged herself out of the arms of her lover so quickly she almost fell. 'Oh no!'

Mal walked past Avery into the tent, his dark gaze fixed intently on the man who had been kissing Kalila. 'And you are—?'

'No! I won't let you touch him!' Her tone infused with drama and desperation, Kalila plastered herself in front of her lover—*was he a lover?*—and Avery braced herself. No doubt there would be a battle for masculine supremacy. Holding her breath, she waited for him to face Mal, man to man, but instead he stayed firmly behind the Princess and then prostrated himself.

'Your Highness—'

Avery's brows rose because she'd expected fists, not fawning. Astonished, her gaze flickered to Mal and their gazes briefly connected. She subdued a ridiculous urge to laugh and then realised that there was nothing funny about this situation. Mal was desperate for this marriage to go ahead. He would fight for Kalila, she was sure of it.

'Get up.' Mal issued the command through clenched teeth and the man stumbled upright, but stayed behind Kalila with his head bowed.

Avery watched in disbelief. What woman in her right mind would choose that cowering wimp over Mal? Not that she wanted to see them fight, but surely he should at least look his adversary in the eye and take control. Where was the strength? Where was courage?

Nowhere, apparently, because the man, scarlet-faced, continued to stare at the floor while Kalila sent him an adoring glance. In the end it was Kalila who braced her shoulders and faced the man she was supposed to be marrying.

'I won't let you lay a finger on him.'

'I have no intention of touching him,' Mal drawled, 'but an introduction would be appropriate at this point, don't you think?'

'This is Karim.' Kalila's voice was a terrified squeak. 'He's my bodyguard.'

'You *have* to be kidding.' Avery stared at the cowering man. 'Your *bodyguard*? But—' She caught Mal's single warning glance and broke off in mid sentence. 'Sorry. I'm not saying anything. Nothing at all. I'm totally silent on the subject. Mute. Lips are sealed.'

'If only,' Mal breathed, returning his attention to the couple in front of him. 'So your "bodyguard" appears to be taking his responsibilities extremely seriously. Presumably he was wrapped that closely around you to protect you from flying bullets?' His biting sarcasm drew an uncomfortable glance from the other man but he didn't speak.

The talking was left to Kalila, who was every bit as red faced as the man next to her. 'Wh-what are you doing here, Your Highness?'

'I was searching for my bride-to-be,' Mal said softly, 'to find out why she'd run away. But apparently I have my answer.'

What?

Braced to defuse serious tension, Avery stared at him. Was that it? *Was that all he was going to say?*

Kalila seemed equally taken aback. 'Your Highness, I can explain—'

'You can call me Mal. I believe I've told you that on more than one occasion. And the situation doesn't merit any further explanation.'

Why wasn't he fighting?

Avery wondered if he had heatstroke. *Something* had affected his brain, that was for sure.

Kalila was still clasping the bodyguard's hand tightly. Probably to stop him running away, Avery thought. 'I can't believe you came looking for me. Why would you do that?'

'Because he's a decent person and he was worried about you,' Avery snapped and then caught Mal's eye again. 'All *right*. It's just that you're not saying anything and it's really hard to stay silent—'

'*Try*,' Mal advised silkily and Avery clamped her jaws shut. Without even realising it, she'd moved closer to him so that now all she had to do was reach out her hand and she'd be touching him. And she wanted to touch him. *She wanted to touch him so badly.*

'We came looking for you because naturally we were concerned that you might be in danger. But I can see that you're fine.' Mal was calm and composed and Avery resisted the temptation to poke him to check he was actually still alive. Surely he should be seething with anger? Burning up with raw jealousy?

Or perhaps he was just in shock. Yes, that had to be it. Shock.

But if he wasn't careful the moment to act would have passed. And if he wasn't capable of taking action, then she'd do it for him. 'What Mal is trying to say is that—'

'I can't marry you, Your Highness.' Kalila blurted the words out. 'It's too late.'

Avery closed her eyes. 'Of course it's not too late! Honestly, you shouldn't make hasty decisions, Kalila. You need some time to think about this. And when you've talked it through I'm sure you'll change your mind because Mal is a fantastic catch for any girl and you're really lucky.'

'This is nothing to do with His Royal Highness—' Kalila avoided Mal's gaze '—I don't want to be the Sultan's wife. I'd be hopeless. I'm shy and I'm not an interesting person.'

Avery gave Mal a look, expecting him to contradict her and when he didn't, she took over. 'That is not true at all. Just because you're shy doesn't mean you're not interesting.'

'You have no idea how hard I find it in crowds. And the Prince doesn't want to marry a mute. He gets really impatient when I don't speak.'

'Of course he doesn't!' Avery drove her elbow into Mal's ribs to prompt him to speak but he remained ominously silent. 'Mal loves you just the way you are.' Her less than subtle hint went unrewarded.

'He doesn't love me,' Kalila stammered, her face scarlet, 'he loves *you*.'

Silence filled the tent.

Avery felt as if someone was choking her. She lifted her hand to her throat, but there was nothing there, of course. Nothing she could loosen to help her breathing. 'That isn't true. He loves *you*. He asked you to marry him!'

'He asked you first.'

Oh, for crying out loud. 'No, he didn't, actually.' Avery spoke through her teeth. 'I don't know what you've heard, but that was all a big misunderstanding. You don't know the details.' *And why wasn't Mal telling her the truth? Putting her right?*

'I do know the details. I was there. I heard what he said. I heard him have a row with that horrible man who runs that oil production company and thinks he's irresistible—'

Avery frowned, confused. 'Richard?'

'Yes, him. He told Mal that you were planning his party and he was going to have you as a bonus. Mal was so angry he punched him. And when he dragged him out of the dirt where he'd knocked him, he told him that he was going to marry you and that you wouldn't be able to run any parties for him, now or in the future, personal or otherwise.'

Avery discovered that her mouth was open.

Slowly, she turned her head to look at Mal, waiting for him to deny it, but still he said nothing. Apart from a faint streak of colour across his cheekbones, he made no response.

Confusion washed over her. She knew he hadn't loved her. He'd proposed to Kalila within weeks of them parting. 'You misunderstood.'

'I was there,' Kalila said quietly. 'There was no misunderstanding. It's the only time anyone has seen Mal lose his cool.'

'Well, Richard can be a very annoying person. I've almost lost my cool with him a million times.' Dismissing the incident as a display of male jealousy, Avery forced herself back to the immediate situation. 'He was obviously trying to wind Mal up and he succeeded, which is why he said all that about marriage… That doesn't have any impact on what is going on here. Of course he wants to marry you. We've just spent two days chasing through the desert trying to find you.'

Kalila looked at her steadily. 'Together.'

'Not together *as such*—' Avery felt her cheeks darken as she thought about their night in the tent '—just because that's the way it worked out.'

'He went straight to you with the problem because he loves you and trusts you.'

'He came straight to me because he thought I might know where you were! That doesn't mean he loves me. He doesn't! I'd be a terrible Sultan's wife. Actually I'd be a terrible wife, full stop. I don't have any of the qualities necessary, in particular the fundamental one of actually *wanting* to get married.' She was stammering, falling over her words like a child practising public speaking for the first time, exasperated by Kalila's insistence that Mal loved her. 'We're just friends. And not even that, most of the time.'

Mal remained silent.

Why on earth didn't he *speak?* And why couldn't Kalila stop talking?

'You're the only woman he's ever loved,' she said. 'He was just marrying me for political reasons. Because it was agreed between our families.'

'Well, political reasons are as good a justification for marriage as any. I've known many fine, successful marriages that started from a lot less than that—'

'Avery—' Mal's voice was soft and he didn't turn his head in her direction '—you've said enough.'

'Enough? I've barely started. And you're not saying anything at all! Honestly, the pair of you just need to—' Her voice tailed off as he lifted his hand and she wondered how it was that he could silence her with a single subtle gesture that was barely visible to others.

Kalila bit her lip. 'You don't need to worry about it. It doesn't bother me that you don't love me, Your Highness. I don't love you either. It says something that we've known each other for years and we've barely spoken. To be honest—'

'*Don't* be honest,' Avery said quickly, interrupting before Kalila said something that couldn't be unsaid. 'Honesty is an overrated quality in certain circumstances and this is *definitely* one of them.'

'I need to say how I feel.' Kalila stuck her chin out and Avery sighed.

'Oh go on then, if you must, but you're not displaying any of the cardinal signs of shyness, I can tell you that. From where I'm standing you'd be fine at a public gathering. The challenge would be allowing someone else to get a word in edgeways.'

Kalila ignored her. 'Mal is gorgeous, of course. But he's also intimidating.'

'That's just his Prince act and he has to do that, otherwise he'd be mobbed by well-wishers, but underneath that frown he's a really gentle, cuddly guy—' Avery caught the lift of his dark eyebrows and cleared her throat 'Well, perhaps not *gentle*, exactly, but very decent. Principled. Good. And—'

'All right, that's enough. We're going to discuss this now and then the subject will never be raised again.' Finally Mal took charge and Avery relaxed slightly.

About time too.

Mal's eyes were fixed on his bride. 'You don't want to be married to a man who will become the Sultan?'

Avery gave a growl of exasperation. What was he *doing*? That was hardly going to persuade Kalila, was it? And, as if to prove her right, Kalila shook her head vigorously.

'No. I'll be hopeless, especially at all those meet and greet things you do. Parties.' She shuddered. 'The very worst of me would be on display.'

Giving up on Mal, Avery intervened again. 'Did your father tell you that? Because honestly, it's nonsense. You have a lovely personality. Stop putting yourself down! You have plenty to talk about. And anyway, all you have to do at these meet and greet gatherings is get people to talk about themselves. That's what I do all the time at my parties. I barely have to say a word. It's stopping people talking about themselves that's usually the problem, not starting them.'

'I'm nothing like you.'

'I know! And that's what makes you perfect for Mal. And you *are* perfect for him.' Avery beamed at her, hoping that her body language would reinforce the positive message. 'The moment I saw the two of you together, I knew you were a match made in heaven.'

Kalila's startled glance made her realise she might have been a bit too enthusiastic. Afraid that her response might have a counter-effect, she moderated her tone. 'There is no "right" personality for being a Sultan's bride. You'll be friendly and approachable and a real hit.'

'But I'll hate it. I will dread every moment.'

'It will get easier with time, I'm sure. I have some girls working for me who were pretty shy when they started and now I can't shut them up. Honestly, Kalila, you're going to be a huge success and very popular. I wish you'd just talked to someone about this instead of running away.'

'I did. I talked to you! You were my inspiration.'

Avery gulped. Heat rushed into her cheeks as she remembered Mal saying something similar. 'Me?'

'Yes. You told me to face my fears and that's what I did. I can't thank you enough.'

Avery made a vow never to give another person advice again as long as she lived. 'I was speaking metaphorically. I didn't actually mean for you to run off into the desert just because you're afraid of it.'

'That wasn't the fear I was facing.' Kalila lifted her chin, surprisingly stubborn. 'The fear I was facing—am still facing—is my father. All my life he's used fear to control me. I've never been allowed to do what I wanted to do. I'm not even allowed to express an opinion.'

Sympathy was eclipsed by her own feelings of panic as Avery watched the situation unravel. 'Your father doesn't even know you're gone yet. Everyone has been covering for you. You haven't actually faced him. You've avoided him.'

'I've faced the fear of him. For the first time in my life, I've done something I know will incur his disapproval. I know there will be consequences and I'm willing to take them. I knew that if I ran off he would never forgive me. He will not have me back in his house, under his roof. I will no longer be his daughter.' Kalila clasped her hands together nervously. 'And that's what I want.'

'Well then, that's perfect, because soon you can be Mal's wife. This doesn't mean you can't marry the Prince. I'm sure there's a way round this that is going to be fine for everyone—' Her voice tailed off because Kalila was staring at her in disbelief and Avery realised how crazy she must sound. Apart from admitting that the last thing in the world she wanted was to be the Sultan's wife, the woman was clearly obsessed with her bodyguard. There was no way on this planet Mal would marry her now. How could he? And truly, she wouldn't want that for him, would she? She, who knew how badly so many marriages ended, would never want one to start in such inauspicious circumstances.

Avery's shoulders slumped. She stole a glance at Mal but he seemed maddeningly calm about the whole thing.

'So this is what you want, Kalila?' His blunt question brought colour pouring into Kalila's cheeks.

'Yes. I'm in love with Karim. I just want to live with him quietly.' She gave her shrinking beau a trembling smile. 'For ever. Happily ever after. I feel so happy.'

'I feel so sick,' Avery muttered but Mal ignored her.

'Fine. If you're sure that's what you want, then I'll make that happen. If your father won't approve the match then you can live in Zubran under my protection. You can have your happy ever after, Kalila, with my compliments.'

'"*You can have your happy ever after*"! What sort of romantic claptrap is that? Have you gone totally mad?' Exasperated and upset for him, Avery followed Mal as he strode from the tent towards the desert. Her head was in a spin. 'You didn't even bother trying to talk her out of it.

If anything you made it easy for her by offering her sanctuary. Why didn't you just offer to conduct the ceremony while you were at it?'

Not only did she not understand it, but Mal seemed in no hurry to explain himself.

'Drop it, Avery.'

'Drop it?' She virtually had to run to keep pace with him. 'Sorry, but did we or did we not just spend two days roughing it in the desert in order to find Kalila and persuade her not to run away?'

'Certainly the intention was to find her. And we did that. Thank you for your assistance.'

Avery gave a murmur of frustration. She opened her mouth to ask him if the sun had gone to his head but he was already several strides ahead of her and she could see that he was angry.

Well, of course he was angry.

He'd found Kalila with another man.

Perhaps that explained his reaction, or lack of it. He was too gutted to respond. And too hurt to discuss it with her now.

She tried to imagine how he must feel, but as someone who had never seen marriage as an attractive option she honestly didn't have a clue. In his position she would have been rejoicing at the narrow escape, but of course he wasn't going to feel that way. He'd wanted this marriage. And as for the business with Richard—

And everything Kalila had said about Mal being in love with her—

Avery stared after him, Kalila's words in her head.

He hadn't been in love with her. She'd presented him with a challenge, that was all. They'd had fun together.

How could he have been in love? The moment they'd broken up he'd become engaged to another woman. He'd started planning his wedding. Those weren't the actions of a man in love.

She glanced towards the car and then back towards his rapidly vanishing figure.

'Damn and blast.' How could she leave him on his own? When he hurt, she hurt. It was like being physically connected and it was a bond she'd been trying to break for longer than she cared to remember.

Muttering under her breath, Avery strode after him, tugging the brim of her hat down over her eyes to shield herself from the blaze of the desert sun and the scrutiny of curious tourists. *Relationships,* she thought. *Why did anyone bother?* Her mother was right. They were nothing but trouble.

As she approached him, she tried to work out what to say.

Better now than in ten years' time...

Lucky escape, my friend...

One in three marriages end in divorce and that's without counting the number that carry on in faithless misery...

Truthfully, she wasn't good at broken relationship counselling.

When friends' relationships broke down her standard support offering was a girls' night in. Or out. Either evening featured copious volumes of good wine combined with a boosting talk about the benefits of being single. By the time the evening was over they were generally talking about lucky escapes and exciting futures. If the malaise continued she dragged them shoe shopping, used her connections to get them a discount on a dreamy hotel in an exotic location and pointed out all the things they could do single that they couldn't do as a couple. Unfortunately she had nothing in her armoury to prepare her for consoling a Prince who had lost his bride.

Normally she considered herself a competent person but right now she felt anything but competent. As she strolled up to his side, his shoulders stiffened but he didn't turn.

Avery stood awkwardly, trying to imagine what he was thinking so that she could say the right thing. She knew how important this marriage had been to him. And now he had to unravel what could only be described as a mess. Despite that, he'd treated Kalila with patience and kindness—probably more kindness than she'd been shown in her life before.

The girl was a fool, Avery thought savagely, tilting her head back and staring up at the perfect blue of the desert sky. For someone dreaming of happy endings as Kalila clearly was, she couldn't have done better than Mal.

Slowly, she turned her head to look at him, her gaze resting on the strong, proud lines of his handsome face. Not knowing what to do, she lifted her hand, hesitated, and then placed it on his shoulder, feeling the tension in the muscle under her fingers. 'I'm sorry. I know how upset you are. And I'm sorry I couldn't fix it.'

'But you had to keep trying.' His voice was harsh and she blinked, taken aback by his tone.

'Er…yes. *Obviously* I was trying to persuade her to change her mind.'

'Then let's just be grateful you didn't succeed.'

'Grateful?' Avery let her hand fall from his shoulder. 'But you *wanted* this marriage! I know you wanted this marriage.'

He turned his head and the look in his eyes made her heart stutter in her chest. His mouth twisted into a cynical smile as he observed her reaction. 'You consider yourself an expert on what I want, *habibti*?'

The look in his eyes confused her. Were they still talking about Kalila? 'You have a wedding planned. We've just

chased across a desert to find your bride. It seems reasonable to assume this is what you wanted and yet now that
she's broken it off you're not putting up a fight and you
don't seem remotely heartbroken.'

There was a strange light in his eyes. 'Heartbroken?'

Exasperated and confused by his lack of emotion, Avery
held back her temper. 'OK, so obviously you're *not* heartbroken because you don't have a heart. Silly me.'

'You think I don't have a heart?' Under the sweep of
thick dark lashes, something dangerous lurked in his eyes
and Avery felt as if she'd just jumped into the ocean and
found herself way out of her depth.

How had she ever become trapped in this conversation?
They were supposed to be talking about Kalila.

'All I know is that you don't seem to be fighting to keep
her. Is it pride?' And she knew all about that, didn't she?
'Because honestly I think you should try and get over that.
She's perfect for you in so many ways. Go back in there
now, give that muscle-bound wimp his marching orders—
and by the way, she needs a new bodyguard because that
one *definitely* isn't fit for purpose—and talk some sense
into her.'

Her words were greeted by a prolonged silence.

Just when it was becoming awkward, he breathed
deeply. 'Are you really that desperate to see me married
to someone else?'

'Yes—' Her heart was bumping and she trod through
the conversation like someone walking on quicksand. 'Yes,
I am.'

There was a hard, humourless slant to his smile. 'Would
that make it easier?'

It would have been a waste of time to pretend she didn't
know what he was talking about. Their eyes locked for a

brief moment but it was long enough for her to know that she was in trouble. 'Let's not do this, Mal.'

But of course he didn't listen. His hand slid beneath her chin and he forced her to look at him. 'We're doing this.' This time his tone was harsh. 'We've wasted enough time and taken enough wrong turnings. Just because we made a mistake once doesn't mean we have to do it again.'

'For crying out loud—' the words were shaky '—five minutes ago you were engaged to marry another woman.'

'That wasn't my choice. This is.'

That didn't make sense to her. Despite duty and responsibility, he was a man who chose his own path.

'What the hell are you saying? Mal—'

'Tell me why you were so determined that I marry Kalila. Tell me, Avery. Spell it out.'

'Because you're the marrying type and because she's perfect for you and because—' she choked on the confession '—and because I thought it would make it easier if you were married.'

Emotion flared in his eyes. 'And did it?'

'No.' The words came out as a whisper. 'No. It didn't. Nothing does. But that doesn't stop me hoping and trying.'

'You don't have to do either.'

Yes, she did. 'Nothing has changed, Mal—'

That clearly wasn't the answer he wanted and he looked away for a moment, jaw tense. 'No? If that's true then it's just because you are the most stubborn woman I've ever met. But I can be stubborn too.' Without giving her a chance to respond, he closed his hand over hers and pulled his phone out of his pocket. After a brief one-way conversation during which he delivered what sounded like a volley of instructions in his own language, he hung up. 'Is there anything in your bag that you need? Because if there is, tell me now.'

'Need for what? Who were you phoning?'

'Rafiq. You remember my Chief Adviser?'

'Of course. I love him. I would have offered him a job on my team if I'd thought there was any chance that he'd leave you. So what completely unreasonable request have you placed in the poor man's lap this time?' As the words left her mouth she heard the sound of a helicopter approach and looked up, her brows lifting as she saw the Sultan's insignia. 'I see you and discretion have parted company.'

'There is no longer a need for discretion. There is, however, a need to get the next part of the journey over as fast as possible.'

'You're leaving in style, Mal, I have to hand you that.'

'*We're* leaving in style.' His grip on her hand tightened. 'You're coming with me.'

It was a command, not a question.

Avery's heart stumbled but whether that was because of his unexpected words or the feel of his fingers locked with hers, she wasn't sure. 'What about Kalila?'

'Can we *stop* talking about Kalila?' His tone was raw. 'She has my protection and I will do my best for her, but right now I don't want to waste any more time thinking about it.'

'I really ought to get back to London. I have the Senator's party to run and I can't just take time off.'

'Of course you can. You're the boss. You can do whatever you like. Call Jenny and put her in charge for a few days.'

'I couldn't possibly do that.' Her mouth was dry and her heart was pounding. 'It's out of the question.'

'Really? The advice you give others is to face your fears—' ebony eyes glittered dark with mockery '—and yet I don't see you facing yours.'

'There's nothing to face. I'm not afraid.'

'Yes, you are. You're terrified. So terrified that your hands are shaking.'

'You're wrong.' She stuffed her hands in her pockets. 'So if you're such an expert you'd better tell me what it is I'm supposedly afraid of.'

'Me,' he said softly. 'You're afraid to be alone with me.'

CHAPTER SIX

MAL was braced for her to throw a million arguments why she couldn't do this but she simply lifted her chin in the air and walked briskly by his side to the helicopter and he allowed himself a smile because although she would have hated to admit it, she was totally predictable. Because he'd challenged her, she just had to prove him wrong.

As the ever loyal Rafiq appeared, Mal delivered a series of succinct instructions, threw him the keys to the vehicle and followed Avery into the helicopter.

There were a million things that demanded his attention, but only one that he cared about right at that moment.

And suddenly he was grateful for her pride and stubbornness because it was only those two things that had her stepping into his helicopter without an argument. It was pride that kept that back straight as she settled into her seat, pride that had her greeting his pilot with her usual warm smile and no visible evidence of tension.

As the doors closed, she turned to him, her gaze cool. 'So here I am. By your side and unafraid. Sorry to disappoint you. You've lost.'

'I'm not disappointed.' And he certainly hadn't lost.

'So where are we going?'

'Somewhere we can be sure of privacy.' He watched as

her shoulders shifted defensively and her mouth tightened as she instinctively recoiled from the threat of intimacy.

'I'm surprised you don't just want to return to the palace. Your wedding plans have fallen apart. Shouldn't you be talking to your father?'

'I've already spoken to him. I told him I will be back in a few days and we can discuss it further then.'

'I would have thought the cancellation of your marriage would have taken precedence over everything else.'

'Not everything.' Not *this*. The most important thing of all.

He realised now how badly he'd got it wrong. He, who prided himself on his negotiation skills, had made so many fundamental errors with this woman who was so unlike any other woman.

He'd been complacent. Sure of himself. Sure of *her*.

It wasn't a mistake he was going to make again.

The helicopter rose into the air and neither of them spoke again during the forty-minute journey. And then he saw the change in her as she finally realised their destination. 'The Zubran Desert Spa?'

She'd used it as a venue for an event a while back. It had been the place they'd moved from friends to something more. It had significance, marking an important milestone in their relationship.

He'd chosen it for that reason. He'd wanted significance. He wanted to tear down every barrier she erected between them and when she turned to face him he knew he'd succeeded.

'Why here?'

'Why not?'

Blame mingled with vulnerability. 'You're not playing fair.'

Could he be accused of dirty tactics? Possibly, but he felt

no guilt. When the stakes were this high, all tactics were justified. He was going to use everything at his disposal to get her to open up. He was going to fight for their relationship, fight *her* if necessary, and he'd keep fighting until he had the outcome he wanted. He hadn't expected to get a second chance but now he had, he wasn't going to waste it.

'I don't play to be fair. I play to win.'

'You mean you have to get your own way in everything.'

'Hardly.' If he'd had his own way they never would have parted. It had been the first time in his life he'd felt helpless.

As the doors to the helicopter opened, they were met by the hotel manager and an entourage of excited staff.

'They've mistaken you for a rock star,' Avery murmured as she reached for her bag and stood up. 'Do you want to break it to them that you're no one important, or shall I?'

'I suggest you don't ruin their fun.'

'When a new employee starts in my office and they're overwhelmed by the people we deal with, I remind them that famous people are all human beings with the same basic needs.'

'Sexual?'

Colour warmed her cheeks. 'How typical of you to pick that need first. Others would have gone for something different.'

'Others haven't just been trapped in a desert with you for two days.' Speaking under his breath, Mal urged her towards the welcoming committee.

'Your Highness, it is a pleasure to welcome you back. We are so honoured that you have chosen to spend a few days with us.' Clearly overwhelmed by the importance of his guest, the manager of the hotel bowed deeply. 'Your instructions have been carried out precisely, but should you need anything else—'

'Privacy.' Mal's eyes were on Avery's taut profile. 'My greatest need right at this moment is for privacy.'

'And we pride ourselves on our ability to offer our guests exactly that. I will escort you straight to the Sultan's Suite, Your Highness, and can I say once again what an honour it is to be able to welcome you.'

The Sultan's Suite. The place they'd spent their first night together.

Avery tried to slow her pace but he gripped her hand firmly as they walked along the curving path that led to the exclusive desert villa. And it was no use pretending that he was forcing her. She was a grown woman with a mind of her own. She could have walked away at any point in the past few hours, but she hadn't. And what did that make her? A fool, definitely.

If only he hadn't accused her of being scared. That comment alone had made it impossible for her to refuse, and—

—he'd made it impossible for her to refuse!

Her eyes narrowed dangerously.

She turned her head to look at him, the movement sending her hair whipping across her back. 'You are an underhanded, manipulative snake.' She kept her voice low so that the manager couldn't overhear but clearly Mal caught the words because he smiled.

'Save the compliments until we are alone, *habibti.*'

'You made that comment about me being afraid because you knew I'd have to prove you wrong.'

'So does that make me manipulative or you predictable?'

The fact that he knew her so well didn't improve her mood. 'I suppose you think you're clever.'

'Desperate,' he murmured, his thumb stroking her palm. 'Desperate would be the word I'd use. Even famous people have needs, you know.'

She did know.

And the contrast between his gentle, seductive touch and the raw desire she saw in his eyes unsettled her more than words could. The heat rushed through her and suddenly she was truly afraid. Not of him but for herself. She'd spent the past months trying to get over him. Hauling herself out of bed every day and reminding herself that she was not going to ruin her life over a man, even a spectacular man. And yet here she was, about to risk it all again.

And now there was no Kalila. There was no virgin bride. Nothing to keep them apart.

Nothing except all the usual reasons.

She tried to snatch her hand from his but his grip was unyielding. 'This is a mistake.'

'If it's a mistake then I'll take it like a man.'

That offered her no comfort because his masculinity had never been in question. From the hard-packed muscle of his wide shoulders to the powerful legs and the iron self-discipline that drove him, he was more of a man than any she'd met.

'You're going to regret this.'

And so was she.

When he'd told her to drop everything and come with him she should have pleaded workload or an event that couldn't possibly continue without her personal attention. Anything that would have got her out of this situation.

But the manager was already bowing again as they reached the doorway of the exclusive villa and it was too late for her to back out.

'The doctor is waiting for you, Your Highness, as instructed.'

Mal murmured his thanks and Avery frowned.

'Doctor?' She tugged her hand free of his and pulled off

her hiking boots. It was a relief to be rid of them because they were heavy and hot. 'Who needs a doctor?'

'You do. I want you checked after that scorpion bite.'

'Oh for goodness' sake, I'm fine.'

'The doctor will decide that.'

'He might send me home,' she muttered in an undertone. 'Have you thought of that?'

'Or he might send you to bed, where you are going to end up either way.'

'You think so? Maybe you're a little over-confident, Your Highness.'

'And you are the most aggravating woman I've ever encountered. The scorpion met its match. Even now it is probably engaged in a session of psychotherapy as part of the recovery process.' Mal stepped forward and there was a brief exchange with the doctor, during which Avery tapped her foot impatiently.

'I am as healthy as a horse.'

'When I hear that from a professional I will be reassured. If you go through to the master bedroom, he will examine you. And try not to take your frustration out on the doctor. He's an innocent party.'

'You think I'm frustrated?'

'I truly hope so. But we'll talk about this later.' Maddeningly cool, Mal strolled towards the bedroom and opened the doors and her heart skidded in her chest because there in the centre was the hand-crafted bed that had witnessed the shift in their relationship from friends to lovers.

The sensual, unashamed luxury of the suite unsettled her as much as the look in his eyes.

'What's the doctor supposed to do? Declare me fit for action?' Her response was flippant and she realised that she hadn't thought about the scorpion bite for hours. She'd been too caught up in all the drama and the swirling mess of her own feelings. She'd been too busy thinking about *him*.

And he knew it.

He hovered while the doctor examined her and Avery almost felt sorry for the man as Mal subjected him to a volley of cross-questioning until finally he was satisfied.

Exhausted, she flopped back against the pillows. 'You terrified that poor man. His hands were shaking. For God's sake, Mal, ease up on people, will you?'

'I just wanted to make sure he was thorough.'

The room was the ultimate in sophistication. Decorated with elaborate woven rugs and antique furniture, the doors opened onto an uninterrupted view of the desert. Last time she was here with him she'd taken a picture of the same view at sunset and made it her screen saver. Seeing it again now made her heart lift and ache at the same time because it brought back memories of a time when life had been close to perfect.

The mattress dipped slightly as Mal sat down next to her. 'You are thinking about the last time we were here.'

'No. I don't do that sort of thing. If you wanted sentimental then you picked the wrong woman. But you discovered that a while ago.' Sliding away from him, Avery sprang from the bed. 'What I was actually thinking is that I need a shower. My hair is full of sand. My clothes are full of sand. Right now I'm more camel than human.' She shot towards the bathroom because it was the only room with a lock on the door, but he caught her easily and pulled her firmly back towards him.

'There is nowhere to run. It's just you and me, *habibti.*'

'And you only have yourself to blame for that. I told you you'd regret it.'

'Do I look as if I'm regretting it?' Smiling slightly, he slid his hands either side of her face, tilting her head. 'Do you really want to fight? Because I'll fight if that's what you want. Or you could listen to an alternative suggestion as to how we can spend this time we have together.'

'No.' The word was meant to be firm and decisive. Instead it sounded more like a pathetic plea and he frowned, the smile fading from his eyes.

'How long are you going to keep pretending this isn't what you want?'

'As long as it takes for you to get the message. What I want is a shower.' Her voice was croaky. And she was terrified. Terrified of the thought of doing this again. Of risking everything. *Of being hurt.*

'Shower first?' He lifted his hand and freed her hair.

'First?'

'I thought you might be hungry.'

'Shower sounds good. But I don't have clothes to change into. You should have thought of that before you kidnapped me.'

His fingers lingered on her hair. 'I can solve that, too.'

'How?'

'Sometimes being a Prince has its advantages.'

Her heart was beating fast but whether it was the fact that he was touching her or the fact that he was standing so close to her, she didn't know. 'So you've been shamelessly using your position and influence to coerce people.'

'Something like that.'

'I'm not impressed. It doesn't work on me.'

'It never did. But you *do* want me. Are you going to admit it?'

'Not until all the sand has blown from the desert.'

His eyes glittered dark. 'Then I'll have to use other means to get the truth from you.'

'You resort to violence now?'

His mouth twisted. '*Not* violence. But you will be honest because I am finished with games.'

They were talking, but words were only part of the communication between them. There was the subtle brush of his hand against her cheek. The meaningful look. The sudden rapid sprint of her heart as it hammered against her ribs. It was useless to pretend he had no effect on her. That she was immune. She was as susceptible now as she always had been. And he knew it. And the fact that he knew it made her furious. Furious with herself. Even more furious with him.

Avery pulled away and stalked over to the bathroom that adjoined the master suite. She knew her way. Had been there before. But even here the memories followed her because they'd used this room for more than a shower. 'You're crowding me and I need time to think. Don't follow me, Mal.'

And because she didn't trust him not to do that, she locked the door. And then spent several minutes just staring at it, knowing he was on the other side and discovering that a locked door wasn't enough to keep the feelings away. And that was because he wasn't the problem, was he? The problem was *her*.

She stripped off her clothes, then walked into the shower and stood under the sharp needles of hot water, washing away two days of hot, sticky travelling in the desert. She lathered her hair in expensive shampoo that smelt like lotus flowers, massaged conditioner and then stood for ages with her eyes closed while the water washed over her.

But she couldn't stay in the shower for ever.

Reluctantly, she turned off the flow of water and wrapped herself in one of the large fluffy towels that were stacked inside a glass cabinet.

Then she turned and found him standing there.

'You forgot that the bathroom has two entrances. You only locked one door.'

'Another man would have taken that as a hint.'

'And you know that how?' His ebony hair glistened dark and his broad shoulders were still damp from the shower he'd clearly taken in another bathroom. He was in the process of knotting the towel around his hips. 'Have you had other lovers in the time we've been apart?'

Other lovers? The question would have made her laugh if it hadn't hurt so much. *He didn't have a clue what he'd done to her.*

She was distracted by the flat planes of his abdomen, as hard as a board and with a tantalising line of dark hair vanishing beneath the towel. 'Of course I had other lovers. Why do you ask? Did you think I'd been pining for you?'

'Be grateful that I know you're lying. And I take it as a good sign that you're trying to protect yourself.'

'Well, if you think you know so much about me, why ask?'

'Because I want you to admit how you feel.'

'Right now? Pretty annoyed. You're in my personal space.'

'You think I'm in your personal space? Try this—' He moved so fast that she didn't see it coming and before she could even murmur his name his mouth was on hers and the chemistry was instantaneous and as powerful as ever. Everything they'd been holding back came rushing straight at them. His hands were on her hips, tugging away the towel and hers were doing the same to his until they were both naked and the only sounds in the room were his harsh breathing and her soft gasps. Abstinence bred desperation and desperation had him scooping her into his arms and carrying her to the bedroom, still kissing, their mouths hungry and demanding as they made up for lost time.

'Only you can do this to me.' He murmured the words against her mouth as he lowered her into the centre of the huge hand-crafted bed. 'Only you, and this time we are doing this properly. No more encounters in the bathroom or desperate snatched moments wherever we can take them.'

She didn't care. She didn't care where they were as long as they were together and when he came down on top of her she immediately rolled so that he was underneath.

'Battle for supremacy?' His eyes glittered dark and she smiled down at him, her lips skimming his because after so long without touching him she needed to touch.

'Can you take it?'

'Can *you*?'

And it was a question she was to ask herself over and over again as he used all his skill and knowledge to drive her wild. She didn't believe in love. She didn't believe in happy ever after. But she believed in *this* and wondered how she'd survived so long without his touch and then realised that she barely had. That every day since they'd parted she'd been starving for him.

He was hard, hot and hers, and being with him again felt crazily good. So good that she was clumsy as she moved against him and of course he took instant advantage of that, rolling and pinning her beneath him.

'I missed you.' He groaned the words against her neck and she closed her eyes because hearing him say it choked her up so badly.

'No, you didn't.'

'Yes, I did. And you missed me too.'

'No, I didn't.'

'Yes, you did. Say those words back to me, Avery. Be honest.' His hand cupped her face. 'It doesn't make you weak to admit it.'

No, but it made her vulnerable. 'I missed having someone to argue with, that's true.' She made the mistake of opening her eyes at that moment and met the heat in his. His mouth curved into a slow, sexy smile of complete understanding.

'Of course, you missed the arguments and that is all. You didn't miss this—' eyes half shut, he stroked a hand down her body and she gasped '—or this—' he moved his hand lower still and this time she moaned '—and you definitely didn't miss *this*.'

This had her writhing under him but he denied her the satisfaction she craved, easing away slightly when she arched her hips against him.

'Do you realise that the only time you show your feelings is when we're in bed together?' His voice was husky and he pinned her arms above her head, holding her captive. 'Apart from the scorpion sting, the only time I've ever seen you vulnerable is when you're in my bed.'

'It wasn't always your bed. Sometimes it was my bed.' Her heart was thumping because of course she was vulnerable. Terrifyingly so, naked in every way. All of her exposed to this man who saw so much and yet still insisted on more.

'Are you going to tell me why you're so afraid?'

'Afraid?' She tugged gently at his hands but he held her firmly. 'I'm not afraid.'

'If you're not afraid then stop trying to free yourself.' His mouth trailed over her shoulder, his tongue slow and explicit as he traced her skin. 'If you're not afraid then you should just trust me not to hurt you. It shouldn't be hard.'

It was the hardest thing in the world, to put her safety in the hands of another person. To trust her heart to the one person in the world who could break it. It was too much to ask. He wanted her to surrender something she couldn't surrender. To submit to something that terrified her because she knew that whatever he gave, he could also take away.

His mouth moved lower, his tongue flicked her nipple and a low moan of pleasure escaped her.

'Mal—'

'Trust me not to hurt you.' He murmured the words against her skin, against her body, already damp from his tongue and shivering with an excitement so intense it was impossible to keep still. She squirmed and her breath caught at the feel of him, the rough hardness of his thigh and the thickness of his penis as his powerful body brushed against hers. The extent of his arousal mirrored hers and she tried to wrap her arms around him and urge him on but he held her hands fast so that she had no choice but to submit to his will.

Struggling to stay in control, to stay in charge, Avery closed her eyes and blocked out the sensual gleam in those dark eyes. As always, he drove her to the edge. Even with her eyes closed she felt restraint slip. She couldn't remember actually why she was trying to prevent this happening. Excitement engulfed her in great waves until she was drowning in sensation, the feelings of her body colliding with her fears.

His tongue flicked over the sensitive tips of her breasts, his touch so skilled that she felt the sensation deep inside her. She squirmed, her hips shifting against the luxurious sheets, but he showed her no mercy. A moan escaped her lips but his response to that was to slide his hand between her legs, to apply his expertise to that part of her that now ached for his touch. And touch her he did, those long, strong fingers shamelessly knowing as he drove her wild, controlling her response and easing back as he felt the first ripple of her body.

'No. Not yet.'

Denied the completion she craved, she moaned against his mouth. 'Not fair.'

'I want you. All of you.' He murmured the words against her mouth and she parted her lips and tried to steal a kiss but with her hands held and her body trapped beneath the powerful strength of male muscle, she wasn't the one in control. He kept his mouth just out of reach of hers, close enough to drive her crazy and make her desperate for his kiss, not close enough for her to take control.

'Mal—'

'I want you to trust me.' He spoke softly but there was no mistaking the command in his voice and had they been in a different position she would have smiled because he just couldn't help himself. Even now, in this position of extreme intimacy, he had to be in control.

'I don't trust anyone but myself.'

'Up until now that might have been true—' His fingers, placed tantalizingly close to that delicate part of her, traced her so gently, so skilfully that the exquisite pleasure swelled to something close to pain. Her body throbbed with her need for him and he knew it. She knew he knew it because she felt his smile against her mouth as he finally lowered his head to hers and gave her what she'd craved. His tongue slid over hers, bold, demanding and unashamedly sensual while all the time his fingers worked magic. And still he held her hands. Still he held her trapped and the ease with which he did it confirmed that physically he was the stronger, but she couldn't allow herself to surrender in the way he wanted her to surrender.

'Let go of me. I want to touch you.'

'No. For now, I'm the one in charge. The sooner you acknowledge that, the sooner I let you go.' His hand pushed her thighs wider and with a single smooth movement he was inside her. Deep, sure but achingly slow and gentle and that control on his part tore at the last straining threads of hers.

She moaned and he withdrew slightly and then moved again, deeper this time, his hand on her hip, controlling her movements. The look in his eyes made it hard to catch her breath and she wanted to close hers, to block him out, but something in her wouldn't allow it so the connection continued, deepening an experience that was already terrifying.

It had never been like this before. The sex had always been amazing and each time had been different but never, ever had it felt like this. Never this close. Never this— *personal.*

He'd never demanded this much from her and she'd never given this much.

She felt the strength of him, the power of him stretching her, possessing her and she wrapped her legs around him, always active, never passive and he smiled against her lips because he recognised that need in her. He knew her so well. He knew all of her and she tried again to block him out because the level of intimacy was terrifying. She was bound, not by the fact that he held her hands, but by the fact that he held her heart. If she begged him, he'd let her hands go. Physically, she'd be free. Emotionally, she knew she'd never be free. He was the only man she wanted. He was the only man she'd ever wanted and those feelings bound her to him as securely as if she'd been handcuffed.

'Stop fighting it—' he kissed her slowly '—stop fighting me and pushing me away.'

'I'm not pushing you. Thanks to you, I can't move.'

'I'm not talking about physically and you know it.' His mouth was still on hers. Gentle and yet demanding at the same time. 'I'm talking about everything else.'

'What else is there?'

'You know.'

Yes, she knew and this time she managed to close her eyes, moaning a low denial. 'You are asking too much.'

'I'm asking a lot. But not too much.'

'You don't know.'

'If there are things I don't know then it's because you've never trusted me enough to tell me. I won't hurt you.'

And she knew he wasn't talking about the physical side of their relationship. He wasn't talking about sex or anything that they were doing right now in this bed. That wouldn't have scared her. What scared her was the fact that he *would* hurt her. Maybe not now, or even tomorrow but at some point in their relationship, perhaps even when she'd started to rely on having him in her life.

He'd hurt her before...

Panic washed over her. 'Mal—'

'I want it all, Avery. Everything you've never given before. I want that from you.' His free hand locked in her hair. 'I won't be satisfied with less than everything.'

She moaned because he was deep inside her and thinking clearly no longer seemed easy and natural. In fact thinking felt impossible as he took her in a slow, sensuous rhythm that drove her wild.

'I want to know about the dream.'

'The dream?'

'Those dreams you have. Tell me—' he breathed the words against her mouth as he broke one erotic kiss and started another '—tell me what it is that makes you moan in your sleep and wake with dark circles under those beautiful eyes.'

She was dizzy from his kisses, melting and desperate from each carefully timed thrust. 'I dream about work—' she moaned as his tongue slid into contact with hers and her senses exploded '—work.'

'Work?' His hand moved down, lower, sliding under her bottom, holding her firm as he deepened his possession. 'It's work that makes you cry out?'

'Yes.' She was on the point of begging because he'd held her at this point for so long and she didn't think she could stand it any longer. She ached with need. She craved him in a way that was indecent.

'You're lying. Tell me what you dream about.' The husky tone of his voice was unbearably sexy and she wondered how he could still string a sentence together when she herself was barely able to give voice to a moan.

'Avery—' Purring her name, he sank deep into her quivering flesh and Avery lost her grip on control, every sense in her body teased to its limits under his skilled touch. As she lost control of herself she realised that her mother had got it wrong. Yes, she could be responsible for her own orgasm, but it was so much better when someone else was. And she could be responsible for her own heart too, but sharing it was the greatest gift she could give and she wanted to share it with this man.

'You,' she gasped as he brought ecstasy crashing down on them. 'I dream about you.'

Mal lay in the dark, wrapped in the scent of her and the softness of her, holding her in the curve of his arm as the rising sun sent arrows of golden light shooting across the desert. Apart from the night of the scorpion sting, this was the first time she'd allowed herself to fall asleep in his arms, as if it were somehow a weakness to do that.

And there was no doubt in his mind that she saw it that way. As if admitting to having feelings for a man somehow threatened who she was.

It was ironic, he thought, because in many ways she was the strongest person he knew and yet he understood that her independence was driven by fear as much as anything. Fear of being let down. Fear of hurt. She'd told him little about her past but what little she'd told him had been sufficient for him to form a picture of a life lived devoid of paternal influence.

He'd read about her mother. About the impressive divorce lawyer who had sacrificed everything on her way to the top. Clearly she'd also sacrificed her relationship with Avery's father because there was no mention of him anywhere, and no doubt that negative experience was responsible for her damaged view of marriage. He told himself that he shouldn't judge, especially given that he knew countless men who had done the same thing. Men who had put their own ambitions before the needs of their loved ones. Marriages died. It was a fact of life.

But they'd made progress.

It wasn't much of a leap to go from 'I dream about you' to 'I love you'.

And he was confident she was ready to make that leap.

She woke to warmth and a safe feeling. Struggling up through clouds of sleep, Avery opened her eyes and the first thing she saw was bronzed skin and male muscle.

Mal.

She'd spent the night with Mal. The whole night. Not just a few hours and not even just sleeping in the same bed, but *with* him, snuggled. Joined. And after months of trying to piece herself back together, piece by broken piece.

Warmth was replaced by dismay. What had she done?

It was like spending a year on a diet and then taking a job in a chocolate factory and binging from dawn to dusk. She was *furious* with herself—and with him for assuming that he could just pick up where he'd left off.

Panic exploded and she tried to wrench herself away

from him but his arms tightened like a steel band, locking her against him.

'What's the matter?'

'I'm suffering a serious case of morning-after regret. Let me go.' Had he always had muscles like this? She strained against his hold but there was no shifting him.

'You're not going anywhere. If there are things you want to say then you can say them here.'

Pressed against his warm naked body with every passing second reminding her of last night and weakening her resolve?

'Let me go.'

'Never.' He didn't open his eyes and a slight smile tilted the corners of his firm, sexy mouth. 'You are running away from me yet again like the coward you are.'

'I'm not a coward.'

'No?' His eyes opened a fraction and he looked at her, his expression shielded by the thickness of dark lashes. 'Prove it, *habibti*. Stay where you are. Do not create the distance your instinct tells you to create. Last night, for once, you were honest. Embrace it. Face the fear.'

'Last night I was an idiot. And I *don't* want this! I had it once before and it was truly horrible.' She shoved him hard and sprang from the bed, her heart racing and panic gripping her like the talons of one of his falcons.

'Horrible?' His tone was several shades cooler. 'You are saying our relationship was horrible?'

'Not our relationship, no, the part when it ended.' Flustered and confused and horribly conscious that she was naked, she grabbed the nearest item of clothing, which just happened to be his discarded shirt. 'You just don't get it, do you?'

He lifted himself onto his elbow, his inky black hair flopping over his forehead. The sheet drifted down, displaying packed muscle and abs as hard as steel. 'Given that you were the one who ended it, no, I don't.'

She thought back to that time and didn't know whether to cry or punch him. 'Never mind.' The words were thickened around the lump in her throat and she pulled on the shirt, covering herself. 'Forget it. I'd be grateful if you'd do your powerful Prince thing and call your helicopter. It's time for me to go home.'

'Wearing nothing but my shirt?'

'I'll change.'

'Don't bother. I'm not letting you go again.' He was so sure of himself and who could blame him after the way she'd folded in his arms only a few hours earlier.

'It isn't your choice, it's mine and I choose not to do this again. I won't make the same mistake twice.' But she'd already made it, hadn't she? She'd already taken more than a few steps down that path. And the wounds of her healing heart were already bleeding again. And that was her fault. Despite everything, she'd allowed them to be ripped open a second time.

'Are you pretending that we're not good together?'

His lack of insight was like a punch to her belly. Her emotions overflowed. 'You don't have a clue, do you? You have absolutely no idea.' She paced to the far side of the bedroom on legs that shook so badly she wasn't confident of their ability to fulfil their purpose. 'We've done this once before, Mal, and when it fell apart it left me in pieces. I was…was broken, and helpless and utterly pathetic and… God, I can't believe I just told you that.' Turning away from him, she covered her face with her hands. 'Just stop this, *please*. I don't want a post-mortem. Last night was last night but that's it. That's all it was. One night. No more. I can't give any more.'

But it was too late. He was already out of the bed and

next to her, gloriously naked and completely indifferent to that fact. 'You were in pieces?' The light humour had gone. In its place was nothing but raw emotion. '*When* were you in pieces? Because whenever I contacted you, you were the most perfect example of someone completely together. I did *not* see a woman in pieces, I saw a woman who didn't give a damn. Until last night that's all I've ever seen when I've looked at you.'

'Well, what did you expect?' She let her hands drop and she was yelling now, completely forgetting to lower her voice and incapable of playing it cool. 'After everything I gave you, you did that to me.'

'Everything you gave me?'

'Yes.' Her voice cracked. 'With you I did something I'd never done with a man before—I gave you my heart and you sliced it up into a million pieces and served it up in public like chopped liver. *"Here, look at this everyone, help yourself."*' That confession was followed by a horrible silence. She waited for him to say something but instead he simply stared at her, his cheeks unnaturally pale.

He swallowed, although that manoeuvre appeared to cause him difficulty. '*You* were the one who ended our relationship.'

'And weeks later you were engaged to Kalila. And news of that engagement was everywhere. I couldn't go on the Internet without having pictures of the happy couple flashed in front of my face. And everyone was watching me, waiting for me to fall apart. *Everyone.* It was like being an exhibit in a zoo. Do you know how hard it was to drag myself out of bed in the morning and face the world? Because I can tell you it was hell.'

He looked shell-shocked. 'Avery—'

'And as if it wasn't bad enough, you then had the gall to ask me to organise the evening party to celebrate your wedding. You had to rub my face in it.' All the emotion that had been locked inside her for so long came flowing out, smothering her and choking her. 'And I had to laugh and smile and say, *"Of course I don't mind,"* to what felt like a million nosy people who wanted to stop and stare at our massive car crash of a relationship. It was bad enough that you asked her to marry you so soon after we broke up, but to ask me to organise the party knowing that I wouldn't feel able to refuse—' she was sobbing now, tears soaking her cheeks as she finally lost control. 'How could you do that? How could you want to hurt me and humiliate me like that? *How could you?'*

Ashen, he muttered something unintelligible and reached for her but she snatched her hand away and dodged him.

'No! There is nothing you can do or say to make this right. I've always thought that long-term relationships were doomed but with you, just for a moment, I was happy. And hopeful. And then you did that.' The words ended on a hiccup. 'And it wasn't an accident. You did it to hurt me. And you did. You *did* hurt me, Mal. And I won't let you do it again.'

CHAPTER SEVEN

MAL stood frozen to the spot, staring at the space where only a moment ago she'd stood. Stunned, he sifted through the words she'd thrown at him, sorting them in order of importance. And when he'd done that, he cursed softly.

Mouth tight, he rapped on the door of the bathroom. The door that she'd locked, of course. 'Avery? Open up. Now.'

When there was no answer, he stepped back and contemplated his options. Examining the lock, he strode across the bedroom and retrieved the bag he'd taken into the desert. The knife felt heavy in his hand and he stared at the blade, wondering if it would serve his purpose. Silently thanking Rafiq who had ensured that he was armed with no end of practical skills, he manoeuvred the knife and successfully unlocked the door.

She was huddled on the floor of the bathroom, her arms locked around her legs, his shirt barely covering the tops of her pale thighs. His entry earned him a scowl. 'So now you can walk through locked doors? Get out.'

'No.'

'It isn't enough to hurt me once? You have to do it again and again?' Her gaze dropped to his hands. 'And with a knife? Is this a new blood sport?'

He'd forgotten about the knife in his hand and instantly he put it down, thinking that he'd never seen her like this before. Never seen her with her emotions so clearly on display. 'I did not hurt you intentionally.' With the same care and caution that he would have approached an injured animal, Mal squatted down next to her. 'I didn't know, *habibti.*' He purposefully kept his voice soft and non-confrontational but that didn't stop the sudden blaze of fire in her eyes.

'Didn't know what? That you are an insensitive bastard? That just means you have a depressing lack of self-insight.'

He chose to ignore the insult because he recognised it for what it was—a last frantic defence from someone who was terrified. 'I didn't know you'd given me your heart. Until today, I didn't think you had. I thought that was a prize I hadn't won. You didn't say anything and I—' he let out a breath '—I failed to pick up the signals.'

'And you're such an expert in body language.'

'Apparently not.'

'You didn't have to be an expert.' The derisive glance she sent in his direction spoke volumes about her view on relationships. 'I was with you for a year. A whole year. What do you think that says?'

'To me it said that we were having a good time.' Mal saw the shimmer of an unshed tear stuck to her eyelashes and his heart clenched. He lifted his hand to brush it away gently with his thumb but she flinched away from him. The shirt she'd grabbed was too big for her and as she flattened herself against the wall of the bathroom it slid down, exposing one pale shoulder. Just a glimpse, and yet it was enough to force him to shift positions for his own comfort. Enough to remind him that this woman affected him in a way that no other woman ever had. 'It didn't tell me that you were in love with me. I didn't presume that and *you* didn't tell me that. Not once did you say those words.'

'Neither did you.'

Was it that simple? *Was that all it would have taken?* 'I was ready to say them. I was ready to ask you to marry me. I had plans. And then you told me it was over and walked away.'

'The first I knew of your "plans" was when a creepy guy who could never keep his hands to himself rang me to make me an offer for my business because he'd heard I was giving it all up to walk five steps behind you for the rest of my life.'

Mal reined in the anger, refusing to be sidetracked. 'I didn't know he'd made an offer on your business.'

'He was taunting me because he knew how much my company meant to me. And I fell for it, of course.' Eyes closed, she let her head fall back against the wall. 'He understood my weaknesses better than you did.'

'And he understood mine.' His muscles protesting at his cramped position, Mal stood up and lifted her to her feet, relieved when the shirt she was wearing slid back into place and covered slightly more of her.

'I thought you were Prince Perfect. You don't have any weaknesses.' Her hair tumbled over her shoulders, softly tangled after a night in his bed. Without her make-up she looked impossibly young and Mal felt something soften inside him. He'd so rarely seen her like this. This was the real Avery, not the businesswoman.

'You think I don't have a weakness?' He slid his hands into her hair and tilted her head. 'My weakness is you, *habibti*. It's always been you. And Richard knew it. He knew exactly what to say to cause maximum havoc. And his plan was a spectacular success. I lost my cool.'

Her beautiful eyes were bruised and wary. 'Sorry, but I just can't imagine that.'

'Try. It was bad.' Mal's mouth twisted into a smile of

self-mockery. '*Very* bad. You want details? Because it wasn't pretty. I lost control, just as Kalila told you.'

'I didn't believe her. You never lose control.'

'Everyone has a breaking point. He found mine with embarrassing ease. I'd planned to ask you to marry me. To do it "properly". I knew we were happy together. I knew you were the woman I wanted to spend my life with. It was an unfortunate coincidence that Richard confronted me before I'd had a chance to have time alone with you.'

She stared at a point at the centre of his chest. 'It might have helped if you'd actually included me in your plans.'

'I'm very traditional. I wanted to ask you in a traditional manner.'

She pulled away, her narrow shoulders suddenly tense. 'Yes, you're traditional. And that brings us full circle. Even if you'd managed to ask me to marry you in the conventional way, face to face, you still would have expected me to give up my business.'

It was the elephant in the room. The thing they'd never talked about because it had seemed insurmountable. Even back then, when he'd been determined to make it work, he'd seen the difficulties because it was absolutely true that to run a business like hers would require a time commitment that the woman who married him would not be able to afford.

Mal hesitated for a beat but even that was a beat too long because he saw her shoulders sag as she took that fatal hesitation on his part as confirmation of her fears. 'I would *not* have expected you to give up your business.' But he saw from her cynical expression that she didn't believe him and he sighed. 'You wouldn't have been able to work eighteen hour days, that's true, but we would have found a way.'

'A way that involved me giving up everything and you giving up nothing.'

'No. We would have talked about it. Come to some mutual agreement, but we didn't communicate as well as we might have done.'

'If that's the case then it's your fault.'

And that made him smile because she sounded so much like herself and it was a relief. 'I agree. My fault. Except for the part that was your fault.' Noticing that the shirt was slipping again, he took her hand and led her out of the bathroom, ignoring her attempts to resist him. 'Sorry, but we need to have this conversation somewhere that doesn't make me think of you naked in the shower if we're to stand any chance of actually resolving this. It would help if you could button the shirt to the neck.'

'You're thinking about sex at a time like this?'

He gave a wry smile. 'Aren't you?'

She dragged her eyes from his shoulders. 'No. You don't turn me on, Your Highness.' His smile drew a shrug from her. 'All right, maybe I *am* thinking about sex, but if anything that makes it worse because good sex cannot sustain a relationship. Good sex does not change the fact that our relationship is impossible.'

'*Not* impossible.'

'We want different things.'

'Then we will compromise. It is just a question of negotiation.'

'In other words you'll bully me until you get your own way.'

They were in the living area now, with its sumptuous furniture and breathtaking views of the desert but neither of them was conscious of their surroundings. Just each other. Avery snatched her hand from his and took refuge in the furthest corner of the sofa, as far away from him as possible.

'What time is the helicopter arriving to pick me up?'

'It's not.' He paused, unwilling to give her the option to leave but knowing that he would never keep this woman by binding her to his side. 'But if you still want the helicopter when we have finished this conversation to the satisfaction of both parties then I will fly you home myself. Fair?'

Her eyes skidded to his and then away. 'Go on then, Your Highness. Slay me with your superior negotiation techniques.'

This time he didn't hesitate. 'You accuse me of being insensitive, and I admit the charge but you share some of the blame because I had no clue as to the depth of your feelings. You never told me. You were so busy protecting yourself—'

'—something I was obviously right to do.'

'No. If you'd trusted me—if we'd understood each other better—' He felt a rush of exasperation as he remembered how much she'd held back. 'Every time I tried to talk to you I came up against this tough, competent, ball-breaking businesswoman. Nothing could shatter that shield you put between yourself and the world.'

'It's not a shield. It's who I am.'

'It's a shield. Why do you think I asked you to organise my wedding party?'

'I thought we were already in agreement on that one. Because you're insensitive.' Her tone was flippant but he saw the pain in her eyes and that pain was matched by his.

'You cut me off.' His tone was raw, his grip on control as slippery as it always was around this woman. 'You didn't even give me the right to reply. You just told me that you weren't prepared to make the "sacrifice" necessary to be my wife—a point which, by the way, hurt almost as much as the realisation that you were not prepared to fight for the survival of our relationship.'

'Relationships end, Mal. It's a fact of life. Fighting just prolongs the inevitable.'

'*Some* relationships end.' He realised just how deeply he'd underestimated the level of her insecurities. 'Others endure.'

'If I want endurance, I'll run a marathon.'

Sensing that the way was blocked, he shifted his approach. 'I once considered you the most open-minded, educated, impressive woman in my acquaintance but on the subject of marriage you are blinkered and deeply prejudiced. How did I not realise that sooner?'

'If this is an elaborate way of shifting blame for the fact that you were cruel enough to force me to plan the celebrations for your wedding to another woman, then you'll need to work harder. I am not to blame for your shortcomings.'

'You didn't even afford me the courtesy of a face to face conversation. You just told me it was over. You refused to speak to me until that final phone call, the details of which are welded in my brain.' He had the satisfaction of seeing her shift slightly. 'That's right. The one when you told me that the only way I was going to be able to speak to you again was if I booked you in a professional capacity. So that's what I did. I booked you.' He watched as the truth settled home. Watched as she acknowledged her part in what had happened.

'I didn't mean it literally.'

'Well, I took it literally.'

'You chose to marry another woman,' she snapped, 'and you expect me to believe that you were broken-hearted? Sorry, but look at the evidence from my point of view. I hear from someone else that we are getting married and that I'm giving up my job, and your response when I say "no" to that less than appealing prospect is to immediately propose to someone else. That merely confirmed everything I already knew about the transitory nature of relationships.'

It all came back to that, he thought and realised that this was the moment he should tell her the truth about his engagement to Kalila. But if he told her, it would be over and he wasn't ready to let her go without a fight. 'I believed our relationship was at an end.' He dragged his hand over the back of his neck, forcing himself to relive those horrible months. 'I thought that was it.'

'And it didn't take you long to recover, did it? If you cared about me that much, why did you ask Kalila to marry you?'

'I didn't ask her. Our marriage was arranged by the Council. That was the deal I made with my father.' That much, at least, was true. All that was missing was the detail.

'The deal?'

'I told him I wanted to marry you—' he sat down on the sofa next to her and took it as a positive sign that she didn't immediately leap out of her seat '—and he predicted that you would refuse.'

She studied her fingernails. 'Your father is a wise man, I always said so, but I fail to see how even he would know that without consulting me.'

'He met you. You'd charmed him as you charm everyone you meet, but he also saw the problems. Perhaps he saw things I was not prepared to confront. He warned me that the sacrifice required would be too great for a woman like you. And it turned out he was right. Because I couldn't marry you, it didn't matter to me who I married. So I let them make the arrangements they wanted to make.'

Silence spread across the room. She lifted her gaze to his.

'You could have said no.'

No, he couldn't have said no.

Mal felt tension spread across his shoulders. 'Why would I? I have to marry. That point is not in question. My father is not in good health and yet under his rule Zubran has achieved an unprecedented level of stability and progress. Our economy is strong, I am taking over more and more of his role and ultimately I will be responsible for the country's future. That is a huge responsibility, but one that I'm prepared for.' He breathed deeply. 'But the prospect would have been more appealing had I been able to do it with you by my side. That was what I wanted.'

Something that might have been shock flickered in those blue eyes.

She tucked her legs under her and made herself smaller. 'So now you're telling me that? Your timing sucks, Your Highness.'

'I would have to agree with that.'

'Why didn't you say it before?'

'Because you would have run faster than a stallion in the Zubran Derby.'

The corners of her mouth flickered. Her lips curved. *Those lovely lips that he couldn't look at without wanting to kiss them.*

'So you suffered when we broke up?'

'Greatly.'

'Good.' There was a gleam in her eyes. 'Because if I went through hell I'd hate to think that you got away free.'

'Believe me, I didn't. I asked you to arrange the wedding party in a last-ditch attempt to get some response from you. A small part of me still hoped that you had feelings for me and I assumed that if you had feelings for me then you would refuse to take the business because it would be too difficult for you to plan an event that celebrated my wedding to another woman.'

'I can't believe you asked me to do that. It was a terrible thing to do. A sign of a sick mind.'

'Or the sign of a desperate man.' He stretched his arm along the back of the sofa. 'I hoped that by being forced to communicate with me, eventually you would crack and admit how you felt.'

'You thought I'd ruin someone else's relationship? You *really* don't know me very well. I wouldn't touch a man who was engaged to someone else.'

'Kalila didn't want this marriage any more than I did. She probably would have been grateful if I'd been the one to back out because it would have saved her from doing it and risking the wrath of her father. And that's enough of that topic. I've had enough of talking about Kalila and the past and the total and utter mess we made of something special. I want to talk about last night.'

'Last night was last night. It doesn't change anything.'

'Last night I saw the real you. And the real you confessed that you dream about me.' Mal drew her to her feet and this time she didn't resist. 'Have I told you that you look cute in my shirt?'

'Stop trying to soften me up.' But her breathing wasn't quite steady. 'We can't do this, Mal. *I* can't do this.' Her voice shook and he realised the fragility of what he was holding in his hands.

'Yes, you can. This is one of those occasions when you're supposed to face your fears.'

Face your fears.

He made it sound so easy and yet it was the scariest thing she'd ever faced.

'You think I'd risk letting you hurt me twice? Do I look stupid?'

'I didn't hurt you the first time. At least not intentionally, and you are at least partially to blame for that fiasco.'

'It's not a fiasco, it's a relationship. That's what happens in relationships. They break. It's a question of how, not whether.' Avery pulled away from him and wrapped her arms around herself. She was still wearing the shirt she'd grabbed and suddenly she regretted not getting dressed and putting on make-up because somehow it was easier to project a different side to herself when she was wearing her warpaint. 'People start off optimistically, thinking that nothing can go wrong, and then eventually it starts to fall apart. The only unknown factor is how and when.'

'That's your mother talking. Your mother the divorce lawyer.'

'You paid someone to dig into my background?'

'No, I looked you up, but I shouldn't have had to. We were together for a year and our relationship was serious enough for you to trust me with at least some basic information about your family, although there was nothing there about your father.'

Of course there wasn't.

'Why does my family matter?' Her heart was thumping at her ribcage. 'You were with me, not my mother.'

'It might have helped me understand you. Is it her profession that makes you so wary of relationships? Is that the reason you didn't introduce us?'

'I don't take people home to meet my mother. We don't have one of those cosy mother-daughter relationships where we shop together and get our nails done.' Nerves made her snappy. 'She wouldn't have embraced you; she would have warned me off. My mother's idea of irresponsible behaviour is a relationship lasting more than a few months and being a Prince wouldn't have earned you points. If there is one thing she hates more than a man, it's an alpha, macho man. You should be grateful I didn't introduce you. It was for your own protection.'

'Do I look as if I need protecting?' He'd pulled on a pair of trousers but his torso was bare, bronzed flesh gleaming over solid muscle.

Distracted by that muscle, Avery almost lost the thread of the conversation. 'All right, maybe it was for *my* protection.'

'She sounds like a formidable woman.'

'Formidable and utterly messed up. Like me, only very possibly worse if you can imagine that. I can see her faults, but that doesn't mean I can dismiss everything she believes because I believe some of it too. When we broke up I *was* a mess.' Remembering it was terrifying. Thinking about how much she'd changed. How much of herself she'd almost given up. Just thinking about losing her business made her break into a sweat. 'I can't do this, Mal. I just can't. My business gives me independence. It's my life and I won't give that up. Seriously, we'd be crazy to even think of doing this again because the ending will be the same.'

'No it won't, because this time we're being honest with each other. This time we're going to understand each other. We'll find a way.' His gaze didn't flicker from hers. 'I love you.'

She felt a lightness inside her. A lightness that spread and grew. She felt as if she could float, spin, dance in the air. 'You love me?'

'Yes. All of you. Even the aggravating parts.' He gave a wry smile. 'Especially the aggravating parts.'

Avery lifted her hand to her throat. This was the moment she was supposed to say it back. Those three words she'd never said to another human being. Those three words that her mother had warned her always made a woman stupid.

'I—' The words jammed in her mouth, as if her body was putting up a final fight. 'I—'

'You—?' Those dark eyes were fixed on her expectantly and she felt as if she were being strangled.

'I really need some fresh air,' she muttered. 'Can we go for a ride?'

Galloping across the desert on an Arabian horse was the most exhilarating feeling in the world. More like floating, Avery thought, as she urged the mare faster. Soon, the sun would be too high, the day too hot for riding or any other strenuous activity, but for now they were able to enjoy this spectacular wilderness in a traditional way. And with Mal by her side it couldn't be anything other than exciting. Being with him was when she was at her happiest, but didn't all relationships start with people feeling that way?

She adjusted the scarf that protected her face from the drifting sand and cast him a look. 'Do I look mysterious?'

'You don't need a scarf for that.' His response was as dry as the landscape around them. 'With or without the scarf, you are the most mysterious woman I've ever met.'

'Somehow that doesn't sound like a compliment.'

'A little less mystery would make things easier.' His stallion danced impatiently and Mal released his grip on the reins slightly. 'We should go back. You'll burn in this sun.'

'I won't burn. You're talking to someone with pale skin who has an addiction to sunscreen.' But Avery turned back towards the Spa and urged her mare forward. 'It's stunning here. Beautiful. But I feel guilty. Do you know how much work I have waiting for me at home?'

'You employ competent people. Delegate.'

'I have to go back, Mal.'

'We both know that your desire to go back has nothing to do with your workload and everything to do with the fact that you're scared.' With an enviable economy of movement that revealed his riding skill, he guided the sleek black stallion closer. 'Tell me about your mother.'

'Why this sudden obsession with my mother?'

'Because when I have a challenge to face then I start by finding out the facts. Was it her work as a divorce lawyer that made her cynical about relationships, or was it being cynical about relationships that fuelled her choice of profession?'

'She was always cynical.'

'Not always, presumably, since she met and had a relationship with your father.'

Despite the heat of the sun, her skin felt cold. Avery kept her eyes straight ahead, feeling slightly sick as she always did when that topic was raised. 'Believe me, my mother was always cynical.'

'That was why her relationship with your father failed?'

She never talked about this. Never, not to anyone. Not even to her mother after that first occasion when she'd been told the shocking truth about her father.

She'd stared at her mother, surrounded by the tattered remains of her beliefs and assumptions. And she could still remember the words she'd shouted. *That isn't true. Tell me it isn't true. Tell me you didn't do that.*

Witnessing the visible evidence of her daughter's shock, her mother had simply shrugged. 'Half the children in your class don't have a father living at home with them. You don't need a father at home or a man in your life. A woman can exist perfectly well by herself. I am living proof of that. Trust me, it's better this way.'

It hadn't seemed better to Avery, who was at that age

where every little difference from her peers seemed magnified a thousand times. 'Those kids still see their dads.'

'Poor them. I've spared you from the trauma of being shuttled between two rowing parents and growing up an emotional mess. Be grateful.'

But Avery hadn't been able to access gratitude. Right then, she would have swapped places with any one of the children in her class. Her mother wanted her to celebrate an absent father but Avery had wanted a father in her life, even if he turned out to be an eternal disappointment.

She'd never again discussed it with her mother. Couldn't bear even to think about the truth because thinking about it made it real and she didn't want it to be real. At school she'd made up lies. She'd even started to believe some of them. Her dad was just away for a while—a successful businessman who travelled a lot. Her father adored her but he was working in the Far East and her mother's job was in London. She'd stopped asking for affection from her mother, who was clearly incapable of providing it, and instead asked for money, the only currency her mother valued and understood. She'd used it to add credence to her lies. She produced presents that he'd sent from his trips. Fortunately, no one had ever found out the truth—that she'd bought all the presents herself from a small Japanese shop in Soho. *That she'd never even met her father.*

And the lie had persisted into adulthood. Until somehow, here she was, a competent adult with the insecurities of childhood still hanging around her neck.

She should probably just tell Mal the truth. But she'd guarded the lie for too long to expose it easily and it sat now, like a weight pressing down on her. 'I don't see my father. I've…never met my father.'

'Does he even know you exist? Did she tell him about you?'

They were surrounded by open space and yet she felt

as if the desert were closing in on her. Avery tried to urge the mare forward into a canter but the animal refused to leave the side of the other horse, and Mal reached across and closed his hand over her reins, preventing her from riding off.

'You've never tried to contact him?'

'No. And he absolutely wouldn't want to hear from me, I can tell you that.' Once again she tried again to kick the mare into a canter, but the horse was stubbornly unresponsive, as if she realised that this was a conversation Avery needed to have and was somehow colluding with the Prince.

And he obviously had no intention of dropping the subject. 'Avery, no matter what the circumstances, a man would want to know that he had a child.'

'Actually, no, there are circumstances when a man would not want to know that and this is one of them. Trust me on that.' But she didn't expect him to understand. Despite his wild years, or maybe because of them, he was a man who took his responsibilities seriously.

'Whatever problems he and your mother had doesn't mean that the two of you can't form a bond. Your mother has turned you against him and I believe that often happens in acrimonious breakups, but their problems are not yours. He has a responsibility towards you.'

'No, he doesn't. I'm an adult.'

'At least he might be able to shed light on what went wrong. He owes it to you to tell you his side of the story.'

'I know his side of the story.' Why, oh why, had she ever allowed this conversation to advance so far? 'I'm happy as I am. I'm too old to adapt to having a dad in my life now. Oh look, more gazelle!' Trying to distract him, she waved her arm but all that achieved was to scare the horses and almost land her on her bottom in the sand.

Keeping his hand on her reins, Mal steadied both horses. 'You are such an intelligent woman. I cannot understand why this issue affects you so badly. You are surrounded by evidence of good relationships. Why must you only focus on the bad?'

Avery rubbed her hand over the mare's soft coat. This she could talk about and maybe if she gave him this, he'd be satisfied and let the rest of it go. 'My mother wasn't what you'd call a hands-on mother.' That had to be the understatement of the year. 'She encouraged me to be independent, so pretty much the only time we met up was dinner in the evening. Five minutes were spent reviewing my grades, and after that she talked about her work, which basically meant that I listened to a million ways for a marriage to die. Every night my mother would talk about her day because she believed it was important that I understood exactly how a relationship could go wrong. I heard about the impact of affairs, job losses, gambling, alcoholism, addictions—*lots* of those in different subsections— I heard about the corrosive effects of lack of trust, about the impact of not listening...the list goes on.' It had seeped into her, becoming part of her. 'I was one of the few five-year-olds in the land who understood the legal definition of "unreasonable behaviour" before I'd even learned to add. Do you want me to carry on? Because I have endless experience, gathered from eighteen years of living at home.'

'And did she ever describe any of the ways a successful relationship could work?' There were layers of steel beneath his mild tone. 'Did she ever talk about that?'

Avery stared straight ahead, through her mare's twitching ears.

There was no sound except the metallic jingle of the bridles and the soft creak of leather.

'No,' she said. 'She never talked about that.'

'Did you have boyfriends?'

'Yes, but I never brought them home. She always believed that most of the factors that contributed to a breakup of a relationship could be easily predicted and she wouldn't have hesitated to point them out.'

'So you were trained to spot the potential pitfalls. You don't enter a relationship waiting for it to go right, but waiting for it to go wrong.'

'I suppose so. But given that a significant proportion *do* go wrong, that's not as mad as it sounds.'

'It sounds like a shocking upbringing for the child of a single mother and it is no wonder you are so wary of relationships.'

'There is nothing wrong with being the child of a single mother.'

'Agreed. But there is plenty wrong with a single mother who chooses to poison her daughter's mind against men based on nothing but her own prejudices.' The stallion shied at some imaginary threat, leaping sideways, nostrils flared. Mal sat firm, soothing the animal with firm hands and a gentle voice.

It took him a moment to calm the animal, a moment during which she had plenty of time to dwell on the strength of his shoulders and the strength of *him*.

Only when he'd calmed the stallion did he look at her again. 'In my opinion she had a moral duty to bring you up with a balanced view of relationships, particularly given that you didn't have an example of a positive one in your own household. You spent your formative years living alongside stories of couples at the most miserable point of their relationship.'

'Yes.' It was the first time she'd truly acknowledged the effect it had had on her. 'I think that's the reason I went into party planning. The end of a relationship was terrify-

ing, but the beginning—that was exciting. I loved glittering events, the dressing up, the possibilities—'

'Possibilities?'

'Yes, so many possibilities, even if only for the short-
term. I know that at my parties, people are happy. I make
sure they're happy, even if that is only transitory. Talking
of which, I assume you want me to cancel arrangements
for the wedding party?' Her fingers were sweaty on the
reins but she told herself it was just the heat.

He stared at her for a long moment, thick lashes framing those eyes that made women lose their grip on reality. 'No. Not yet.'

'But—'

'You were the one who wanted to ride.' He released her
reins and urged the stallion forwards. 'Let's ride.'

CHAPTER EIGHT

THEY made love in the still waters of their secluded pool under the warm glow of the setting sun. Afterwards, they dined overlooking the dunes, their private feast illuminated by flickering candles.

They hadn't spent enough time like this, he thought. The madness of their lives had interfered with their relationship. It had prevented the intimacy needed to develop trust.

'You look beautiful in that dress.' He topped up her glass with the chilled champagne he knew was her favourite.

'I suppose you think you're clever for producing it in the middle of the desert?'

'Not clever, no. Fortunate. And not the wardrobe part, that was easy, but the fact that you are here to wear it.' He'd never been so unsure of a relationship. *Never so unsure of a woman.* 'I wasn't sure you'd stay.'

'The Crown Prince of Zubran not sure of someone or something? This must be a whole new experience.' Her eyes teased him and he had to force himself to stay in his seat and not rush this. Timing was everything. And his timing had been wrong before.

'It is a fairly new experience. And not one I'm enjoying.'

'You know your problem?' Glass in hand, she leaned forward, the movement accentuating the tempting dip between her breasts. 'Life has been too easy for you. Your playboy past has spoiled you. You've had it easy.'

'My father and my late uncle would agree with you, but you'd all be wrong.'

She put her glass down and rested her chin on her palm, studying him across the table. 'When has a woman ever said no to you?'

'You did.'

The humour in her eyes faded. The caution that was never far from the surface reappeared, and she sat up and dropped her hands into her lap. 'You don't like to be crossed. You like to get your own way. That's probably what this is all about.'

'That is *not* what is going on here and you know it.'

'Have you ever had to work at a relationship with a woman?'

'Is that a serious question?' He heard the irony in his tone. 'Because if it is, I think you already know the answer to that.'

Her fingers slid slowly round the base of her glass. 'You're a complicated man, Mal.'

'This from a woman renowned for keeping her relationships superficial.'

'A sensible strategy. For some reason I didn't apply it with you and look how that turned out.'

'All relationships have rocky moments.'

'Well, forgive me if I chose not to become another ship wrecked on your shores, Your Highness.' Her tone was flippant but there was a bleakness in her eyes that tore at him and suddenly he knew he had to risk more if he was expecting that of her.

'I'm sorry I hurt you. That was never my intention.'

'I'm not sure if that makes it better or worse.'

'Better. I was so in love with you.' Admitting it was

hard, particularly as he'd been raised not to share his thoughts and feelings outside the family circle. But he wanted her to be his family and he knew if there was to be any hope of that, he had to give. 'I'd never felt that way about a woman before. I'd never been in love. It scared me as much as it scared you because it changed everything. I wasn't prepared for it.'

Neither of them took any notice of the meal. The food remained untouched and forgotten on the table between them.

'I know—' her mouth flickered '—you needed a virgin princess.'

'It was *you* I needed.' His tone was raw. 'You. From the first day I met you, in charge of that enormous event and yet so cool that I could have put ice on you and it wouldn't have melted. I'd been careful, so careful, about choosing the women I spent time with.'

'Your reputation suggests otherwise.'

'My reputation only tells one part of the story.'

She toyed with the stem of her glass. 'Let's face it, Mal, you wanted me because I wasn't impressed by your rank or the size of your wallet. I was turned off by it because in the past I've found that men like you generally think they have a free pass when it comes to women. I said no. And you were arrogant enough to see me as a challenge.'

'Arrogant? You saw that as arrogance? Yes, there were women—' and he couldn't even remember them now because next to her there was no one '—but there will always be women who are attracted by wealth and the opportunity to mingle with the famous and the influential, but that's one single part of the life I lead. Then there is the other part—' he paused because this degree of honesty was so alien to him '—the part that means your choices are rarely your own and the part that requires you to serve others while forfeiting your own wishes and invariably your privacy too. You want to trust people, so you do and then you make a mistake and you learn that trust is a luxury afforded to other people. It's a hard lesson, but you learn to trust no one except your immediate family.'

She was still now, the humour gone from her eyes as she listened. 'Mal—'

'You learn how it feels to go through life alone and because you *are* alone you are forced to develop confidence in your own decisions. And that isn't easy. In the beginning you're afraid that all those decisions are wrong.' Remembering, he gave a humourless laugh. 'You wait for the world to fall apart and for everyone to discover that just because you are a Prince doesn't mean you know what you're talking about. You want to ask advice, but you don't dare because to display such a lack of confidence would be a political error. It's back to trust again, and you remember that you can't afford to do that. So you make the decisions alone and you make them with confidence and you learn not to question or hesitate because when you do, people lose faith in you. Is that arrogance?' He lifted his head and looked her in the eyes, wondering if anything he'd said made any sense to her. 'I see it more as a product of a lifetime of making decisions alone.'

She was silent for a moment. Then the corners of her mouth flickered. 'Well, that's put me in my place.' Her tone was light but her expression was serious. 'You never told me this.'

'No. And I should have. When you and I argued, I was more myself than I have ever been in my life before. I found myself trusting you.' He reached across the table and took her hand. 'Suddenly I was contemplating something I'd always thought unobtainable. Sharing my life and my future with someone I could love and someone I knew could cope with the life I lead. For once what I wanted coincided with what my father wanted for me. I made the decision the way I've made every other decision. By myself. I told my father and he was supportive.'

'You were sure of me.'

'I was sure you loved me as much as I loved you, even though you hadn't told me that. I was about to tell you how I felt and ask you to marry me—' The memory came along with a rush of frustration. 'I had the ring in my pocket on the night I met Richard and he taunted me. Implied that you and he—'

'I have better taste in men than that.'

'I know. I overreacted and it cost me the only relationship that would have worked for me.'

'That wasn't the reason.' She eased her hand out of his and sat back in her chair. 'I was raised to see marriage as something that damaged a relationship. Something that removed choice and meant nothing but personal sacrifice. Being with a man meant giving up part of yourself. I tried moving past that. Tried telling myself that it didn't always happen that way and with you I'd begun to believe it—' she stared at the bubbles rising in her glass and then back at him, her gaze frank and honest. 'But then I took that call from Richard and instead of seeing it for what it was—a manipulative attempt to break us up—I chose to let it feed all my insecurities. You can find evidence for anything if you want to and I took this as evidence that our relationship couldn't work. That you were taking over my life. Making decisions for me. You wanted me to give up my job. I was waiting for a reason to run, and he gave it to me.'

'*I* gave it to you. I see that now. I was so used to making decisions on my own that I failed to share my thoughts and that was a fundamental error to make with a woman like you. I underestimated the depth of your insecurities and I—' he gripped his glass '—I overestimated your feelings for me.'

'Maybe the first is true, but the second—' she lifted her head and gave him a faltering smile '—no. You didn't overestimate. I did have those feelings. You were right about that. But the feelings weren't enough to cancel out the insecurities.'

'And now?' He hardly dared ask the question. 'Are those feelings enough for you to overcome everything your mother taught you? Can you forget One Thousand and One ways for a marriage to die and instead think about ways it can work?'

The only sound was the relaxing sound of water that came from the ornamental fountain by the pool.

Then she stood up abruptly and walked to the edge of the pool, her back to him. *Like a wild animal disturbed,* he thought, watching in silence.

'Don't do this, Mal.'

'I *am* doing it.'

She wrapped her arms around herself even though the evening was oppressively warm. 'Why can't you leave it alone? Why does it have to be marriage?'

'Because for me there is no other possible outcome. It has to be marriage. But, unlike you, I don't see that as a negative. I love you. You're the only woman I want to spend my life with so marriage is logical to me.' He rose to his feet, careful to give her time. He rescued her chair, but she didn't sit down. Just stood there, looking at him over her shoulder as if she was deciding whether it was safe to stay. Whether she should run or not. *Hunted and hunter.*

'I am an independent woman—'

'You're a frightened woman.' He curved his hand around her waist and pulled her against him. It felt like progress when she didn't pull away. 'It's time to separate what your mother told you from what you know to be true. I love you. You have to believe that I love you. I want you to marry me.' He felt the fear ripple through her but he kept his arm round her and held her.

She placed her hand flat against his chest, as if it was essential to keep some distance even now, during this most intimate of conversations. 'You want to kill what we have stone-dead?'

'It doesn't have to be that way. It's not going to be that way for us.'

'People say that—' There was desperation in the way she blurted the words out. 'They make promises and exchange rings and believe that it's going to last, and then it doesn't. Relationships fail all the time. How can you possibly know what you'll want, or feel, in the future?'

'When you started your business, were you afraid of failing? Did it ever occur to you that perhaps it was better not to try in case it didn't succeed?'

She looked up at him and then looked away again. 'No, of course not. But that's different.'

'Businesses fail every day, *habibti*. If yours had failed—'

'I wouldn't have let it fail.'

'Exactly. You wouldn't have let it fail. That is the reason your business is flourishing in this economic climate. Because of your determination. Because when something feels wrong, you deal with it. You flex. You compromise. And you will bring all those skills to our marriage and it will be a success.'

'Marriage is different than business.'

'But the same qualities are required for both. You start with a burning passion, and that burning passion is what keeps things alive if problems arise.' He could see her weighing it up, pitting his words against her ingrained beliefs and he held his breath because he had no idea how that fight would end.

'I'm scared—' She covered her face with her hands and leaned her forehead against his chest. 'I can't believe I'm admitting that.'

'I'm pleased you're admitting that. For once you're being honest. I can work with that. Now all I have to do is get you to admit that you love me.' He closed his hands around her wrists and drew her hands away from her face so that he could look at her. 'Is it unreasonable to hope that one day you'll actually say those words to me?'

There was humour in her eyes. And something else. Something warm he'd always hoped to see when she looked at him.

'I don't think your ego needs the boost.'

He lowered his head, smiling against her mouth as he brushed his lips over hers. 'Try me. Let's see what happens.'

'We're too different. We want different things.'

'I want you. You want me. What's different about that?'

Her fingers were locked in the front of his shirt. 'You'd expect me to give up my job.'

'Not true, at least not in the sense that you mean.' He trailed his fingers down her neck, touching the diamonds she wore at her throat. *His diamonds.* 'You are a master of organisation—that is why your parties are always such a success. You can juggle a million projects at once. You have consummate social skills and you know just what to say to put people at ease. You are beautiful, poised, generous and warm. All these are perfect qualities for the role of Sultan's wife.'

'Are you asking me to marry you or are you offering me a job?'

'I haven't asked you to marry me yet. I'm leading up to that.'

'Oh.' She was trembling against him. 'So you're offering me a job. You're asking me to give up everything and in return you give up nothing.'

'Life is all about perspective, *habibti*. Some would say I was offering you everything.'

The dimple appeared at the corner of her mouth. 'You have a high opinion of yourself, Your Highness.'

'I'm sure a life spent with you will cure me of that.' Hoping that he'd judged the moment perfectly, he slid his hand into his pocket and pulled out the ring. 'Last time I did this badly—'

'If we're talking about a marriage proposal, you didn't do it at all.' Her tone was light but the look in her eyes was panic and he took her face in his hands and kissed her gently.

'Breathe.'

'I'm breathing.'

'I want you to marry me, not because I want to ruin your life, but because I want to make it happy. I want to make *you* happy.'

'Now that is arrogance, Your Highness—' But her eyes were fixed on the ring. 'Was it Kalila's?'

The fact that she would ask him that question intensified his guilt. 'I am willing to concede that sensitivity towards your feelings has not been my strong point, but even I would not be so thoughtless as to give a gift I bought for one woman to another. It belonged to my great-grandmother.' Unsure of her response to that, he paused, watching as her face changed. 'She had a long and happy marriage, so perhaps you'll consider that auspicious.'

Carefully, she took it from him, turning it so that the stone winked in the sunshine. 'It's exquisite.'

'But will you wear it?'

She hesitated for what felt like a lifetime but which was, in reality, only seconds. 'This is huge.'

'The diamond or the commitment?'

'Both?' But his words drew the smile he'd been hoping for and he took ruthless advantage of that and slid the ring onto her finger.

'It doesn't feel huge. It feels right. It fits, *habibti*. It's an omen.'

'I don't believe in omens and neither do you.'

'But I believe in *us*. And I want you to believe in us, too. Will you marry me?' He tilted her face and she stared up at him, more vulnerable than he'd ever seen her.

'Yes.' She stumbled over the word. 'But if you hurt me, I'll kill you.'

He laughed. 'That sounds fair to me.' And if she still hadn't said that she loved him, he told himself he had to be patient.

They spent two more days in the desert. Two days during which they only left the bed to swim, ride and eat. Days during which Avery was conscious of the weight of the ring on her finger. She was aware of it all the time, aware of *him* all the time. And the feelings inside her were a stomach-churning mixture of excitement and trepidation.

But already the Palace machine was rolling into action. Arrangements were being made for her to become his bride and although it made her feel uneasy and out of control, she understood. Because of who he was, it had to be that way.

'Don't they mind that it's not Kalila?'

'Turns out that there was more to Kalila than either of us knew. I'm informed that she married her bodyguard within hours of us leaving.'

'What?'

'I would have preferred she waited. It would have been easier for her to let me take responsibility, but I suppose she was afraid that her father might find a way to stop her.'

'Or perhaps she needed to take responsibility for her own decisions.' Avery understood that, but it didn't stop her being concerned for Kalila. 'What will her father do now?'

'He can't do much. Rafiq is arranging for them to come back to Zubran, at least for the time being. But I don't want to talk about Kalila right now. I promise she won't suffer for her decision.' He lowered his mouth to hers. 'I want to think about us, and if we are discussing a wedding, I want it to be ours. Talking of which, do you intend to invite your mother?' The question was asked casually but there was no such thing as casual when it came to discussing her relationship with her mother.

'No. I've told you—we're not really in touch much now.'

'Perhaps a wedding would be a good time to reconcile.'

He had no idea. 'Believe me, my mother would be the very last person anyone would choose to invite to a wedding. Not if they want it to be a happy event.'

'And your father? I was thinking that this might be a perfect time to make contact.'

'No.' Suddenly cold, she pulled away from him. 'I'll give you a list of people I'd like to invite. Friends and people from work.'

'In other words you don't want to talk about your father.'

'That's right.' Closing down the conversation, she slid from the bed and pulled on a silk wrap, knotting it firmly at the waist. 'Not all families are like yours, Mal. I wish you'd try and understand that.' Without giving him an opportunity to respond, she walked through to the bathroom and locked the door.

And this time he didn't follow her.

Was this the start of it? she wondered, leaning her head

back against the door and closing her eyes. Was this how it happened? The first crack. And then another crack, until the cracks became a rift, and the rift became a canyon and suddenly there was nothing between them but space that couldn't be bridged.

'It is *not* going to happen the way you're thinking.' His dry tone came from the other doorway and she felt a rush of exasperation with herself for forgetting about the second door, but also relief because she hated feeling the way she was feeling.

'Please tell me that your apartment in the Palace doesn't have two doors in the bathroom.'

He crossed the room to her, lean, powerful and confident. 'It doesn't, but unless you stop trying to knock down what we are building with every thought you have, then I'm going to remove all the walls and we will be living open-plan. I know which part of our conversation had you running from my bed and I won't mention it again. If you don't want to trace your father then that is your decision, but if you ever change your mind then let me know. I will use my contacts to find the truth.'

She already knew the truth but any guilt she felt at not revealing that was drowned out by more urgent feelings as he pulled her into his arms and brought his mouth down on hers.

And afterwards, hours afterwards as they lay in the darkness in sheets tangled from their loving, she told herself that it didn't matter, that it didn't make a difference, but the feeling that she was somehow deceiving him stayed with her and it was still with her when they finally landed in Zubran City.

The Old Palace, the Sultan's official residence, was a fascinating labyrinth of private courtyards, soaring ceilings and opulence built on the shores of the Persian Gulf.

Avery had planned parties in the most luxurious and exclusive venues in the world, but nowhere had left her quite as breathless as this place. The Palace was beautiful, but her real love was the gardens, particularly the water gardens that provided a cooling sanctuary from the blistering desert heat.

It became her favourite place to escape from the madness and chaos of the wedding plans, none of which seemed to require her input. As someone used to running things, it felt strange not to have a role in what was surely the biggest event of her life.

While Mal was occupied with state business, Avery flew back to London to see clients and deal with aspects of her own business that Jenny couldn't handle. Far from being concerned about Avery's marriage to Mal, her friend was delighted. Together they agreed to a few changes to the running of the business, giving Jenny more day to day control. Avery returned to Zubran knowing her business was in safe hands and feeling slightly redundant. It was a strange feeling. She loved her work and was proud of her achievements, but she knew that for her it wasn't just a means to independence, but a shield against intimacy. She'd been afraid to share herself, afraid to trust, and her mother would have said that was a sensible approach. Until a few weeks ago, Avery would have agreed.

That was before she realised how good it felt to love and be loved. And she *was* loved, she was sure of that.

Mal loved her.

How could she doubt it? He loved her so much that he couldn't wait to marry her. There was no hesitation on his part. He was so sure of himself and of her and that made her feel wanted in a way she'd never been wanted. Her mother's only contribution as a parent had been to teach her that it was better to live her life alone. She'd never mentioned the richness of a life shared and Avery was starting to appreciate the flavour of that.

Ten days after they'd arrived back at the Palace she'd taken coffee and her work down to her favourite spot and was sitting in the shade reading through a document Jenny had sent through to her when Mal found her.

'The entire Palace is searching for you.'

She closed the document she was reading. 'I wasn't hiding. I like it here. I love the water gardens. The sound is so soothing.'

'The gardens were a wedding gift for my mother. She liked the sound, too. She told me that it was the one place in the madness of the Palace and her life that she could be sure of finding peace.'

'I can understand that. It's very soothing.'

'Do you need soothing? Are you stressed?' He sat down next to her and she realised how tired he looked. Since they'd arrived back in Zubran he'd been in endless meetings, his presence required almost continuously either by the Council or by his father.

'I *should* be stressed. Marriage and me. Can't believe I'm saying those two words in the same sentence and not freaking out and running through the Palace screaming.' Laughing at herself, Avery twisted the ring on her finger, realising that it no longer felt heavy. It felt *good*.

He breathed deeply and took her hand in his. 'You have no idea how relieved I am that you're not freaking out.'

'I trust you. And I love you.' She curled her fingers around his and smiled. 'Did you hear that? I said, "I love you." And now I just said it again. That's twice in as many minutes. I'm getting good at it.'

'It's practice.'

'Not practice. Trust.' She watched as a butterfly settled on the border of flowers next to her and opened its wings to the sun, trusting that no harm would come to it while it stole the moment for itself. 'Trust is like a door. I always assumed that keeping that door closed kept you safe, but now I see that opening it can let in good things. Things I've never felt before.'

'Avery—' He seemed unusually tense and she kissed him.

'Although we were together for that year, I didn't really understand the level of responsibility you face. I didn't understand the pressure. Everyone wants a piece of you and you have to juggle so many things. I think my job is busy, but yours is stupid. And everyone comes to you expecting a decision. I see now why you behaved the way you did when horrid Richard tried to goad you. As far as you were concerned, you'd already made that decision and moved on to the next. You were decisive because you loved me.'

He cupped her face in his hands. 'I do love you. Don't ever forget that.' He kissed her and then stood up. 'These party organising skills of yours—do they extend to children's parties?'

'You want to hold a children's party?'

'My mother was patron of a charity devoted to equal educational opportunities for all. Once a year we hold a giant children's party.' He gave a helpless lift of his shoulders. 'I confess that running it doesn't play to my skills.'

Pleased to finally have something positive to do, Avery smiled. 'Just as long as you don't expect me to do a balloon release or hire fifty swans. What's my budget?'

'Change the day.' Mal faced the Council, staring at faces aged with worry and experience, faces that had been part of his life for as long as he could remember. 'Even if you shift it by a week, that would work.'

'Your Highness, we cannot do that. You know that circumstances do not allow us any flexibility.'

He did know. He'd been living with those 'circumstances' for a decade. He also knew how Avery would react if she found out what that date signified.

And then the door to the Council chamber opened and she stood there, fire in her eyes, and he knew that, somehow, from someone, she *had* found out.

Across the room, their eyes met and he stood, forcing himself to absorb the silent accusation that flowed across the room like a lethal mist.

So that was it, then. Regret stabbed him along with disappointment and frustration at the timing. Maybe if they'd had a little longer in this phase of their relationship. Maybe if those fragile strands of trust had been given time to strengthen…

He addressed the Council. 'Leave us.'

Something in his tone clearly communicated itself to them because they rose instantly, those men for whom duty exceeded all other priorities, exchanging worried glances as they shuffled from the room. He knew there would be mutterings, but he didn't care. The only thing he cared about was the woman holding his gaze.

She stalked into the room, her heels tapping on the marble floor of the Palace that had housed his ancestors for centuries. She'd come to reject him, as a small part of him had known she would—reject her role as his lover, his wife, *his princess*.

The irony was she looked regal; this woman who had turned his life upside down from the moment he'd met her walked with the confidence of a Queen.

The moment the door closed behind the last Council member, she pounced. 'In the middle of planning this party, I had a very illuminating conversation with one of the Palace staff. Were you going to tell me?'

He didn't pretend not to know what she was talking about. 'I was afraid you would misinterpret the facts.'

'That is *not* an answer. *Were you going to tell me?*'

'I hoped I wouldn't need to.'

'So if I hadn't found out, that would have been all right?'

'Yes, because it has nothing to do with my feelings for you. It has nothing to do with us.'

'But it has everything to do with our marriage, doesn't it?' Her voice was a traumatized whisper. 'You demanded that I trust you, and I did. I've never done that before, but with you I made that leap.'

'Avery—'

'You told me so much about yourself, Mal. But you didn't tell me the most important thing of all, did you? That you *have* to be married, and that your marriage has to take place by the end of the month. And it seems everyone knows that but me.' Her laugh was agonised. 'Whenever I felt doubts, I looked at the evidence to prove that you loved me. I said to myself, *He can't wait to marry me.*'

'That is true. I do love you and I can't wait to marry you.'

'But the *reason* you can't wait has nothing to do with the depth of your feelings and everything to do with the terms of your late uncle's will.'

'I made no secret of the fact that I have to marry.'

'No, but you made it sound like a general thing, not something specific. You didn't mention the will. You didn't mention that you have to have a bride by a fixed date. It doesn't even matter who the bride is, does it?' Her voice rose. 'Just any bride will do in order to fulfil the terms of your uncle's will.'

'I repeat, that has no bearing on us.'

'So, postpone the wedding. Change the date.'

He didn't tell her that he'd been trying to do exactly that. 'You don't understand.'

'I understand that I was a pawn and so was Kalila.'

'Kalila was an attempt by the Council to fulfil the terms of my uncle's will, that's true, but she was fully apprised of the reasons behind the marriage right from the start.'

'So you were happy to tell her and not me?'

'The circumstances were different. The only reason I proposed marriage to Kalila was to fulfil the terms of my uncle's will.'

'No wonder she ran.' Her chin lifted. 'What I don't understand is why you felt able to tell her, and not me.'

'I was honest with her about the terms of our marriage and I have been equally honest with you.'

'That isn't true.'

'Yes, it is.' He saw the flicker of surprise in her eyes at his savage response but he was past caring. Past hiding anything. 'My reason for marrying you was love, but because you never believed in that love, because you never believed in *us*, I didn't dare tell you about the terms of my uncle's will. I knew you would use that as more food for your wretched insecurities as you have done before, so I told myself that I would tell you when our relationship had progressed a little further, when we had strengthened the bond, when I was confident that what we had could withstand a confession like that.'

She stood still, absorbing that. Her chest rising and falling as she breathed. 'You should have told me.'

'Apart from the element of full disclosure, my uncle's will had no bearing on our future. I would have married you anyway. The timing of that is immaterial.'

'But it isn't immaterial, is it?'

'I will tell you a story and you will judge.' Mal paced to

the far side of the room and stared out of the pretty arched window that looked down on the stables. 'My grandfather had two sons. Twins. The right of succession naturally passes to the eldest twin—' he turned, watching her face to be sure she understood the impact of his words '—but no one knew who that was.'

'I don't understand.'

'There was a crisis during the birth. An obstetric emergency. People were so concerned about the welfare of the mother that somehow the midwife who delivered the twins lost track of which was born first. A matter of little importance, you might think, but you'd be wrong. Unable to think of any other solution, my grandfather decided to divide Zubran and give one half to each son, on the understanding that whichever of them had a son first, he would be the successor. It meant that ultimately the land would be united again. And that was me. My uncle had no children, so there was only me and he was concerned by my partying and what he saw as my decadent lifestyle.' His mouth twisted as he recalled the bitter exchanges they'd had over that particular subject over the years. 'My father tried to assure him that my actions were nothing more than the normal behaviour of a young man. For a short time they fell out over it, but then they agreed a compromise. My uncle agreed to name me as his successor in his will, providing that I was married by the age of thirty-two. If by that age I hadn't settled down, then the succession would go to a distant cousin.'

'Which would keep the land divided.'

'Yes. I always knew I would have to marry because it was essential that Zubran be reunited as one country, but I'd always assumed it would be a political marriage based on nothing more than economic gain. I've met many women, but not a single one who I would have wanted to spend a lifetime with. Until I met you.'

Her eyes met his. 'Why didn't you just tell me this before?'

'If I'd said to you, "I have to be married by the time I'm thirty-two," would you have listened to anything else I said? You, who are always looking for evidence to endorse your view that all relationships are doomed? Tell me you wouldn't have interpreted that as a sign I was pursuing you for less than romantic reasons, just as you are now.' He saw her shift slightly and gave a derisive smile. 'Precisely. I would have lost you on day one and I had no intention of doing that. So I kept quiet until day two, and then until day three and I let the relationship run and hoped that if you found out, *when* you found out, the bond we shared would be sufficiently deep for you to trust me. Yes, the date by which I have to marry is almost here. It matters to my father and my people that Zubran becomes one country again. And it matters to me. But none of that has any bearing on my feelings for you and *that* is why I didn't mention it.'

'And if I had said no? What then?'

It was a question he hadn't wanted her to ask. A question he hadn't even wanted to ask himself because there really was only one answer. 'I would have married someone else. When you're wealthy and well connected there is always someone who is willing to sacrifice romance for reality. And now, no doubt, you will go away and add that to your armoury of reasons why our marriage would fail. No doubt you will hear the voice of your mother warning you that a man who needs to marry is a man whose marriage is doomed.' He threw it out there and waited for her to throw it back at him, to tell him that of course she didn't think that, but she was ominously silent and he saw the telltale sheen in her eyes.

'Mal—'

He was afraid to let her speak in case this was the moment when she told him it was over. 'Has it occurred to you that your mother could have been wrong? You're not even willing to entertain the idea of contacting your father, but it might be helpful. It might shed light on their relationship. Perhaps it wasn't all him, perhaps it was *her*; have you thought of that? Perhaps she killed her own relationship, the way she has tried to kill all of yours simply by the way she raised you.'

Her face was white, as if he'd suggested something shocking.

Watching her with a mixture of exasperation and despair, Mal wondered why this was such a block for her.

Was she afraid that she'd track down her father, only for him to reject her all over again?

Was that what he was seeing in those beautiful blue eyes?

She stood still as if she wanted to say something and then she gave a little shake of her head, turned and walked towards the door.

Mal resisted the temptation to stride after her and turn the key in the lock. 'This isn't about the fact I didn't tell you about my deadline to get married. It isn't about any of that. It's about you, Avery. *You.* Once again you are looking for excuses to run. You are expecting it to fall apart, just as your mother no doubt did with your father. Are you really going to kill what we have in the same way that she did?'

Say no. Say no and stop walking.

But she didn't stop walking and he felt a heaviness in his chest, an ache that refused to go away.

'I will be there tomorrow, ready to marry you,' he said

in a thickened tone, 'because that is what I want and because I believe in us. Despite everything, I believe in us.
The question is, do you believe in us too, *habibti*?'

Finally her steps slowed. He saw her shoulders move
as the breath rippled through her and then she increased
the pace again and walked from the room without a backward glance.

CHAPTER NINE

It was a night without sleep. She stayed up. Saw both sunset and sunrise as she sat alone in the water garden, feet bare, hair loose, tucked away in a place that no one would think of looking, apart from Mal, and he hadn't bothered.

I will be there tomorrow, ready to marry you.

But how could she do that now that she knew he *had* to get married? It explained everything. The speed with which he'd put that ring on her finger; the fact that he'd asked her so quickly after his relationship with Kalila had collapsed. It wasn't to do with the depth of his love for her. It was all to do with his uncle's will.

He hadn't been honest.

Avery turned her head. Inside the Palace, lights burned as an army of staff busied themselves with final preparations for the wedding of the Crown Prince and Miss Avery Scott. Miss Avery Scott, the woman who'd been raised to believe that a woman was stronger without a man, that a life was happier, and more secure, if it were lived alone. That the only guarantees and promises worth believing were the ones you made to yourself.

No, he hadn't been honest with her. But she hadn't been honest with him either, had she?

As if on cue, her phone beeped and she found a text from

her mother. They hadn't spoken for months. She opened it—there was only one line

Heard rumour you're getting married. Don't do anything stupid.

Don't do anything stupid…

Her eyes filled. It was exactly what she needed to see. What had she been thinking? What had she been doing? There was no way she could put herself through that pain again.

Avery stared at that message for a long time. Then she slipped on her shoes. Even the tranquil sound of the fountains in the water garden couldn't soothe her.

Her mother was right.

It was really important not to do something stupid.

She found Mal sprawled on the balcony of his bedroom, apparently oblivious to the buzz of excitement that gripped the rest of the Palace. But that was because only the two of them understood that this wedding might not happen.

He took one look at her, his dark gaze sweeping over her, taking in her jeans and the casual shirt she was wearing and his sensual mouth hardened. 'So that is your decision. Thank you for not waiting until I was standing in front of a thousand guests to break the news to me.'

'I'm not here about the wedding. I'm not here to talk about us. This is about me. There's something I have to tell you about me.' She took in the roughness of his jaw and the shadows beneath his eyes. 'You didn't sleep last night either.'

'Did you really think I would? Just say what you have to say, Avery.' The chill in his voice was less than encouraging but somehow she forced the words out.

'I have to tell you about my father. I should have told you before, but it's not something I've ever discussed with anyone.' And it felt terrifying to discuss it now but he was already sitting up. Paying attention.

'What about your father?'

She could hear the splash of water from the fountain that formed the centrepiece in the courtyard beneath them. 'He didn't leave, Mal. He didn't walk out on me or abandon me. He wasn't a high-powered businessman frequently out of town, which is what I used to tell my school friends.' One by one she sliced through the lies she'd created over the years and watched them fall, leaving only the truth. 'I'm not afraid of marriage because my own parents' marriage failed. That isn't what happened.' She'd come this far but, even so, saying those last words felt hard. She waited for him to say something. To prompt her in some way, but he didn't.

He just watched and waited and in the end she turned away slightly because saying this was hard enough without saying it while looking at him.

'The man who fathered me was never part of my life. Or part of my mother's life.'

'He was a one-night stand? Your mother became pregnant by accident?'

'It wasn't an accident.' Did she sound bitter? She was amazed that, after so many years, she could have an emotion left on the topic. 'My mother doesn't have accidents. Everything she does in life is calculated. She plans everything. She controls everything. Her relationship with my father played out exactly the way she wanted it to play out.'

'And he was fine with that? He made her pregnant and wasn't interested in being part of your life?'

'That's right.' The condemnation in his voice made her nervous about telling him the rest. She paused, trying to find words that didn't make it seem quite so cold and clinical. 'But it wasn't the way you're imagining it. My mother didn't have a relationship with anyone. I don't know my father's name.'

'He was a stranger?'

'In a manner of speaking. I may not know his name, but I do know his clinic code.'

'Clinic code?' He looked confused and she couldn't blame him for that. It was hardly the first thing that came to mind when discussing someone's parentage.

'My mother used donated sperm.' It was easier to say than she'd thought it would be, given that she'd never said it before.

'Donor sperm? She had infertility issues?'

'No. No infertility issues. Just man issues. She wanted to cut the "man" part out of the deal.' She glanced at him, looking for shock, disgust, any of the emotions she'd anticipated seeing, but there was nothing.

'She struggled to trust men so when she chose to have a child of her own, she chose to have one alone?'

If only. Avery felt her throat thicken. 'That wasn't it, either. I truly wish it were. At least then I would have known I was loved by at least one of my parents. But the truth is I was another of my mother's social statements. She wanted to prove that a woman doesn't need a man for anything, not even to produce a baby, although obviously that wasn't what she told them in the clinic. She was determined to prove that she could do it all by herself, and she did. The trouble was, she forgot that her experiment was permanent. Once she'd proved her point, she was stuck with me. Not that she let that interfere with her lifestyle, you understand.'

As Mal rose to his feet, she backed away with a quick shake of her head.

'Don't speak. I n-need to finish this now or I won't ever say it,' she stammered. 'I've never said it before and it's…

hard because I'm used to being a confident person and I am confident in my work, just not about this.'

'Avery—'

'My childhood was nothing like yours. It was nothing like anyone's. Your family was close and tight-knit. You had two parents, cousins, uncles and aunts. Even when you disagreed, you were a unit. And yes, I'm sure there were huge pressures, but you shared those pressures. I'm sure that being a Prince must occasionally have been lonely but even when you were lonely you knew there were people around you who loved you. You knew who you were and what was expected of you. You *belonged*.'

He opened his mouth, but then caught her desperate look and closed it again.

Avery's mouth was dry. 'I didn't have that. On the outside my family looked fine. Single mother. No biggie. Loads of people have that, right? I hid the truth about my father because I thought it was so shaming that my mother couldn't sustain a relationship for long enough even for a single bout of sex, but what really affected me wasn't the fact that I didn't have a father, but the fact that I didn't have a mother, either. All I had was a woman who taught me how to be a version of her.'

'Avery—'

'Most of the time I *hated* her.' It was the first time she'd ever admitted that. 'There was no affection because she saw that as weakness. No involvement in my life. We spent mealtimes together, during which she talked about her work and about how lucky we were to have avoided that complex relationship trauma. And I vowed I wasn't going to be like that. I vowed that my relationships would be normal, but she'd done her job well and the only thing that was ever in my head at the start of a relationship was, *How will this end?* She taught me how to live alone. She didn't tell me how to live with other people. And it never really mattered. Until I met you.'

'Why didn't you tell me this before?' His tone was raw and this time when he pulled her into his arms she didn't resist. 'All that time we spent together—all the times I brought up the subject of your father and you never once mentioned it.'

'Because I've kept it a secret for so long from everyone. And you mattered to me more than anyone I'd ever met. It wasn't just that I was ashamed. I was afraid that if you knew, it would kill what we had.' Admitting it was agony. 'I was afraid that if you knew the truth about me, you wouldn't want me any more. You know who you are. Your ancestors are Sultans and Princes. You can trace your family back for centuries. And I'm—' Her voice cracked and she gave a despairing shrug. 'I don't even know who I am. I'm a… I'm the result of my mother's unofficial social experiment.'

He took her face in his hands and rested his forehead against hers, his gaze holding her steady. 'You're the woman I love. The only woman I want.'

She hadn't dared hope that she would hear that. 'Even now you know?' She discovered that her cheeks were wet and she brushed her palm over her face self-consciously. 'I'm crying. I never cry.' Her voice was unsteady and his was equally unsteady.

'I'm not marrying you for where you came from. I'm marrying you for who you are and who you are going to be. You are a bright, talented, very sexy woman who will make a perfect Princess. I don't care about your past, except for the degree to which it affects our future. Can you shut out everything she ever taught you and believe in us, no matter what? Or are you going to walk away?'

'Last night she sent me a text. She'd heard I was getting

married and she told me not to do anything stupid. And I realised that she was right. It *is* important not to do something stupid—' she felt him tense and, because she saw pain flicker into his eyes, she carried on quickly '—and it would be stupid not to marry you. It would be the stupidest thing I've ever done.'

He breathed in sharply. 'Avery—'

'I love you. That's why I took a risk with you the first time, because I cared for you so much. And it's why I'm here now. I was upset when I found out that you had to get married by a certain date, that's true, but I only needed a few minutes alone to realise that everything you told me made sense. And it's partly my fault that you didn't tell me because I'm so screwed up. I *do* believe you love me but when you've believed yourself unlovable for so long, it's hard not to doubt that. I love you—' the words caught in her throat '—I really love you. And if you still want me, then I want to marry you.'

'*If* I still want you?' He hauled her against him and held her so tightly she could hardly breathe. 'There is no "if". There never has been an "if" in my mind. I have always been sure. *Too* sure, which was why I messed it up so badly the first time. And I did mess it up.' He eased her away from him and smoothed away her tears with his thumbs. 'I understand that now. You accused me of arrogance and perhaps I was guilty of that but most of all I was guilty of being too sure of us. I knew we were perfect together.'

'I'm pleased to hear you think I'm perfect.' She laughed up at him and he smiled back, but it was a shaky smile. The smile of someone who had come close to losing everything that mattered.

'You know your problem? You're arrogant.'

'A moment ago I was perfect.'

'You're perfect for me.'

A warm feeling spread through her. 'I've never had that.' Her voice faltered as he kissed her. 'I don't honestly think anyone has ever loved me before. Apart from Jen. And most of the time I drive her mad.'

'Not so mad that she didn't agree to fly out for our wedding.'

Avery stared at him. 'She—?'

'My plane lands in the next hour. She is on it. She can help you get ready and she has strict instructions to call me if one word of doubt crosses your lips.'

'It won't.'

'What if your mother texts you again?'

'She can't. I dropped my phone in the fountain.' Her voice faltered. 'But I *am* afraid of messing everything up. I don't know anything about making a relationship work. Nothing.'

'There is only one thing you need to know about making a relationship work and that is that you don't give up.' His fingers slid into her hair, strong and possessive. 'Whatever you feel, you tell me. You shout, you yell, anything, but you never walk away. Never.'

It should have felt terrifying but instead it felt blissfully good. 'My mother told me that marriage was a sacrifice, but it feels so much more like a gift.'

His eyes gleamed. 'I look forward to unwrapping you, *habibti*. And in the meantime, do you think you could change into something that will make the unwrapping more fun? Everyone would be disappointed to see the elegant Avery Scott wearing jeans on her wedding day.'

She curled her hand into his shirt and pulled him towards her. 'You want the dance of the seven veils?'

'That sounds like the perfect way to begin a marriage.'

* * *

'Where exactly are we going? Could someone please tell me what's going on?' Avery was so nervous she felt sick. 'Jen?'

Her friend shook her head. 'This is one event you're not organizing, Avery. Just relax.'

'I'm not a relaxed sort of person.' Despite the air conditioning in the limousine, her palms felt damp and her stomach was a knot of nerves. 'I'm supposed to be marrying Mal so it would be great if someone could tell me why we're driving in this car *away* from the Palace and with blacked-out windows so I can't even see where I'm going.'

'It's a surprise. You're controlling, you do know that, don't you?'

'I'm efficient, not controlling. I get things done. And it's hard to get a wedding done when the groom is in one place and the bride is in another.' Just saying those words made her heart race. Bride. Groom. *She was getting married.* 'And you, by the way, are supposed to be on my side.'

'I'm on your side. You're scared, Avery.' Jenny reached across and took her hand. 'Don't be. It's the right thing. I never saw two people as right for each other as you and Mal. And I've seen a few.'

'I haven't.' Avery's teeth were chattering. 'I haven't seen any.'

'You can borrow some of mine. OK, so there's Peggy and Jim—they're clocking up sixty years. True, neither of them has their own teeth left but that hasn't been a barrier to lasting happiness. Then there's David and Pamela—' Jenny ticked them off on her fingers '—a happier couple you never did meet. And Rose and Michael—they just celebrated sixty years.'

Avery stared at her, confused. 'What are you talking about?'

'I'm listing all the people I know whose marriages have

lasted more than sixty years so that you don't sit there with a list of your mother's divorce cases in your head.'

Avery moved the hem of her wedding dress so that it didn't catch in her heel. 'You *know* all those people?'

'My Aunt Peggy does. They all live in her retirement home.'

'But—' Avery looked at her in exasperation. 'What does this have to do with my wedding to Mal?'

'I was distracting you before you exploded with fear.'

'I'm not afraid!'

'Yes, you are. But you're facing your fear and that makes me so, so proud of you. And I really want to hug you right now but I daren't ruin your hair and make-up because you look stunning.' Jenny's eyes glistened and she sniffed and flapped her hand in front of her face. 'Oh look at me! I'm going to ruin my own make-up and everyone will think your best friend is a panda. You are a lucky woman, Avery Scott. Mal is gorgeous. He was the one who insisted on all this. The whole Palace has been in an uproar, changing everything on his orders.'

'Changing everything? Changing what?' Completely confused, Avery realised that the car had stopped. 'Where are we?'

The door opened and Rafiq stood there. 'Welcome. Can I help you with your dress, Your Highness?'

'I'm not Your Highness yet, Rafiq, but thank you.' With Jenny helping, Avery stepped out of the air-conditioned limo and gasped. 'The desert?' She blinked in the blaze of the sun. For a moment she just stood, overwhelmed by the savage beauty of the golden landscape. She never grew tired of looking at it. Never. 'But the wedding was going to take place at the Palace.'

'But you love the desert,' Rafiq said quietly. 'Although this has to be a public affair, His Highness was insistent that it should also be personal. The wedding itself is for the people, but this part—this is for you. '

Avery heard Jenny sniff but she ignored her. 'But...oh... isn't everyone angry that they had to come to the desert and stand in the heat?'

'Angry that their future Queen loves their country as they do?' Rafiq gave an indulgent smile. 'I hardly think so. And now everyone is waiting for you. Are you ready?'

Avery stared at the sea of faces. She was used to large gatherings, but never one where the attention was focused on her. She felt a sudden rush of nerves. 'Where's Mal?'

'I'm right here.' He was standing behind her, stunningly handsome in flowing robes, his eyes gleaming dark and the smile on his face intended only for her.

Even the unflappable Rafiq was shocked. 'Your Highness! Convention states that—'

'I don't care about convention, I care about my bride.' Mal took her hand in his and lifted it to his lips, his eyes holding hers. 'Are you afraid, *habibti*?'

She should be.

She was giving him everything. Her love, her trust and her heart. But the moment she'd seen him standing there, she'd been sure and the feeling filled her and warmed her. 'I'm not afraid. I can't believe you did this for me.'

'I couldn't change the date, but I could change the place.' The words were for her and her alone. He managed to create intimacy despite the crowd watching and waiting. 'Are you pleased that we're marrying in the desert?'

'Yes. You know I love it. I had our picture on the computer. It was the first thing I saw in the morning.'

'I did the same. And every time I saw that picture I dreamed of this moment.'

Her eyes filled and she gave a strangled laugh. *'Don't make me cry!'*

'Never.' As he lowered his head towards her, she closed her eyes and lifted her mouth to his but Jenny gave a shriek and intervened.

'What are you *doing*? You can't kiss her! You'll mess up her make-up and she'll look terrible in the photographs. Stop it, the pair of you. Rafiq, *do* something.'

'Sadly, it seems I am powerless, madam. A fact I have long suspected.' But there was humour in his voice as he bowed to Jenny. 'May I escort you to your seat? The others are already waiting.'

'Others?' Avery glanced at Mal. 'Who? I don't have family.'

'But you have friends.' He spoke softly, his eyes gentle. 'Many, *many* friends, all of whom want to wish you well and would not miss this, the most important party of your life.'

She glanced through the crowd of people, now silent and curious, and saw faces she knew. So many faces. All smiling at her.

'You have some seriously cool friends, I'll give you that,' Jenny muttered under her breath. 'Chloe is probably going to pass out.'

Mal smiled. 'Chloe has already passed out. Twice. I have someone looking out for her.'

Jenny glanced at Avery in despair. 'She passed out last week at the Senator's party. Which was a great success, by the way. The doves were sweet. I hope you're having doves.'

'We will have doves for our fiftieth anniversary,' Mal breathed, 'and now, if no one objects, I'd like to marry the woman I love in the company of the people who love her.'

'Can we walk up there together?' Avery slipped her hand in his and he smiled down at her.

'I would have it no other way, *habibti*.'

Rafiq looked desperate. 'But Your Highness, tradition states that the bride should be brought to the groom. That is how the marriage begins.'

'Not this marriage.' His voice was deep and sure. 'This marriage begins the way it will continue. With the bride and groom side by side as equals. Are you ready?'

Avery smiled. 'I've never been more ready for anything in my life.'

* * * * *

Marriage Behind the Façade

LYNN RAYE HARRIS

Lynn Raye Harris read her first Mills & Boon® romance when her grandmother carted home a box from a yard sale. She didn't know she wanted to be a writer then, but she definitely knew she wanted to marry a sheikh or a prince and live the glamorous life she read about in the pages. Instead, she married a military man and moved around the world. These days she makes her home in North Alabama, with her handsome husband and two crazy cats. Writing for Mills & Boon is a dream come true. You can visit her at www.lynnrayeharris.com.

CHAPTER ONE

I⊤ was done. Sydney Reed dropped the pen and stared at the documents she'd just signed.

Divorce papers.

Her heart hammered in her throat, her palms sweated. Her stomach cramped. She felt as if someone had taken away the last shred of happiness she would ever, ever know.

But that was absurd. Because there was no happiness where Prince Malik ibn Najib Al Dhakir was concerned. There was only heartache and confusion.

Though it irritated her, just thinking his name still had the power to send a shiver tiptoeing down her spine. Her exotic sheikh. Her perfect lover. Her husband.

Ex-husband.

Sydney shoved the papers into the waiting envelope and buzzed her assistant, Zoe. Why was this so hard? It shouldn't be. Malik had never cared for her. She'd been the one who'd felt everything. But it wasn't enough. One person couldn't feel enough emotion for two. No matter how hard she tried, Malik was never going to love her. He simply wasn't capable of it. Though he was a generous and giving lover, his heart never engaged.

Of course it didn't. Sydney frowned. It wasn't that he

couldn't love—he just couldn't love *her*. She was not the right woman for him. She never had been.

Zoe appeared in the door, her expression all business.

"Call the courier. I need these delivered right away," Sydney said before she could change her mind.

Zoe didn't even acknowledge the tremble in Sydney's fingers as she handed over the thick sheaf of papers. "Yes, Miss Reed."

Miss Reed. Not Princess Al Dhakir.

Never Princess Al Dhakir again.

Sydney nodded, because she didn't trust herself to speak, and turned back to her computer. The screen was a little blurry, but she resolutely clenched her jaw and got on with the business of selecting property listings to show the new client she was meeting with later.

She'd been such a fool. She'd met Malik over a year ago when someone on his staff had called her parents' real estate firm to arrange for an agent to show him a few properties. She hadn't known who Malik was, but she'd quickly familiarized herself with his background before their appointment.

Prince of Jahfar. Brother to a king. Sheikh of his own territory. Unmarried. Obscenely wealthy. International playboy. Heartbreaker. There had even been a photo of a sobbing actress who claimed she'd fallen in love with Prince Malik, but he'd left her for another woman.

Sydney had gone to the appointment armed with information and, yes, even a dose of disdain for the entitled sheikh who broke hearts so carelessly. Not that she thought he could ever be interested in her. She wasn't glamorous or movie star gorgeous or anything even remotely interesting to a playboy sheikh.

But oh, the joke was on her, wasn't it?

Malik was so charming, so suave. So unlike any man she'd ever met before.

When he'd turned his singular attention on her, she'd been helpless to resist him. She hadn't wanted to resist. She'd been flattered by his interest.

He'd made her feel beautiful, accomplished, special—all the things she definitely was not. A dart of pain lodged beneath her heart. Malik's special gift was making a woman feel as if she were the center of his universe; as long as it lasted, it was bliss.

Her mouth compressing into a grim line, Sydney grabbed the listings from the printer and shoved them into her briefcase. Then she shrugged into the white cotton blazer hanging on the back of her chair. She refused to feel sorry for herself a moment longer. That part of her life was over.

Malik had been happy to be rid of her—and now she was taking the final step and cutting him from her life permanently. She'd half expected him to do it in the year since she'd left him in Paris, but he clearly didn't care enough to make the effort. Whatever the reason, Malik's heart was encased in ice—and she was not the one who could thaw it.

Sydney let Zoe know she was leaving, stopped by her mother's office to say good night and headed out to her car. It took over an hour in traffic to reach the first house in Malibu. She parked in the large circular drive and glanced at her watch. The client would be here in fifteen minutes.

Sydney gripped the steering wheel and forced herself to breathe calmly for a couple of minutes. She felt disjointed, unsettled, but there was nothing she could do about it now. She'd sent the papers; it was the end.

Time to move on.

She went inside the house, turning on lights, opening heavy curtains to reveal the stunning views. She moved as if on autopilot, fluffing the throw pillows on the furniture, spraying cinnamon air freshener and finding a soft jazzy station on the home entertainment system.

Then she walked out onto the terrace and scrolled through the email on her phone while she waited. At precisely seven-thirty, the doorbell rang.

Show time.

She took a deep breath before marching to the door and pasting a giant smile on her face. *Always greet the client with warm enthusiasm.* Her mother's first rule of engagement. Sydney might not be the best salesperson the Reed Team had, but she worked the hardest at it. She had to.

Sydney was the odd duck in the Reed family of swans, the disappointing daughter. The one who made her parents shake their heads and smile politely when what they really wanted to do was ask her why she couldn't be more like her perfect sister.

The only thing she'd ever done that had made them so proud they'd nearly popped was to marry a prince. But she'd failed at that, too, hadn't she? They didn't say anything, but she knew they were disappointed in her.

Sydney pulled the door open, her smile cracking apart the instant her gaze collided with the man's standing on the threshold.

"Hello, Sydney."

For a minute she couldn't move, couldn't speak. Couldn't breathe. She was mesmerized by the dark glitter of those burning, burning eyes. A bird sang in a nearby tree, the sound oddly distorted as all her attention focused on the man standing before her.

The man she hadn't seen, other than in photos in the papers or video clips on television, in over a year.

He was still spectacular, damn him. He was the desert. He was harsh and hard and beautiful. He'd been hers once.

No, he had not. It had been nothing more than an illusion. Malik belonged to no one but himself.

"What are you doing here?" she forced herself to ask.

"Isn't that obvious?" Malik responded, one dark brow lifting sardonically. "I'm looking for a house."

"You have a house," she said inanely. "I sold it to you last year."

"Yes, but I've never liked it."

"Then why did you buy it?" she snapped, her pulse roaring in her veins.

His dark eyes glittered hotly. She almost took a step back, but held her ground beneath the onslaught of his gaze. My God, Malik was all man. There had never been anyone like him in her life. So tall and dark and powerful. Malik walked into a room and owned it. There was never any question who was in charge when Malik was around.

And she had been just as vulnerable to his power as anyone.

He'd *owned* her. He would own her still, had she not realized how destructive a life with him would be. Had she not decided she couldn't give herself so utterly and completely to a man and still mean so little to him.

Pain rolled into a hard knot in her belly.

One corner of his mouth lifted in a grin, though there was no humor in his expression. "I bought it because you wanted me to, *habibti.*"

Sydney's feet were stuck to the floor. Her stomach churned with emotion, and her eyes stung. So much pain and anger in seeing him again. She'd tried to inure herself to his presence in the world by reading every article about him she could find, even when they stabbed her in the heart with tales of his latest conquests. She'd told herself it would only be a matter of time before he returned to L.A. and that if she ran into him again, she would sniff haughtily and act like an ice princess.

And wasn't she doing a fine job of that now?

Sydney stepped away from the door, determined to cloak herself in disdain. She did not need him. She'd never needed him. She'd only thought she had.

Riiight…

Inside, she was a mess. Outside, she was cool. As cool as he was. "And you always do what people want you to do, don't you?" she said.

Malik walked inside and shut the door behind him. "Only if it amuses me."

He took up all the space in the foyer, made it seem far too intimate. She could smell his soap, that special blend he had made in Paris. Her eyes skimmed over him. His suit was custom made, of course. Pale grey. The powder blue shirt beneath his jacket was unbuttoned just enough to show the hollow of his throat.

She knew what that spot tasted like, how it felt beneath her tongue.

Sydney pivoted, moved toward the floor to ceiling windows across the room. Her heart beat triple time. Her pulse throbbed. Her skin felt tight. "Then perhaps it would amuse you to buy a house with such a gorgeous view. I could use the commission."

"If you need money, Sydney, you only have to ask." He sounded so cool, so logical, so detached, as if he were telling his valet that he didn't care whether it was the red tie or the maroon today.

Bitterness flooded her. So typical of him. Nothing engaged Malik's emotions, not really. Her mistake had been in thinking she was different somehow.

Ha. Joke's on you, girlfriend.

She turned back to him. "I don't want your money, Malik. Now why don't you get out before my real client arrives? If you have anything to say to me, you can say it through my lawyer."

The heat in his eyes didn't waver. Her stomach clenched. Was it anger or a different kind of heat she saw there?

"Ah yes, the divorce," he said disdainfully, as if he were talking to a naughty child.

Anger, then. He wasn't accustomed to her fighting back. Because she never had before.

Not until today, when she'd slid her pen across that signature line.

Sydney crossed her arms over her chest. She knew it was a defensive gesture, but she didn't care. "I didn't ask you for anything. Just your signature on those papers."

"So you have signed them finally." There wasn't the least trace of sorrow or surprise in his voice.

Always so calm and cool, her desert lord. It infuriated her that he could be so unaffected.

Her blood felt thick in her veins. Heavy. "Isn't that why you're here?"

It had only been a little over an hour since she'd given the papers to Zoe. It was possible they'd been delivered to Malik in that time—but even if they had, how had he found where she was and gotten here so quickly?

She'd just assumed that was why he'd come. Comprehension unfurled. She felt stupid for not realizing it sooner. He must have known she'd been having the papers drawn up. Though why it mattered to him, she wasn't sure. "There is no client, is there? You set this up."

It was precisely like him to do so. Malik orchestrated things. If he didn't like something, he had it changed. If he wanted something, he got it. He spoke the words, and things happened as if by magic. It was the kind of power that most people would never possess.

He inclined his head. "It seemed the best way to meet with you. Less likely to cause a scene for the paparazzi."

Hot anger threated to scorch her from the inside out. And something else as well. Something hot and dark and secret. Something she recalled from the sultry nights with him, the hours spent tangled together in silken sheets, his body entwining with hers, thrusting into hers, caressing hers.

Why could she never look at this man without thinking of it?

It was the one place where he'd been raw and open with her—or so she'd thought. She knew better now.

Sydney closed her eyes, swallowed. Her skin was moist with perspiration, so she went to the terrace doors, flinging them open to let in the clean ocean breeze. It was always too hot when Malik was near.

She didn't have to turn to know he was right behind her. He vibrated with an energy that she'd never been able to ignore. When Malik walked into a room, she knew it. The hairs on the back of her neck prickled. Her blood hummed. Part of her wanted to turn and go into his arms, wanted to feel the extraordinary bliss of a night in his bed at least one more time.

She despised that part of herself. She wasn't that weak anymore, damn it! She was strong, capable of resisting the animal part of her that wanted this man without reason. Without sense.

But she had to resist—or pay the price.

Sydney whirled, taking a step back when she realized he was closer than she'd thought. "You never bothered to get in touch with me," she said, her voice cracking in spite of her determination. "You let all these months go by, and you never once tried to contact me. So why are you here now?"

His eyes flashed, his lean jaw hardening. He was so very, very beautiful. It wasn't an incongruous word when applied to a man who looked like Malik did. Jet dark hair, chiseled features, honed body, bronzed skin that looked as if he'd been dusted in gold. The most sensuous lips God had ever created. Lips that knew how to bring her to the brink of screaming pleasure again and again.

A tiny shiver crawled down her spine. She should have known a man like him could never truly be interested in her.

"Why would I chase you down, Sydney?" he demanded, ignoring her question. "You chose to leave. You could have chosen to come back."

She drew herself up. Of course he would think that way! Because he hadn't been affected by her going. "I had no choice."

Malik snorted. "Really? Someone made you walk out on our marriage? Someone forced you to run from Paris in the middle of the night with one suitcase and a note left on the counter? I'd like to meet this someone with such power over you."

She stiffened. He made her sound so ridiculous. So childish. "Don't pretend you were devastated by it. We both know the truth."

He brushed past her to stand in the open door and look at the ocean while her heart died just a little with each passing second as she hoped, ridiculously, that he might contradict her.

Why did a small part of her always insist on that rosy naiveté where he was concerned?

"Of course not," he stated matter-of-factly. Then he turned and speared her with an angry look, his voice turning harsh. "But I am an Al Dhakir and you are my *wife*. Did you not consider for one moment the embarrassment this would cause me? Would cause my family?"

Anger and disappointment simmered together in her belly. She'd hoped he might have missed her just a little bit, but of course he had not. Malik didn't need anyone or anything. He was a force of nature all his own.

She'd never understood him. That was only part of the problem between them, but it was a big part. He'd been everything exotic and wonderful and he'd swept her off her feet.

She still remembered the moment she'd realized she was in love with him. And she'd thought he must feel the same since she was the only woman he'd ever wanted to marry.

How wrong she'd been. It hadn't taken very long for her naive hopes to be ground to bits beneath his custom soles. Her eyes filled with angry tears, but she refused to let them fall. She'd had a year to analyze her actions and berate herself for not demanding more from him.

From *life*.

"That's why you're here? Because *you're* embarrassed?" Sydney drew in a trembling breath. Adrenaline surged in her blood, but she was determined to maintain her cool. "My, my, it certainly took you a long time to get worked up."

He took a step toward her. Sydney thrust her chin out,

uncowed. Abruptly, he stopped and shoved his hands into his pockets. The haughty prince assumed control once more as he looked down his refined nose at her. "We could live apart, Sydney. That is practically expected, though usually after there is an heir or two. But divorce is another thing altogether."

"So you're embarrassed about the divorce, not about me leaving," she stated. As if she would ever consider having children with him. So he could leave her to raise the kids while he dallied with mistresses?

No way. She'd been such a fool to think their lives could be normal when they came from such diverse backgrounds. He was a prince of the desert. She was plain Sydney Reed from Santa Monica, California. It was laughable how deluded she had been.

"I've let you have your space," he continued. "But enough is enough."

Sydney felt her eyes widening. A bubble of anger popped, sending fresh heat rushing through her. "You *let* me have my space? What the hell is that supposed to mean?"

His eyes flashed. "Is that any way for a princess to talk?"

"I'm not a princess, Malik." Though technically his wife *was* a princess, she'd never felt like one, even when she'd still been happily married to him. He'd never taken her to Jahfar; she'd never seen his homeland or been welcomed by his family.

She'd never even *met* his family.

That should have been her first clue.

Shame flooded her, made her skin hot once more. How naive she'd been. When he'd married her, she'd thought he'd loved her. She'd had no idea she was simply an instrument of his rebellion. He'd married her because she'd been unsuitable, no other reason. He'd *wanted* to shock his family.

She'd simply been the flavor of the moment, the woman warming his bed when the idea occurred to him.

"You are still my wife, Sydney," he growled. "Until such time as you are not, you will act with the decorum your position deserves."

Sydney's stomach was doing flips. She clenched her fists at her sides, willing herself not to explode. What good would it do?

"Not for much longer, Malik. Sign the papers and you won't have to worry about me embarrassing you ever again." Or that she wasn't good enough for his family's refined taste.

He closed the distance between them slowly...so slowly that she felt as if she were being hunted. Her instinct was to escape, but she refused to give him the satisfaction. She stood her ground as the ocean crashed on the beach outside, as her heartbeat swelled to a crescendo, as he came so close she could smell the scent of his skin, could feel his breath on her face.

His fingers snaked along her jaw, so lightly she might have imagined it. His eyes were hooded, his expression unreadable. She fought the desire to close her eyes, to tilt her face up to his. To feel his lips on hers once more.

She was not that desperate. Not that stupid.

She'd learned. She might have been blindly, ignorantly in love with him once—but she knew better now.

His voice was a deep rumble, an exotic siren call. "You still want me, Sydney."

"I don't." She said it firmly, coldly. Her legs trembled beneath her, her nerve endings shivering with anticipation. Her heart would beat right out of her chest if he kept touching her.

But she would not tell him to stop. Because she would not admit she was affected.

"I don't believe you," he said.

And then his head dipped, his mouth fitting over hers. For a moment she softened; for a moment she let his lips press against hers. For a moment, she was lost in time, flung back to another day, another house, another kiss.

An arrow of pain shot through her breastbone, lodged somewhere in the vicinity of her heart. Was she always destined to hurt because of him?

Sydney pressed her hands against the expensive fabric of his jacket, clenched her fingers in his lapels—and then pushed hard.

Malik stepped back, breaking the brief kiss. His nostrils flared. His face was a set of sharp angles and chiseled features, the waning light from the sunset hollowing out his cheeks, making him seem harder and harsher than she remembered.

Sadder, in a way.

Except that Malik wasn't sad. How could he be? He didn't care about her. Never had. She'd been convenient, a means to an end. Impressionable and fresh in a way his usual women had not been.

The slow burn of embarrassment was still a hot fire inside, even after a year. She'd been so thoroughly duped by his charm.

"You never used to push me away," he said bemusedly.

"I never thought I needed to," she responded.

"And now you do."

"Don't I? What's the point, Malik? Do you wish to prove your mastery over me one last time? Prove that you're still irresistible?"

He tilted his head to one side. "Am I irresistible?"

"Hardly."

"That's too bad," he said.

"Not for me, it isn't." Her head was beginning to throb from too much adrenaline, too much anger.

He pushed a hand through his hair. "It changes nothing," he said. "Though it might make it more difficult."

Sydney blinked. "Make what more difficult?"

"Our marriage, *habibti*."

He was a cruel, cruel man. "There is no marriage, Malik. Sign the papers and it's done."

His smile was not quite a smile. "Ah, but it's not so easy as that. I am a Jahfaran prince. There is a protocol to follow."

Sydney reached for the door frame to steady herself. A bad feeling settled into her stomach, making the tension in her body spool tighter and tighter. Her knees felt weak, making her suddenly unstable on her tall designer pumps. "What protocol?"

He speared her with a long look. A pitying look?

By the time he spoke, her nerves were at the snapping point.

"We must go to Jahfar—"

"What?"

"And we must live as man and wife for a period of forty days…"

Dying. She was dying inside. And he was so controlled, as always. "No," she whispered, but he didn't hear—or he didn't care. His eyes were flat, unfeeling.

"Only then can we apply to my brother the king for a divorce."

CHAPTER TWO

SYDNEY slipped out the door and sank heavily onto a nearby deck chair. Beyond, the Pacific Ocean rolled relentlessly to shore. The surf roiled and foamed, the sound a muted roar as the power of the water hit the beach.

That was Malik's power, she thought wildly. The power to rush over her, to drag her with him, to obliterate what she wanted. That had been part of the reason she'd left, because she'd somehow let her sense of self be pulled under the wave that was Malik. It had frightened her.

That and hearing what his true feelings for her had been. Sydney shuddered.

Finally, she pulled her gaze from the water, which was now turning orange with the sun's setting rays. Malik stood beside her chair. His jaw seemed hard in the waning light, as if he, too, were trapped and trying to make the best of it.

"Tell me it's a joke," she finally said, squeezing her hands together over her stomach.

His gaze flickered to her. His handsome face was so serious, so stark. Even now she felt a twinge of something, some deep feeling, as she looked at him. She refused to examine what that feeling might be; she simply didn't want to know. She wanted to be done with him, finished.

Forever.

"It is not a joke. I am bound by Jahfaran law."

"But we weren't married there!" She laughed wildly. "I've never even *seen* Jahfar, except on a map. How can I possibly be bound by some crazy foreign law?"

He stiffened, but she didn't really care if she'd insulted him. How dare he show up here after all this time and tell her they would remain married until she lived with him for forty days—in the desert, no less! It was like something only Hollywood could think up.

The irony made her laugh. Malik looked at her curiously, but didn't seem to mistake the laugh for real humor. At least he could tell that much. Maybe forty days wouldn't be so bad after all.

Who was she kidding?

"I won't do it," she said, drawing in a deep breath heavy with salt and sea. "I'm not bound by Jahfaran law. Sign the papers and as far as I'm concerned, we're through."

He shifted beside her chair. "You might think it's that easy, but I assure you it is not. You married a foreign prince, *habibti*."

"We were married in Paris." Quickly, by an official at the Jahfaran embassy. As if Malik were afraid he might change his mind if it didn't happen fast. Bitterness ate at her.

That was precisely what he'd been thinking.

"Where we were married matters not," Malik said in that smooth, deep voice of his that still had the power to make her shudder deep inside. "But it does matter by *whom*. We were married under Jahfaran law, Sydney. If you ever wish to be free of me, you will come to Jahfar and follow the protocol."

Sydney tilted her head up to look at him. He was gazing down at her, his expression indecipherable. Anger surged in her veins. "Surely we can find a way to fake it. Your brother is the king!"

"Which is precisely *why* we cannot fake it, as you so charmingly say. My brother takes his duty as king very seriously. He will hold me to the letter of the law. If you wish to be divorced, you will do this."

Sydney closed her eyes and leaned back against the cushion. Dear God. It was a nightmare. A giant, ironic joke from the cosmos. She'd married Malik hurriedly, secretly. There'd been no royal wedding, no fairy tale day with music and beautiful clothes and pageantry.

There'd been the two of them in a registry office at the embassy. A fawning official who called Malik *Your Royal Highness* and bowed a lot. A wide-eyed woman, Sydney remembered, who'd registered the marriage and asked them to sign.

She'd almost felt as if it weren't real, but then the newspapers had picked up on it and suddenly she and Malik were splashed across the tabloids. The attention hadn't died by the time she'd left. And then it followed her back to L.A., finally disappearing a few weeks later when she'd refused to talk to anyone.

Oh, she knew her picture had appeared a few times over the last year, but the paparazzi were far more interested in Malik than they were in her. He was the news. She was a casualty.

And not even a very interesting one.

The last thing she wanted was to remain tied to him, to have the media take a renewed interest in her down the road because Malik caused an international stir of some sort and they wanted to know how his poor wife was handling it. Or, worse, what happened when Malik found someone else he wanted to marry, and he needed her to go to Jahfar for a divorce when he had a current lover in tow?

No. Way. In. Hell.

"Fine," Sydney sniffed. "If that's what it takes, I'll go."

A shiver dripped into her veins. She could get through forty days, if that's what it took to officially end this. Because there was nothing left between them, no danger to her heart any longer. The damage had already been done. There was an iron cage where her heart had once been.

"We can leave tonight. My plane is ready."

Goose bumps crawled across her skin. What had she just agreed to? Panic spread inside until she was quivering with it. "I can't be ready that fast. I need time to put things in order."

The last time she'd dashed off with Malik she'd left her life in disarray. This time, she was putting everything in order before going anywhere. Because this time she would be stepping back into her life without the pain and disorientation of last time.

She'd gone without much thought, because he'd asked her to, and then when he'd asked her to stay, to marry him, she'd impulsively agreed. She'd given no thought to her life back in Los Angeles. A fact that her family never mentioned, but that she knew was very much on their minds whenever they looked at her. She was the impulsive one, the artistic one—the one who could leap without looking but then paid the price later.

And what a price it had been. She'd been a wreck. She'd asked herself in the early days after her return home if she'd been too hasty, if she should have stayed and confronted him, but she always came back to the same thing: Malik regretted marrying her. He'd said so. What was there left to say after that?

She might have loved him, but she would not be anyone's cross to bear. And she'd definitely felt like a burden in the week after his confession. He'd changed, and she simply hadn't been able to take it anymore. She'd never thought a year would pass without any contact between them, but that had only proven he did not want her in his life any longer.

"How much time do you need?" he asked, his voice tight.

"At least a week," she answered automatically, though in fact she knew no such thing. But she wanted to be in control this time. Needed to be in control. It wasn't much, but it was something.

"Impossible. Two days."

Sydney bristled. "Really? Is there a timeline, Malik? A celestial clock somewhere that insists we must do this on a specific timetable? I need a week. I have to make arrangements at work."

And she had to check with her lawyer, just in case she could find some sort of legal loophole that would change everything.

Malik gazed down at her, his dark eyes gleaming hotly. Intensely. She waited almost breathlessly for his answer. Malik was proud, haughty. Aristocratic and used to getting his way. If only she'd told him no when he'd suggested she marry him—but it had never crossed her mind. She'd been too awestruck, and far too much in love with the man she'd thought he was.

Though it was a little late, she would not blindly accept his decrees ever again.

"Fine," he said, his voice clipped. "One week."

Sydney nodded her agreement, her heart pounding as if she'd just run a marathon. "Very well. One week then."

He turned to gaze out at the ocean again. Then he nodded. "I'll take it."

She blinked. "Take what?"

"The house."

"You haven't really seen it," she exclaimed. It was a gorgeous house, one that she only wished she could afford in her wildest dreams, with spacious rooms and breathtaking ocean views. It was the kind of house where she could be inspired to paint, she thought wistfully.

But Malik had only seen the exterior, the main living space, and this terrace. For all he knew, the bedrooms were tiny closets, the bathrooms a 1970s throwback with mustard and orange tiles and psychedelic black fixtures.

Malik shrugged. "It is a house. With a view. It will do."

Inexplicably, a current of anger uncoiled inside her. He was careless when he wanted something. Accustomed to getting whatever he wanted when he wanted it.

Like *her*.

In Malik's world, there were no consequences. No price to be paid when things didn't work out the way you expected. There was only the next house, the next deal.

The next woman.

Dark anger pumped into her. "I'm afraid that's impossible," she said. "There's already an offer."

Malik was unfazed. "Add twenty-five percent. The owner will not turn that kind of money down."

"I think they've already accepted the offer," she said primly. But guilt swelled inside her as soon as she voiced the lie. The owners were entitled to the sale. Her anger at Malik was no excuse to deprive them of it. "But if you'll give me a moment, I can call and see if there's a chance."

Malik's dark eyes burned into her. "Do it."

Sydney turned away and walked across the terrace. She called the listing broker just to make sure there were no offers, and then strolled back to Malik when she finished. "Good news," she said, though it galled her to do so. "If you can come up half a million, the property is yours."

Because he was too smug, too careless, and she couldn't let him ride roughshod over her. It was a rebellion of a sort to jack up the price. She refused to feel guilty. In fact, she would donate her portion of the commission to charity. At least Malik's money could do someone some good.

"Fine," he murmured. "Whatever it requires."

Bitterness swelled in her veins. "And will you be happy here, Malik? Or will you regret this purchase, too?"

She didn't say what she was really thinking—that he regretted her—but it was implied.

"I never regret my actions, *habibti.* If I change my mind later, I will simply get rid of the property."

"Of course," she said stiffly, shame pounding through her. "Because that is easiest."

Malik could discard whatever he wanted, whatever he no longer needed or desired. He'd spent a lifetime doing so.

His expression didn't change. He looked so haughty, so superior. "Precisely. You will write up the papers, yes?"

"Of course."

"Get them now and I will sign them."

"You don't want to read them first?"

He shrugged. "Why?"

"What if I increase the price another million?"

"Then I would pay it," he said.

Sydney opened her briefcase and jerked a blank offer form from inside. As much as she despised him in that moment, as much as she despised his arrogance and nonchalance, she couldn't succumb to the temptation to take him for a spectacular ride. She quickly wrote in the price, and then shoved the papers at him.

"Sign here," she said, pointing.

He did so without hesitation. She couldn't decide if he was simply arrogant and uncaring or stupidly trusting. A split second later he looked up at her, his eyes sharp and hard, and she knew that stupidly trusting was not the correct choice.

This man not only knew what the fair market price of the property was, he also knew that she'd inflated the price—and he was willing to pay it.

"One week, Sydney," he said, his voice sending a shiver through her body. "And then you are mine."

"Hardly, Your Highness," she said, though her voice shook in spite of her determination not to let it. "It's simply another business arrangement. Forty days in Jahfar in exchange for a lifetime of freedom."

He bowed his head in acknowledgment. "Of course," he said. "You are quite correct."

And yet, as he walked out and left her standing alone with the ocean crashing in the background, she had the sinking feeling that everything about this arrangement was going to be far more complicated than she wanted it to be.

At least for her...

CHAPTER THREE

It took a week and half to get her life organized, and then to board a flight for Jahfar. Malik was not happy, as his messages indicated more than once, but Sydney refused to feel a moment's worry about it. After he'd left her in the Malibu home—*his* Malibu home now—she'd quickly phoned her lawyer.

Jillian had tried to help, but in the end there was nothing she could do. An American divorce wouldn't do the trick. When she'd originally drawn up the papers, she'd warned Sydney it might not be enough. Sydney had just hoped against hope that it would be. Even if it hadn't been, she hadn't expected an archaic law like the one mandating she live with Malik in Jahfar for forty days.

Forty days. My God.

Sydney sipped the champagne a flight attendant had brought for her. Her first class seat was comfortable, though the flight was full and she certainly wasn't alone. She could have flown on Malik's private plane, but she'd chosen to fly commercial instead. He'd been furious, but she'd held fast to her determination to do so. In the end, he'd gone to Jahfar a few days ahead of her.

Her stomach tightened nervously, and she took another sip of the champagne.

Jahfar. What would she find when she arrived? What would she feel?

It was Malik's home, and she would in some ways be at his mercy. But she was determined to maintain as much control over her life as possible, which was why she'd insisted on making her own arrangements. Yes, it would have been easier to fly with Malik and let him take care of everything.

But she refused to give him that much control.

The plane touched down in Jahfar a couple of hours after dawn. The moment they taxied to the gate, Sydney realized how foolish her thoughts had been. Because nothing was under her control any longer. A flight attendant hurried to her side, hands clutched together in front of her body. The woman seemed nervous, afraid. And then she bowed deeply.

A heavy feeling settled in the pit of Sydney's stomach.

"Princess Al Dhakir, please forgive us for not realizing you were aboard."

"I…" Sydney blinked, her skin heating with embarrassment. "No, that's fine," she said, recovering herself though her heart throbbed painfully. "I didn't wish it to be known."

She felt so pretentious, but what else could she say? There was no explaining, no telling these people not to refer to her as a princess. They wouldn't understand.

The woman bowed again before a man came forward and collected Sydney's carry-on bag from the overhead compartment. Everyone else remained seated as she exited the plane first, her cheeks burning hot. She had an overwhelming urge to strangle Malik when next she saw him.

Which proved to be far sooner than she expected.

The international airport in Port Jahfar teemed with people clothed in both Jahfaran and Western dress, but they fell away like water from a ship's bow as a man and his entourage cleaved through them. The man was tall, dressed in the flowing white *dishdasha* and traditional headdress of Jahfar. At his waist was a curved dagger with a jeweled hilt—surprising in an airport, and yet not so much considering where they were.

And who he was. She realized with a shock that the magnificent man in traditional clothing was actually her husband. Heat softened her bones, flooded her core. She'd never seen Malik in Jahfaran clothing. The effect was...extraordinary.

He was every inch a sheikh. Exotic, dark, handsome. Magnificent.

Malik strode toward her with that arrogant gait of his, his dark eyes burning into her from afar so that she felt the urge to shrink inside herself and disappear. She looked like hell—felt like hell—after so many hours in the air.

And he was like something out of a fairy tale.

Oh, if only she could turn time back an hour or so and change clothes, fix her hair, her makeup.

Why, Sydney? What would be the point in that?

Malik might have made love to her again and again over the two months they were together, but he'd clearly been slumming for his own purposes. Supermodels and beauty queens were more to his taste.

Sydney thrust her chin out. She would not cower or hide. She would not be ashamed.

There was nothing to be ashamed of.

Malik came to a halt before her, his entourage carefully surrounding them both, protecting them, without coming too close.

Her throat felt as dry as sand as his gaze slid over her. "Here I am," she said somewhat inanely. "As promised."

Immediately, she wished she hadn't been the first to speak. It was as if she'd given away some slice of invisible ground in their war with each other, as if she'd arrayed her forces on this particular field of battle and then failed because of something so obvious such as not arming them with weapons.

But it was because of him, because he was making her nervous as he studied her. No doubt he was regretting his impulse to inform anyone she was his wife. She was too casual in her white cotton tank, navy jacket, jeans and ballet flats. A princess should look more polished, like a movie star. She should be sporting Louboutins on her feet, carrying an Yves St. Laurent handbag and wearing the latest Milan fashions.

Well, she wasn't truly a princess and there was little point in pretending to be one for the next month and ten days.

One dark eyebrow arched as he studied her. "Yes, here you are."

Sydney's heart skipped several beats at once, making her feel momentarily light-headed. She splayed her hand over her chest, breathing deeply to regulate the rhythm.

Malik looked alarmed. "What is wrong? Do you need a doctor?"

She shook her head. "No, I'm fine. Just a few skips. Happens sometimes, usually when I'm tired. It's nothing."

Before she had time to do more than squeak a protest, he swept her off her feet and into his arms, cradling her against his chest as he turned and barked orders to the men surrounding them.

"Malik, for God's sake, put me down! I'm not hurt," she cried.

He didn't listen. She considered kicking her legs and fighting, showing him just how strong she was, but decided that bringing them both to the ground with a struggle was counterproductive.

"Please put me down," she begged as he began to move. "This is embarrassing."

People were staring at them, pointing, whispering. Malik seemed not to care. It was stunning to be held against him after so much time. Like plunging into a swimming pool with all your clothes on. He was hard, strong, and the heat of his body reminded her of another kind of heat they'd once shared.

He glanced down at her, his handsome features stark against the dark red background of the headdress framing his face. No one would ever mistake this man for anything other than a prince, she thought wildly. He was so sure of himself, so full of life and heat and passion.

She'd missed that.

No.

No, she was *not* going there. She didn't miss Malik. She didn't miss a single thing about him.

"We are not going far," he said. "I will put you down as soon as we are somewhere quiet, so you may rest."

She turned her head away as his long strides ate up the distance. The entourage hurried along with them, in front of them, their passage through the airport like the ripple of a giant wave. Soon, they were passing between sliding glass doors and into a quiet suite with plush chairs, tables and a bar at one end. Soft music played to the empty room. The lights in here were low, the air cool against her heated skin.

Malik set her down in one of the chairs. A glass of cold fizzy water appeared before she'd even blinked.

"Drink," he ordered, settling into the chair beside her and picking up the glass.

"I've had plenty to drink," she said, pushing his hand away. "Anything else, and I'll explode."

He looked doubtful. "Jahfar is hot, *habibti*. It can sneak up on you before you realize it."

"Water is not my problem, Malik," she insisted. "I've just flown all the way from L.A. I'm tired. I'm stressed. I want a bed and six hours of uninterrupted sleep."

She'd slept a little on the plane, but not enough. She'd been too nervous.

And with good reason. The man staring back at her now, this hard, hawklike being who seemed so remote and unapproachable—so regal—could make a lion nervous. Were they really married? Had she ever shared a tender moment with this intimidating man?

"Then you shall have it," he said. He nodded to a man who turned and disappeared through another door. A few minutes later, he took her hand—as she tried desperately to block the prickling heat of skin on skin—and led her out the same door and into an elevator. Then they were exiting the airport through a private entrance and climbing into a Mercedes limousine.

It was almost like the past, only Malik was dressed in white robes and a headdress instead of a tuxedo. He looked so cool and exotic while she felt frumpy and hot. She tugged at her jacket, drawing it off and laying it on the seat beside her.

Malik's eyes dropped to her chest, lingered. She felt his gaze as a caress, felt her body responding, her nipples tightening inside her bra. Lightning sizzled in her core. She crossed her arms and turned to look out the window.

"Where are we going?" she asked as the limo slid into traffic. In front of them, a police car with whirling lights blazed a trail. The windows were tinted dark, but the light outside them was still so bright. It would be blinding, she realized, were she out in it. And hot, as he'd said.

"I have a home in Port Jahfar. It is only a few minutes away, on the coast. You will like it."

Sydney leaned her head against the window. It was odd to be here, and exciting in a way she hadn't anticipated. In the distance, stark sandstone mountains rose against the backdrop of the brilliant sky. Date palms dotted the landscape as they rode into the sprawling city. The buildings were a mix of modern concrete, glass and sandstone.

She realized that the hills in the opposite direction weren't actually hills, but sand dunes. Undulating red sand dunes. Along their base, a camel train trod single file toward the city. It was the most singularly foreign moment she'd ever experienced.

The car soon left the stark landscape behind as they passed deeper into the city. Eventually they turned— and suddenly the sea was there, on her right. They rode a short distance along the coast, with the turquoise water sparkling like diamonds in the sun, and then they were turning into a gated complex.

Malik helped her from the car and ushered her inside a courtyard cooled with tiny jets spraying mist that evaporated before it hit her skin. The air was thick, hot. It wasn't unexpected, or even anything she'd never experienced before—and yet it was different in its own way.

Or maybe she was just too tired.

A woman in a cotton *abaya* appeared, bowing and speaking to Malik in Arabic. And then he was turning to her as the woman melted back into the shadows from whence she'd come.

"Hala says that your room is prepared, *habibti*. You may sleep as long as you wish."

She'd expected that a servant would show her the way, but Malik took her elbow—no matter how lightly he touched her, she still burned—and guided her into a huge sunken living area and down a hallway that led to a small suite. The outer room had cushions arrayed around a central table, a rosewood desk in one corner and two low-slung couches that faced each other across a fluffy white goat-hair rug. The bedroom featured a tall bed covered in crisp white cotton linens that beckoned seductively.

"I need my bags," she said, realizing suddenly that she had nothing to change into. They'd left the airport without collecting her luggage.

"They are on the way. In the meantime, you will find all you need in the bathing room." He gestured to another door. Sydney walked into the spacious bath, marveling at the sunken tub, a shaft of sunlight coming from high up in the ceiling and illuminating the marble. The light picked out the red and gold veins of the stone, sparkled in the glass mosaic tiles surrounding the tub.

"I trust it meets with your approval."

Sydney whirled, his voice startling her, though it shouldn't have. She'd known he was behind her, watching her from the door.

"It's lovely," she said, swallowing hard. Why did it feel so surreal to be here like this? She'd agreed to come, known it was necessary, and yet she felt off balance, out of her element in a way she hadn't expected.

And why not? This is Jahfar, not Paris, she told herself. *Not Los Angeles.*

Malik crossed to her, cupped her face in his hands while her heart thundered in her ears.

She meant to protest, she really did, but her voice froze in her throat.

"There is nothing to fear, Sydney," he said. "We will get through this."

When he lowered his head, her eyelids fluttered closed automatically. Because she was tired, of course. No other reason.

He chuckled softly, his lips brushing her forehead while her pulse throbbed. The sound speared into her heart, reminded her of a different time when she still believed in a fairy tale ending with the handsome prince.

"Don't," she choked out as his lips moved to her temple.

An instant later, he released her and took a step backward. "Of course," he said, his voice thicker than it had been only a moment ago. "As you wish."

Sydney put a shaking hand to her throat, dropping it again when she realized how frightened and helpless it made her seem. She was neither of those things, though she was most definitely nervous. She'd loved him. She'd been through hell because of him. This situation was strange, unnatural.

For them both, she thought. He would probably prefer to be with his current mistress instead of her, the wife he'd thought he was rid of.

"I think it's best if we don't...touch," she said.

He arched an elegant brow. "You are afraid of a little touch, Sydney? And here I thought I was resistible."

He was mocking her. Naturally. She lifted her head. "There is no purpose to our touching, Malik. We aren't happily married. We are nothing to each other. Not anymore. I realize I'm an inconvenience to you, but I just want to get this over with. You don't have to pretend otherwise to make me feel more comfortable."

His dark eyes flashed with emotion. "I see. How wise you have grown, Sydney. How very jaded."

"I always thought you liked jaded women," she retorted—and felt instantly contrite. If she were trying to make him believe they could behave with cool civility for forty days, she'd just failed abominably.

He leaned against the door frame, but she didn't make the mistake of thinking him relaxed. No, he was carefully—and tightly—controlled. It had been one of the things that had driven her the most insane about him, that ability to shut down his emotions and rein them in so hard that he was nearly inhuman.

"I did not realize you cared," he said softly. Mockingly, still.

Sydney flicked her hand as if brushing away a fly. "I don't."

He straightened to his full height. "Let us not descend into games, *habibti*. You have had a long night of travel. Bathe, rest. I will see you when you are prepared to be reasonable."

Her temper spiked at the condescension in his tone. "I'm not playing games, Malik. I came, didn't I? I'm here because I want this over with. Because I want to be free of you forever." She flung the last at him, unable to stop herself from saying the words.

His jaw hardened, his eyes flashing hot once more. "You will get your wish," he growled. "But first I will get mine."

Her stomach flipped. "Wh-what do you mean?"

He looked so menacing. "Scared, Sydney? Afraid of what I will exact from you now that you are here?"

She swallowed, her throat thick with emotion. "Of course not."

His gaze slid down her body, back up, his eyes hot on hers. His voice came out as a sensual drawl that made heat flare in her core. "Then perhaps you should be."

CHAPTER FOUR

MALIK was in a bad mood. He sat in his study, working on minute details that were mind-numbing and boring and meant to distract him. They did not.

He shoved back from the computer and turned his head until he could see the sparkle of the sea beyond the windows.

She was here. His errant wife. The one woman he'd thought might be different, might make him happy— but who, instead, had run away from him. He was not accustomed to women running away from him.

It had been a singular moment when he'd realized she'd truly gone.

He'd raged. He'd made plans. He'd sworn to go after her and drag her back by force if necessary.

And then he'd thought, *no.*

She'd walked out. Let her be the one to come back. Instead, she'd started divorce proceedings.

Yet he still wanted her. His body desired hers, regardless of his wishing otherwise. From the moment she'd opened the door to the house in Malibu, he'd wanted her with a fierceness that surprised him after so much time.

Especially considering how very angry he still was with her.

But she'd looked so virginal, so pure, in her white

jacket and pale pink dress. Her long legs had been displayed to perfection, enhanced by the nude-colored high heels she'd worn. He'd imagined those legs wrapped around him as he thrust into her body.

It had taken every ounce of control he'd possessed not to press her. Because he'd known that she still wanted him every bit as much as he wanted her.

Her body wanted him, but her heart did not. And that was what had stopped him, both then and today.

He squeezed the pen he held until it cracked, its jagged edge slicing into his finger. A drop of blood welled on the tip. He grabbed a tissue from the box sitting on his desk and swiped the blood away.

Sydney Reed—Sydney Al Dhakir, he corrected—was so beautiful, so very luscious, so bad for his control. From the first minute he'd seen her, he'd wanted her. She'd been aloof…but only at first. When he'd finally gotten her into his arms, she'd burned so hot he'd known that once with her wasn't enough.

She probably wasn't the most beautiful woman he'd ever known, but he couldn't actually remember another being more compelling to him. Her skin was as pale as milk, her hair the color of the red dunes of the Jahfaran desert. Her eyes were like a rain-gray sky, the kind of sky one often found hanging over Paris in winter.

While others might find rain depressing, he found it unbearably lovely.

Especially when it was reflected in her eyes.

Malik swore softly. He'd known, when he'd impulsively married her, that it could not last. Because he'd married her for all the wrong reasons, not least the utter dismay it would cause his family. That, and he'd wanted her with a fierceness that had shocked him.

The phone clanged into the stillness, making him

jump. Though he could let his secretary get it, he preferred the distraction to his chaotic thoughts.

"Yes?" he barked into the receiver.

"I hear that your wife arrived today," his brother Adan said.

"That's correct," Malik replied somewhat stiffly. "She is here."

He'd kept her away from Jahfar for a reason. Now that she was here, he had no choice but to share her with his family. Though he'd thought there might be a bit more time before that happened. Malik frowned. His brothers would be polite, but his mother certainly would not.

"And do you plan on bringing her to the palace?"

Malik ground his teeth. He hadn't told Adan why Sydney was here. He hadn't told anyone. "Perhaps in a few days. Or not. I have business in Al Na'ir."

"Surely you can spare an evening. I wish to meet her, Malik."

"Is that a command?"

There was no pause whatsoever. "It is."

How very easily Adan had slipped into power. He hadn't been the heir to the throne, just as Malik had not been a part of the ruling family, until their cousin had died in a boating accident and Adan suddenly found himself the heir to their uncle. When their uncle died a year later, Adan had ascended the throne as king.

He'd been a good king. A just king.

"Then I will bring her. Though not today. She is tired from the journey."

"Of course," Adan replied. "We will see you for dinner tomorrow night. Isabella looks forward to it."

"Tomorrow night then."

Their goodbyes were stiff, formal, but Malik had expected nothing different. They'd had such a barren childhood, with nannies and a kind of rigid formality that was not conducive to warmth between them. Oh, Malik loved his brothers—and his sister—but theirs was not an easy relationship.

He wasn't quite sure why. There'd been no huge trauma, no major falling out. Just a quiet distance that seemed impossible to breech. The more time moved on, the wider the chasm.

Perhaps that was why he'd been so drawn to Sydney. She'd made him feel less alone, and he'd been addicted to that feeling. But that was before she'd betrayed him, before she'd proven she was no different than anyone else in his life.

Malik checked his watch. It had been over six hours since he'd brought her here. He debated calling Hala to check on her, but decided he would do so instead. He would not hide from her, would not shrink from the raw emotions still rolling between them like a storm-tossed sea.

He found her on the small terrace off her room, her long hair loose and flowing down her back, the wind from the sea ruffling the auburn strands. She'd put on a fluid cream-colored dress that skimmed her form. It was slightly darker than the milk of her skin, but it made her look ethereal. Like an angel.

She turned her head as he approached, setting down the coffee she'd been cupping in both hands. Her expression went carefully blank, but not before he saw the yearning there.

It gutted him, that yearning.

"Are you feeling refreshed?" he asked.

"I am, thank you," she replied, glancing away again.

He pulled out the chair opposite her, setting it at an

angle so he could view the sea and her face at once if he so chose. "Your luggage is intact, I take it?"

"Yes. Everything arrived."

She picked up the coffee again, her long fingers shaking as she threaded them on either side of the cup. He did that to her, he realized. Made her as skittish as a newborn foal.

It reminded him of the first time they'd made love. She hadn't been a virgin, but she hadn't been terribly experienced, either. Everything he did to her had been a revelation. Soon, she'd been bold and eager for more.

His body hardened instantly.

This was the problem, he thought, with no small measure of anger. This need that flared every time he was with her. He'd ceased trying to understand it long ago. He'd never been the sort of man to be ruled by his penis—until Sydney came along and turned everything upside down.

He blew out a disgusted breath and turned to stare at the container ship gliding into port in the distance. It wasn't simply the physical that drew him to her.

No, he'd been dissolute long before Sydney came along. He'd indulged every appetite, every whim. It had been great fun.

At first.

But in the last couple of years, the more he'd pushed the envelope, the emptier he'd felt.

And she seemed to fill that emptiness somehow.

"I'm going to need internet access," she said, cutting through his thoughts. "I have work to do while I'm here."

"There is Wi-Fi," he told her. "I will have someone give you the password."

"Thank you." Her fingers drummed against the side of the cup. He heard her draw breath, as if she was planning to speak, but she said nothing. Several more times she tried, until he finally speared her with a look, pinning her into place.

"Say it, *habibti*."

She was looking at him with those big grey eyes, her long lashes sweeping to her cheeks and back up again as she let her doubts war with her desire to speak.

Then she bit her lip, and he forced himself not to turn away. Forced himself to deal with the slice of pain that shafted into him, the flood of desire that pooled low in his groin.

He would conquer this ridiculous need.

She was a woman, like any other. She was not special, or different. She possessed nothing that he couldn't obtain elsewhere. Whatever pull she had on him, whatever imagined void she seemed to fill…she was not irreplaceable. No woman was. He knew that better than most.

Her expression changed by degrees, turned fierce, and he knew she'd made up her mind. He relished her fierceness. It was far better than wide-eyed defeat.

"I want to know why you never brought me here," she burst out, gesturing at him, her hand encompassing his entire body as she swept it up and down. "This is who you are—the clothes, the desert—but you never let me see it."

She leaned toward him then, her eyes stormy. "Did I embarrass you *that* much?"

There, she'd said it. She'd finally put voice to the pain that had been nagging her since the moment she'd arrived and seen him dressed in traditional clothing. This was who he was. This was his life, his heritage, and he'd never allowed her to be a part of it.

She *knew* why, but she wanted to hear him say it. She wanted him to admit to her that he'd regretted taking her for his wife. Her heart thundered, her pulse throbbed and her breath razored in and out of her chest. She *needed* to hear him say it.

To her face this time.

Not that she was in any danger of forgetting, of succumbing to his considerable charm, but she wanted the pain front and center so long as she was here. If she kept it there, it would act as a shield.

He'd removed the headdress between the time she'd seen him earlier and now. His dark hair was wavy, thick, and she remembered threading her hands into it, pulling his mouth down to hers as she lay beneath him in their bed.

Her heart turned over at the thought. Warmth gathered in her belly. A knot of something she dared not name tightened in her core.

No. Those memories had nothing to do with now.

"You did not embarrass me." Malik's handsome face was carefully blank, and though the words were what she wanted to hear, she did not believe them. He was too stoic, too detached. "We would have come here eventually."

"Eventually," she repeated, unable to keep the bitterness from her voice. He would not tell her the truth, even now. Had she truly expected it?

"What do you wish me to say, Sydney?" he demanded. "It was not foremost on my mind, I have to admit. I was more concerned with how long I had to wait until the next time I could get you naked."

Sydney set the coffee cup down, grateful that she didn't clang it into the saucer. "Why can't you just admit the truth?"

His dark eyes flashed, his expression hardening. "Why don't you tell me what this truth is and stop beating around the bush, as you Americans say?"

"You know what it is. You just won't say it."

He got to his feet, gazed down at her with that cool disdain she'd come to hate. He'd always shut down whenever she'd pressed him about anything. And she'd been so blinded by love that she hadn't seen it for the warning sign it was.

"If this is how you plan to spend the next forty days, we will never be divorced," he said.

She lifted her chin. She'd never really confronted him about anything. They hadn't been together long enough to truly argue, and she wasn't a confrontational person. But she was feeling so frustrated, so disoriented being here with him now, and she was fed up. Fed up with hiding behind a mask, with worrying that she didn't fit in or that she was embarrassing to those she cared about. She'd been trying to fit in since she was a child, and she was suddenly unwilling to do it with him for even a moment longer.

"Why is it suddenly my fault? Why am I the one causing the problem? You're the one who can't admit to the truth."

"I don't do drama, Sydney," he growled. "Either say what you so desperately want to say, or be quiet."

Fury roiled in her belly like a living thing. She pushed her chair back and stood, unwilling to allow him to stare down at her. Or to stare down at her from so great a height, she amended, since he was still taller than she was.

Fine, he wanted to hear it, she was not holding back a moment longer. She'd already held back for far too long.

Time hadn't eased the pain, but it had at least allowed her to come to terms with it.

"I think you *were* ashamed of me," she accused him. "And I think you didn't want to bring me here because you regretted marrying me."

His laugh was bitter. "And this is why you left me? Why you walked out in the middle of the night? Because of your own insecurities?"

"I left a note," she said, and felt suddenly ridiculous. A note? She'd packed her suitcase and fled because she'd been hurt, confused and suddenly so unsure of herself. She'd needed time to think, time to process everything. She'd never thought, never believed for a moment, that an entire year would pass without any communication from him. She'd been impulsive, reckless.

But she'd had to go. What choice was there?

"A note that said nothing. Less than nothing."

"Then why didn't you call me and ask for more?"

He took a step closer, his arms rigid at his sides. "Why would I do so, Sydney? *You* left me. You left. You chose to flee. You did not do me the courtesy of speaking to me first."

Sydney was trembling, but not from fear. A hard knot formed in her gut, her throat. The words wouldn't stay inside her. The bitterness she'd held in for a year came spilling out. "I heard you, Malik. I heard you tell your brother that you regretted marrying me. You were on speakerphone, in your office—"

The words died, simply died. She couldn't continue. His face said it all.

"*This* is why you ran away like a child? Because of something you heard me say in a private conversation that you had no right to listen to?"

She swallowed. Her throat felt as if it were lined with

razor blades. How dare he try to make her feel guilty! "You can't turn this around, Malik. You can't make it about me listening in on your private call when you plainly said you'd made a mistake. I wasn't trying to listen. I came to remind you that we were due at the opera at seven."

He looked so cold, so remote in that moment. She felt as if she'd violated his privacy when in fact *she* was the one who had every right to be upset. Damn it, he'd said he'd made a mistake! She'd been so desperately in love with him that she'd given up everything to go with him. Like some giddy schoolgirl with her first crush, she'd left her friends, her job and her home and followed him halfway around the world.

Because he'd asked her to. Because she'd believed he was the right man.

And then, when he'd suggested they marry, she'd been the happiest woman in the world. A little niggling voice had whispered doubts, but she'd ignored them. She'd been blind, thrilled, happy—and it had all come crashing down, just as she'd known deep inside that it must.

Girls like her didn't get the fairy tale prince, not really. She was pretty, she supposed, but she wasn't elegant. She wasn't sophisticated enough for a man like Malik. She'd ridden the wave as far as it would take her, and then she'd had to go before it crushed her.

"You did not leave that night," he said. "I remember the opera. It was *Aida*. You did not go for another week at least."

"Because I kept hoping it was a mistake! I kept waiting—"

His gaze sharpened when she didn't finish the sentence. "Waiting for what?"

She couldn't answer. Because she'd been waiting for

him to say he loved her. A foolish hope in light of everything that happened.

They'd gone to the opera that night, her heart feeling as if it were being ripped in two, and then they'd returned home. He'd had business to attend to, he'd said, and she'd gone to bed alone. She'd lain awake, waiting for him, but he never came. She'd finally fallen asleep as the sun was creeping into the sky, her heart still breaking.

She'd learned in the week that followed that a heart did not break cleanly or quickly. It happened slowly, agonizingly, by degrees.

And it wasn't a sharp feeling, but a dull throbbing one that refused to go away. It was the kind of pain that permeated your entire body, your soul, and left you wanting to fall asleep and not wake up until it was in the distant past and you didn't feel anymore.

Malik grew cold, detached. He spent his days closeted in his office, or traveling on business. He became darker, quieter, harder to read. But at night, he would slip into their bed and take her again and again, the pleasure so hot and intense that it took her breath away.

Soon, she'd started to think she'd misunderstood his conversation. And one night, when she was boneless and spent, her heart throbbing with conflicting emotions that were killing her inside, she'd let spill the words she'd been feeling for weeks but hadn't been brave enough to say yet. She'd told him she loved him.

Sydney closed her eyes. Even now, the memory hurt.

He'd said nothing. It was as if he hadn't heard her, but she knew he had because his grip on her tightened for the briefest of moments.

She didn't know what she'd expected, though she'd

had a vague hope he would tell her he loved her, too. When he said nothing, her last hope was crushed.

"Nothing. It's nothing."

His hand shot out, his finger tipping her chin up so he could gaze into her eyes. He was angry, yes, but he was also brimming with some other emotion she couldn't quite pin down. Her skin sizzled beneath his touch. Would there be a mark when he pulled his hand away? Would she be forever branded with the imprint of his finger?

"Do not lie to me. Not now." His voice was hard, dark, full of leashed fury.

"What does it matter, Malik?" she asked tiredly. "We're finished. It's over. What happened a year ago isn't important. It won't change anything now."

"Tell me, Sydney," he demanded.

She almost said it. Almost spilled her deepest desire to him. Her most foolish and misguided wish.

But he would pity her if she did. Right now, she still had her dignity. If she tore away that last veil, admitted her plaintive hope, she would reveal the depth of her foolishness to him.

Sydney jerked away, took a step backward as she crossed her arms over her chest. "You don't have the right to ask. And I'm not answering. It's *over.*"

He stared at her, his jaw grinding—and then he swore. Explosively.

She took another step backward, both appalled and fascinated. She'd never, ever seen Malik lose his cool. Not once in the short time she'd known him. He was a passionate man, but a supremely regulated one. His rigid control never shattered.

"It's not over," he growled moments later, his accent thicker than she'd ever heard it. "Because you are here,

Sydney, in Jahfar. You are my wife for forty days. And I *will* have satisfaction."

She had no idea what that meant, but she shivered as he turned and swept away from her in a magnificent swirl of white robes. The air crackled in his wake, and she found herself sitting in her chair, staring after him, not quite remembering when she'd sat down.

Her stomach was hollow, her nerves stretched taught, almost to the breaking point. Coming here had been a mistake. Such a huge, huge mistake. She should have tried harder to find another way.

But what other choice had there been? It was the law.

And she *had* to get through it. They both did.

But she was beginning to doubt that either of them would make it through unscathed.

CHAPTER FIVE

SHE did not see Malik for the rest of the day, nor did she see him the next morning. In some respects, it reminded her of their days in Paris, after the first couple of heady weeks when they'd been inseparable. Except this time it didn't hurt so badly. She knew what to expect now, knew he did not love her.

Nor did she love him.

Malik was a prince, but he was also a businessman. He was lord of his own territory within Jahfar—Al Na'ir, she believed it was called—and he worked hard to make it profitable and self-sustaining. There was oil throughout Jahfar, but Al Na'ir had the richest wells. She remembered that he'd been working on a deal to modernize Al Na'ir's oil industry when they were in Paris.

Sydney logged on to her computer and did some work on new listings that were coming up. In the past couple of years, she'd somehow become the office's web guru. In truth, she loved playing with the site's design. It wasn't quite the same as painting pictures, but she hadn't done that in years anyway. A twinge of wistfulness crawled through her, but she pushed it away and concentrated on the website.

This at least was something of which her father could approve. Something useful and practical, unlike art.

She'd even thought of taking some classes in graphic design, of working to create things for people. It wasn't the same as painting, but it was artistic—and you could make money doing it.

She made a few last changes, and then uploaded the new page to the website. The blazing purple graphic she'd created for The Reed Team stood out, her parents' smiling faces gazing at her so confidently.

Now theirs was an admirable marriage. John and Beth Reed had met in college and been inseparable since. They'd married within a year, had two children, started their business and built it into something they could be proud of. Alicia, her older sister, was an overachiever like their parents. She was blond, stunning and wildly popular when they were still in school. As an adult, she hadn't stopped excelling: a Rhodes scholar, Alicia had graduated at the top of her law class. She was a huge asset to The Reed Team now that they'd branched into commercial real estate.

Sydney slapped the laptop closed with more force than necessary. The old sibling rivalry was alive and well. She loved Alicia and applauded her success. But she'd always felt like the odd duck in her family of swans. She was the only fair-skinned redhead, the only artistic type, the only one who didn't get a visceral charge out of making business deals. When she was little, she'd thought she was adopted—but now she knew it wasn't true. She had her mother's bone structure, her father's eyes. She was a Reed all right.

But she was still the odd duck.

Lunch arrived sometime after the noon hour, served by Hala and a man who stood mutely by with the tray of food as Hala retrieved dishes and arranged them on the low table in the living area of Sydney's suite.

There were dishes of olives, hummus, baba ghanoush, and grilled lamb with tomatoes that was served over fragrant basmati rice. Hala bowed and backed away, the man with her following suit. When they were a certain distance from her, they pivoted and hurried out the door.

Sydney blinked, and then shook her head slowly. The only time Alicia had been the tiniest bit envious of her was when she'd started to date Malik. If her sister could see this, she would no doubt turn pea-green.

Except that appearances were certainly deceptive. There was nothing to be jealous of, unless Alicia had a burning desire to live with a man who turned her inside out—and not in a good way—for the next forty days. Since Alicia's current boyfriend basically worshipped the ground she walked on, Sydney doubted she'd want to trade places. Who would?

Sydney frowned. She had to stop comparing her life to Alicia's perfect one. It did no good and only made her feel worse.

"They do you honor because you are a princess," Malik said, and Sydney whirled to find him entering her rooms from the terrace. Today he was wearing a pair of khaki trousers and a crisp white shirt. Not so exotic as the *dishdasha*, but still unbearably handsome. Even in Western dress, he somehow managed to look as if he'd just ridden in from the desert on the back of a fiery Arabian steed.

Sydney's heart kicked up several notches as he met her gaze, her skin heating by degrees until she knew she must have been red in the face.

She couldn't help it. She was flustered, embarrassed and angry. Not a good combination.

"I wish they wouldn't," she said. "It makes me uncomfortable."

His sensual mouth flattened. "I know this. Why do you think I did not bring you to Jahfar before?"

Sydney tilted her chin up. "If that was your reason, why couldn't you have told me? Seems awfully convenient to say that now, Malik."

He strode toward her. She stood her ground until the last second, until he was nearly upon her. Just as she turned to flee, he sank onto the cushions arrayed around the table. She stared down at him, her heart still fluttering like mad. What had she thought he was going to do? Grab her and toss her over his shoulder? Take her to his bedroom and have his wicked way with her?

A tiny part of her whispered, *yes, please.* She ignored it as she moved to the other side of the table. Malik grabbed a piece of flat bread and dipped it into the lamb-and-tomato dish. Then he speared her with a look.

"Think what you wish, Sydney. You seem determined to do so anyway."

She stood there, undecided what to do next. She didn't like the fact that what he'd said made sense. Had he really considered her feelings last year? Had he tried to spare her the intense scrutiny that went with being his wife here in Jahfar?

Was it possible? Or was he just very good at making her feel petty?

She watched him eat, watched the slide of his throat as he swallowed. For a moment, she considered leaving. But where would she go? And why? It would simply make her seem even pettier than she already did.

Besides, the smell of the food was driving her insane. It'd been a while since breakfast, and her stomach was about to eat itself. She sank onto the cushions opposite him. "I don't recall asking you to join me for lunch," she said, reaching for a dish.

"In fact, you are joining *me*," Malik replied, lounging sideways on an elbow. "I instructed Hala to set lunch in here."

Sydney looked away and popped an olive into her mouth. It was too intimate, eating with him like this. They'd shared meals before—some of them in bed—but this time was different. Harder because of the emotion she felt being here now. Knowing she'd given him everything, believed in him, and he'd only ever given her a very superficial part of him.

"Why?" she said. "I could have come to the dining room—or wherever you usually eat. Or I could have eaten alone. That would have been fine, too."

"Yes, but tonight we dine with my brother and his wife. I had thought we could use this opportunity for instruction."

Sydney coughed as the next olive lodged in her throat. "Your brother—the king?" she managed to ask when she'd swallowed it. "And his queen?"

"The king and queen of Jahfar, yes. They wish to meet you."

Heat prickled her skin again. She was so completely unprepared for everything this life entailed. No matter that it was temporary. Dinner with a king?

A king who had not been pleased with Malik for marrying her. "Is that a good idea? I'm not really here to stay."

He shrugged. "Probably not, no. But we are commanded to attend. My brother is curious, I imagine."

"Curious?"

"About the woman who enticed me to give up my cherished bachelorhood. Though she now wishes to divorce me."

Sydney cast her gaze down. The lamb she'd taken a

bite of had been delicious—now it was more like a lump of sod in her mouth. "Please don't," she said.

"Don't what? Speak the truth?"

"You make it sound as if you are hurt. But you aren't, Malik. Your pride perhaps, but not you. Not your heart."

She could see out of the corner of her eye that he'd gone still. "How well you know me," he said, his voice containing that hint of mockery she hated. "I'm amazed at your insight."

Sydney closed her eyes and sighed deeply. "I don't want to do this right now," she said. "Can't we just eat?"

"We can," he finally said, reaching for another piece of bread. He tore it in half, handed one side to her. His fingers brushed hers as she accepted it, a tingle of fire rippling up her arm in response.

Why couldn't there have been another way? Why did she need to be here in Jahfar, living in Malik's house, eating with him, gazing at his once beloved face across a table and knowing their relationship was in its death throes? And now, as if it weren't painful enough, she would have to face the brother who knew that Malik regretted marrying her in the first place.

Beyond humiliating.

Sydney dipped the bread in the sauce the way he did, scooped meat and rice up together. She made the mistake of glancing at him after she'd put the food into her mouth. He was watching her intently, his dark eyes smoldering as they held hers.

Her stomach flipped. "What?" she said when she'd managed to swallow. "Do I have sauce all over my chin?"

"Not at all." He took another bite of the food while she focused on the variety of dishes instead of him. "I was thinking that you seemed to appreciate your first taste of Jahfaran cuisine."

She was confused, nervous, and angry with herself for being so. Confused because he watched her so intently and she didn't know why. Nervous because she imagined he was cataloguing her flaws. And angry because she cared.

"It's good," she said. "I'm enjoying it very much."

Or as much as possible when the man who'd turned her world upside down sat across from her as if nothing bad or hurtful had ever happened between them.

"I am glad," he replied. "But tonight I imagine the fare will be more familiar to you. The queen is half-American and will no doubt wish to make you feel comfortable."

"That's really not necessary," Sydney said. "I like trying new things."

His gaze sharpened, and she knew with a certainty he wasn't thinking of food. "Yes, I remember this."

Sydney glanced away, her face reddening. The bad thing about being so pale was that there could never be any doubt when she was embarrassed. Everyone knew.

"You will need to wear an *abaya* tonight," Malik said while Sydney sent up a silent thank you that he did not pursue that line of the conversation. "I have ordered several for you to choose from. If we had more time, I would have them custom made. But the seamstress will be able to tailor one to fit for tonight."

"There's no need to have anything custom made," she said. "It would be a waste of money. And I will pay for the necessary garments myself."

"You are so determined not to accept anything from me. You were not always this way, I recall."

Sydney tugged at the napkin on her lap. It was true

that she'd never protested when he'd spent money on her before. It hadn't seemed necessary then. She'd never asked him for gifts, but she'd never turned them down, either. "I see no sense in it. I don't want to feel like I owe you for anything."

"How odd," he said, his jaw tightening as he stared at her.

"Why is that odd?"

"Does this prohibition against owing me only extend to financial matters? Because I feel as if you still owe me something for the way you left like a thief in the night."

It was a direct hit, and yet it made her angry instead of remorseful.

"What could I possibly owe you for that?" she flashed. "You could have called me. You could have come after me. You did nothing. Because you knew you'd made a mistake, Malik. Because you wanted to be free of me but you didn't know how to do it!"

It hurt to say it, but it was true. He'd made a mistake, and she'd done the dirty work for him by leaving before he could push her away.

He looked so coolly furious in that moment. "Do you honestly believe I lack the necessary courage it would take to extricate myself from a marriage I no longer wanted?"

It didn't seem like him, and yet what else could she think? If he'd cared, he wouldn't have waited a year to come after her. Which he'd only done because she'd initiated divorce proceedings.

"I don't know what to believe." It was nothing more than the truth.

"The correct answer, Sydney, is no."

She pushed back on two hands and glared at him. "Then why did you say you'd made a mistake? Are you trying to tell me I didn't hear you correctly? Because I'm fairly positive I did."

A muscle in his cheek flexed. His eyes burned into her. "No, you did not hear incorrectly."

In spite of the fact she knew it to be true, a sharp pain pierced her heart to hear him finally say it. As if she didn't already know. As if she were hearing the words again for the first time. Ridiculous to feel so much when she'd had a year to think about what he'd said to his brother. And how he'd reacted when she'd confessed her love.

Malik stood. "I said the words, Sydney, though I did not intend for you to hear them. It was never my intention to hurt you."

Her head tilted back as she gazed up at him. Tears pressed at the corners of her eyes, but she'd be damned if she let one fall while he stood there. She would be strong, unfeeling.

Just like him.

"Then I'm not sure what we have left to talk about. You said you'd made a mistake. And now we're divorcing. Everything has worked out perfectly for you."

"Yes," he said softly. "Perhaps it has."

He glanced at his watch. He looked so cool, so controlled, while she felt like a mess inside. Her stomach fluttered, her chest ached and she was no longer hungry.

"The clothing will be here in an hour. Choose what you like. Pay me if you wish. I care not." He inclined his head. "Until tonight."

Sydney had an overwhelming urge to throw something at his retreating back. Instead, she punched one of the pillows lining the seating area. It didn't help.

Malik felt nothing. She felt everything. And this was only day two.

CHAPTER SIX

SYDNEY dressed with care in the turquoise silk *abaya* she'd chosen from the selection the seamstress brought. She did not wear a headscarf, but she did twist her hair into a loose knot and secured it with a couple of rhinestone pins. She wore her own shoes with the outfit, a pair of kitten-heeled strappy sandals that didn't give her the height she would have liked but were very comfortable and modest.

She kept her makeup subtle, concentrating on her eyes and adding a touch of pink gloss to her lips. When she was satisfied she looked presentable, she grabbed her small clutch and went to meet Malik.

He was standing in the entryway, waiting. She hesitated when she caught sight of him, but he looked up just then and she could do nothing except stride boldly forward. He'd always been gorgeous in a tuxedo, but tonight he made her heart ache with longing. He wore a black *dishdasha*, embroidered at the sleeves and hem in gold thread. His *keffiyeh* was the traditional dark red. Somehow the framing around his face succeeded in drawing her attention to his mouth.

That bold, sensual mouth that had taken her to heaven and back.

She looked away, determined not to think about it.

And yet she could feel the heat rising, flaring beneath her skin. Between her thighs. A tingle of sensation began deep inside, whether she wanted it to or not.

How could she still be attracted to him when he'd hurt her so badly? He didn't want her, not really. He'd thought she was a mistake. It was too much like growing up in the perfect Reed family, where she was the imperfect one. The mistake. Her family was blond, tanned, gorgeous, ambitious, successful. She was none of those things.

"Do not fear, Sydney," Malik said, mistaking her inability to look him in the eye for shyness. "You look lovely. The king and queen will not find fault with you."

"Thank you," she replied. Because there was nothing else to say. Not without sounding pitifully insecure and needy.

Soon, they were exiting the house and climbing into a sleek silver Bugatti. The engine roared like a tiger as Malik accelerated onto the thoroughfare. She turned her head, gazed at the city lights instead of at him. The sports car was super expensive, but the interior was small. He sat so close to her. Too close.

She could smell his skin, the scent of his shampoo. She could feel his heat as if he were curled around her.

Or maybe that was her heat as her body reacted to him.

His voice sliced into the silence. "My brother does not know why you are here."

Sydney whipped her head around to stare at him. For a moment she wondered if she'd heard him correctly. But no, that was what he'd said. "You didn't tell him about the divorce? Why not?"

Malik's fingers on the wheel were strong, sure. She

dragged her gaze from them and concentrated on the stubborn set of his handsome jaw.

"Because it is our business, not anyone else's."

She could only gape at him. "But we've been apart for over a year. Don't you imagine he's suspicious?"

"People do attempt to reconcile, Sydney." He glanced into the rearview mirror, changed lanes smoothly and quickly. "Unless you wish to spill our personal problems tonight, I suggest you pretend to be happy."

Pretend to be happy. As if a river of hurt had not passed between them. As if she could simply flip a switch and act as if her heart hadn't broken because of this man. "I'm not sure I can do that."

He shot her an exasperated look. "It's not difficult. Smile. Laugh. Don't glare at me."

She folded her arms across her breasts. "Easier said than done," she muttered.

Malik's fingers flexed on the wheel, his tension evident. "It's one night, Sydney. I think you can handle it."

Ten minutes later, they were driving through the palace gates and pulling up to the massive entry. Malik told her to wait, then came around and helped her from the car. He tucked her arm into his and led her toward the entry. All along the red carpet lining the walkway, men in uniform bowed as they passed.

And then they were inside the palace, and Sydney was trying very hard not to crane her neck. She'd seen opulence before, of course. She'd shown houses to the very rich, and she'd lived with Malik for a month in Paris. She knew what wealth could do.

But this place was more than she'd expected. Crystal chandeliers, mosaic tiles, Syrian wood inlaid with mother-of-pearl, Moorish arches and domes, delicate paintings on silk, marble floors.

Her heels clicked across the tiles, the sound echoing back down to her from the vaulted ceiling. "Did you grow up here?" she asked, and then wished she hadn't spoken. Her voice sounded very loud in the silent rooms, as if she'd shouted the question rather than whispered it.

"No," he said curtly. His body was tense, but a moment later she sensed a softening in him. As if he were trying to follow his own advice and pretend they were not on the edge of disaster. "My family was not in the direct line for the throne. Adan came to power when our cousin died, and then our uncle afterward. It has been an adjustment for all of us, but for him most of all."

"'Uneasy lies the head that wears a crown'," she quoted.

"*Henry the Fourth, Part Two*," Malik said without pause.

"I didn't know you liked Shakespeare." They'd gone to the opera a couple of times, to the ballet once—but never to a play. Why had they never discussed Shakespeare? She'd wanted to study literature and art in college, but her parents wouldn't hear of it. It was a business degree or no degree.

Liberal arts majors worked in the food service industry, according to her father. Business majors made the world go around.

"There's a lot you don't know about me, *habibti*."

But before she could ask him anything else, they reached a door with two guards stationed on either side. One of the guards opened the door, and then they were entering what looked to be a private area that was infinitely homier than the palace they'd passed through.

A very attractive, but otherwise normal-looking couple came to greet them. It took Sydney a few moments to realize this was the king and queen of Jahfar. The pregnant queen, with her long tawny hair streaked with sun-kissed highlights, looked more like a California girl than Sydney did.

"Call me Isabella," the queen said when Malik introduced them. Sydney instantly liked Isabella. King Adan, on the other hand, was imposing. He and Malik were the same height and breadth, but Adan looked harder, harsher, more serious. The weight of that crown, no doubt.

And possibly the weight of his disapproval of her. Sydney dropped her gaze as he studied her. He was no doubt remembering that phone call. Hearing Malik tell him again that he'd made a mistake when he'd wed an American girl with no money or connections.

"Welcome to Jahfar, sister," the king said, kissing her on both cheeks. "You are long overdue for a visit."

"I—thank you, Your Majesty." She could feel the color rising, creating twin spots of flame in her cheeks.

Malik took her hand, pulled her to his side and anchored an arm around her. She was grateful for it, if only for the way it diverted Adan from studying her so intently. His gaze swept over them both, and then he was turning and leading the way to the dining room.

He was so like Malik. Intense, dark, handsome. They were clearly brothers, both with the same bronzed skin, chiseled bone structure and rich voices. And yet there seemed to be a coolness between them, a reserve.

Sydney thought she must be wrong at first, but all throughout the dinner she noticed how formal they were with one another. Like business associates rather than family.

It was Isabella who was the social butterfly, who smoothed the conversation when it reached a rough patch, who kept them talking when it seemed there was nothing else to say. She was warm and witty and full of personality.

For the first time, Sydney didn't feel so intimidated by what she thought life as a sheikh's wife must entail. Isabella was nothing like Sydney had expected—and that was a good thing.

When dinner was over, Isabella suggested they take coffee on the terrace—but not before she asked Sydney to accompany her to the nursery to check on her son.

"The truth is that I wanted to talk to you alone," Isabella said as she closed the nursery door behind them after their visit.

"Oh," Sydney said. "All right." She was still feeling entranced by Rafiq's dark curls, with the way he'd been lying on his back, his head to one side and his little leg kicked up. She'd not actually thought much about children with Malik, though she'd expected they would have had them after they'd been married for a while.

Now the thought made her heart squeeze tight.

Isabella took her hand and led her to a sitting area tucked away in an alcove. "I know it's probably difficult for you," Isabella said once they'd sat down facing each other. "It's not easy to put a marriage back together after so much time away. But I want you to know it's possible. Al Dhakir men are worth the trouble, even when you think you'd cheerfully strangle them and leave them for dead."

Sydney made herself smile. "Did the king give you trouble?"

Isabella laughed. "Far more than you'd like to hear about, though I think I was probably the one who caused the most trouble. But we survived it. And you can, too. Give Malik a chance. He's a good man—they all are—

but they don't always know how to reach out to the ones they love."

Love. Now that was definitely not an issue with Malik since he did not love her. But Sydney wasn't about to say so, especially when she could see how much the king absolutely adored his wife. His eyes smoldered when he looked at her. His expression lit up. He touched her often, even if it was just a light touch of his hand on hers.

Once, she would have given anything for Malik to feel that way about her. It was too late now, but she wouldn't say so to the queen.

"I'll remember that," she said, dropping her eyes from the earnest look in Isabella's. The queen truly believed what she said, and while Sydney was glad it had worked out for them, she knew it was hopeless for her and Malik. You couldn't put back together what had never been there in the first place.

Isabella squeezed her hand. "Good. Now why don't we go have that coffee, hmm?"

Thunder woke her in the middle of the night. Sydney sat up in alarm, her heart pounding, certain she hadn't heard correctly. This was a desert country—they didn't have thunderstorms. Or did they?

Another crash sounded, and then a flash of lightning. Sydney grabbed her robe and stumbled from the bed. A hot gust of wind rippled her clothing as she opened the doors and stepped onto the terrace in her bare feet. The stones were still warm from the afternoon sun. Another flash of lightning lit the sky, illuminating the sea and the thunderclouds hanging over the water.

It had taken her hours to fall asleep. Jet lag was partly to blame. Malik was the other part of the equation. They'd driven back to his home in silence after dinner with the king and queen. Sydney had wanted to ask him questions about the evening, about his family, but she'd been unable to find her voice.

She'd kept expecting him to speak to her, but beyond a cursory question about how she'd enjoyed the food, he'd said nothing else. When they'd arrived, he'd bid her a good night and left her standing alone in the entry.

Another gust of wind blew her hair across her face. She shoved it to the side and breathed deeply of the rain-scented air. It reminded her of storms back home when she was a kid, of the way she'd made up stories in her head about giant knights slaying fire-breathing dragons in the sky.

Her father had said she was too fanciful. Alicia had always laughed and gone back to playing office with her dolls.

"It looks worse than it is."

Sydney spun to find Malik sitting at the other end of the terrace. He unfolded his frame from a chair, stalked toward her. Her heart was already hammering from the thunder, but it kicked up several notches as another flash of lightning illuminated the sky.

Dear God, Malik wasn't wearing a shirt.

Sydney swallowed as he came to halt in front of her. "Will it actually rain?"

He tilted his head up, exposing his throat as he gazed at the sky. She remembered nibbling that throat. Sucking the skin there. A dart of sensation throbbed between her legs. She could feel herself growing wet, feel the aching heaviness of sexual arousal. His chest was broad, sculpted with muscle. Lightly sprinkled with hair that tapered into a *V*, leading the eye down, down, down to the waistband of the faded jeans he wore.

Sydney jerked her gaze back up, but not quite in time.

Malik was watching her, his dark gaze smoldering with intensity.

"Like what you see?"

She tossed her hair over her shoulder again. Why lie? He'd see right through her anyway. "Yes. But it doesn't matter if I like it or not, because I'm not traveling that road again."

His chuckle was a sexy vibration in his throat. "It won't rain here tonight, but we could quench our thirsts in other ways. I'm sure you remember how good it was between us, Sydney."

"I don't care," she said, her voice catching at the end.

He reached out with one hand, tucked a strand of hair that had blown free behind her ear. A shiver ran the length of her. He was different now. Not as reserved as earlier. After they'd left the palace, he'd been silent, tense. She'd wanted to know why, but she'd been unable to ask.

"You used to care. Very much. I remember that you couldn't get enough of me."

"People change, Malik. I've changed."

"Have you?"

"I think we both have."

"Perhaps these changes will only make it better," he said, his voice too seductive for comfort.

She *was* mesmerized. Oh, how she *wanted*. But it was a bad, bad idea. Once she stumbled down that path, she wouldn't be able to turn around again. Because he was addictive.

"I doubt that," she said firmly, as much to him as to herself.

His smirk told her she'd made a mistake. "Yes, perhaps you are right. It could hardly get better. How many ways did you give yourself to me? How many times?"

"More than enough," she answered, proud of herself for being able to reply when his words called up a wealth of erotic memories in her mind.

"I'm certain we could think of a few more things to try," he said.

She shook her head. "It won't work, Malik. You can't talk me into going to bed with you."

"Who said anything about a bed?"

A crash of thunder reverberated off the water and Sydney jumped. Malik caught her as she stumbled into him. He held her close, his heart thundering as fast as her own. His big body was so solid, so comforting. She felt like an ice cube dropped into warm water. She was thawing, melting, losing herself.

It had always been so with him. He had only to touch her, and she responded.

He shifted—and she felt the press of his erection against her body. Without conscious thought, she leaned into him. Malik sucked in a breath.

"Careful, *houri*," he growled in her ear. "Or you will find yourself in my bed before you know it."

She wanted to be there. Ached to be there. One more night with Malik, one more night feeling more alive than she'd ever felt in her life, more cherished...

No. He did not cherish her. He never had.

"I'm sorry," she said, pushing away from him. He let her go without protest, his arms dropping to his sides.

Her skin sizzled from the contact with him, her pulse throbbing—in her temples, between her legs.

"I'm sure it would be fabulous, but I'd still regret it in the morning," she told him. "It won't change anything between us. And it would make the remaining time together even more difficult."

"So we cannot be, how do you say, friends with benefits?"

A twinge of sadness curled through her. "We've never been friends. I think we skipped that part altogether."

Malik shoved a hand through his dark hair as he blew out a frustrated breath. "No, perhaps not."

Sydney bit the inside of her lip. That was not an admission she'd expected from him. "I feel like I know nothing about you."

"You know the most important things."

"How can you say that? I know nothing! Until tonight, I didn't even know you liked Shakespeare."

"I went to university in England. Shakespeare was inevitable."

"See, I didn't even know that much."

He spread his arms wide in frustration. "Then what do you wish to know? Ask me, and if I can, I will tell you."

Another peal of thunder sounded over the ocean. It was less violent now, less surprising. What did she want to know about Malik? Everything, and nothing. Everything because she knew nothing, and nothing because she didn't want to open herself back up to the pain of caring for him in any way.

But curiosity won out over restraint. "I'd like to know why you and your brother are so uncomfortable together."

He closed his eyes briefly. Pinned her with a hot glare. "Of course you would ask this. And I have no answer for you. We were close as children, but drifted apart later. Our lives were…formal."

"Formal?"

"You lived in a house with your parents, yes?" When she nodded, he continued, "We had nannies, and we did

not always live in the same house. Our mother was…
nervous, let us say. Children were too much for her."

"Too much?" A knot was forming in the pit of her
stomach as she imagined the Al Dhakir children growing up without their mother.

She could see tension in the set of his shoulders, the
thrust of his jaw.

"We saw her, but we were to be on our best behavior
when we did. She preferred socializing with her friends
to children. I think it was not quite her fault, really. She
was young when she and my father married, and the ba-
bies came right away. She didn't know what to do with
us, so she retreated behind the veil of wealth and privilege she was afforded."

"And your father?"

He looked sad. "A good man. Very busy. And very
formal. I think he had little time for my mother, and so
she had little time for us."

Sydney thought of her own parents, of how much
they loved one another and how happy her childhood
had been. Yes, she felt like the cuckoo in the nest, but
she'd always been loved. Even when her parents were
slightly alarmed by her tendencies, or disappointed in
her inability to be more like Alicia, they loved her.

"But he must have loved her if he married her."

Malik's laugh was unexpected. "This is how marriage
is supposed to work in *your* culture, *habibti*. Here, one
marries for duty. For family alliances. To consolidate
power and land. My father married the woman who had
been arranged for him. And then he did his duty and got
her with child."

Sydney felt sad. It was all so cold, so unfeeling. And
yet it was the Jahfaran way. Who was to say America
was any better? People married all the time for love—

and love did not always last. You only had to look at the national divorce statistics to realize that.

And she was about to become another one. Odd in a way.

"You have not asked the most obvious question," Malik said, cutting through her thoughts.

She was still trying to process the idea of marrying someone she did not love in order to ally her family with another. "What is that?"

His gaze glittered. "You have not asked if I had an intended bride," he said, his soft voice in contrast with the sharp edge in his gaze.

Sydney's stomach flipped. An arranged marriage for Malik? She'd never thought of it. And yet...

"Did you?" she managed to ask.

His smile was bittersweet. "Of course I did. I am a Jahfaran prince."

CHAPTER SEVEN

SHE was looking at him with a wealth of hurt in her rain-grey eyes. Malik cursed inwardly. He'd never intended to cause her pain, and yet he'd failed miserably on that score.

Too many times to count.

"You had a fiancée?" she said.

He shrugged casually, though he felt anything but casual. "Dimah was not my fiancée in the sense that you think of a fiancée."

She shook her head, her long red hair rippling like silk in the night. The wind wasn't gusting so badly now and she was no longer shoving hair from her face. The silk of her robe clung to her frame, the breeze contouring the fabric around the peaks of her lush breasts.

His body was painfully hard. Had been since she'd walked onto the terrace, the wind blowing her robe open and exposing her legs. Legs he'd had wrapped around him a lifetime ago.

Legs he wanted wrapped around him again. Now. Tonight.

It had been too long. Far too long.

"I don't know what that's supposed to mean," she said, oblivious to his torment. "You were supposed to marry someone. You married me instead. Why?"

Malik drew in a sharp breath as her words sliced through the fog of his thoughts. The hurt was still there, the horror. The guilt.

He hadn't talked about it with anyone, hadn't wanted to. It was over and Dimah was dead. Nothing he said or did would bring an innocent girl back.

Lightning flashed again, illuminating Sydney's face. She looked confused, worried. For him, he realized with a jolt. She was worried *for him*.

He did not deserve her sympathy.

"She died," he said, surprising himself with the words he'd never spoken to another.

Sydney grasped his hand, squeezed. He felt the jolt of sensation down to his toes. What was it about this woman that always, always got to him? He needed nothing, needed no one. Not even her.

But he wanted her. Wanted the way he felt when she was near, when she touched him with her soft hands, smiled at him. When Sydney looked at him, he didn't feel like he wasn't worthy of being loved.

"I'm so sorry," she said.

"It is not your fault. It happened a long time ago." He'd been barely twenty at the time. Young and foolish.

"And you did not marry anyone else."

"I did not have to, no." He hadn't wanted to marry Dimah. They'd known each other since they were children, and had always been intended for one another. But Malik hadn't wanted her. Dimah was like a wraith, following him at a distance, hanging on his every word, looking at him as if he were the only person in the world besides her.

As they'd gotten older, her behavior changed, but only slightly. She became subtler with her adoration, but it was still there. He'd felt as if she were suffocating him, though he rarely saw her and never spent time alone with her.

And then he'd thrown a fit when his father had summoned him and told him it was time for the wedding to take place. He'd been angry, and he'd gone to Dimah, railed against her.

"She killed herself," Malik said, remembering. "Because I told her I hated her."

He didn't miss the sharp intake of breath, the little gasp. She would despise him even more now.

"Oh, Malik." And then she squeezed his hand again. It was meant to be comforting, but the gesture was somehow more important to him than that. More profound. "It wasn't your fault."

He could still see Dimah's face. The way he'd crushed her dreams. "How could it not be? We were to be married, and I told her I hated her—because without her, I wouldn't be forced to do this thing."

"You aren't responsible for her actions," Sydney insisted. "No one is. She made a choice."

Malik could only stare. He wanted to believe, but he would not do so. Because he deserved to feel the pain of what he'd done. "She would not have made this choice if I'd quietly done my duty."

"You don't know that."

Her fingers were threaded through his now. He wondered if she knew it. He raised their clasped hands, turned hers over until he'd bared her pale wrist. Pressed his mouth there because he'd been dying to do so.

He felt the shudder pass through her. But it wasn't a shudder of revulsion.

"Why are you so willing to forgive me this terrible crime?" he asked. "You of all people should know how selfish I can be."

"I—" She dropped her gaze from his. He felt…disappointed somehow. Because now she would agree with him. There was no other choice. "Everyone is selfish from time to time. It doesn't mean you're at fault for what your fia— What Dimah did."

A surge of feeling blazed inside. She was wrong, of course, but he loved that she defended him. Was that why he'd gone against everything he'd known was right and married her?

He remembered meeting her, remembered the way her long legs had intrigued him as she'd walked in front of him and talked about the houses she was showing him. And then she would turn from time to time, quite surprisingly, and glare at him. As if she were daring him to say something, anything, that would give her the excuse she needed to end the appointment.

He'd been captivated, not only by her fierceness, but also by the way she dealt with him. As if he weren't the least bit attractive to her. He'd found that novel, considering the way women usually behaved when they discovered they were dealing with a bachelor prince.

Not that he didn't enjoy the fawning, the coyness, or even the downright bold ways in which women usually approached him.

But he'd never been treated with thinly veiled hostility. And it had intrigued him.

"How good you are to defend me," he murmured against the delicate skin of her wrist. "I remember that you did not always feel so charitable toward me."

Her head came up then, her eyes sharp and blazing with emotion. "I still don't. But I don't think you should blame yourself for another's actions, no matter how dramatic."

"Is it not my fault that you left me in the middle of

the night with hardly an explanation? Is it not my fault that you are here, now? I cannot be blameless in everything, *habibti*, though I appreciate that you would make me so."

"I—I made my own choices," she whispered harshly.

Lightning blinked in a chain of succession over the sea. It was like a series of lights being turned on for only a second before flashing out again. Thunder followed, but it was farther away and no longer seemed to frighten Sydney. She was watching him with eyes that were full of emotion. The air crackled with electricity, but he wasn't sure if it was the storm or the tension between them.

He wanted to pull her into his arms again, wanted to find out. He could lose himself for a few hours.

An impossible wish, however. She hated him. And he probably deserved it.

He let go of her hand, stroked along the skin of her throat with a finger. She swallowed convulsively, but made no move to stop him.

"Ah, but now you see the trap you have set for yourself, yes? In exonerating me of the crime of Dimah's death, you must also hold me blameless for your flight. For our estrangement. And that you cannot do."

Her eyes flashed. "Stop putting words in my mouth, Malik."

He would love to put something else there. He was not so bold as to say so.

"I only speak the truth."

She blew out a breath, tightened the belt of her robe. The outline of her breasts made his mouth water. "Neither of us is blameless," she said. "Neither is perfect." She rubbed a hand over her eyes. "I could have done things differently. I probably should have. I should have been more direct with you. Instead, I allowed you to control everything."

His head came up. "I was not aware of this. I remember you challenging me on more than one occasion."

She snorted. "For little things, Malik. Nothing big. Nothing important. And I should have."

"Yes, you should. I would have welcomed it."

Her laugh was soft, surprising. "Would you now? I hardly think so, oh, mighty prince of the desert."

"You mock me," he said, and yet he wasn't bothered by it. On the contrary, he found it amusing. Refreshing.

"No, I'm merely pointing out the truth."

He clasped her shoulders. His blood rushed from the simple contact. "The thing I liked about you from the beginning was your lack of pretense. You did not pretend to be overwhelmed by me."

She laughed. "God, no. I think I did everything but insult you to your face. I was a bit, um, hostile."

"Because you did your homework," he said, remembering what she'd told him once they'd started to see each other.

She looked down, clasped her hands together in front of her. "You didn't need yet another woman falling at your feet. Though it didn't take long for you to make me do just that, did it?"

Something sharp stabbed him in the chest. He remembered her surrender, remembered the sweetness of it. He'd never once believed it to be because she was weak. "I took your indifference as a challenge."

"Some challenge," she said bitterly. "It took you less than a week to succeed in making me forget my resolve."

"You are angry with yourself for this, yes?" Pain throbbed inside him. Filled him.

She regretted her capitulation. Regretted him.

A burning need to possess her, to make her forget every moment of hurt feelings between them, rose up inside him like a wave.

Why now? Why here? She did not want him any longer, as she'd been only too happy to tell him more than once since her arrival. He should have pursued her when she'd left Paris, should have refused to allow more than a day to go by where they did not speak about her reasons for leaving.

He'd been a fool.

"It would have been better for us both had I shown more restraint. We would not have to endure this time together now."

Her words stung. *Endure.* He did not like to think too deeply about that word, or the impact it'd had on his life thus far. There were many things in this life to be endured. It was not altogether pleasant to be one of them.

"And yet we shall." Sudden weariness washed over him. The evening had been a strain, in more ways than one, and Sydney was still looking at him with a kind of wariness that gutted him. He had no more patience for it. If he did not leave her now, he would scoop her up and take her to bed, prove that she could still be mastered by his touch.

And neither of them would gain anything by such a demonstration.

Malik took a step backward, bowed to her. "It is late, *habibti.* You need your rest."

Then he pivoted and strode away from her. Back to his bedroom. Back to his solitude.

Sydney did not sleep well. There were things she wanted to ask Malik, things she'd meant to say when they'd stood on the terrace together. He'd been so approachable for once, so raw in his feelings. It was a side of him she'd never seen before. She'd been drawn to him—a dangerous feeling—and she'd wanted to know more.

But he'd shut down again. Withdrawn. Left her standing there with the wind and lightning and her tangled emotions.

She'd considered following him, but dismissed the thought as foolhardy. He would be angry if she did so. Not only that, but how could she control what might happen if she followed him to his bedroom?

Because she was so weak where he was concerned. She could still feel his chest where she'd pressed her palms against him. The hard contours, the blazing heat of his skin, the crisp hair. She'd ached with want. With memories of bliss.

And when she finally did fall asleep, she was troubled by dreams of him, by the agony in his voice when he'd told her about Dimah. Why had he never told her before? Why, in the weeks they'd been together, had he never told her?

It was another symptom of everything that had been wrong between them. Everything she'd been too blind to see. They'd barely known one another, subsisting instead on reckless passion and heated lovemaking. That could only last so long before it burned itself out.

After a restless night, she awoke early. The sun was just creeping into the sky when she showered and dressed in a fitted mocha sheath and a pair of gladiator sandals. Then she put her hair in a ponytail and applied the barest of lipstick and mascara before making her way to the dining room.

Her heart thudded in her throat as she paused outside the door. She could hear Malik's smooth voice as he spoke with one of the staff. Sydney sucked in a deep breath and walked into the room.

Two sets of eyes turned to look at her. Malik's dark gaze was angry, but it was the woman with him who drew Sydney's attention. She was slender, elegant, expensively dressed—and livid.

Definitely not a staff member.

She turned back to Malik, spewed a tirade of Arabic at him while gesturing to Sydney.

"Mother," Malik said at last, his voice harder than she'd ever heard it, "we will speak in English for the benefit of my wife."

His mother? Oh, God.

The other woman glared at her. "Yes, English. And you say this girl is not unsuitable to be an Al Dhakir? She does not even speak Arabic!"

"Language can be learned. As your command of English proves."

His mother bristled in outrage. "You should have done your duty, Malik. Your father let you off too easily after Dimah died. Adan found you a suitable bride, at my request, but you would not do what you should." The rings on the princess's fingers glittered in the morning light as she took a sip of her coffee.

"I preferred to find my own bride. Which, as you see, I have done." Malik looked murderously angry as he came over and snaked an arm around her. Sydney had no idea what his intent was—she was still stunned by the news that Adan had found Malik a bride, and that he'd refused to marry her.

When Malik pulled her close and dropped a kiss on her lips, Sydney could only gasp.

"Mother, you will greet my wife properly. Or you will leave."

"Malik," Sydney began, "that's not necessary."

His grip on her tightened. "It is completely necessary. This is our home."

His mother got to her feet in an elegant flurry of fabric and jewels. "I was leaving anyway."

Sydney watched Malik's mother start for the door. Her pulse was pounding. Her head throbbed. She felt suddenly hot, uncomfortable. This woman was Malik's mother—and she despised Sydney, not for any other reason than because she was a foreigner who had married her son.

No wonder he'd been reluctant to bring her to Jahfar. But she couldn't let him do this, couldn't allow there to be hard feelings between mother and son on her account. Not when there was no reason for it.

"Tell her the truth, Malik," Sydney said, stepping away from the circle of his arm. She had to play this cool. Collected. She could feel Malik's disapproval as she went and poured a cup of coffee for herself.

Malik's mother stopped and turned to her son. "Tell me what?"

Malik looked furious. And not with his mother this time. "Now is not the occasion," he growled.

"When would you suggest is a better time?" Sydney asked. "Tell her what she wants to hear. Don't torture her."

Malik's mother looked from her son to Sydney. She was a small woman, slim and graceful, with the same hawklike eyes as her sons. She looked fierce, proud. Also like her sons, Sydney thought.

"Malik?"

He didn't look at his mother. Instead, he was looking at her. Glaring at her. "Sydney and I are discussing a divorce."

It wasn't quite what she'd wanted him to say, but it was enough. It certainly had the desired effect, as his mother seemed to visibly melt with relief.

"Very sensible of you," she said. She turned to where Sydney stood with her coffee. "I'm happy to see that you do have some sense after all. You must know you don't belong here."

Sydney tilted her chin up. "I know it very well."

She'd once hoped against hope that it wasn't true, but she knew she didn't belong in Malik's life. She'd had a year to figure it out. And even if she hadn't, the last couple of days had driven the message home with sonorous finality. Sydney Reed was not meant to be a prince's wife.

Malik's mother nodded before sweeping from the room in a cloud of perfumed silk. Malik did not follow. He stood there, scowling. Sydney pulled out a seat and sank down into it.

She felt remarkably calm somehow. As if she'd faced the deadly storm and come out on the other side stronger for it. And yet, there was a slight tremor in her hand as she set her cup down.

"There is no need to glare at me, Malik. She was going to find out eventually."

"Yes, but when I wanted her to."

He was coldly furious, she realized. Her sense of having survived the storm began to ebb. "Why keep it a secret from everyone? It's not like we're trying to make this relationship work. We're coexisting for a purpose. I don't want to pretend this is something it isn't."

She didn't want any false hope, any magical thinking that would have her starting to believe there was something more between them. Her heart couldn't take it. A shiver slid across her skin, left goose bumps in its wake.

Because, yes, that was a problem. Being here with him, living with him, being inundated with memories—she was in danger of wanting too much, of believing there was a chance he could love her in return.

Love her in return?

Sydney shoved that thought away with all her might. She would not go there, would not dwell on the past and her feelings then. She did not love Malik. Not anymore. She couldn't.

How could she, when their conversations lately had proven she'd never really known him at all?

"Once you have finished your breakfast," Malik said softly—too softly, "you will need to pack your things."

The coffee cup arrested halfway to her mouth. Her heart dropped into her toes. "You're sending me away?"

He looked almost cruel. "That would not please you, would it?"

"Well, um, it would mess up the, uh, the divorce," she said lamely, her heart thudding a million miles a minute.

"Never fear, Sydney. You will get your precious divorce." The last word was hard, cold. Bitter. "But I have business that is long overdue in my sheikhdom. We are traveling to Al Na'ir without delay."

CHAPTER EIGHT

THEY traveled by helicopter. Malik piloted the craft with the expertise of someone who had done so many times before. Yet another thing she had not known about him, Sydney thought sourly. He sat in the pilot's seat of the military-like craft, his copilot beside him. They wore headsets and communicated from time to time, with each other and with what she presumed was a flight control tower somewhere.

Sydney sat in the back and gazed out the window at the scenery below. The landscape whisked by in the two hours it took to reach Al Na'ir, the red dunes and sandstone cliffs becoming more and more imposing as they flew. For once, she wished she'd bothered to look up Al Na'ir on the map. She knew nothing other than what Malik had once told her—that it was oil-rich and remote.

When the helicopter finally began its descent, she was stunned to see there was nothing around it. They landed on a rocky outcrop, the desert undulating in all directions. The land was barren, stark. There were no buildings, no house.

But there was a Land Rover, she noted with relief. A white vehicle sitting not too far from the landing area. The rotors slowed to a gentle *whop-whop-whop*. Malik

descended, and then came to the rear of the helicopter
and opened her door. A blast of hot air hit her in the face,
taking her breath along with it.

What kind of barren hell was this?

"Where are we?" she managed to ask, grasping
Malik's hand and letting him help her to the ground.
She'd changed into a white cotton *abaya*, because he'd
told her it would provide better protection from the elements, and a pair of ballet flats. The rocks beneath her
feet were hot. The sun bore down on her head, its rays
intense. It had not yet reached its zenith, but it was already scorching.

His dark eyes gave nothing away. "We are in Al
Na'ir."

"But where in Al Na'ir?" she pressed. Because this
was so remote she could almost believe they were the
only people on the planet. It was a frightening feeling
in some ways.

"We are in the Maktal Desert, *habibti*. It is the most
remote area of Jahfar."

Sydney swallowed. "And why are we here? Is there
more to Al Na'ir than this?"

"Much more. But we are here because I have business."

She eyed the Land Rover. "Where do we go from
here?"

"There is an oasis about an hour's drive away. We
will find shelter there."

Shelter. Sydney tried not to let her fear show. She'd
never been anywhere so menacing before. "Why did we
not simply fly there?" she asked as he reached into the
helicopter and grabbed her suitcase.

The copilot came around and helped gather their
luggage.

"Sandstorms are a problem. We cannot fly into the deepest desert because the sand will disrupt the engines. We would crash, Sydney. Here, we are on solid rock. It's as close as we can get to where we have to go."

"And is driving safe?"

"So long as the engine does not overheat, yes."

They carried the luggage to the Land Rover and stowed it. Malik said something to his copilot in Arabic. The man replied before bowing deeply. Then he was striding toward the helicopter and climbing inside.

"Get into the car, Sydney," Malik said. She did as he asked, buckling herself in as he slipped into the driver's seat. The rotors on the helicopter began to beat harder— and then the craft was lifting off and banking toward the horizon.

Sydney's heart felt as if it would beat out of her chest. The helicopter was gone, and she was completely alone with Malik in the middle of a harsh desert. If the engine died, would anyone find them?

"Why did he leave?" she asked.

Malik turned to her. "The helicopter cannot stay in the open. If there's a storm, the sand will gum up the engines. When we are ready to leave, it will return."

"And when will that be?"

"A few days, perhaps. No more than a fortnight."

A fortnight? She did the mental calculation—two weeks. Two weeks in the desert with Malik? She hoped it would not come to that. At least in Port Jahfar, she'd felt as if she could escape into the city if she needed time away. There was shopping, culture, activities.

But out here?

The journey to the oasis took longer than an hour. The sun was high overhead, but Malik did not have the air-conditioning cranked on high. It was warm in the Land Rover, though not oppressive.

"To keep the engine from overheating," he explained, though she did not ask.

They took a fairly flat path through the dunes, though occasionally they rolled up one impossibly high dune to slide down the other side. When she saw a stand of palm trees in the distance, she breathed a shaky sigh of relief.

They pulled to a stop beneath some trees as a group of black-clad men came toward the SUV. They were strong men, fierce men, with piercing dark eyes and sun-wizened features. And they were armed, Sydney noticed, with daggers and pistols clipped to their leather belts.

"Bedu," Malik said. "They will not harm you."

"I didn't think they would," she replied. Though they did look quite menacing.

Malik climbed from the car and spoke with the Bedu. The men bowed and made obeisance, and then a couple of younger boys were collecting the luggage and carrying it away. Malik came and helped her from the car, and then they were moving across the oasis and toward a large, black tent set beneath a stand of palms.

A shimmering pool of clear water gleamed in the sunlight in the center of the oasis. On one bank, a group of camels and horses stood contentedly, swishing flies with their tails. It was so odd to drive through a stark landscape, and then to come upon water in the middle of seemingly nowhere.

"Where does it come from?" she asked.

Malik followed her gaze. "From a reservoir in the sandstone deep below the surface. It has been there for millennia," he said. "At one time, this oasis was a vital stop on the trade routes between Jahfar and the north. It is what made the Maktal navigable."

Sydney imagined the oasis swirling with activity, camel trains coming and going as they followed the trade routes. There was a touch of romanticism to the idea, and yet she knew it would have been a hard life, a life filled with deprivation and danger. Much better to be here today. To arrive by air-conditioned car rather than on the back of a camel.

As she watched, three women trekked to the pool's edge and began to dip out water into a large trough. Sydney stopped when she realized they were washing clothes.

Malik came to a halt beside her. "It is their way," he said, as if he knew the sight surprised her.

"It's so surreal. What would they think if they knew about washing machines?"

Malik laughed. "They might be less impressed than you would imagine. This is a way of life that is very ancient."

So much for romanticism.

They continued walking toward the tent. The men who'd led the way were waiting at the entrance. Malik spoke to them, and then they were moving away, toward another group of tents at the other end of the oasis. Machinery began to hum nearby. It surprised her, though perhaps it should not have.

"Did they know you were coming?" she asked, shading her eyes to watch them go.

"I have not been here in quite some time. No, they did not know I would arrive today. But this is my land, and I am their sheikh, and therefore they are prepared for me."

He held the flap open for her and Sydney ducked inside. The confines of the tent were hot, the air still. Malik strode past her and did something she couldn't see. Then a fan blasted on high. It didn't cool the air much, but it moved what was there.

"There is a generator," he explained. "It won't run an air-conditioning unit, but it will run fans and lights. And refrigeration," he added. "It has only just been switched on, but soon there will be cold beverages."

"Amazing," she replied. A generator in the desert? That explained the machinery she'd heard. "But why this oasis, Malik? What's here for you?"

Because she was baffled. If there were a large oil industry nearby, they would have power and workers and the infrastructure to support them. There would be no need for a tent in the middle of a desert that seemed about as far from anywhere as you could get.

He looked away, busied himself with turning on other fans. "I have neglected to visit the Bedu. It was time I came."

Sydney licked her lips. "It could not have waited?"

He turned, speared her with hot dark eyes. "No."

Sydney let her gaze wander over the tent. It was luxurious, she realized, with bright carpets on the floors and walls, hammered brass tables and even a low-slung couch. What she didn't see was a bed.

"Where do I sleep?" she asked.

"There is a bedroom."

She looked around, realized there was a shadowed opening that must lead to another section of the tent. And then what he'd said sunk in. "A bedroom? As in one?"

"Yes, one."

Her pulse kicked into high gear. One bed. "That won't

work," she said, hoping her voice didn't sound as husky as it felt.

"I cannot create another bedroom, *habibti*. This is what is."

"I'm not sleeping with you."

He sauntered toward her, finally halting only inches away. She could feel his heat enveloping her. Her gaze landed on his mouth. That gorgeous, sensual mouth. His lips were full, firm, oh, so kissable.

"Perhaps you should," he said, his voice a sexy purr. "Perhaps we should explore every nuance of this marriage before ending it permanently."

"You can't mean that." Her heart was pounding, her stomach flipping. Need was pooling in her blood, filling her veins, making her body throb. She could feel the wetness between her thighs, the ache of arousal.

"I might. After this morning's display, I'm beginning to think I've acquiesced far too easily to your demands."

Sydney blinked. "My demands? You're the one who forced me to come to Jahfar! I'm simply trying to get through this without a lot of pain for either one of us."

His eyes narrowed. "You have changed, Sydney. You did not used to be so…cynical."

She swallowed. "I'm not cynical. I'm just practical."

"Is that what they call it now?"

"You're still angry with me because of your mother," she said after a tense moment of silence in which she wasn't quite sure how to respond. "I'm sorry if you didn't agree, but I couldn't let there be hard feelings between you when there was no need for it."

His sudden laugh was harsh, startling. "I'm afraid you failed, my dear. There have always been hard feelings between my mother and I, and there will continue to be long after you are gone. Your outburst did nothing to relieve that."

She hurt for him, for the casual way in which he could say that he and his mother were at odds. But then she remembered what he'd said about his childhood, and all she felt was sadness. He'd been raised in wealth and privilege, but he'd never really known what it was like to have a close-knit family. His was all about duty and tradition—without any consideration for love and connection.

She thought of what his mother had said this morning about finding Malik another bride—and it felt as if a puzzle piece suddenly clicked into place. *Of course*.

"You married me because you didn't want to marry the bride they'd picked out, didn't you?"

"I married you because I wanted to."

"But doing so got you out of another arranged marriage."

He hesitated a fraction too long. "It doesn't matter."

"It does to me," she said, her heart throbbing with hurt. She'd been convenient, nothing more. If he'd been dating some other woman at the time, he would no doubt have married her instead. Anything to throw a wrench into his family's plans.

"Perhaps I married you because I felt something," he said, his voice dipping. "Did you ever consider that possibility?"

An ache of a different kind vibrated in her heart. "You're just saying that. Don't."

Because she couldn't take it, not now. Not when she'd spent the last year apart from him, not when he'd failed to contact her even once during their long separation. Those were not the actions of a man who felt anything.

Never mind the conversation she'd overheard with his brother. A conversation he did not deny having.

His eyes gleamed in the darkened tent. "You know me so well, don't you, Sydney? Always positive that you have my motives pegged. My emotions."

"You don't have any emotions," she flung at him. He stiffened as if she'd hit him, tension rolling from him in waves.

Her heart lurched, her throat constricting against a painful knot. She shouldn't have said that. This was a man who'd told her, with such anguish, that he'd been responsible for the death of a girl.

Malik felt things. She knew he did.

But she still doubted he'd ever felt much for her. Nevertheless, that did not give her the right.

She dropped her gaze from his, swallowed. There was no moisture in her mouth. "Forgive me," she said. "I didn't mean that."

He sounded stiff, formal. "I think we both know you did."

You don't have any emotions.

Malik couldn't put the words out of his head, no matter how he tried. The sun had sunk behind the dunes hours ago now, and the desert air chilled him. He sat with a group of Bedu who'd gathered around a fire, smoking *shishas* and drinking coffee. He let their talk wash over him, around him. He spoke when necessary, but always his mind was elsewhere.

You don't have any emotions.

He had emotions, but he'd learned at an early age to bury them deep. If you didn't react, no one could hurt you. He'd stopped crying for his mother when he was three, stopped crying for his nanny at six.

And he'd grown determined, the older he got, that no one would force him to do what he did not want to do. Ever. He'd had little choice when he was young, but once he'd reached the age of majority, he'd been determined to make his own decisions, regardless of what his family thought.

He was the third son. His recalcitrance would be annoying, but not shattering. Indeed, his father, beyond the marriage with Dimah, had seemed in no rush to arrange another wedding for him. But once Adan became their uncle's heir, his mother grew determined to see each of her sons married and producing heirs. No doubt to consolidate their family's grip on the throne.

As if it were necessary. There were at least four Al Dhakirs who could inherit—and there would soon be more since Isabella was pregnant.

He'd always intended to take a proper Jahfaran wife. When he was ready. But first he'd wanted to have fun.

You have no emotions.

He could still see Sydney's face, the paleness of her skin. She'd looked drawn, tired. Her voice had shook as she'd accused him of marrying her to avoid another arranged marriage.

He'd denied it, and yet—

She had not been entirely wrong. He'd known what awaited him in Jahfar when he'd met her. He'd simply been putting off the inevitable.

But then she'd become a part of his life, and he'd wanted her in a way he'd wanted no one else. And, for one brief moment, he'd thought, *why not?*

He'd known how she felt about him. And he'd never once believed he was taking advantage of those feelings. He was a wealthy prince, considered one of the most eligible bachelors in the world, along with his brothers.

The woman he married would be fortunate. Honored. He was a great prize, a catch beyond compare.

Malik frowned. He'd been proud, arrogant, certain he was right. Certain he was making her life better when in fact he seemed to have made it worse.

She'd loved him once. He knew that she had, even if she'd only said the words on their last night together. She'd loved him.

But not enough. If she had, she wouldn't have run away.

His grip on the *shisha* tightened. There was nothing left between them now but passion. She might not love him, but she did want him. He would have to be made of stone not to know it. He could feel the electricity between them when she was near, feel the way she quivered with anticipation. When he touched her, she leaned into his touch. And she fought with herself until she won the battle and pushed him away.

His body ached with need for her. He remembered her touch, her scent, the feel of her beneath him. He missed that. He wanted to possess her again, wanted to own her mouth and her lush body. Wanted her to admit she wanted him, that maybe they had unfinished business left between them.

He'd brought her out here because he was angry. But also because he wanted to leave behind all the distractions of Port Jahfar. Out here in the desert, there was nothing but space and time.

Nothing to distract them. Nothing to interfere.

Malik climbed to his feet and thanked the Bedu for their hospitality. Then he stalked toward the tent where he'd left his wife.

* * *

Sydney lay in the big bed beneath a pile of furs. She'd been shocked at how cold the air grew after the sun went down. Malik had sent a Bedouin girl with food earlier, but she hadn't seen him since earlier in the day when he'd left her alone in the darkened tent with her heart in her throat.

Why could they not be in a room together without wounding each other? Why did every conversation between them degenerate into a battle of words, of old hurts flung so carelessly?

Sydney shoved a hand behind her head, stared up at the darkness. A small light burned nearby, throwing a purple glow into the room. She'd thought it was an oil lamp at first, had even managed to say the words in Arabic, but the Bedu girl smiled and shook her head as she flipped a small switch in the back.

A sound in the other room lodged her heart in her throat. She sat up, dragging the covers up with her. Waiting. What if it wasn't Malik? This was a wild, untamed place—even her cell phone didn't work, much to her dismay. What would she do?

A long shadow appeared on the wall, and then a man stepped into the room.

"Malik?" Her voice was little more than a whisper.

"You are awake," he said.

Relief made her sag into the mattress. "Yes. It's so quiet here." Not just that, but she'd been wondering about him. Worrying about him.

He began to remove his clothing. She could see the fabric whisper over his head, see the gleam of his bare chest in the lamplight. Her breath caught in her throat.

"I—I didn't know when you'd be back. I'll move to the couch in the other room."

He sat on the edge of the bed and pulled at his boots.
"No," he said, and her heart skipped.

"No? I won't sleep with you, Malik, and I won't have
sex with you," she said in a heated rush.

"So you keep saying. But I don't believe you, Sydney."
He stood, still wearing the loose trousers he'd had on
beneath the *dishdasha*. They hung low on his lean hips,
tied at the waist with a drawstring. His hipbones pro-
truded from the waistband, and her mouth went dry.

Oh, dear God. His abdomen was as tight as ever, his
chest sculpted with lean muscle. His body was perfect.

Her heart throbbed. And, God help her, her body was
responding.

"You won't force me," she blurted.

He put his hands on his hips. "No, I won't. But I won't
have to, will I?"

Before she knew what he was planning, he grabbed
her foot and dragged her down until she was lying flat
on the bed. And then he was on top of her, his body hov-
ering over hers but not quite touching.

His head dropped, his lips skimming her throat. She
splayed her hands against his chest, intending to push
him away—except that she didn't quite manage to do
so. Heat seared her, glorious heat.

She arched her neck, bit her lip to stop the moan that
threatened.

"You want me," he said, his voice a sensual rumble
against her skin. "You burn for me."

"No," she replied. "No…"

"Then push, Sydney," he urged heatedly. "By God,
push me away. Or I won't be responsible."

CHAPTER NINE

SYDNEY was frozen, like a small animal trying to hide from a much larger predator. She wanted to be strong, wanted to push him away —and she didn't. She wanted him with a fierceness that no longer surprised her. She wanted him inside her, his powerful body moving with precision, taking them both to heaven and back.

Her fingers curled, her eyes closing. Oh, how it hurt to want her desert prince so badly. To know that she would never truly have him, even if she offered herself up here and now.

She thought he would kiss her, thought that her inability to move would bring him to her and begin what she wanted oh so desperately.

Instead, he rolled away from her.

Sydney blinked back tears—of frustration, of anger, of sadness? She was no longer certain. Being with Malik again confused things. Confused her.

"Why did you leave, Sydney?" He sounded almost tormented. "We had *this*—and you left."

"You know why," she said, pushing the words past the ache in her throat.

"No, I don't. I know what you told me—that you overheard my conversation—but why did that make you go? Why didn't you confront me?"

"Confront you?" she choked out. "How could I do that? You humiliated me!"

"Which should have made you angry."

"It did make me angry!"

He rolled onto his side to face her. "Then explain to me how you thought leaving would fix the problem."

Sydney scrambled up to a sitting position. Shame flooded her. How could she say it? How could she explain that she'd always known she wasn't good enough for him? That she knew it was too good to be true? It had always been a matter of time before he no longer wanted her.

So why did you agree to marry him?

"I was upset," she said. "Hurt. You didn't want me, and I wasn't about to stay and pretend I didn't know it. And then, then…" She couldn't finish, couldn't speak about their last night together when she'd told him how she felt and been met with silence. It was too humiliating, even now.

"When did I say I didn't want you?"

She thought back. He'd never actually said those words, had he? But what else could he have meant when he said marrying her was a mistake?

She shook her head. He was trying to confuse her, and she wouldn't allow it. She had to hold onto her anger, her pain. "You told your brother you made a mistake. What was I supposed to think?"

He reached for her hand, took it in one of his. She tried to pull away, but he wouldn't let her. "I did make a mistake, Sydney. Because I married you without giving you a chance to realize what this kind of life entailed. Did you know my mother would despise you? That you would always be an outsider in Jahfar? Did you have any idea what being my wife would entail? I gave you no chance to discover these things."

Her heart hurt. Her head. Her throat felt like sand. "Are you really trying to tell me that you were only thinking of me when you said it? Because, if so, why didn't you come after me? Why didn't you call?"

"You left me, Sydney. No other woman has ever done so."

She couldn't believe what he was saying. And yet she could. Because Malik didn't love her. His pride had been hurt, but not his heart. He was not about to come after her when it was a matter of pride alone. She bit her lip to stop the trembling. Damn him!

She shook her head again. "It doesn't matter, though, does it? Even if we'd talked about it then, we're still wrong for each other. It would have never worked out." She swallowed. "A divorce is the right thing to do."

"Maybe it is," he agreed. "But the terms have changed."

Her heart fell to her toes. "I don't understand."

He sat up, faced her. His voice, when he spoke, was firm. "If you want this divorce, you're going to live with me as my wife."

She couldn't stop the gasp that caught in her throat. "That's not what we agreed to back in California!"

"This is the desert, *habibti*. Conditions change. We either adapt or die."

"But—but—this is blackmail," she bit out, fury vibrating through her. How dare he change the terms midcourse!

"I am aware," he said coolly. "But it is my price. If you don't agree, you are free to leave. We will simply remain married for all eternity."

Sydney struggled to calm her breathing. She was absolutely livid. And frightened.

"You would like that, I suppose." It would forever keep him from his family's matchmaking attempts, which he probably considered a good thing.

"Not particularly. It would require me to break our marriage vows since I refuse to spend the rest of my life celibate."

Sydney snorted. "As if you haven't done so already." She'd read the papers, seen the pictures of him with other women. She was not so naive as to believe he'd spent the last year completely alone.

"Ah, yes," he practically snarled. "Once more, you know me so well. You are quite an expert on my behavior. Whenever I am uncertain how to proceed, I should ask you in future. You will know unerringly what I should do."

"Stop it!" The words tumbled from her, laced with bitterness and pain. "Don't lie to me, Malik. Don't treat me like I'm stupid."

He swore, long and violently, in Arabic. "What about the way you treat me? As if I have no honor, as if my word means nothing."

"I didn't say that!" He turned things around on her, made her feel wrong for saying such a thing—and yet she'd seen the papers, seen the pictures of him with other women. How could the evidence be wrong?

"But you did." She could feel the anger vibrating from him, the indignation. A thread of doubt began to weave its way through her brain. "Do you know what I think, *habibti*? I think you are little more than a spoiled child. You refuse to deal with anything. You only wish to run away when life gets difficult."

A sharp pain lodged in her breastbone. "That's not true."

But she feared it was. She'd grown so accustomed to hiding behind masks, to hiding who she was and what she wanted. It had been the only way to survive, to be like everyone else.

To make her parents proud.

She was afraid to say what she wanted, afraid she would be rejected or ridiculed.

He reached out, his fingertips sliding along her cheekbone. "You have to grow up sometime, Sydney. You have to face your fears."

The lump in her throat was too big to swallow. "You're trying to change the conversation. It was about you, about your women—"

His hand dropped away again. The air between them grew frosty. "Yes, of course. Now please tell me how many women I've had. I seem to have forgotten."

His voice was tight with anger, but she refused to be intimidated. It felt wrong somehow to continue, and yet she blundered on. "There were pictures. You and Sofia de Santis, for one."

"Sofia is genuinely beautiful. She is also engaged—to a woman."

Sydney sucked in a breath, the fire of humiliation creeping up her neck. She was only glad it was dark and he couldn't see. How had she missed the news that Sofia de Santis was a lesbian?

"What about the Countess Forbach? There were several pictures of you together."

"No doubt because I attended many of her charity balls where I donated money to her causes. She is also, I must say, happily married to the count."

"You have an answer for everything," she said.

"And you have an objection."

"You can't really just expect me to believe everything I read was a lie—"

"Why not? Did any of these *news* articles appear in a real paper? Or were they splashed across the pages of the tabloids you grabbed at the checkout stand?"

"Why are you doing this?" she asked, anger and fear overwhelming her. Because he made sense and she didn't like it. Because if she believed what he said, she had to question everything about herself, about the way she'd run from Paris and hidden from the problem, convincing herself with each passing day that she had been right to go. "Why can't we just do what we were doing, endure this forty days and be done? Why do you have to make it into something more just to torment me?"

He grabbed one of the pillows from beside her and punched it. She flinched in the darkness, but he only tossed it down and stretched out, tucking it beneath his head. "What good has maintaining the status quo gotten us so far? We live as man and wife, or you return to L.A. without your precious divorce."

"That's not much of a choice," she whispered.

He yawned. "Nevertheless, it is the choice before you."

She sat there, aching, not knowing what else to say, how else to convince him. How would she ever survive being his wife again? How would her heart survive? He would destroy her. Once more, the wave that was Malik was dragging her under.

And there was nothing she could do about it.

"I'm going to sleep on the couch," she finally said,

needing to say something, needing to contradict him, if only for the time being.

His only answer was a soft snore.

Sydney reluctantly trudged to the couch and fell asleep. She didn't want to leave the warm, soft bed—or the heat of the man beside her—but she felt as if she had to take a stand, no matter how temporary. But when she awoke the next morning, she was in the bed, snuggled beneath the covers—and Malik was gone.

It embarrassed her to think that he must have carried her there, and that she'd slept through the whole thing. How was that possible? But clearly it was.

She rose and went to wash in the bathing area, which was remarkably well-fitted for a desert tent, complete with a shower stall and solid surround, then dressed in a cool white *abaya* and sandals. The same girl from last night—Adara—brought her breakfast, which she ate in the living area while watching satellite television.

There was a news piece on a Hollywood couple, and she watched with interest as the familiar scenery of L.A. slid by. Remarkably, she didn't feel homesick for it, though she did wish for her own apartment—her own things. She wondered what her parents were doing. They'd been happy when she'd told them she was going to Jahfar with Malik. Having a prince for a son-in-law was quite good for business, it seemed. She hadn't the heart to tell them the truth.

She knew they would be disappointed in her when she returned alone, but the one thing about her family was they would never say so. In fact, they'd never said a word about her choices for as long as she could remember.

Unless it was a business decision, her parents said

nothing. Her sister had always been her closest confidante—but Alicia had been tangled up with a new boyfriend for the past six months and was rarely available if she wasn't at work. Sydney had wanted to talk to her sister about what spending time with Malik again would mean, but Alicia could never take her calls.

Jeffrey needed her, or Jeffrey had other plans. Alicia would say a hurried goodbye, and the phone would go dead. Though they worked in the same building, lunches were also out because Alicia spent them with Jeffrey.

Sydney had a sudden feeling she should call Alicia, but her cell phone didn't work out here in this remote location. She would have to wait until Malik returned and ask him if there was a way to make a call. She assumed there had to be, since he had satellite television.

When she got bored of television, she ventured outside. The heat was staggering. She pulled the head covering tighter and walked toward the gleaming pool in the center of the oasis. The oasis seemed empty, but she knew it was not. The black tents of the Bedu were still erected on one end of the area, and occasionally she saw movement as a child darted outside and back in again.

Sydney skirted the far edge of the pool, intending to walk all the way around. It wasn't far, but at least it was a bit of exercise. A group of camels lay beneath the palms, tethered to a line, watching her progress while they chewed their cud.

At some point, she realized it was getting harder to breathe. She sucked in air that nearly scorched her lungs. Sweat trickled between her breasts. Her throat seemed to close against the heat, quickly devoid of all moisture. Finally, she stumbled to the foot of a palm and sank to the ground.

She put a hand over her stomach. It was beginning to ache, and her head felt fuzzy.

A few moments later a noise grabbed her attention and she looked up again. A horse and rider blotted out the sun. The horse was dark, brown or black, and finely made. Its nostrils flared wide, and red tassels dripped from its breastplate and bridle. One hoof pawed the ground impatiently. The rider, clad from head to toe in black, separated from the horse and sprang to the ground beside her.

"Sydney." The word was muffled behind the black fabric wrapped over his face. But the eyes...

"Hello, Malik," she said. "I was taking a walk."

Malik swore. And then he swept her into his arms and strode toward the tent. She expected he would set her down on the couch, get cool water for her, but he carried her through the tent and into the small bathing area. Once there, he turned on the water and pushed her under it fully clothed.

Sydney gasped as cold water rushed over her, soaking her to the bone. "What are you doing?"

He ripped away his face covering. "The heat is too dangerous. You should never have gone out in it."

"For heaven's sake, Malik, I was barely outside five minutes! I'm not dying!"

Though she might if he kept the cold water running on her like that—except that it sort of felt good sluicing over her. Perhaps she'd been hotter than she'd thought.

"You were overcome." One hand held her firmly under the water. His sleeve was soaked, but the rest of him remained dry as he refused to let her go.

"It was only a moment! I needed to sit."

"Where did you think you were going? This is the

Maktal Desert! You could have been killed, if not by the heat, then by a scorpion or a viper."

A viper? Sydney shivered, and not from the water.

"I just wanted to go somewhere other than this tent! I was bored, and you weren't here...." She trailed off, realizing how ridiculous she sounded. Exactly like the child he'd accused her of being only last night.

"A very good reason to risk your life," he growled.

Sydney closed her eyes, fury and frustration welling within her. She had to do something or burst with it. Without thinking about the possible consequences, she cupped a hand and slung water at Malik. It hit him in the face, dripped down over his tanned features. One drop clung to his lower lip, and a dull ache began in her core.

No.

She would *not* want him. She lashed out again, slinging more water at him, soaking the front of his *dishdasha*.

"This is how you wish to play?" he asked dangerously. Then he shoved the dark covering from his hair, let it fall as he pushed her all the way under the spray, water rolling over her face for the first time.

Sydney came up sputtering. And furious.

She reached for him, wrapped her hands in the fabric of his clothes. She didn't expect she could move him, but she threw all her weight backward—and he stumbled into the shower. Water plastered his dark clothes to his body, and Sydney burst into a fit of giggles at the look of surprise on his face.

"How do you like it?" she asked.

His face was thunderous—but then he shoved his wet hair back and grinned at her. Her heart lurched. "I like it just fine," he said, his gaze dropping over her. Sydney glanced down—and squeaked in surprise. Her white garments were transparent. It wasn't quite like being naked, but close enough. The fabric clung to her, outlining her breasts, the dark nipples, the shadowed cleft between her legs.

She looked up again, met his hot gaze. The raw lust she saw there threatened to double her over with need. Everything was happening so fast, the atmosphere between them changing, becoming more charged, more desperate.

"Malik," she choked out as he closed the distance between them. She wanted him—and she didn't. It terrified her to think of making love with him again—and it terrified her to think of *never* doing so.

She didn't know what he would do—but she realized his hand was shaking as he reached out. Shaking as he palmed her breast, his thumb brushing over the jutting peak of her nipple. Sensation streaked through her. Flames licked at her belly.

The water did nothing to cool this fire eating her up inside. Because nothing could cool her now. The fire needed to burn out, and the only way it would burn out…

"You've done it now, *habibti*," Malik said, smiling roguishly.

Her heart thrummed. "D-done what?"

He took her hand in his, pressed his lips to her upturned palm.

And then he placed her hand against his chest before sliding it oh, so slowly down his body.

CHAPTER TEN

THE wet fabric molded to his perfect frame, delineating muscle and sinew—but Sydney didn't need to see how the fabric clung to know he was hard.

The evidence—powerful, impressive, mouth-watering—thrust against her palm.

She couldn't take her eyes off his beautiful face. His eyes were bright, his jaw set in stone as if he were enduring a great torment. Sydney's body was aching, melting, throbbing with need. Touching him like this...

She swallowed. She knew that she had only to drop her hand away and he would turn and go.

Instead, she traced the hard ridge, her pulse thundering in her ears. He sucked in a breath, his eyes burning even brighter if that were possible. Then he pulled her to him, wet body to wet body, his arm hard around her. He hesitated only a moment before he dipped his head and covered her mouth with his.

There was never any doubt she would open to him. Her lips parted, her tongue tangling with his on a moan. He gripped her tight, kissed her with all the pent-up frustration and want that had been building between them.

His hands began to move on her body, divesting her of her clothes. She wanted to laugh—with joy, with nervous anticipation. This was Malik, her husband. The man she'd loved.

For one wild moment, she thought she should have said no, should have stopped him.

But it was too late now.

Too late.

She would play with fire and hope she survived.

As her clothes peeled away, the air from the fans cooled her even more. Goose bumps prickled across her skin. Malik broke the kiss to let his eyes travel her body. She dropped her gaze, self-conscious and unsure.

"You are beautiful," he said, his voice husky. And then he picked her up and sat her on the waist-high ledge surrounding the shower.

His dark head lowered. He took one tight nipple in his mouth, sucking it lightly while she squirmed and gasped. She could feel her sex tightening, swelling, aching with need for this man.

As if he knew it, he slipped a finger over her, caressed her silky curls, traced her outer lips. His finger glided into her moist heat, and she groaned with pleasure.

"Ah, Sydney," he said, "I've missed this."

Her heart squeezed even as pleasure rippled through her. *I've missed this.* Not, *I've missed you.*

But her thoughts fractured as he sunk a finger into her. A second joined the first, and then his thumb parted her, ghosted over her clitoris. She thought she would weep from the painful need he evoked. It had been so long, too long....

"Malik—"

"Yes," he murmured. "Yes. I have not forgotten even a moment of making love to you. I know what you need, *habibti*. I know what you want."

His mouth closed over her other stiff nipple, and she

threw her head back as he sucked harder this time. A sharp current of pleasure spiked from her nipple to her clitoris, making her moan with need. He repeated the motion again and again, driving her insane for him.

She wanted him. Fiercely. Now. Deep within her, driving her—driving them both—toward completion.

But he would make her wait for it. She knew that.

Malik was the consummate lover. He was attuned to her body as if it were his own. He knew how to make her shudder and jolt and beg and cry. He knew how to wring every last bit of sensation from her, until she was utterly spent. Until all she could do was lay boneless and content and wait for her strength to return.

It had always been this way with him, this headlong rush into hedonism that was so unlike her. Nothing had ever made her want to abandon herself to pleasure. Nothing but Malik.

It frightened her, this dark need for him. She shouldn't be here, shouldn't be allowing herself to fall so hard again—but she was powerless to stop it from happening. She didn't *want* to stop it from happening. If she had to crash and burn, what a way to go...

His fingers moved in and out of her body, his thumb working against her sensitive bud until she knew she would fly apart at any moment.

But it was too soon. She didn't want to go over the edge yet. She'd waited so long now that she wanted to prolong the pleasure for a little longer. Prolong the torture.

"I want to see you," she cried. Somehow, she did not know how, she managed to form the words. Managed to speak them.

His dark eyes gleamed bright as he straightened. His fingers ceased their torture. "Then strip me, *zawjati*."

She looked at his traditional Jahfaran clothes, at the wet black material, and frowned. "I don't know how."

"I will help you."

She hopped off the ledge and he guided her hands to the fastenings. It took her only a moment to figure out how to rip them open. And then she was peeling the wet robes off, revealing his naked torso while he chuckled at her.

"So eager. I like this."

She couldn't stop herself from touching him, from running her hands over the peaks and valleys of muscle and sinew. The hard planes of his body that made her mouth water, made her long to press her lips just there and taste him again.

Malik might be wealthy and privileged, but he was a son of the desert. The kind of man whose strength wasn't feigned, but real strength forged from the harshness of the environment he came from.

Though he probably maintained his physique in a gym, he didn't look like the kind of man who jogged on sterile treadmills or lifted cold bars of steel. He looked as if he'd been formed during hot, hard work beneath a blistering sun.

Sydney frowned at the trousers and riding boots he wore. Those boots weren't coming off easily, and she didn't want to wait. She untied the trousers and slipped them open until they hung low on his hips.

And then, because she couldn't help herself, she pressed her hot, open mouth to his nipple as she found the hard ridge of his erection and squeezed. Malik sucked in a sharp breath, his hands coming up to cup her head.

"This won't last if you keep doing that," he warned her.

Sydney smiled against his skin. She loved knowing

she could make him dance on the edge of control. And when he lost that control…oh, God, it was spectacular.

The water was no longer flowing over them. She wasn't sure when he'd turned it off, but she was glad. Now, all she could taste was Malik. The warm honey of his skin. That combination of soap and man that she loved so much.

She trailed her tongue down the valley between his pectorals, skimmed over his tight abdomen. And then she freed him from his trousers and took him in her mouth while he made a sound that wasn't quite human.

His entire body stiffened. She glanced up. His head was tilted back, the muscles in his neck corded tight, as if he were fighting for control. His hands gripped the back of her head, fisted in her wet hair.

She swirled her tongue around the silky head of his erection. Her hand shaped him. He was like velvet and diamonds. So soft, and so hard at once. She wanted to bring him to completion this way, but he wasn't going to allow it.

He pushed her away, put his hands around her hips, and lifted her onto the ledge again. She clung to him, her mouth finding and fusing with his, their tongues tangling deeply and urgently.

And then she felt him, felt the hot head of his penis as he began to push inside her. She shifted her hips so she could take him deeper. She was impatient, needy. Greedy.

Malik held her hard, the tips of his fingers digging into her hips. She knew it was because he needed to hold onto his control, no other reason. He'd always been so rigidly controlled, even here—until he broke and let the passion overwhelm him.

She welcomed the fierceness of his passion. Craved it. Could not wait for the storm to break.

Sydney wrapped her arms around his neck, arched her body toward him. She wanted to drink him in, wanted all of him. *Now.*

But Malik was still in control. He pressed forward slowly, so slowly—and then he thrust to the heart of her, making them both groan with the exquisite pleasure of his possession.

He broke their kiss, pressed his lips to her jaw, her throat, while she clung to him. He didn't move, but she could feel the length of him throbbing deep within her. It was exquisite, this joining. She remembered why she'd been helpless before, why she'd followed him halfway around the world. Why she'd believed enough to marry him, though a part of her had known the truth.

She wasn't a weak woman, wasn't a particularly sensual one—except with Malik. Whatever he wanted, when they were like this, she would give.

Her hands slipped over his shoulders, down his back, trying to bring him closer as she arched and wiggled her hips toward him. His intake of breath was sharp.

"Sydney," he said, his voice broken. On the edge.

Exactly as she wanted him.

"Now, Malik," she urged. "Now."

He gripped her hips harder still—and then he withdrew, pulling so far out she thought he was planning to leave her insatiate and aching.

And then he thrust forward again, joining them once more. Sydney wanted to laugh with joy—and yet her breath froze, her lungs incapable of filling as the pleasure washed over her in blistering waves.

He thrust again, and then again—and her body caught fire until she was shuddering, until her very fingertips sizzled with the force of her orgasm. She was caught, too quickly, her entire being folding in on itself before bursting into a million liquid shards.

She knew she cried his name, knew that he was feeling a special kind of male triumph in that moment. He owned her, body and soul, and he knew it. She wanted to damn him for it, but she couldn't.

She wanted more—more Malik, more pleasure, more of his hard length thrusting into her.

She knew—without asking, without words—that he'd regained his strength. That somehow her surrender was required for him to be in control again.

Such exquisite control.

"Are you all right?" Malik asked.

Sydney shook her head, buried her face against his throat. His pulse throbbed in his neck, letting her know that he wasn't quite as controlled as she'd thought after all. The pieces of her slid together, reformed into something that she didn't quite recognize.

Or rather, something she *did* recognize, and dreaded. A woman who *needed*.

Malik tilted her chin back with a finger. His eyes searched hers, and the concern she saw there made her heart lurch. "Did I hurt you?" he asked, his voice so tender.

"No," she said. Then again, stronger, "No."

There were different kinds of hurts. But she knew he was talking about physical pain, and that was definitely not a problem. Emotional pain was another story.

"Good," he said. "Because I need you, Sydney. I need you."

And then he was kissing her again, and she was opening to him, taking him deep inside. He held her hips hard, thrusting into her, their bodies melding together. His strokes were deep, expert, driving.

She gave herself up to him, gave herself up to the rhythm and beauty of it. Sydney wrapped her legs around him, arched her body so that her breasts could press against his bare chest.

His mouth moved over her throat, his voice saying words in Arabic, and then he bent and took her nipple in his mouth, pulling hard so that the spike of pleasure shot to her sex. She was on fire for him, her body primed and ready for another shattering orgasm.

She felt as if she were swelling with something too wonderful to be contained, as if she would fly apart any second. Malik's thrusts grew more frenzied, his hold on her tighter.

And then his hand slid between them, finding her sweet spot, sending her over the edge.

She splintered apart in one long wave, coming with a gasp, his name spilling from her lips.

It did not end there. She was holding on to him, shuddering, her legs wrapped high around his hips as continued to pump into her. But his strokes were slower, more deliberate.

Not so frenzied.

And she knew he was drawing this out, giving her every moment of pleasure he could while waiting to take his own.

"Malik," she said. But it came out as a sob.

"Again, Sydney. I want to watch you come again."

She squeezed her eyes tight, tried not to focus on the sensations beginning to build in her core. Because she would be senseless in his arms if she let him keep taking her over the edge like this.

"I can't," she cried.

"You know you can." It was a firm command.

And then he lifted her up, his big hands splaying across her bottom as he carried her out of the bathing room and into the bedroom. Their bodies were still joined. His gaze was hot on hers, intense. She wondered how he did it, how he kept such a tight rein on his need.

But she pushed the thought away because she didn't want to go there. Didn't want to consider that she might not mean anything to him, that he was capable of this because he had no emotional attachment.

Because it was just sex.

He put a knee on the bed, tumbled her back onto the mattress. And then he was withdrawing from her, sliding down her body. Before she could protest, he slid his thumbs into her sex, spread her open.

His tongue touched her hot flesh, his mouth closing over her clitoris. He suckled the sensitive flesh there with the same intensity as he'd shown to her nipples. His tongue darted over her, his teeth nibbling oh, so gently.

Her release sucked the air from her lungs. She sobbed his name, begged him to stop.

But not because it hurt, and not because she didn't like it.

It was simply too intense, too soul-shattering. She would never be free of him this way. Never be able to love another man, to be with another man if this is what she had to remember.

"Again," he said, before driving her once more to the peak.

When she came again, he crawled up her body, kissing his way over her sensitive skin. He was still wearing the riding boots, his black trousers open at the waist and hanging low on his hips.

Sydney could only stare. He was an erotic fantasy, a

desert lover come to claim her. She was aching, quivering with need. The pale maiden ready for the possession of her dark lover.

"Do you want me, Sydney?"

"You know I do."

"That wasn't enough for you?" he asked silkily.

She shook her head against the pillows. She knew she must look wild, her hair plastered to her head from the shower, her skin flushed with the glow of amazing sex. But she didn't care.

She needed him inside her. Needed him to breathe.

He urged her up, turned her so that she was facing away from him on all fours. He stroked her sex, kindling the flame again until she was panting with need.

And then he plunged into her. Sydney arched backward, her hair fanning across her back. Malik wrapped an arm around her waist, held her against him as he thrust into her body. His other hand found her, moved expertly against her slick flesh.

It was raw, earthy, and she loved it. He could have taken her gently, reverently, but instead he'd taken her with all the power and wildness he possessed.

It wasn't fairy tale lovemaking—but she didn't want fairy tale lovemaking. She wanted *this*.

This raw need that scorched her from the inside out. That branded her as a sexual being who craved the kind of release that only this man could give.

She came again in a hot, hard rush, collapsing against him while he held her steady and pumped into her body. This time, he followed her, his body stiffening as he moaned her name.

She loved the sounds he made when he was stripped of his control, the way his body jerked and shuddered. *She* did that to him. It made her feel powerful, needed.

His fingers stroked along the column of her spine, his touch reverent. He collapsed onto his back, and she turned so that she could face him. He reached up to push away a hank of her hair that had fallen across her face, and then cupped the back of her head and pulled her down for a lingering kiss.

"You've destroyed me," he murmured.

But what she was thinking was that he'd destroyed her. It didn't matter what happened, how many days they spent together, whether they made love or studiously avoided touching one another—she felt something for this man that was never going to dissolve. Time and distance hadn't managed it so far, though she'd convinced herself that it had.

Tears pricked the backs of her eyes. One afternoon in his arms, and the truth was too blinding to ignore.

CHAPTER ELEVEN

WHEN Malik awoke, the tent was dark. He moved his foot, grateful that he'd at least managed to get out of the riding boots at some point. Beside him, Sydney was curled into a small ball. He lifted onto an elbow, smiled as he gently drew her curtain of hair from her face. He'd always loved the way she slept.

She lay on her side, her body curled as tight as it could be, as if she were trying to make herself smaller. He frowned for a moment. It was very much like Sydney to try and make herself disappear. He'd known, when they were together, that she often tried to go unnoticed.

She truly believed that she was without any remarkable qualities, which he found both interesting and baffling. He'd never known a woman who was more remarkable, or more certain she was not.

He stretched and climbed from the bed naked, in search of the food they'd left on a table nearby. It was cold in the desert at night, but he was still too hot to bother covering up. He found flat bread and olives, a bit of cheese. He didn't need much, but he needed something if the way his stomach was growling was any indication.

Sydney didn't stir. And no wonder. It was a mystery that he could.

His body was sated, content—his mind was not. He thought back to that moment in the shower when she'd taken him in her mouth. He'd nearly come apart then and there, but somehow he'd managed to keep it together long enough to regain control of himself.

He felt a moment's guilt for the way he'd taken her once they'd made it to the bed. But he'd been so on edge, so unsure of himself and so raw with the wounded feelings he'd buried down deep that he couldn't lie in her arms and spill himself into her body with her soft limbs wrapped around him and her cries in his ear.

He'd needed to take her like an animal, needed that slight disconnect that turning her away from him would give.

Except that he'd failed rather spectacularly. Because it didn't matter how he made love to Sydney, she still managed to crack him wide open until his feelings were so raw that he wasn't sure how to deal with them.

When he'd recovered sufficiently, he'd dealt with them by taking her again, this time as they entwined their bodies together, limbs tangling, hands clasping, tongues dueling for supremacy. Her cries of ecstasy fueled some hidden fire in his gut that only made him want to push her further and further over the edge.

Malik pushed a tired hand over his eyes, rubbed his arm against his face. It had been a very long afternoon, punctuated by bouts of sleeping combined with the sort of lovemaking that turned him inside out each and every time. He didn't care to examine why, though he knew he would have to at some point.

All he knew was that Sydney was a fire in his body like no other woman had ever been. He was addicted to the rush he felt whenever he was inside her, addicted to the way she made him feel better than he'd ever felt in his life. With her, he felt…right.

Somewhere during it all, they'd managed to eat.

He'd told her last night she would be his wife again. He didn't know precisely why he'd done it, except that he'd been angry with her for being so determined to push him away again. She'd walked out on him once, and he'd been too proud to go after her. He should have done.

He should have chased her all the way to L.A. and reminded her why they were so good together.

But she was here now, and he wasn't going to let her go again without making very sure she understood precisely what she would be giving up.

"Malik?"

"Over here," he said. "Do you want something to eat?"

She pushed herself up in the bed and yawned. "No thanks. What time is it?"

Malik shrugged. "I'm not sure. I haven't checked. It's probably earlier than it should be."

"What do you expect? We did sleep part of the day away."

"Is that what we did?" he asked, making his way back to the big bed and the warm woman waiting for him.

She laughed. "Sometimes."

"How are you feeling?"

She lifted her arms in a sensual stretch. "Tired. Sore."

He'd hoped she would say *happy*. He told himself not to care that she did not.

"Perhaps we should have taken it slower," he said instead.

"I'm not sure that was possible."

No, probably not. He'd never been very good at maintaining his control with her. "Nevertheless, you almost

succumbed to heat stroke. I should have been more careful."

She shook her head. "And yet here I am, remarkably
alive and unaffected by your callous treatment of me."

He tried not to laugh. It didn't work. "I should love
to treat you callously more often."

She sighed. He didn't like the wistfulness he heard
in the sound. Something was coming that he'd prefer
to leave alone for the time being. He was not, however,
going to get his wish.

"It was beautiful, Malik. Wonderful and amazing, as
always. But how does sleeping together help the situation?"

Her words pricked him. He had no idea what happened next, how making love to her fit into his life beyond this very moment, and he didn't want to think of
it. They'd had an extraordinary day together, getting to
know each other's bodies again, feeling the emotion that
burned between them as they did so.

Being inside Sydney wasn't just about sex. He knew
that, but he didn't know what else to call it. How to say
it. He knew she was determined to move forward with
the divorce, determined they could not build a life together, and he couldn't think of one good reason why
she was wrong.

Except that it *seemed* wrong somehow. Why couldn't
they figure it out? Why couldn't they take it a day at a
time and try to build something more lasting?

"It helps me feel calm," he said lightly, because he
wasn't prepared to take the conversation any deeper.

She blew out a breath. "Does it make you feel anything else?" she asked, her voice smaller than it had
been.

He pulled her to him then, stretched out over top of

her, his mouth finding the sweet skin of her throat. "You know it does, Sydney."

Her fingers slipped over his shoulders, a small moan issuing from her as he licked the flesh of her neck and then blew softly on the wet spot. "But I *don't* know it," she said. "I have no idea what you feel. All I know is we have this amazing chemistry in bed together. But that's not enough, is it?"

"It's a start." He didn't want to talk about feelings, not right now. The idea of it created a hard knot of tension deep in his belly. "Why question our good fortune?"

He palmed her breast, tweaked a nipple as she gasped. "Malik," she breathed. "This is serious."

"I know. Very serious." He claimed her lips, delved inside with his tongue. She kissed him ardently, her hands threading into his hair as her body arched.

He was growing hard again. He knew the moment she realized it, because she gave a little moan. And then she tilted her hips up and ground them against him.

"Temptress," he said, and then he bent his head and took the hard bud of her nipple into his mouth.

"Oh—I can't think when you do that."

"Then don't think. Feel."

"But Malik," she said on a half groan. "I want to talk to you. I want to know you. I want more than just this."

He lifted his head. Irritation was growing inside him. Frustration. And a sense of panic that was completely foreign to him. "I ache for you, Sydney. I've ached for a year. Is this not enough for you?"

She didn't say anything for a long moment. "No," she said. "It's not enough."

Malik rolled away from her with a groan. He put his arm over his face, covering his eyes. His body throbbed, but that was nothing compared to the piercing throb of his heart.

"We've been down this path before," she said. "And look where it got us."

Malik sat up and began to hunt for his trousers. "If you will remember, *habibti*, you ran away." He knew he sounded cold, but he had to. It was that or cave in to the hot emotion in the air—and he wasn't ready for that. He would never be ready for that.

"I did run. And maybe I was wrong, but you share some of the blame, too."

"Yes, I know this." He found the trousers, shoved a leg in first one side and then the other before standing and pulling them up to fasten them.

"That's it?" she said. "You're leaving? You'd rather have sex or walk out than talk to me?"

She sounded bitter. And angry.

"Right now, yes."

She got to her knees in the middle of the bed. He tried not to look at the way the dim light from the lamps limned the silky skin of her breasts. The way it kissed her curves, disappeared in the shadowed cleft between her thighs. She put her hands on her hips, and his gaze shot up to her face, more for self-preservation than anything else.

"You're unbelievable, you know that? You talk about me running away, but what about you? You can't face any conversation that might be about the way you feel."

He stood there, clenching his fists at his sides. Willing himself to be calm and methodic about this. He thought back to his childhood, to those days when he'd longed for someone—*anyone*—to tell him he was loved, valued. Wanted for more than dynastic reasons. For more than reasons that were only about tradition and duty.

His father was proud. He cared for his children in his own way, but he wasn't demonstrative. And his mother…

Malik frowned. His mother had no maternal feelings whatsoever. Children were a duty, something one produced before handing them over to be raised accordingly. She only became interested in him when he was old enough to do what he wanted without recourse.

He'd never talked about his feelings because there was nothing to talk about. No one to talk about them with. Since he'd become a man, he'd heard those three words often—*I love you*—but always from women whose motives he did not trust. Women who wanted to trap him for his wealth and position, not for who he was at heart.

And who was he, really? What great prize was he?

Malik ground his teeth in frustration. "Our relationship didn't break down overnight. I don't imagine it can be fixed overnight, either."

"Relationship? Is that what you call this? I thought it was just sex."

"What do you want from me, Sydney? We've been apart a year. Do you expect a declaration of true love?"

"No," she cried quickly. Too quickly. "That's not what I want. Not what I expect."

And yet he knew she did. She was a woman who was open with her feelings, even when she thought she wasn't. Her every emotion was written on her face. He couldn't be like her, even if he wanted to. He was too used to protecting himself, denying himself.

What happened if he tore down the walls between him and the world? "I'm not sure I can be what you expect," he said. "I can only be what I am."

"How do you know what you can do," she said sadly, "if you won't even talk about it?"

* * *

The next morning, Malik announced they were leaving. Sydney looked up from the tray Adara had just brought in for them, her heart sinking into her stomach.

"But we've only just arrived. I thought you had business to conduct."

Malik's handsome face was studiously blank. "I've done what I needed," he said. "We're moving on to the city of Al Na'ir. You will be more comfortable there."

"And by done what you needed, do you mean enticing me into your bed again?" It was the wrong thing to say, but she couldn't seem to stop herself.

His jaw looked harder than granite. "That was so very difficult to do, wasn't it? No, Sydney, that is not what I mean."

She lifted her chin. No, it hadn't been difficult, just like it hadn't been difficult when she'd met him last year.

"Be ready in an hour," he said. She thought he looked as if he would say something else, but instead he turned and went back outside. Sydney balled her hand into a fist and punched one of the cushions on the couch.

She had no one to blame but herself. She'd known what being with Malik again would mean, and she'd fallen headlong into hedonism anyway.

Her body was still languorous from their intense lovemaking of yesterday. She'd lost track of how many times they'd awakened from a nap to sink into each other again. It had been a day of excess, of pleasure so intense she'd wanted to weep from it.

It had also been a day in which she'd realized that nothing had changed for her. She was still in love with Malik. She'd pushed him to talk, but it hadn't quite been fair of her. Only a few days ago, he'd told her about Dimah, about his family and his relationship with them when she'd asked.

Compared to what they'd talked about before, it had been a lot of revelations in a short span of time. Malik did not open up easily. She knew that, but she'd been feeling so vulnerable after realizing how she still felt about him.

She'd wanted to know he was affected, too. That some part of him wanted more than just sex. The way he'd touched her in the shower, his hand trembling—it had to mean something, didn't it? And after, when he'd been so focused on her pleasure, so determined to make her feel good—what had he said? *I have not forgotten even a moment of making love to you.*

Even now, the words had the power to make her shiver.

She'd been certain he must feel *something*—but Malik was not the sort of man to talk openly about his feelings. He never had been. Sydney bit her lip. She had no idea where things stood between them now. Just because they'd had sex, it didn't mean that everything was grand.

It didn't mean they could leave Jahfar and forget about the divorce. Nor did she want to. She'd given up everything when she'd married him—and then she'd given up her self-respect while she'd waited for him to say he loved her, to contradict what he'd told his brother on the phone.

She would not be so weak again. Loving someone didn't mean you were capable of having a relationship with them, especially if they didn't have the same level of commitment to it as you.

Sydney gathered her things together and shoved them into the small suitcase she'd brought. It wasn't very hard to do so since she hadn't brought a lot. Within the hour, they were in the Land Rover and heading out of the oasis. Sydney turned to look back at the stand of palms with the cool, clear water and the black goat-hair tents arrayed around it. A child stood behind one of the palms, arms wrapped around the tree, watching them go.

Inexplicably, hot tears rose to her eyes. Not because she was going to miss the oasis terribly—she hadn't been there long enough to get attached to it—but the child represented a kind of innocence she would never have again. It was impossible not to be tossed about by the vicissitudes of life when you got older. And impossible not to long for a simpler time when your heart was breaking.

Sydney blinked away the tears as she turned to concentrate on the rolling sand before them. The desert was blinding, but the windows were tinted and helped to cut the glare. Waves of heat rippled in the distance. Malik had the air on, but only barely. She knew it was to keep the engine from overheating.

"How long will it take?" she asked.

Malik shrugged. "About two hours."

They lapsed into silence then. Sydney stared out the window, but her eyes were growing heavy. She hadn't had nearly enough sleep last night. She tried to keep them open, but finally gave up to the inevitable and dozed off.

She awakened with a start, what felt like only a short time later. Something didn't feel quite right. She blinked, sitting up higher. And then she realized—

The Land Rover wasn't moving. And Malik wasn't inside any longer.

In a panic, she grabbed for the door pull and yanked hard. The vehicle sat at an angle that tilted her door down so that it swung wide very quickly when the latch was released.

Sydney barely caught herself before she tumbled onto the sand below.

"Careful," Malik said, and her thudding heart gave a little leap. He hadn't left her.

She closed her eyes. Dear God, she wasn't alone.

"Why did we stop?" she asked, climbing down from the vehicle to join him.

The Land Rover sat in the minimal shade of a giant dune. She glanced up, realizing the sun was still fairly high overhead. It was past its zenith, which meant it was after the noon hour at least.

She brought her gaze back to Malik, her pulse thrumming quickly, her blood pumping hard. She didn't know if it was fear, or the adrenaline from nearly falling into the sand.

Malik leaned against the side of the Land Rover. His head was wrapped and his dark gaze burned steadily as he stared at her.

This couldn't be good....

"We did not stop on purpose, *habibti*. We have broken down."

CHAPTER TWELVE

THE hours passed slowly in the desert. Sydney gazed up at the horizon for the hundredth time, wondering where their rescue was. Malik had told her not to fear because he had a satellite phone and a GPS transmitter. They were not lost, and not unrecoverable.

But they were all alone, and likely would be for some hours yet. There had been a sandstorm to the north, which cut them off from Al Na'ir city. And Al Na'ir city from them.

A hose had broken, and there was no spare. Malik seemed calm enough now, but she knew he would have sworn violently when he realized it.

Yet he'd let her sleep through the whole thing.

Sydney perched on a chair in the sand and made whorls with her foot. It was hot, but not as bad now that the sun had fallen deeper and deeper in the sky. The shadow of the dune was long, and they were in it. Thankfully.

"Drink some water," Malik said, handing her a fresh bottle from the cooler in the back. Not that the water was icy cold, but it had been refrigerated in the oasis and put into a chilled container for their trip.

Sydney unscrewed the top and took a sip. "Will they

come soon?" she asked, wiping her hand across her mouth.

Malik looked toward the horizon. Then he turned back to her. "The truth is that I don't know. It may be morning before anyone can make it."

"Morning?" She tried not to shudder at the thought. A night in the desert. In a Land Rover. Not exactly her idea of a fun vacation.

Malik shrugged. "It will be fine. So long as the storms don't turn south."

"And if they do?"

He speared her with a steady look. "That would be bad, *habibti*. Let us hope they do not."

A few minutes of silence passed between them again. "Malik?"

He turned to look at her. He was every inch a desert warrior, she realized. Tall, commanding and as at home in this harsh environment as he was in the finest tuxedo.

"Yes?"

"Did you spend much time in the desert when you were growing up?"

She thought he might not answer, might consider it too personal in light of their conversation last night, but he nodded slowly. "My father thought that his boys should all understand and fear the desert. We came many times, and when we reached a certain age, we underwent a survival test."

She didn't like the way that sounded. "A survival test?"

He took a drink of his own water. "Yes. We were left at a remote location with a survival pack, a compass and a camel and told to find our way to a certain point. None of us ever failed."

"But if you had?"

"None of us did. If we had, I imagine my father would have sent someone to retrieve us before we died."

Sydney swallowed. She couldn't imagine such a thing. How could you send your own children into danger?

"I don't understand your life at all." It was so foreign to her, so otherworldly. She'd been protected, educated, guided. She'd never been tested.

Perhaps she should have been. If she had been allowed to choose for herself, even if the choice was wrong, then maybe she'd have learned to trust herself more.

"And I don't understand yours," he replied.

She took a deep breath. "Then tell me what you want to know about me. I'm an open book, Malik." Because, if she were open with him, if she were willing to talk, then maybe he would do the same. Maybe they could learn to understand each other. It was a long shot, but she had nothing left to lose.

His gaze grew sharp. Considering. "I want to know why you have no confidence in yourself, Sydney."

Her stomach flipped. "I don't know what you mean. That's ridiculous."

"You do. You work for your parents, at a job you despise, and you think you are not worthy of more. They've taught you that you are not worthy of more."

"I don't despise my job." But her throat was dry, her ears throbbing as the blood pounded in them. "And my parents only want the best for me. That's all they've ever wanted."

She'd attended the finest schools, taken culture and deportment lessons, learned to ride horses, play piano. Her parents had given her everything she needed to be successful.

They were wildly successful, a perfect couple—and

their children would be perfect, too. The perfect Reed family.

"You do despise your job," he said firmly. "You're good at it, but it's not what you want."

Her eyes burned. "How do you know what I want?"

"Because I pay attention. You don't miss your job when you are away. You would rather play with your designs on the computer."

Her pulse was racing, throbbing, aching. "How do you know that? I've never told you that."

"Because I know more than you think, Sydney."

She could only stare at him, wondering. And then it dawned on her.

"You had me watched," she said, her throat suddenly threatening to close up. "You spied on me."

His gaze glittered. "I did have you watched. For your safety, *habibti*. You are my wife, and just because you chose to leave me, that did not mean you would not be of interest to people."

She couldn't believe what she was hearing. And yet it suddenly made terrible sense. She'd always wondered why no one ever bothered her, why the paparazzi left her alone. She was the wife of a renowned international playboy, and no one ever hounded her for pictures or quotes.

She should have known. Anger welled inside her. "You had me watched, but you never called me yourself."

"I have already stated it was so."

"I realize that," she snapped. "It just sounds so unbelievable, even for you. As if picking up the phone and calling me was such a monumental task."

"We have discussed this before," he said evenly. "The answer has not changed since the last time."

Sydney crossed her arms and looked out over the red desert. So much time wasted, and all because of pride. *Both of you*, a little voice said.

"You made sure no one bothered me, didn't you? The paparazzi, I mean."

"Yes."

She thought of the media in L.A., the way they hounded the stars, the way nothing ever seemed to stop them from getting one more picture, a picture they hoped would be embarrassing or shocking enough to earn them big money on the open market. She wasn't a celebrity, but he was. She would have definitely been on their radar for her connection to him alone.

But for Malik's intervention. He should not have been able to do it. But he had.

"How?"

"Money is a strong motivator, Sydney. And power. Never forget power."

She looked down, at the whorls her foot was making in the sand. Emotion threatened to choke her, but she would not let it. He had done it for his own purposes, not for her. She couldn't think it was more than it was.

"Well, okay then." She sucked in a breath, and then another. "But what makes you think I have no confidence? I meet with clients as wealthy as you on a regular basis. And I've sold a lot of real estate. You can't do that without confidence."

"Tell me about your family," he commanded.

She looked at him askance. "Why? What's that have to do with this discussion."

"Humor me."

She folded her hands in her lap, her emotions in riot. "What is there to tell that you don't already know? My parents are passionate about their real estate business and they've built it into one of the most successful firms in L.A. My sister is incredibly smart. She'll take over the business one day, and she'll make it into something even better than it already is."

"And you?"

She ran her tongue over her lower lip. "I'll help her."

"Help." He said it as a statement, not a question. "Why don't you take over? Or why don't you be her partner?"

Sydney rolled her neck. She was beginning to feel like this was the inquisition. And she wasn't enjoying it, regardless that she'd said she was an open book. Apparently she was not so open as she claimed. "I *will* be her partner. That's what I meant."

"But not what you said."

"And your point would be?" She arched an eyebrow, tried her best to look haughty. Hard to do when you were sweaty and tired.

"My point is that you can't think of yourself in control. You think your sister is the better businesswoman—"

"Because she is," Sydney said. "There's no shame in admitting it." Not that it didn't prick her sometimes to think she wasn't the one her parents counted on, but that's just how it was. She was valuable in her own way.

"You told me once that you wanted to study graphic design and art."

"I did?"

"In Paris. Shortly after we were married. We went to dinner at that little café on the Seine, and you told me you had always wanted to design things for people. Websites, logos, advertising."

She remembered now, remembered that night when she'd been drunk on love and tipsy from too much wine. Her entire life had seemed to be waiting for her, a long stretch of time in which everything would be perfect be-

cause she'd married her own Prince Charming. She'd felt
nervous and she'd wanted to impress him, because she
was beginning to realize the import of what she'd done
when she'd married him. He was not simply a man who
happened to have a title. He was a prince in all senses
of the word.

He'd made her feel insignificant, though he'd not said
a word to make her feel that way. It was his presence, his
bearing. The knowledge that she was out of her depth
and would no doubt lose her appeal once he realized
how very boring she was.

"There's nothing wrong with that," she said. "Graphic
design is a legitimate business."

He scoffed. "That's your father talking, trying to form
you into something he can understand. Something he can
approve of." His voice dropped. "But that's not what you
really want, Sydney."

Her heart was pounding, threatening to leap from her
chest. Sweat beaded on her skin, and not from the heat.
Her palms were clammy as she wiped them down the
fabric of her *abaya*.

"I honestly don't know what you're talking about—"

He moved then, grabbed her by the shoulders and bent
so that his face was only inches from hers. "I've been
inside your apartment. I've seen the paintings on your
walls that have your signature. And I watched you in
the Louvre, the Jeu de Paume, the Orangerie. You want
art, Sydney. Beautiful, magical art. It's what you want
to do, whether it's to paint or to simply own a gallery
of your own where you showcase collections you have
selected—"

"No," she cried, pushing him away. "You're wrong!"

"Am I?"

She could only stare up at him, her body hurting with

the truth of what he said, her mind rebelling. It was so…
crazy. There was no money in such a thing, no future.
The paintings on her wall were from a different time in
her life, when she'd still thought she might find a way
to do what she wanted. They had been part of that cultural education she'd received: enough to educate, but
not enough to corrupt.

But she was no one, nothing. How could she dare to
paint, dare to claim she knew art well enough to run a
gallery?

Her parents would be horrified. Alicia would frown
and shake her head. Sydney, flighty Sydney, off on one
of her fantastical mind trips again. Being an imperfect daughter. A disappointing daughter. An *ungrate-
ful* daughter.

She put her face in her hands and took deep breaths.
She would not cry. It was ridiculous to cry. Who got
upset over such a thing? Lots of people worked jobs they
hated in order to pursue the hobbies they loved on the
side.

Except that she'd even denied herself that. She'd never
pursued art, as if it were an abomination to do so.

No. She'd never pursued it because once she started,
she was afraid of where it would lead. Of the obsession
it might become.

The Reed Team needed her. Her parents. Alicia. They
counted on her.

But if that were true, a voice asked, why had she left
them so easily when Malik had asked her to the first
time?

"Sydney." His voice was soft, his hands gentle on her
arms. He pulled her palms from her face.

She sniffled. "It's a fantasy, Malik. I can't afford to be
a starving artist. I don't even know what I would paint."

He smiled then, his hand sweeping wide. "What about this? The dunes are beautiful, are they not?"

"They are." She gripped his arm. "But I haven't painted in years. I'd be terrible."

"Does it matter?"

Did it? Was this really something she could do?

"I—I guess not." What did being terrible matter so long as you enjoyed it? Lots of hobbyists would never be professionals, but that didn't stop them from enjoying their hobbies. "So long as I don't quit my job," she added. She tried to smile, but it shook at the corners.

"Was that so hard to admit? You aren't doing what makes you happy, Sydney. You're doing what makes other people happy. You have to put yourself first for once. Stop caring what they think."

"You make it sound so easy. But it's not, Malik. I still have responsibilities." And the expectations that went with those responsibilities.

"You also have a responsibility to yourself."

Sydney gazed up at the sky. It was growing darker now, and much more quickly than she'd thought it would. "Do you always put yourself ahead of your responsibilities?"

"This is not what I said. You confuse the matter." He took a drink of water from the bottle he held. She watched the slide of his throat, her body heating irrationally as she did so. Everything he did was sexy, and she was like an addict looking for her next fix. It irritated her, especially now.

"What about your arranged marriages? Those were a responsibility, weren't they?"

He leveled his gaze at her. His expression was troubled, but he quickly masked it. "They were. The second one does not trouble me. But the first…"

He shook his head. "I failed miserably when I blamed Dimah for forcing me into it. It wasn't her fault. It was our parents, our tradition. Not her. And if I hadn't been so cruel to her, if I had married her without the bitterness, she would be alive today."

Sydney felt rotten for bringing it up. Why had she done so?

She knew why. Because she was feeling raw, exposed and maybe even a little bit confused. He'd held her over the coals, and she'd wanted to strike back. Except that it wasn't nice. Or fair, in this case.

"I'm sorry, Malik. I shouldn't have brought it up."

He shrugged. "Why not? I have called you to task. It's your turn."

"Yes, but it's painful for you." And she didn't like being deliberately cruel.

He looked severe. "Only because a young girl died. If she had not, I would regret nothing of what I said to her. And I might have been selfish enough to walk out before the marriage was finalized. Or I might have married her and made her miserable."

Sydney sighed. "It's tragic what happened to her. But I can't believe it's completely your fault. Perhaps she was simply unstable. Perhaps she needed help and no one saw it."

"I'm not sure her death was intentional."

Horror threatened to close her throat. "What makes you think so?"

She didn't think he would answer, but then he finally sighed and spoke. "She sent me a text message earlier that day. She claimed she would do something drastic if I didn't call her."

"And did you?"

He turned his head away, gazing into the distance.

And then he shot to his feet, his entire body vibrating with tension.

"What?" Sydney cried, standing and grabbing his arm. "What is it?"

The sky was darker than before. Toward the horizon it was purple—and the purple was growing, spreading upward. Sydney's bones liquefied. That wasn't right at all. Darkness spread from the top down once the sun was behind the horizon. But this…this was like the sky was being swallowed from the bottom up.

Malik turned then and pushed her toward the door to the Land Rover. "Get inside, Sydney. Roll up your window and close the vents."

She did as he instructed, her heart pounding with adrenaline. Malik got in beside her and began to do the same.

"It's a sandstorm, isn't it?" she said, turning to him. Shivering at the size and menace of the thing. She did not know what it was capable of, but she remembered that Malik had said it would be bad if the storm reached them.

He nodded, and then turned to look out the back window at the oncoming darkness. She followed his gaze, her heart sinking. The darkness was coming fast. The sky would soon disappear inside it.

"Will we die?" she asked, feeling suddenly very small.

Malik snapped toward her, his dark gaze hard, intense. Then he cupped her jaw and gave her a swift kiss. "No, we will not die. I promise you, Sydney."

CHAPTER THIRTEEN

"How can you promise that?" she cried.

His jaw hardened, his eyes glittering in the darkness. "Because I have seen this before. We will be fine. But we will be uncomfortable for a while."

She wasn't quite sure she believed him, but she desperately wanted to. Sydney turned to face the front of the car again. Bits of sand flecked against the paint, while ahead of them the sky was still clear. But it wouldn't last long. Soon, they would be buried in sand. Her heart lurched. She hoped they wouldn't *literally* be buried in sand.

Within fifteen minutes, she could barely see the Land Rover's hood. A trickle of sweat slid between her breasts. It was stifling in the confines of the SUV, but not unbearable. And she took comfort in knowing the temperature would cool dramatically in the next hour or so as the sun went down.

"Tell me what's the worst that could happen," she said.

He looked at her, his expression carefully neutral.

"I need to know, Malik."

He nodded. "We could be buried. The dune is close, and depending on the direction of the wind, it could blow onto us, covering us."

Her heart throbbed painfully. "And then what?"

"We try to dig out."

"Oxygen?"

"There are a few bottles packed away. Like hikers use at altitude," he explained.

"So we could survive a while."

"Yes."

Sydney shivered. She hoped it didn't come to that. But her heart wouldn't stop thudding, her stomach churning with dread. She turned to look out the windscreen again. The sand had swallowed them whole, and her stomach fell.

She put her fist to her mouth, chewed on her knuckle. It was an unconscious gesture, but when she realized what she was doing, she didn't stop.

"I called her," Malik said, drawing her attention once more. He sat with one hand on the bottom of the steering wheel, his head leaned back against the headrest.

She hadn't forgotten what they'd been talking about before the storm, but she hadn't thought he intended to answer the question. Though perhaps he was only trying to distract her from the storm. "You did?"

He rolled his head against the seat to look at her. Her insides squeezed at the expression on his face. He was still tormented by what had happened to Dimah. Though it hurt to see him this way, she knew there was nothing she could do to take away the pain.

"I did." His fingers flexed on the wheel. "And I was angry. I told her to stop being so dramatic. I told her there was nothing she could do to make me want our marriage."

Sydney reached out impulsively and put her hand on his. "I'm sorry. I know I keep saying it, but I don't know what else to say."

"There is nothing else to say. I was wrong, and I hurt her." He pressed a thumb and forefinger to his temples. "It was nearly ten years ago and I still feel guilty. I will always feel guilty."

The storm howled over them with even greater force then, stunning her and making her jump as she felt the strength of it against the SUV. Malik did not react, and she took some comfort from the fact. Perhaps it was nothing. When he looked worried, she would worry.

"I think that's very normal," she said, raising her voice to be heard over the wind. "If you didn't feel a little bit guilty, if you didn't think of her at all, you would not be the kind of man you are."

"And what kind of man is that, Sydney?"

She swallowed hard. What could she say? That he was the kind of man she could love? How would that help? "A good man. A man who cares that he hurt someone."

He reached out and caressed her cheek. Her skin prickled from his touch, a trail of fire following in the wake of his fingers. "I hurt you."

She dropped her gaze from his. "Yes."

"It's not what I wanted to do."

"It would have happened eventually," she said, her throat feeling tight.

His fingers stilled. "And what makes you say this?"

Could she tell him? The wind howled around them, the storm buffeting the Land Rover, blocking out most of the light, making her heart pound and her stomach clench. And she thought, *Why not? What is there to lose?*

And then, *We could die out here.*

But she would not die without saying what she needed to say.

She lifted her chin, looked him in the eye. She would

not hide from him. Not now. "Because I loved you, Malik, and you did not love me."

There, she'd said it, and even if she hadn't quite said it properly, she'd told him what was in her heart. It was almost a relief to do so. And terrifying at the same time. What would he say?

He stroked her cheek again, his expression softer than she'd ever seen it. "I cared for you, Sydney," he said. "I still do."

Pain uncoiled a thorny tendril inside her. They could die tonight, no matter what he promised her, and that was all he felt. He *cared*.

It was something, she argued. Something more than he'd ever said before. And yet it left her feeling empty, sad.

"That's not enough," she finally said.

"It's what I have, Sydney. Feelings aren't…easy for me."

She put a hand to her chest, tried to hold in the hurt. "I *need* more. I want more. And if you can't—*couldn't*," she corrected, "give it to me, then I would have been hurt regardless of your intentions."

"I gave you everything I had," he said. "Everything I was capable of."

"Did you?" She laughed, but the sound was harsh. Bitter. "I think it's an excuse, Malik. I think you've spent a lifetime not feeling anything. That your upbringing made you afraid to feel because you were always afraid your feelings wouldn't be returned."

He looked furious—and he looked wild, hunted. As if he wanted to escape.

Knowing she was hitting so close to the mark only spurred her recklessly forward. "Your brother doesn't seem to have a problem with his feelings! Look at him with his wife—"

She stumbled to a halt, her emotions churning, her eyes pricking with angry, frustrated tears. Yes, look at King Adan with his wife. She would give anything to have what they had. She deserved that kind of love. Everyone did.

"My brother is not me." He sounded stiff, formal, and she recognized it for what it was: Malik retreating behind his walls.

"Don't you think I know that?" she cried. She sucked in a shaky breath. "I think you feel, Malik, but I also think you're still punishing yourself for Dimah's death, among other things."

His gaze glittered. "You have no idea, Sydney. You only think you do."

"Then why on earth don't you tell me?" she demanded, hot emotion threatening to overwhelm her. "Tell me, so I know what it is about me that's not good enough for you!"

The words hung in the air between them, heavy and pendulous. Neither of them moved or spoke for a long moment. She hadn't meant to say such a thing, and yet she'd been unable to stop the words from escaping.

Malik swore. And then he reached over and dragged her onto his lap. She pushed against him, tried to escape, but he held her with arms like bands of steel. Her belly was on fire—with shame, with anger, with unbelievable pain. It had hurt to say those words. And if she spoke again, even to tell him to let her go, she was afraid she'd burst into sobs.

Everything was racing out of control. The storm. Her feelings. Her reaction to him. She was tired and frustrated and angry and confused, and so many other things that she couldn't even name them all.

She wanted this to be easier. She wanted to love a man and have him love her in return. Normal. She wanted normal.

Temporarily defeated, Sydney turned her face into his chest, clutched him with her fist. Angry tears leaked down her cheeks.

Though she tried to hide it from him, Malik knew she cried. He reached up, caught a tear on his finger. "Have you ever thought," he said in her ear while she curled against him, silent tears dripping, "that maybe I am not good enough for you?"

Before she could answer, he tilted her chin back, claimed her mouth. Her mind whirled. She didn't intend to soften, didn't intend to kiss him back—but she did. It was inevitable.

What if they died tonight? What if the storm covered them and they never got out?

"You are good enough for a king, Sydney," he whispered harshly. "Never doubt it."

He pillaged her mouth, taking everything she would give him, and still demanding more. They kissed for what seemed like hours but was in fact only minutes. Sydney's body responded as it always did, softening, melting, her sex flooding with moisture and heat. She could feel Malik's response, his erection thickening beneath her thigh. She couldn't help but move against him. She loved to feel the answering hardness there, loved to hear his groan.

He tore his mouth from hers. "Do you want me, Sydney?" His voice broke at the end, a sound so needy and forlorn that it sliced through her defenses.

She'd never known him to sound so uncertain. "Yes," she answered. "Oh, yes."

He stripped her of her clothes until she sat in his lap in nothing but her bra and tiny lace panties. Then he buried his face in her cleavage, inhaling her scent, before slipping the cups off and teasing her breasts into merciless sensitivity. She threw her head back, thrusting her breasts forward for his pleasure.

"It's getting bloody hot in here," Malik said a few moments later.

"You're still wearing all your clothes."

"Indeed."

He managed to shrug out of the *dishdasha*, baring his gorgeous chest. His gaze on her body was so hot, so sensual, that she wondered how she didn't go up in smoke.

He slipped a finger beneath the waistband of her panties, found her wet and ready for him. But instead of removing her panties the usual way, he simply wrapped his fists in one side and tore them open with a swift tug.

"Malik!" It shocked her, that raw power. And thrilled her.

His eyes glowed in the gathering darkness. "I don't want to wait."

Neither did she. He freed himself from his trousers and then she was straddling him, sinking down on top of his glorious hardness. He filled her completely, made her shudder with sheer joy.

"There is nothing like this," he said, his chest rising and falling rapidly, as if he were holding onto control by the barest edge. "Nothing like being with you."

Then he gripped her hips and drove up into her, his thumb sliding across her sensitive bud in rhythm with his thrusts. Sydney threaded her hands into his crisp black hair, tilted his head back and fused her mouth to his, taking him the way he took her.

Relentlessly. Joyfully. Completely.

The pleasure spiraled higher and higher until she broke with it, coming in a long wave that held her in its grip far longer than she expected. It felt so good it almost hurt, and she cried out when it ended.

Malik was still so gloriously hard as he stroked her back with his fingers. "This is what happiness is," he said. "Being with you like this."

He'd never said as much before, but she wanted him to say more. He was as aware of the storm outside as she was, as worried that it might be their last time together. He had to be.

"Oh, Malik," she said. "Don't you understand it by now?"

In answer, he claimed her mouth roughly. And then he was driving into her again, stoking her body to incredible heights once more. At the last possible moment, he slipped his hand between them, found her again. Sydney flew over the edge with a cry that was torn from her throat.

A cry that sounded suspiciously like "I love you!"

Malik pulled her down to him, kissed her hard as he found his release in her body. His hips thrust into hers until he was spent, and then his kiss turned tender, gentle. As if he were a storm that had spent its fury and was now caressing the very land it had ravaged.

Sydney's pulse pounded in her ears. She knew what she'd said, what she'd been unable to keep inside. The emotion was so strong, buffeting her as much as the storm buffeting the Land Rover. She felt raw, exposed.

Malik pushed her damp hair from her face. "That was amazing," he said. "Thank you."

"Is that all?" she asked, her heart flipping in her chest, her throat aching from the giant knot forming inside.

His brows drew down. "What do you wish me to say, *habibti*?"

That was the moment, she thought, when her heart shattered into a million pieces. They were caught in a deadly storm, possibly permanently, and Malik felt nothing beyond supreme sexual satisfaction.

"Did you hear what I said to you?"

He swallowed, the only visible reaction. "I did. And I am happy for it." He stroked the underside of her breast. "But they are only words. Actions mean much more than words, don't you think?"

Sydney reared back. "The words are nice, too, Malik. Sometimes, the words are necessary."

"Anyone can say those words," he said. "It does not make them true."

"They are true for me."

He closed his eyes. "Sydney. Please, not now."

She climbed off him and gathered her clothes, hurriedly slipping into them again. "When? When is the right time? Or are you hoping we don't live through the night and then we never have to talk?"

His expression grew chilly. "Don't be dramatic."

"Dramatic? I said I love you and that's dramatic?" Her eyes stung with emotion. With pain. He wanted to marginalize her feelings for him and she hated it.

He jerked his trousers closed. "Do you want me to say I love you, Sydney?" His eyes flashed, his chest heaving as he stared at her. "Would that make you happy?"

He leaned forward and caught her chin, forced her to look at him. "I love you," he said, though it came out as a growl. "Is that what you want to hear?"

She pushed his hand away and huddled near the door

as the sand pelted the SUV. "No," she said to the glass. "Because you don't mean it."

His laugh was hollow. "And you said the words were important."

The storm howled for several hours, and the temperature dropped so that it was no longer so hot inside the Land Rover. A battery-powered lantern burned softly in the dark. Sydney stole a glance at Malik. He lay back against the seat, his eyes closed. His chest was still bare. But then so was hers, with the exception of her bra. It had been too hot to remain wrapped in her clothes, so she'd slipped the garment off again.

It was growing more comfortable now. Almost chilly.

Sydney reached for the fabric she'd discarded and slipped into it. Malik stirred then, his dark eyes snapping open as if he'd not been sleeping. He took in her form, and then peered out the window. She tried to pretend the lack of emotion in his gaze didn't bother her.

"The storm is nearly over," he said, his voice rough with sleep. "Soon, we may open the windows again."

"That's good," Sydney replied crisply, though she wouldn't feel any true relief until the air cleared and they could see the sky.

"You are okay?" Malik asked.

"I'm fine," she said, her voice a bit sharp.

He blew out a breath. "I'm sorry," he said. "I did not mean to hurt you."

Sydney shrugged. "It doesn't matter, Malik."

He subsided into silence again, and she felt hot and prickly all over. Not from heat, but from frustration and embarrassment. She'd confessed her stupid, naive feelings for him—and he'd thrown them back in her face. It mattered more than she would ever admit.

Sydney turned toward the window, pillowing her head on her hands, and closed her eyes. She hadn't been able to sleep yet, but maybe she would if she kept trying. She didn't feel like she had them closed for long before Malik spoke her name.

"Yes?" She blinked at him, yawning. Maybe she had slept after all.

"The storm has passed. I need to try your door, Sydney."

"My door?"

"Mine will not open. The sand is holding it closed."

Her anxiety spiked. What if they were trapped? Oh, God...

"Let me," she said firmly, needing to do something. "I'm right here."

He hesitated only a moment before nodding. "You must be careful. First, let the window down very slowly, just a fraction." He turned the key in the Land Rover, and she pressed the button. Thankfully, there was enough power to do the job. Sand flooded into the window the moment she had it open and she automatically pressed it back up again.

"No, let it down once more. If the sand lessens, that is a good sign."

"And if it keeps pouring in?"

"Then we have a problem," he told her. She liked that he didn't lie, but at the same time, she'd almost rather not know.

She pressed her face to the glass, shading her eyes. "But I can see darkness out this window. I think. If it were covered in sand, wouldn't I be able to see it?"

"Yes, but if the dune is unstable, it could collapse and send sand over us. What came in the window is from above. But I don't know how much is on top of us."

Great.

Sydney took a deep breath and tried the window again. The sand poured in once more, but it lessened very quickly until there was nothing more coming in. Though she was sitting, her knees wobbled.

"Roll it down farther and stick your hand out. Carefully. See if you can feel sand."

She did as he asked, reaching down and trying to touch the ground with her fingertips. "I don't feel anything."

Malik let out a breath. "Good. Now let me try. My arms are longer."

He leaned over her, his bare chest a fraction of an inch from her face. Sydney closed her eyes and tried not to breathe as Malik tested the sand. A moment later, he opened the door. Relief puddled inside her as it swung gently outward.

"We aren't trapped," she said. "But how is that possible when the sand was pouring in?"

"It came from the roof. Now climb out very carefully, then tell me what you see."

Sydney slipped out of the SUV. The ground was a lot closer than it had been, and she stumbled when she hit. The cold air washed over her, sending goose bumps crawling across her skin. Above, the sky was clear, the stars winking down in the billions.

But the Land Rover...

She shivered. "It's half-buried," she said. "Your side." And more than his side. Three quarters of it was hidden by sand, in fact. She could see where the sand had slid from the roof and into her window. It hadn't been a whole lot, she realized now, but it had seemed like it at the time.

Malik crawled out to join her. He studied the scene for a long moment. The Land Rover looked like one of those Michelangelo sculptures, the ones that were never finished and looked as if they were trying to break free of the rock. Only a portion of it showed—the passenger side—while the rest was buried beneath tons of sand.

"We were lucky, *habibti*," Malik said quietly.

She wrapped her arms around her body. "We could have died, couldn't we? If it had lasted just a while longer…"

He turned to her, his expression fierce. "It did not. And we are well."

"The power of it," she marvelled. It was staggering. She was trapped in the middle of a vast desert with Malik. They were so small, so inconsequential. Their problems were nothing out here.

"The desert is not a place for amateurs."

She huffed in a breath. "Doesn't it bother you at all? That we could have died?"

"We did not," he said roughly. "And we will not. I promised you that."

"Don't you *feel* anything?" Angry tears sprang into her eyes and she dashed them away with the back of her hand.

He was looking at her, his expression sadder than she'd ever seen it. "Yes. I feel regret, Sydney."

Her blood slowed in her veins. "Regret?"

"I should never have brought you to Jahfar."

Inexplicably, his words pricked her. "You had to. We have to be together until we can get the…the divorce," she finished, stumbling over the words.

He shook his head. His jaw was hard, his eyes bright. "I'm letting you go."

She was confused. "But the forty days—"

"A lie."

* * *

She looked at him as if he'd grown another head. "A lie?"

"An exaggeration," he said. "The law was a real one, but Adan and his government changed it in their reforms. It was written at a time when our society was more feudal, and it was intended to give some protections to women. A former queen talked her husband into writing the law when her sister was wedded, bedded and repudiated in the space of two days. I believe there was a war over the incident, in fact."

"Why?" she asked. She was beginning to tremble, but whether from the cold or from anger he couldn't say. "Why did you do it?"

He slashed a hand through the air. "Because I had to," he said. "Because you walked out on me and I was angry."

"You lied to get revenge?"

No, that was not at all what he'd done. But he couldn't say the words, no matter how he tried. He couldn't tell her that he'd needed her to come back to him. That he'd needed *her*.

Because it was dangerous to need people. If you needed people, they could wound you. Stab you in the heart.

"No, it was not revenge." He reached into the Land Rover to retrieve the satellite phone. It should work now that the storm had passed.

"I don't understand you," she said.

He turned to her. "I believe we have already established that we do not understand one another."

Her stormy eyes flashed. "I had to rearrange my entire life to come to Jahfar."

"You are my wife, Sydney. You agreed to do this when you wed me."

It wasn't a good enough reason, but nothing of what

he'd done when he'd gone to Los Angeles had made sense to him at the time. He'd gone because he'd known she was meeting with an attorney.

But he had not known what he would do when he went to the house in Malibu that night.

"Yes, but that was before you called me a mistake! Before I knew that you wished you had not married me."

Malik hissed. Of all the stupid things he could have done, that had been right at the top, regardless that she'd never been meant to hear it. Because he knew she was the youngest child, that she felt like an underachiever next to her sister, and that she didn't believe in herself as much as she should. He'd known it all because she'd told him, whether she'd intended to or not.

She was strong and beautiful and loyal, and she usually put her family's needs and feelings before her own. She hadn't been accustomed to doing something solely for herself. He was convinced that marrying him in Paris had been the most rebellious thing she'd ever done.

Not that her parents had objected to that event. When they'd discovered their daughter had married a foreign prince, they'd been enthusiastic.

Too enthusiastic. He'd never told her, but they'd wanted to throw a huge party for her and Malik when they returned to California—and invite all their firm's clients. He'd put an end to that scheme, determined they would not use their daughter's marriage as an opportunity to pump up their business. If the party wasn't to celebrate Sydney's happiness, then it wasn't happening under his watch.

"I have explained this to you," he said stiffly. "I will not do so again."

Because it made him angry to think of it. Of what he'd said, of her listening outside the office door. It had not been his finest moment, even if his intentions had not been bad.

She swallowed hard and he knew she was determined not to cry. He did not make the mistake of thinking that she cried out of weakness. It was anger, pure and simple.

"You brought me out here for nothing," she said. "And worse, you made me—"

She pressed a hand over her mouth, turned away from him. He couldn't bear it, couldn't bear that he'd upset her. He grasped her shoulders, turned her into his arms. She balled up her fist and hit him in the chest, but it wasn't hard and he didn't let her go.

She hit him again, and he only held her tighter. She wasn't trying to hurt him. She was furious, hurt. And he deserved it. He deserved everything she did to him.

Her voice drifted up to him, muffled from where she'd pressed her face against his clothing. "You made me love you again, Malik. I would have been fine if you'd just given me a divorce and left me alone, but you had to drag me into your life again. I was almost free of you."

He stroked her hair, held her against his heart. "I am going to let you free. If it's what you still want."

Perversely, he hoped she would say no—but he'd given her no reason to do so. Even now, he couldn't seem to find the words to tell her he wanted her to stay.

She didn't say anything for a long moment. "Yes," she said, so softly he had to strain to hear. "Yes, it's what I want."

CHAPTER FOURTEEN

Los Angeles was a whirlwind of color, light and sound compared to the desert of Jahfar. She dreamed of the Maktal Desert sometimes, of the deep umber sand, sky like the finest sapphires and the blinding white sun.

But mostly she dreamed of a man. Sydney stood at her kitchen counter after a long day at work, eating takeout from a container and trying not to think about Malik. It wasn't working. She set the container down and put her head in her hands.

Why did she dream of Malik after all he'd done? It had been a month since she'd left Jahfar. He had called her once. They'd spoken for a few minutes, but the conversation was stiff and uncomfortable for them both.

When it had ended, she knew he wouldn't call again. She stared at her cell phone lying on the counter, considered calling him instead. She missed him, missed his smile, his seriousness, the way he held her and caressed her while they made love. The way he looked at her when he told her that happiness was being with her.

Sydney sniffed. She felt tight inside, as if she'd swallowed too many emotions that were fighting to get out. But she had to shut them down, didn't she? Because if she let herself feel the pain, she might lie in bed for the rest of her life.

It was going to take time. A lot of time.

She thought wistfully of the small artist set she'd bought in an art store over the weekend. She'd been too embarrassed to ask for help, as if she were doing something elicit, so she'd bought a kit that promised it contained all the paints and brushes she needed to get started.

She had yet to open it. It was tucked away in her guest room, her own guilty little secret.

Tonight. Tonight she would open it. She might not remember how to paint a tree or a flower, but she would try. At least she would try.

Art and work could coexist. Malik had been right that she needed to do something for her. That she needed to put herself first sometimes.

She'd done that when she'd left Jahfar, though it was the hardest thing she'd ever done.

She'd had no idea how quickly it would happen, but as soon as their rescuers had arrived in the desert, Malik had put her in one of the four cars and told the driver to take her to his home in Al Na'ir. She could still see his dark eyes, the way he'd looked at her when she'd climbed into the car that would take her away from him. He'd seemed resigned.

A second car had followed, but Malik stayed behind with the others. It was the last time she'd seen him. She'd bathed and changed in Al Na'ir, and then she was on a plane to Port Jahfar. Once there, Malik's private jet had whisked her out of the country before she could even catch her breath.

Her doorbell rang. The sound made her jump, her heart leaping into her throat.

Malik.

Was it possible? Had he come for her this time? She

pushed her hair from her face, straightened her skirt and hurried to the door, her heart pounding a million miles a minute.

But when she looked through the peephole, it wasn't Malik. Her sister stood on the other side, her head down so that Sydney couldn't see her face. Sydney undid the locks, disappointment spiraling inside her. She didn't really want to talk to anyone just now, especially not someone in a happy relationship.

But she couldn't pretend she wasn't home when it was her sister standing there. It wouldn't be right.

"Thank God you're here," Alicia said when Sydney pulled the door open.

Sydney blinked. Alicia was a mess. Her mascara ran down her face, her hair uncharacteristically mussed. Her entire body trembled, from the roots of her hair to the tips of her fingers. "Oh, my God, what happened?" Sydney exclaimed.

Alicia's lip quivered. "I—I just need to come in for a while. Can I?"

"Of course!" Sydney stepped back and let her sister in, then slotted the locks back into place. She hadn't been thinking straight since the moment she'd thought it might be Malik.

And seeing Alicia looking so upset had temporarily stunned her. Alicia was never anything less than poised.

Alicia went and sat on the couch. Then she doubled over and began to sob. Alarm raised the hairs on the back of Sydney's neck. She rushed to her sister's side and hugged her close.

"My God, Alicia, what is it? Did something happen to Jeffrey?"

That only made Alicia sob harder. Then she looked up and Sydney noticed it for the first time: Alicia's eye was red, as if someone had hit her. Soon, it would turn black and blue, but for now it was a blazing, ugly red.

A sharp feeling of panic sliced into her, turned her into a babbling idiot. "Honey, were you attacked? Should we call the police? Where's Jeffrey?"

Stop, a little voice said. *She needs you to be calm.*

It was shocking to think that Alicia needed her. But she did. Somehow Sydney managed to stop gibbering and simply hugged her tighter. "Just tell me when you're ready, okay?"

"It's Jeffrey," Alicia whispered a few moments later, her lip trembling. "He hit me."

The bottom fell out of Sydney's stomach. "He hit you? But he loves you so much!"

Alicia flinched. "He doesn't, Syd. He really doesn't. Jeffrey only loves himself." She stood and began to pace the room, shredding the tissue she'd dragged from her purse.

Sydney was having trouble processing everything—Alicia's eye, the ugly things her sister was saying—but she knew one thing for certain. "We need to call the police," she said firmly. Because no way in hell was that bastard getting away with this.

No way in hell!

"I can't," Alicia said, halting. Her eyes were wide, her lip trembling anew. "I can't. Everyone will think I'm so stupid. Mom and Dad will be so disappointed in me—"

Sydney shot to her feet and went to put an arm around her sister. "It's okay, Alicia. No one will think that. Everyone knows how smart you are."

Alicia's laugh contained a note of hysteria. "Sydney. Smart women don't stay with men who beat them."

Ice settled in the pit of her stomach. "This wasn't the first time?"

Alicia shook her head. "No."

"Sit down, tell me everything." Sydney guided Alicia to the couch and went to get her a cold drink from the refrigerator. Alicia was a health nut, but Sydney settled on a syrupy sweet soft drink with a slice of lemon anyway. Because sometimes you needed something sweet.

Alicia took the drink and sipped at it. They spent the next hour talking before Sydney persuaded her to go to the police. First she'd had to convince Alicia that she wasn't stupid, that men like Jeffrey were insidious. They took control subtly, and then not so subtly.

Sydney finally got Alicia down to the car and drove her to the police station.

It turned into a long night: the police interviewed Alicia, took her statement and swore out a warrant for Jeffrey's arrest. When it was done, Sydney brought Alicia back to her apartment and tucked her up in the guest room.

Sydney poured a glass of wine and sat on the couch. She was numb, absolutely numb. She'd been so wrong. About everything. She'd thought that Jeffrey was in love with Alicia, that the reason her sister never had time for lunches or girls' nights out or anything else was because she was so happy. But instead, Jeffrey had been controlling her. He flew into rages when she wasn't available to him. He had to know where she was at all times. He didn't want her to talk to anyone, not even her family. He was jealous of her time with anyone else.

And then he hit her. When his rage subsided, he cried and swore he would never do it again, that he loved her so much and would never hurt her.

Jeffrey spoke the words, but he did not mean them.

Words mean nothing. Actions do. That's what Malik had told her, what he believed.

Her heart throbbed with feeling. Maybe she'd been too stupid to see the truth. She'd been so focused on the words that she'd not paid as much attention as she should to the actions. Why had he taken her to Jahfar when it wasn't necessary in the first place?

She was still angry over that. Angry that he'd manipulated her. If he'd wanted to try to fix their relationship, why hadn't he just said so?

Sydney rubbed the back of her neck to try and ease the tension. *Had* he wanted to fix the relationship? Was that why he'd dragged her to Jahfar? Taken her out to the oasis?

Malik was an amazing man. Confident and sure, with the looks and the money to do whatever he wanted in life. Was he truly that insecure that he couldn't come out and say what he wanted from her?

Or maybe it wasn't insecurity. She thought of the night she'd gone to dinner at the palace. How formal and distant Malik and his brother were, like business associates rather than family.

And the next morning, when his mother had been in the dining room, berating him for marrying a foreigner. There'd been no feeling there, no connection other than a bloodline and the tolerance that went with that relationship. Malik did not like his mother as a person, though Sydney thought that he must be fond of her in some way. He'd defended her treatment of him as a child by pointing out that she'd been a child herself. A naive, lonely child who'd turned into a shallow and bitter woman.

Malik wasn't insecure. But he had, Sydney was certain, lacked love in his life. His mother was not the sort to hug her children and tell them she loved them.

Shame flooded her. What an idiot she'd been. She was too stubborn, too insistent on playing the wounded party. She ran away and then waited for a call that never came, convincing herself that she wasn't good enough. Wasn't important or special or loved. She was making it all about her when in fact it was about them as a couple. How they dealt with each other. How they understood— or failed to understand—each other.

She was behaving like a child, as Malik had accused her of doing. And she'd done it again that day in the desert when he'd told her he'd lied about the law. She'd been so hurt and betrayed that when he'd asked if she wanted to leave, she'd said yes. She'd paid no attention to the way he was holding her, to the fact he was actually admitting what he'd done and offering her freedom if that's what she wanted.

She still wasn't sure that meant he loved her, but it might be a start. And she was a fool for sitting here and nursing her wounded feelings when she should be calling him and trying to see if there was any way they could build something lasting together.

She loved him, damn it, and you didn't abandon the people you loved. Even when you thought they were abandoning you.

Love is not love, which alters when it alteration finds, or bends with the remover to remove.

Shakespeare had been a wise, wise man.

Sydney snatched up her phone and found Malik's number. Her finger trembled as it hovered over the call button. But then she punched it and waited as the connection was made, her heart hammering in her chest, her throat, her temples.

Please be there. Please.

But he wasn't. The phone rang several times before going to voice mail. Sydney hesitated, not knowing what to say. In the end, she clicked off the line without saying a word. Disappointment gnawed at her. She would call back. She would leave a message. But first she tried to compose what she should say, what sort of message she should leave for him.

The words wouldn't come.

Words mean nothing.

Sydney groaned. Just when they meant everything, at least to her, she couldn't find the right ones to save her life. Maybe Malik was right. Actions were more important.

The next few days were a blur. Sydney tried Malik a few more times, when she had a spare moment, but he never answered. Panic began to coil inside her. What if he was finished with her forever? What if his silence was deliberate?

Fortunately, her sister was doing better. Alicia had gone to their parents' home, more because they'd insisted than because she'd wanted to, and she'd gotten a restraining order against Jeffrey. Work was crazy without Alicia and their mother, who had stayed at home to dote on her daughter twenty-four hours a day.

Sydney's father was handling it well, but he'd been shell-shocked by the news. He still came to the office, but he seemed to need her to handle many more things than she ever had before. It was both surprising and frustrating. Surprising because she'd never realized how much he trusted her, and frustrating because she'd bought a ticket to Jahfar.

A ticket she was never going to use at this rate.

But within a week, Alicia and their mother were both back at work. Alicia's eye was covered with heavy makeup, but she moved as briskly and efficiently through her tasks as always. No one said anything about Jeffrey.

Sydney sat at her desk and clicked on an email from her mother. A potential new listing in Malibu. Her heart skipped a beat, but the address wasn't the same one as the home she'd sold to Malik. It was two doors down. She thought about going to her mother's office and asking if someone else could take the appointment, but she decided against it. She would get through today, and then she would catch the late flight to Jahfar.

She simply couldn't put it off another minute. The Reed Team was a well-oiled machine, even if they'd had a hiccup recently. Her father had relied on her, and she was grateful, but it hadn't been necessary. The other agents and lawyers took up the slack and made everything run efficiently. She could escape for a few days at least.

When she told Alicia what she was planning, her sister merely hugged her and wished her good luck.

"You don't mind if I go?" Sydney asked.

"Of course not." Alicia squeezed her hand. "I'm fine, and I want you to go. Go get that prince of yours before some other woman snaps him up."

Sydney shuddered at the thought.

"But you are going out to Malibu later, right?" Alicia asked from the door of Sydney's office. "I don't think anyone else is available, and Mom says it's an important listing."

"I'm going," Sydney said. "There's enough time."

Alicia seemed relieved. "Good."

Once Alicia was gone, Sydney's mind began to race with everything she needed to do before she boarded the plane tonight. She had a meeting with a client at three, and then she would drive to Malibu. Once she toured the home and took the listing details, she'd have just enough time to dash home and throw some things together before heading to the airport.

Her stomach churned. What if Malik wasn't in Jahfar? She had no idea whether or not he was, but she knew where he lived and she knew that when she arrived he would be alerted. And then he would return, and she would tell him she was a fool.

And she would pray it wasn't too late.

Around five-thirty, Sydney parked her car in the driveway of the Malibu home. The house Malik had bought was just up the street. She'd passed it coming in. There'd been no activity, no cars in the drive. Not that she'd expected there would be. She fully expected Malik would sell the home in the next few months.

But it did have a gorgeous view. It was the kind of home she'd have bought if she'd had Malik's money. A dream home. She could almost picture the two of them enjoying the sunset...and then enjoying each other. A flash of heat rocketed through her at the thought. Right now, the possibility of being with Malik again seemed remote and unreal.

But she was determined to try.

Sydney grabbed her briefcase and straightened her skirt before walking up the stairs to the door. She'd chosen a long sea-green sundress today and paired it with a white bolero sweater and low-heeled sandals. She would have to change into something a bit warmer for the long flight to Jahfar.

Excitement bubbled in her veins. And fear. What if Malik turned her away? What if he was through dealing with a childish wife? What if he was the one who wanted to move on now?

Sydney shook her head. No, she would not think like

that. She would take the frightening leap and let everything happen as it may.

Sydney punched the doorbell, pasting on her best smile as she did so. The door jerked open. A dark-haired man stood in the entry, his presence making her nearly jump out of her skin.

She blinked, certain she wasn't seeing him right. But no, he looked like Malik. Except he wasn't Malik. He was tall, golden-skinned. His chiseled features were familiar, and not familiar. Handsome, like an Al Dhakir male.

Her heart began to pound.

"Hello, Sydney," he said in a distinctly Jahfaran accent. "I am Taj."

"I…" She swallowed, blinked again. He must have thought she was an idiot. "I'm pleased to meet you," she said at last, though her throat was as dry as the Maktal Desert.

Taj smiled. He was, of course, breathtaking. "I have heard a lot about you," he said, golden-voiced, golden-skinned, golden-smiled.

"You have?"

"Naturally. My brother talks of little else."

She stopped in the spacious entry. Tears of relief pricked the corners of her eyes as her pulse thundered out of control. "Malik? Is he here?"

Taj tucked her hand into his arm and started toward the terrace. "Why don't you come and see for yourself?"

Taj led her across a cavernous living room decorated all in white and onto the terrace. A profusion of flowers bloomed in containers, their bright colors framing the golden beauty of the man standing near the pool. Behind him, the ocean glistened in the late afternoon sun. Seagulls swooped in the distance, their piercing cries carrying on the currents.

Sydney's heart turned over. Malik wore a tuxedo, of all things, and his hands were shoved into the pockets of his trousers. She wanted to rush into his arms, and yet she was paralyzed. She'd tried to find him for days, and here he was. Right here. So close to her and yet so far.

"If you will excuse me," Taj said, "I must change clothes."

Sydney nodded, but her throat had closed up and she couldn't speak. Words, how silly. Who needed words? She couldn't think of anything to say, even if she could manage to force the words out.

Malik's gaze flickered behind her. He nodded once, and then focused his attention on her again. His dark eyes were hot, intense. She loved the way he looked at her. She loved him.

But did he love her?

And yet she was so relieved he was here, because she hadn't been sure she would actually see him again. What if he'd turned her away without seeing her first?

But here he was. Her beloved. Her handsome, handsome husband. Emotion welled in her.

He crossed the distance between them and stopped. She'd thought he was going to put his arms around her, but they remained at his side. She ached for him to touch her, to speak. Her skin was so tight, so confining. She wanted to slip into him, become a part of him.

She wanted his heat and his power the way she'd had it in the desert. Her dress suddenly felt too hot, in spite of the breeze coming off the ocean. She wanted to strip. Right here, right now. She wanted so many things, and she had no idea where to start—or if he'd want to hear any of it.

"It's good to see you again, Sydney," Malik said, his voice caressing her name so sweetly. The way he'd caressed her body. The way she wanted him to caress her body again.

"I bought a ticket," she blurted. Oh, God, where did that come from? Why had she said that? But her brain was refusing to function right. He was here, and she wanted to tell him everything, wanted to spill all her secrets and feelings and hope he felt the same.

He looked puzzled. "A ticket?"

She closed her eyes briefly. Clutched her briefcase. She needed something solid, something to remind her this was real. "To Jahfar," she said, feeling embarrassed and stupid and ridiculous all at once. "I leave tonight."

"Ah, I see. That will be a shame."

"A shame?"

He reached out, his fingers ghosting over her cheek. She tried to lean into the caress, but it was too fleeting to do so. "I had hoped you would attend a party with me."

"A party?" She looked down at her clothes. "I—I'm not dressed for a party."

"I took the liberty of picking something out for you," he said softly.

Sydney swallowed. This was crazy. Nothing made sense, and once more he wasn't saying anything she understood. A party?

"What kind of party is it?" she asked, her throat aching with all she wanted to say. All she didn't know how to say.

"It's for us. It's a celebration."

Her pulse tripped along at the speed of light. If she

kept feeling so many emotions, she was going to explode from the strain. "What are we celebrating?"

He smiled, and her belly lurched. Then he slipped an arm around her, pulled her in close. She tilted her head back to look up at him. Her grip on the briefcase loosened as he took it in one hand and tossed it onto a chair.

His sensual lips curved. "I know it is presumptuous of me, but I had hoped we could celebrate our marriage. Our lives together. Our happiness."

A tear slipped down her cheek. "Malik—"

He put a finger over her lips. His heat seared her. Her body responded to his touch as if it had been starved for him. She felt liquid inside, fluid. Hot.

"Let me speak. This is hard for me, *habibti*. I am not accustomed to speaking of feelings." His golden skin flushed, a muscle in his cheek jumping. But his eyes… his eyes were filled with things she'd never noticed before.

"Words are cheap. Words are meaningless. And yet I know there is value in them, when they are sincere. I've heard many cheap, meaningless words in my life. It has made me immune to words, perhaps. To my detriment, at least where you are concerned."

He drew in a sharp breath. "I did not say what I should have said to you, and I have regretted that. I should have told you that my world went dark when you left it a year ago. That my pride kept me from coming after you when I should have. That I let too much time pass because I kept hoping you would come back to me. How could you not come back to me? I am Prince Malik Al Dhakir."

He was mocking himself. She put a hand over his mouth to stop him. She didn't like hearing him speak that way. "Don't, Malik. Don't berate yourself. We've both done stupid things. I should have never run the way

I did. I was a child, as you said. I was impulsive and stupid."

He smiled then. "I like you when you're impulsive."

"How could you? I behaved like an idiot."

"But you also married me in one of those impulsive moments. Unless, of course, you think that was a stupid move. And I wouldn't blame you if you did."

She shook her head. Then she looked down, at where her palms rested on his lapels. The fabric of his tux was soft, expensive. He smelled expensive, looked expensive. So regal, so handsome.

And she was so plain. Plain Sydney Reed.

He tilted her chin up. "Stop that, Sydney."

"Stop what?"

"Thinking you aren't good enough."

"That's not what I was thinking." But she was, of course. She dropped her forehead to his chest. "I'm working on it, Malik. It's a lifetime habit and I can't change it overnight."

"Listen to me, Sydney." She looked up again, her breath catching at the intensity in his gaze. "You are the finest person I know. The kindest, gentlest and least selfish. I want to be with you. I want you in my life, today and always. But it won't always be easy. You have met my mother. She will not change her mind about you, but know that I don't care. I only ever cared for the way you would feel to know this, not because I was embarrassed or ashamed or regretful of *you*."

Everything he said made her heart swell. "Your mother doesn't bother me. So long as you want me, I could care less what she thinks." She bit her lip. "You do want me, right? You want to be married to me?"

He looked slightly exasperated. "Have I not said this?"

Sydney laughed softly. "I'm just double-checking."

"What is there to check? I have told you how I feel, what I want. What I have always wanted."

She reached up and ran her fingers along his jaw. There was more she needed to know, though it didn't change the way she felt about him. "Why did you marry me, Malik? Was it to get out of another arranged marriage? Was I the most convenient choice? Or was it something more?"

He looked suddenly fierce. The breeze whipped up then, ruffling his hair. She ached to smooth it, but did not do so.

"I did not want to marry my mother's choice, no. But I am far too old for her to truly be able to force me to do something I do not want."

"But your brother—"

"Even a king cannot force a marriage if both parties do not agree."

She felt as if a great weight had been lifted, as if there were no longer anything holding her down and she would fly away on a current of joy and happiness if Malik did not keep his arms around her.

"I love you, Malik. That's what I was coming to Jahfar to say. And I know you care for me. I know because of the things you do, not because of the words you say. I completely understand now."

"I'm not quite sure you do," he said softly. "But I intend to show you." And then he bent and kissed her, his mouth hot and possessive and so sexy it hurt.

She wound her arms around him, arched into him, her body greedy for him. He held her hard, tilting her head back as he kissed her so thoroughly she knew she would never be the same again. She wanted to rip his tuxedo off, get to the golden skin and smooth muscles beneath. She wanted to work her way down his body, take him in her mouth and then work her way back up again.

She wanted him inside her. She wanted to sleep curled up with him, and wake in his arms. She wanted to eat with him, laugh with him, be in the same room with him even if they weren't doing or saying anything.

"Ahem."

Malik squeezed her to him, his tongue delving into her mouth one more time before setting her away from him. Taj stood in the entry, looking resplendent in a tuxedo. He grinned, a brow arching in good humor.

"So you have decided to forgive my idiot brother, Sydney? This is very good, as he would have been embarrassed to arrive at the party alone."

"Taj," Malik warned.

Sydney laughed. "I think there are two idiots here, but yes, we're going to the party together."

"Wonderful," Taj said. "Then shall we move along? Sydney needs to change, and our chariot awaits."

CHAPTER FIFTEEN

EVERYTHING went perfectly, though perhaps it should not have. Malik was very aware that he'd not said quite everything to her that he needed to say. He was still choking when it came to baring his heart, to stripping it raw and giving her the power to slay him.

He'd told her the truth, that he needed her and desired her and that his life was hell without her. But that wasn't the extent of it. It was more than that. Deeper and more beautiful than he'd ever imagined.

He was a headstrong man. It had taken him far too long to admit to himself just why he needed her in his life. He'd been in love with her almost from the beginning. Not from the first moment, of course. Then he'd only wanted to get her naked. He didn't apologize for it.

But somewhere along the way, she'd become vital to him. He'd known it deep down, even while he'd talked himself into thinking that he enjoyed her company and wanted her with him because she didn't demand anything from him.

She'd been fresh and innocent in a way he'd never been, and he'd been drawn to her. From the first moment they made love, he'd felt the connection to her. She had felt it, too. That's what had made them both so reckless.

He'd feared losing her, so he'd married her. And she had feared losing him, so she ran away when she thought she might. What a pair they made.

He watched her across the room. She was so beautiful and vibrant. She glowed with life and happiness. He'd thought, when he'd let her go in the desert, that he would never see her again.

She looked up and caught his eye, smiled that smile that drove him crazy for her. It was as if she smiled only for him, her eyes lighting, her entire face glowing with love.

Love. It was real, her love. He'd never been loved before, but now that he had, he wasn't ever letting a day go by without rejoicing in that love. Basking in it.

His eyes skimmed over her, over the claret silk dress he'd picked. It was strapless, skimming her curves like a lover, glimmering like the stars on a clear desert night. She'd pinned her hair up, revealing the graceful column of her neck. Driving him wild.

He wanted to bite her. Gently, teasingly, making her moan and beg while he primed her body with his mouth and hands.

The hotel he'd chosen for the party was very exclusive, very *riche*. Their guests ate hors d'oeuvres, sipped champagne and laughed like they were having a good time. Soft light illuminated the room, caressed the form of the woman he loved. He couldn't take his eyes off her. Sydney stood near her sister, her arm looped in Alicia's, smiling at something the gentleman talking to them said.

A hard rush of anger filled him when he thought of what Sydney had told him about her sister's boyfriend. Malik had already made a call. Jeffrey Orr would never bother Alicia again. As much as it disgusted Malik to do so, he'd made sure the man got a job transfer he couldn't refuse. He should be in the bottom of a prison cell, but instead he was getting a pay raise in a new location halfway around the world.

Malik would keep tabs on him, though. If he tried to harm another woman, he would find himself in the bottom of a cell. Because the country he was going to was a lot more intolerant than this one.

Sydney looked up and caught his eye. Her smile made him ache. It *was* only for him, he realized, that soft curve of the lips that said how much she wanted him. Needed him.

Loved him.

God, he was a lucky man.

She gave her sister a squeeze and then made her way over to him. He worked to smooth his expression, his emotions roiling inside as if he were a green boy who'd never been with a woman. He wanted her desperately, and he wanted her to know what he'd done to protect her sister. Thinking of Alicia made him angry all over again.

"What's wrong, Malik? You look as if you could chew nails."

He slipped an arm around her, anchored her to him as he dipped his head to kiss her. He would never tire of showing off his beautiful wife. "It is nothing. A business deal."

He wouldn't spoil the atmosphere of their party, but he would tell her later when they were alone. He didn't think she would be angry at what he'd done, but he couldn't be sure. And yet he would do the same thing again. No man should treat a woman the way Jeffrey

Orr had treated Alicia. If he'd been Jahfaran, the punishment would have been infinitely swifter.

"You were very sneaky," she said, smiling up at him. "I had no idea you were even in town. Alicia and my parents kept the secret quite well."

"They love you very much. They are proud of you."

"For what? For getting a rich and handsome husband?" She was teasing him, but he was deadly serious.

"No. For being who you are, Sydney."

He could tell she didn't quite believe it, but he would have a lifetime to convince her of how amazing she was. She would believe it eventually, just as he'd learned to believe he was deserving of love.

Her eyes sparkled in the soft light and he knew she was holding back tears. "I tried to call you."

"I'm sorry," he said. "By the time I realized I'd missed your calls, I was here and the plans were in motion."

"You could have called me," she said.

He squeezed her to him. "No, I could not. I don't do well over the phone, as you very well know."

She rolled her eyes. "Oh, Malik, you have to learn sometime. It's not all that hard."

"Maybe it is," he murmured in her ear. "Maybe it's *very* hard."

Her breath drew in sharply. "Do you think it would be scandalous if we left now?"

He made a show of checking his watch. As if he weren't dying to get her alone as well. As if he had all the time in the world.

"I think we can safely go home now," he said.

She grinned up at him, and his breath caught. How had he ever allowed her to leave him? How had he lived even a moment without her?

He lowered his head and kissed her. He intended it to be brief, but the instant their mouths touched, it was like setting a match to a fuse. She was soft, warm, delicious. His tongue delved into the recesses of her mouth, claimed her boldly and completely. She was *his*. Forever.

The sound of cheering and clapping brought him back to reality. He broke the kiss, more annoyed than anything.

Sydney ducked her head against him, her cheeks turning scarlet. "I think we should go *now*."

Malik laughed. "And so we shall."

He bade everyone a good night before leading Sydney to the waiting limo. They were suddenly very quiet as the limo pulled away from the hotel. She moved to the other side of the car and he kept his place near the door. If he touched her in the darkened interior, they would go up in flame.

And he wanted to do this right. He wanted a bed, flowers, candles, champagne. He wanted everything to be perfect for her.

"I'd ask why you're staying over there," she said, her soft voice cutting into the night. "But I think I know."

"I'm only a man, Sydney. I can only handle so much before I snap."

She purred in the darkness, and he hardened instantly. "I can't *wait* for you to snap."

When they finally reached their destination, she looked at him wonderingly. The Malibu house gleamed in the moonlight as the limo came to a stop in the circular drive, its engine still humming quietly.

"It seemed appropriate," he said with a shrug. "It is where we began this journey the second time. I am quite fond of it."

They didn't make it to the bedroom. As soon as the front door closed behind them, they were in each other's arms, kissing, touching, removing clothes, revealing their bodies as they revealed their souls to one another.

Malik wanted to worship her properly, but everything seemed to go too fast. In no time, he was carrying her to the couch and laying her on it as she shifted her hips up to him and pleaded with him to end her torment.

"We need to slow down," he said. Panted, really.

"No, no, I don't want to."

She wrapped her legs around him, her heels in his buttocks. He hesitated, wanting to remember this moment, the rightness of it. The way she looked as she lay beneath him naked, her nipples still glistening from his mouth, her lips swollen from his kisses. Her hair wild and free, tumbling down her back in a riot of flame.

Beautiful. *His.*

"Malik, please," she said. "Stop teasing me."

And that was it. He surrendered. Utterly and completely. Malik lifted her to him and drove into her molten heat.

Bliss. Comfort. Rightness.

Love.

Sydney had never been so happy in her life. She lay wrapped in Malik's arms, her body spent, her heart full. They'd found their way to the bed, but not before he'd opened the sliding glass doors to the outside. A soft breeze from the ocean whispered over them. It wasn't cool, not after they'd been so incandescently hot together, but it was welcome.

The ocean crashed on the beach below, the waves

eternal and endless. She'd thought of Malik as a wave, a relentless wave dragging her below the surface.

She'd been wrong.

He was relentless, but he wasn't dragging her down. He was lifting her up, asking her to accompany him. To be by his side always.

She could do that. She intended to do that.

She turned in his arms, saw that he was awake. Watching her. Her heart did that little flip it always did when he was near.

"What are you thinking?" she asked, tracing his lip with her thumb. It hurt to love him so much, but she would learn how to live with the pain. It was a good pain to have.

"I am thinking there are no words to describe this moment with you. But I have to say the best ones I have, because they will come the closest to it."

Sydney ran her hand over his chest, up into his hair. She loved touching him. Could never get enough of touching him. "Then they will be perfect, Malik. Because I know you would not use them otherwise."

His white teeth flashed in the darkness. "Then I shall say them."

He turned her onto her back, rose above her on an elbow and traced the line of her collarbone. Her skin tingled with pleasure. Though she should be burnt out by now, tongues of flame licked her from the inside out. How very quickly she wanted him again.

She put a hand on his chest, felt the hard beat of his heart.

"I love you Sydney. You made me believe in love when I didn't think I ever would. And though I fear the words are not adequate, I love you."

"Oh, Malik," she said through a haze of tears, her heart squeezing tight. "They are perfect."

"I am still, however, a proponent of action," he said, dipping his head to suckle her nipple into his mouth.

"Oh, yes," she gasped, clasping his head to her as her body spiraled higher. "So am I…"

* * * * *

A Secret Birthright

OLIVIA GATES

Olivia Gates has always pursued creative passions—singing and many handicrafts. She still does, but only one of her passions grew gratifying enough, consuming enough, to become an ongoing career—writing. She is most fulfilled when she is creating worlds and conflicts for her characters, then exploring and untangling them bit by bit, sharing her protagonists' every heart-wrenching heartache and hope, their every heart-pounding doubt and trial, until she leads them to an indisputably earned and gloriously satisfying happy ending.

When she's not writing, she is a doctor, a wife to her own alpha male and a mother to one brilliant girl and one demanding Angora cat. Visit Olivia at www.oliviagates.com.

To all my Romance World friends.
Authors, editors, fans and reviewers.
I don't have enough words to thank you for
being who you are, and for being there for
me when I most needed friends.

One

"I don't want to see another woman. Ever again."

A long moment of silence greeted the fed-up finality of Sheikh Fareed Aal Zaafer's declaration. His companion's empathy and exasperation hung heavy in the stillness.

Then Emad ibn Elkaateb sighed. "I *am* almost resigned a woman isn't in the cards for you. But because this isn't about you or your inexplicable personal choices, I have to insist."

Fareed's laugh was one of incredulous fury. "What *is* this? *You,* who brought me damning proof on each imposter? You're now asking me to suffer another one? To grit my teeth through more pathetic, disgusting lies? Just who are you and what have you done with Emad?"

Suddenly the decorum Emad maintained dissolved. Fareed blinked. Emad rarely budged in giving him the "dues of his birthright," insisted it was an integral part of *his* honor as Fareed's right-hand man to observe Fareed's position as his prince.

Now Emad's expression softened with the indulgence of twenty-five years of being closer to Fareed than his family, friends and staff in his medical center combined. "Anticipating your disappointment was the only reason I objected to the…scheme that brought upon you all of those opportunists. On any other account, I can't begin to fault your methods. My own haven't produced results either. Hesham hid too well."

Fareed gritted his teeth on the upsurge of frustration and futility. Of grief.

Hesham. The sensitive soul and exceptional artist. And out of Fareed's nine siblings, the youngest brother and the most beloved.

It was their father and king's fault that Hesham had hidden. Over three years ago, Hesham had returned from a long stay in the States to announce that he was getting married. He'd made the mistake of believing their father might be persuaded to give him his blessing. Instead, the king had flared into an unprecedented rage. He'd forbidden Hesham to contact his fiancée again, or to consider wedding anyone not chosen by their royal house.

When Hesham refused to obey him, the king's fury had escalated. He'd ranted that he'd find the American hussy who'd tried to insinuate herself into the royal line and make her wish she'd never plotted to ensnare his son. As for Hesham, he wasn't letting him dabble in his pointless artistic pursuits and shirk his royal duties anymore. This was no longer about what or whom Hesham chose to amuse himself with. This was about heritage. He wouldn't let him taint their bloodline with an inferior union. Hesham *would* obey, or there would be hell to pay.

Fareed and his brothers and sisters had intervened on

their brother's behalf, then had worked together to release him when their father had placed Hesham under house arrest.

Hesham had wept as he'd hugged them and told them he had to disappear, to escape their father's injustice and to protect his beloved. He'd begged for their word that they'd never look for him, to consider him dead, for all of their sakes.

None of them had been able to give that word.

But even though each had tried to keep track of him, with Fareed the one who'd gone to the greatest lengths, Hesham had all but erased himself from existence.

A new wave of rage against their father scorched his blood.

If it hadn't been for the oath he'd taken to serve his people, he would have left Jizaan, too. But that wouldn't have been a punishment for their father. He wouldn't have cared about losing another son. All he'd said after Hesham's disappearance had been that he cared only that Hesham did nothing to disgrace their family and kingdom. Fareed believed that their father would have preferred to see Hesham and any of his future children dead before that came to pass.

What had come to pass had been even worse.

After years of Fareed yearning for any contact with him, Hesham's call came from an E.R. in the States. Hesham had called him only to use his last breaths to beg for a favor. Not for himself, but for the woman for whom he'd left his world, who'd *become* his world.

Take care of Lyn, Fareed...and my child...protect them...tell her she's everything...tell her...I'm sorry I couldn't give her what she deserves, that I'll leave her alone with...

There'd been no more words. He'd almost bloodied his

throat roaring for Hesham to tell him more, to wait for him to come save him. He'd heard only an alien voice, telling him his brother had been taken to surgery.

He'd flown out immediately, dread warring with the hope that he'd be in time to save him. He'd arrived to find him long dead.

Learning that Hesham had been in no way responsible for the accident had deepened his anguish. An eighteen-wheeler had lost control and decimated eleven cars, killing many and injuring more. Grief had compromised his sanity, yet he'd fought it to offer his services. As an internationally recognized surgeon and one of the leading experts in his field, he had been gratefully accepted, and he'd operated on the most serious neurological injuries, had saved other victims as he hadn't been able to save Hesham.

It had been too late by the time he'd learned that a woman had been with Hesham in the car. She'd had no injuries, no identification, and had left the hospital as soon as Hesham had died. Descriptions had varied wildly in the wake of the mass casualties.

With a bleeding heart, he'd taken Hesham's body back to Jizaan. After a heart-wrenching funeral, which the king hadn't attended, Fareed had launched a search for Lyn and the child.

But Hesham *had* hidden too well. It seemed he'd been erasing each step as he'd taken it. Investigations into the new identity he'd assumed had revealed no wife or child. Even the car he'd died in had been a rental under yet another name.

After a month of dead ends, Fareed had taken the only option left. If he couldn't find Hesham's woman, he'd let *her* find *him*.

He'd returned to where Hesham had died, placed appeals in all the media for the woman to contact him. He'd kept his message cryptic so only the right person would approach him. Or so he'd intended…

Women had *swamped* him.

Emad had weeded out the most blatant liars, like those with teenaged children or with none, and still advised Fareed not to waste his time on the rest. He'd been certain they'd all turn out to be fortune hunters. Being a billionaire surgeon and desert prince, Fareed had always been a target for gold diggers. And he'd invited them by the drove.

Fareed couldn't comply, couldn't let anyone who remotely answered the criteria go without an audience.

He'd felt antipathy toward every candidate before she'd opened her mouth. But he'd forced himself to see each performance to its exasperating end. He believed Hesham, the lover and creator of beauty, would have fallen in love only with someone flawless inside and out, someone refined, worthy and trustworthy. But what if Hesham hadn't been as discerning as he'd thought?

But after a month of agonizing letdowns, Fareed had gone home admitting his method's failure. He'd known any new attempt would fail without new information to use. For two more months, he'd been driven to the brink on a daily basis thinking his brother's flesh and blood was out there and might be in need.

He'd groped for a sanity-saving measure, answered a plea from a teaching hospital in the States to perform charity surgeries. A part of his schedule was always dedicated to charity work, but he'd never tackled so many within such a tight time frame. And his work at his own medical center was too organized to provide solace. For the last four weeks he'd lost himself in the grueling endeavor that had managed to anesthetize his pain.

Today was the last day. And after the distraction provided by the crushing schedule, he dreaded the impending release like an imminent jump off a cliff...

"Somow'wak?"

Emad's prodding "Your Highness" brought him out of his lapse into memories and frustration.

Fareed heaved to his feet. "I'm *not* seeing any more women, Emad. You were right all along. Don't go soft on me now."

"I assure you I'm not. I've been sending the women who've come asking for an interview with you away."

Fareed blinked. "There's been more?"

"Dozens more. But I interviewed them in your stead without inflicting even a mention of them on you."

Fareed shook his head. Seemed his desperate measure would haunt him for Ullah only knew how long. "So what's new now? Don't tell me you're suddenly hoping that my 'grief-blinded gamble' might, 'against all rationality and odds,' bear fruit?"

Emad's lips twitched at Fareed's reminder of his reprimands. *"Somow'wak* has an impeccable memory."

"Aih, it's a curse." A suspicion suddenly struck him. "Are you telling me you want me to start this...*farce* all over again?"

"I want you to see this one woman."

Fareed winced at the look that entered his eyes. Emad wouldn't look at a lion with more caution.

Jameel. Great. He was losing it. He huffed in disgust at his wavering stamina. "Why this one? Why is she special?"

Emad sighed, clearly not appreciating needing to explain his conviction. "Her approach was unlike any other. She didn't use the contact number you specified in the ad but has been trying to reserve an appointment with you through the hospital from the day we arrived. Today they told her that you were leaving and she started weeping...."

Fareed slammed down the dossier he'd picked up. "So she's even more cunning than the rest, realized that the others' approach hadn't borne fruit and tried to get past your screening by conning her way to me through my work. And when *that* didn't work, she made a scene. Is that why you want me to see her? Damage control? To stop compounding the 'scandal I created for myself and my family'?"

Emad's dark eyes emptied of expression. "I wouldn't want to resurrect that mess after I managed to contain it. But that's not why. The people in reception today are new. They only heard the story of her waiting around for the past four weeks in case you had an opening in your schedule from her disjointed accounts. When they couldn't deal with her, they sent for me, and I...saw her, heard what little she'd been able to say. She...*feels* different from the rest. Feels truly distraught."

Fareed snorted. "An even more superlative actress, eh?"

"Or maybe the real thing."

His heart boomed with hope, once, before it plummeted again into despondence. "You don't believe that."

Emad leveled his gaze on him. "The real thing *does* exist."

"And she doesn't want to be found," Fareed growled. "She must know I've turned the world upside down to find her and she didn't come forward. Why would she decide to show up when nothing has changed?"

"Maybe nothing we know of."

Fareed closed his eyes. Emad's calm logic was maddening him. He was in a far worse condition than he'd realized if anything Emad, of all people, said or did had him within a hair's breadth of going berserk. It seemed he'd distracted himself at the cost of pushing himself to a breakdown.

Emad's deep tones, so carefully neutral, felt like discordant nails against his restraint. "But what we do know is that Hesham's Lyn is still out there."

And what if that woman down there was her?

He closed his eyes against hope's insidious prodding. But it was too late. It had already eaten through his resistance.

This woman most probably wasn't; but really, what was one more performance to suffer? He'd better get this over with.

He opened his eyes as Emad opened his mouth to deliver another argument. He raised his hand, aborting it. "Send her up. I'm giving her ten minutes, not a second more. Tell her that. Then I'm walking out and I'm never coming back to this country."

Emad gave a curt nod, turned on his heels.

He watched him exit the ultramodern space the hospital had given him as his consultation room, before he sagged in the luxury of the leather swiveling chair. It felt as if he'd sunk into thorns.

If more fake, stomach-turning stories about his brother were flung in his face, he would not be responsible for his actions.

He glowered at the door. He'd seen all kinds. From the sniveling to the simpering to the seductive. He had an idea which type this one would be. The hysterical. Maybe even the delusional.

He steeled himself for another ugly confrontation as the door was pushed open. Emad preceded the woman into the room.

But he barely saw him. He didn't hear what Emad said before he left, or notice when he did.

All he saw was the golden vision approaching until only the wide desk stood between them.

He found himself on his feet without realizing he'd moved, only one thought reverberating in his mind.

Please, don't be Hesham's Lyn!

The thought stuttered to a standstill.

B'Ellahi, what was he thinking? He should be wishing that she was, that his search was over.

It shouldn't make a difference that her drowned sky-at-dawn eyes dissolved his coherence and the sunlight silk that cascaded over her bosom made his hands ache to twist in it. It didn't matter that the trembling of her lush lips shook his resolve and her graceful litheness gripped his guts in a snare of instant hunger. If she turned out to be Hesham's Lyn…

His thoughts convulsed to a halt again.

He wanted her to be anything *but* that. Even another imposter.

B'Ellahi, why?

The answer churned inside him with that desire that had surged out of nowhere at her sight.

Because Hesham's Lyn would be off-limits to him. And he wanted this woman for himself. He wanted her…

As he'd wanted her the first and only time he'd seen her.

He *remembered* her now!

It was the total unexpectedness of seeing her again, let alone here, that had thrown him at first. That, and the changes in her.

That time he'd seen her, her luminous hair had been scraped back in a severe bun. She'd been wearing makeup that he now realized had obscured her true coloring and downplayed her features. A dark suit of masculine severity had attempted to mask her screaming femininity.

She'd been younger, far more curvaceous, yet somehow less ripe. Her vibe had been cool, professional…until she'd seen him.

One thing remained the same. Her impact on him. It was as all-consuming as it had been when he'd walked into that conference room.

He vaguely remembered people scurrying to empty a place for him at the front row. She'd been at the podium. It wasn't until the stunning effect she'd had on him ebbed slightly that he realized what she'd been doing there.

She'd been delivering the very presentation he'd gone to that conference to attend, about a drug that helped regenerate nerves after pathological degeneration or trauma. He'd heard so much about the outstanding young researcher, the head of the R & D team. He'd had a mental image to go with her prodigious achievements, one that had collapsed under its own inaccuracy at the sight of her.

He'd held her gaze captive as he'd sat grappling with impatience for the presentation to be over so he could approach her, claim her. Only his knowledge that the sight of him had been as disruptive to her had mitigated his tension. His pleasure had mounted at seeing her poise shaken. She'd managed to continue, but her crisp efficiency had become colored by the self-consciousness he'd evoked. Every move of her elegant body and eloquent hands, every inflection of her cultured delivery, *everything* about her had made focusing on the data she'd been conveying a challenge. But her work had been even more impressive than he'd anticipated, only deepening his delight with her….

"Is it all a lie? Are *you* a lie?"

He almost flinched. That red wine-and-velvet voice.

It had taken hearing it to know it had never stopped

echoing in his mind. Now it was made even more potent by the raggedness of emotion entwined in it.

But had she said…?

The next second her agitation cascaded over him, silencing questions and bringing every thought to a shocked halt.

"Is your reputation all propaganda? Just hype to pave the way to more reverence in the medical field and adulation in the media? Are you what your rare detractors say you are? Just a prince with too much money, genius and power, who makes a career of playing god?"

Two

Gwen McNeal heard the choking accusations as if they came from a disembodied voice. One that sounded like hers.

It seemed the past weeks had damaged what had been left of her sanity. She'd made her initial request for a meeting with it already strained. But as time had ticked by and her chances of meeting him had diminished, her stamina had dwindled right along.

She'd thought she'd be a mass of incoherence when she was finally in his presence.

Then she was there, and the sight of him had jolted through her like a lightning bolt. The intensity of his gaze, of his impact, had slashed the last tethers of her restraint.

She'd just accused him of being an over-endowed sadist who lived to make lesser beings beg for his intervention.

At least the unchecked flow had stopped. All she could

do now was stare in horror at him as he stared back at her in stupefaction. And realize.

He *was* what she remembered. Description-defying. Or there had to be new adjectives coined to describe his brand of virility and grandeur. Seeing him felt like being catapulted into the past. A past when she'd known where her life was heading. A life that had been derailed since she'd laid eyes on him.

Ever since, she'd told herself she'd exaggerated her memories of him, had built him up into what no one could possibly be.

But he was all that. It was all there, and more. The imposing physicality, the inborn grace and power, the sheer influence. She had no doubt time would continue to magnify his assets until he did become godlike.

One thing time hadn't enhanced, though. His effect on her. How could it when that had been shattering to start with?

Then he moved. The move itself was almost imperceptible, but the intention behind it, to come closer, when that would engulf her even deeper into his aura, intensify his effect, went off inside her like a clap of thunder.

Desperation burst from her in a new rush of resentment. *"Five minutes?* That's what you allow people in your presence? Then you walk away without looking back? Do you smirk in satisfaction as they run after you begging for a few more moments of your priceless time? Do you enjoy making them grovel? That's how much regard the world's leading philanthropist surgeon really has for others?"

A slow blink swept his sinful lashes down, before they lifted to level his smoldering gaze on her.

"I actually said ten minutes."

She'd thought his voice had been hard-hitting in the videos she'd seen of his interviews, lectures and educational surgeries. In reality, the depth and richness of his tones, the potency of his accent, the beauty of his every inflection made the words he uttered an invocation.

"And when I said that…"

She cut him off, unable to hear more of that spell. "So you granted me *ten* minutes instead of five. I can see how your reputation was founded, on such magnanimous offers. But I've wasted most of those ten minutes. Do I start counting down the rest before you walk away as if I'm not here?"

He shook his head as if it would help him make sense of her words, and L.A.'s winter afternoon sun slanting through the windows glinted off his raven mane. "I won't do any such thing, Ms. McNeal."

Her heart gave one detonation. He…he…he *remembered* her?

The world receded into a gray vortex. A terrible whoosh yawned in her ears. Everything faded away as she plunged in a freefall of nothingness.

Something immovable broke her plummet, and she found herself struggling within the living cables that encompassed her, reaching back to the reprieve that oblivion offered.

"*B'Ellahi*…don't fight me."

The dark melody poured into her brain as she lost all connection with gravity, was swathed in hot hardness and dizzying fragrance. She opened her eyes at the sensation and that face she'd long told herself she'd forgotten filled her vision. She hadn't forgotten one line of symmetry or strength, one angle or slash or groove of nobility and character and uniqueness. Sheikh Fareed Aal Zaafer would be unforgettable after one fleeting look. Secondhand exposure would have been enough. But that firsthand encounter had been indelible.

But if she'd thought his effect from a distance the most disruptive force she'd ever encountered, now that she filled his arms, he filled her senses, conquered what remained of her resistance.

A violent shudder shook her. He gathered her tighter.

"Put me down, please." Her voice broke on the last word.

His eyes moved to her lips as soon as she spoke, following their movements. Blood thundered in her head at his fascination. His hands only tightened their hold, branding her through her clothing.

"You fainted." His gaze dragged from her lips, raking every raw nerve in her face on its way back up to her eyes.

She fidgeted, trying to recoup her scattered coordination. "I just got dizzy for a second."

"You *fainted*." His insistence was soft like gossamer, unbending as steel. "A dead faint. I had to vault over the desk to catch you before you fell face down over that table."

Her eyes panned to where she'd been standing by a large, square, steel-and-glass table. Articles were flung all over the floor around it.

Even though she'd never fainted in her life, no doubt formed in her mind. She had. And he'd saved her.

The bitterness that had united with tension to hold her together disintegrated in the heat of shame at her behavior so far. All she wanted was to burrow into his power and weep.

She couldn't. For every reason there was. She had to keep her distance at all costs.

He was walking to the sitting area by the windows as if afraid she'd come apart if he jarred her. What did was the solicitude radiating from him.

She pulled herself rigid in his hold. "I'm fine now...
please."

He stopped. She raised a wavering gaze to his, found it
filled with something...turbulent. Then it grew assessing,
as if weighing the pros and cons of granting her plea.

Then he loosened his arms by degrees, let her slide
in nerve-abrading slowness down his body. She swayed
back a step as soon as her feet found the ground, and her
legs wobbled under her weight, as if she'd long depended
on him to support it. His hand shot out to steady her. She
shook her head. He took his hand away, gestured for her
to sit down, command and courtesy made flesh and bone.

She almost fell onto the couch, shot him a wary glance
as soon as she'd sought its far end. "Thank you."

He came to tower over her. "Nothing to thank me for."

"Just for saving me from being rushed to the E.R., probably with severe facial fractures, or worse."

His spectacular eyebrows snapped together as if in pain,
the smoldering coals he had for eyes turning almost black.
"Tell me why you fainted."

She huffed. "If I knew that, I wouldn't have."

His eyes drilled into hers, clearly unsatisfied with her
answer. "You're not alarmed that you did faint, at least
you're not surprised. So you have a very good idea why.
Tell me."

"It was probably agitation."

His painstakingly sculpted lips twisted. "You might
be a renowned pharmaceutical researcher, Ms. McNeal,
but I'm the doctor among us and the one qualified to pass
medical opinions. Agitation makes you more alert, not
prone to collapse."

He wouldn't budge, would he? She had to give him
something to satisfy his investigative appetite so she could

move on to the one subject that mattered. "It—it was probably the long wait."

He still shook his head. "Eight hours of waiting, though
long, wouldn't cause you to be so exhausted you'd faint.
Not without an underlying cause."

"I've been here since 4:00 a.m…" His eyebrows shot up
in surprise. And that was before she added, "yesterday."

His incredulity shot higher, his frown grew darker.
"You've been sitting down there for thirty-six hours?"

He suddenly came down beside her, with a movement that should have been impossible for someone of
his height, his thigh whisper-touching hers as those long,
powerful fingers, his virtuoso surgeon's tools, wrapped
around her wrist to take her pulse. Her heartbeats piled
up in her heart before drenching her arteries in a torrent.

He raised probing eyes to her. "Have you slept or even
eaten during that time?" She didn't remember. She started
to nod and he overrode her evasion. "It's clear you did
neither. You haven't been doing either properly for a long
time. You're tachycardic as if you've been running a mile."
Was he even wondering why, with him so near? "You
must be hypoglycemic, and your weak pulse indicates your
blood pressure is barely adequate to keep you conscious. I
wouldn't even need any of those signs to guide me about
your condition. You look—depleted."

From meeting her haggard face in the mirror, she knew
she made a good simulation of the undead. But having him
corroborate her opinion twisted mortification inside her.

Which was the height of stupidity. What did it matter if
he thought she looked like hell? What mattered was that
she fixed her mistake, got on with her all-important purpose.

"I was too anxious to sleep or eat, but it's not a big deal.

What I said to you is, though. I'm sorry for…for my outbursts."

Something flared in his eyes, making her skin where he still held her hand feel as if it would burst into flame. "Don't be. Not if I've done anything to deserve this…antipathy. And I'm extremely curious, to put it mildly, to find out what that was. Do you think I left you waiting this long out of malice? You believe I enjoy making people beg for my time, offer it only after they've broken down, only to allow them inadequate minutes before walking away?"

"No— I—I mean…no…your reputation says the very opposite."

"But your personal experience says my reputation might be so much manufactured hype."

Her throat tightened with a renewed surge of misery. "It's just you…you announced you'd be available to be approached, but I was told the opposite, and I no longer knew what to believe."

She felt him stiffen, the fire in his eyes doused in something…bleak. She'd somehow offended him with her attempts at apology and explanation more than she had with her insults.

But even if she deserved that he walked away from her, she couldn't afford to let him. She had to beg him to hear her out.

"Please, forget everything I said and let me start over. Just give me those ten minutes all over again. If afterward you think you're not interested in hearing more, walk away."

Fareed crashed down to earth.

He'd forgotten. As she'd lambasted him, as he'd lost himself in the memory of his one exposure to her, in his delight in finding her miraculously here, then in his anxiety when she'd collapsed, he'd totally forgotten.

Why he'd walked away from her that first time.

As she'd concluded her presentation and applause had risen, so had everyone. He'd realized it had been the end of the session when people had deluged him, from colleagues to grant seekers to the press. He'd wanted to push them all away, his impatience rising with his satisfaction as her gaze had kept seeking him, before darting away when she'd found him focused on her.

And then a man had swooped out of nowhere, swept her off her feet and kissed her soundly on the lips. He'd frozen as the man had hugged her to his side with the entitlement of long intimacy, turned her to pose for photos and shouted triumphant statements to reporters about the new era "their" drug would herald in pharmaceuticals.

He'd grabbed the first person near him, asked, "Who's that?"

He'd gotten the answer he'd dreaded. *That,* a Kyle Langstrom, had been her fiancé and partner in research.

As the letdown had mushroomed inside him, he'd heard Kyle announcing that with the major hurdle in their work overcome, there'd soon be news of equal importance: a wedding date.

The knowledge of her engagement had doused his blaze of elation at finding her, buried all his intentions. His gaze had still clung to her receding figure as if he could alter reality, make her free to return his interest, to receive his passion.

Just before the tide of companions had swept her out of sight, she'd looked back. Their eyes had met for a moment.

It had felt like a lifetime when the world had ceased to exist and only they had remained. Then she'd been gone.

He'd seen her again during the following end-of-confer-

ence party. The perverse desire to see her again even when
it oppressed him had made him attend it. He'd stood there
unable to take his eyes off her. She'd kept her gaze averted.
But he'd known she'd been struggling not to look back.
He'd finally felt bad enough about standing there covet-
ing another man's woman that he'd left with the party at
full swing.

He hadn't returned to the States again until Hesham.

He'd replayed that last glance for months afterward.
Each time seeing his own longing and regret reflected in
her eyes. And each time he'd told himself he'd imagined
it.

He'd long convinced himself he had imagined everything. Most of all, her unprecedented effect on him.

It had taken him one look today to realize he'd completely downplayed it. To realize why he'd been unable to
muster interest in other women ever since. He might not
have consciously thought it, but he'd found no point in
wasting time on a woman who didn't inspire the white-
hot recognition and attraction this woman had.

Now she'd appeared here, out of the blue, had been
waiting to see him for a month, her last vigil lasting a day
and a half of sleepless starvation. She'd just said she was
here because he'd "announced he'd be available to be approached."

Had she meant his ad? Could it be, of all women, this
one he'd wanted on sight, hadn't only been some stranger's
once, but Hesham's, too?

If she had been, *he* must have done something far worse
than what she'd accused him of in her agitation. What else
would that be but some unimaginably cruel punishment
of fate?

He hissed, "Just *tell* me and be done with it."

She lurched as if he'd backhanded her. No wonder. He'd sounded like a beast, seconds away from an attack.

Before he could form an apology, she spoke, her voice muffled with tears, "I lied—" She had? About what? "—when I said ten minutes would do. I *did* keep asking reception for any moments you could spare when they said full appointments were reserved for patients on your list. I now realize they couldn't have acted on your orders, must have done the same with the endless people who came seeking your services. But I was told you're leaving in an hour, and that long might not do now either and…"

He raised his hands to stem the flow of her agitation, his previous suspicions crashing in a domino effect.

"You're here for a *consultation?*"

She raised eyes brimming with tears and…wariness? Nodded.

Relief stormed through him. She wasn't here about the ad, about Hesham. She was here seeking his surgical services.

Next moment relief scattered as another suspicion detonated.

"You're sick?"

Three

She *was* sick.

That explained everything. The only thing that made sense. Terrible sense. Her desperation. Her mood swings. Her fainting.

She had a neurological condition. According to her symptoms, maybe…a brain tumor. And if she'd sought him out, it had to be advanced. No one sought him specifically except in conditions deemed beyond the most experienced surgeons' skills. In neurosurgery, he *was* one of three on earth who'd made a vocation of tackling the inoperable, resolving the incurable.

But a month had passed since she'd first tried to reach him. Her condition could have progressed from minimal hope to none.

Could it be he'd found her, only to lose her again?

No, he wouldn't. In the past, he'd walked away from her, respecting the commitment she'd made. But disease, even what others termed terminal, *especially* that, was what he'd dedicated his life to defeating. If he could never have her, at least he would give the world back that vibrant being who'd made giving hope to the hopeless her life's work....

"I'm not sick."

The tremulous words hit him with the force of a bullet.

He stared at her, convictions and fears crashing, burning.

Had she said...? Yes, she had. But that could mean nothing. She'd already denied knowledge of why she'd fainted. She could still be undiagnosed, or in denial over the diagnosis she'd gotten, hoping he'd have a different verdict....

"It's my baby."

This time, only one thing echoed inside his head. *Why?*

Why did he keep getting shocked by each new verification that this woman had a life that had nothing to do with him? That she'd planned and lived her life without his being the major part of it?

Often he'd found himself overwhelmed by bitterness without apparent reason. He now admitted to himself what that reason had been. That he still couldn't believe she hadn't waited to find him, had accepted a deficient connection with someone else.

But that sense of betrayal was ridiculous, had nothing to do with reality. Her marriage *had* been imminent when he'd seen her. So why did it shock him so much that she had a baby, the normal outcome of a years-old union?

And that baby was sick. Enough to need his surgical skills.

His heart compressed as he realized the reason, the emotions behind her every word and tear so far. The same desperation he'd once felt, to save someone whose life he valued above his own.

How ironic was it that her intensely personal need for his purely professional services had made her finally seek him out?

He'd long given in to fate that had deemed that their paths diverged before they'd had the chance to converge. But to have her enter his life this way *was* a punishment, an injury. And he wasn't in any condition to take more of either.

If it had only meant his own suffering, he would have taken any measure of both. But he held his patients' lives under the steadiness of his hand, their futures subject to the clarity of his decisions. He couldn't compromise that.

Now he had to deal her the blow of refusing her baby's case. He would make sure her baby got the very best care. Just not his.

He inhaled a burning breath. "Ms. McNeal..."

As if feeling he'd let her down, she sat up, eyes blazing with entreaty. "I have Ryan's investigations with me, so maybe minutes will do. Will you take a look, tell me what you think?"

She only wanted his opinion? Didn't want him to operate on her baby? If so...

Again, as if she felt him relenting, she scrambled up. He noticed for the first time the briefcase and purse she'd dropped. All he'd seen had been her. In spite of everything, his eyes still clung to her every move, every nuance, and his every cell ached with long-denied impulses.

He saw himself striding after her, catching her back, plastering her body against his, burying his fingers in the luxury of her golden cascade of hair, sweeping it aside to open his lips over her warm, satin flesh. What he'd give for only one taste, one kiss...

She was returning, holding the briefcase as if it contained her world, her dawn-sky eyes full of brittle hope.

Ya Ullah, how was beauty like that even possible?

He'd never been attracted to blondes, never preferred Western beauty. But to him, she was the embodiment of everything that aroused his wonder and lust. And it was only partially physical. The connection he felt between them, that which needed no knowledge or experience, just *was,* was everything he wanted. When he couldn't have her.

She started fumbling with the briefcase's zipper as she neared him, and another idea occurred to him.

If this would be only a consultation, he owed her a full one after all the suffering she'd endured for the mere hope of it.

He should also give himself a dose of shock therapy. Seeing her with her baby, with her whole *family,* might cure him of this insidious malady he'd been struck with at her sight.

He stayed her hand with a touch, withdrew his as if contact with her burned him, and before he tugged her against him.

"I won't be able to give you an opinion based on those investigations. I don't rely on any except those done to my specifications." Alarm flared in her eyes. He couldn't believe the effect her distress had on him. It…physically hurt. He rushed to add, "Anyway, my preferred and indispensable diagnostic method is a clinical exam. Is your baby downstairs with his father?"

Her gaze blipped, and she barely suppressed a start.

Before he could analyze her reaction, she murmured, her voice deeper, huskier, "Ryan is with his nanny at our hotel. They both got too tired and Ryan was crying nonstop and disturbing everyone, I had to send them away."

Agitation spread across her features like a shadow. "I thought I'd bring them back as soon as I got an appointment with you. But the hotel's near the airport, and at this time of day, even if I'd told Rose to come as soon as I knew you'd see me, it would have taken her too long to get here. I didn't even tell her, because Mr. Elkaateb said you had only minutes to spare. That's why I said an hour won't do...."

He raised a hand, stopped her anxiety in its tracks. "I'm going home on my private jet, so the timing of my departure is up to me. Call your nanny and have her bring Ryan over."

Her eyes widened. "Oh, God, thank you..."

A hand wave again stopped her. He hated the vulnerability and helplessness gratitude engendered in others, was loathe to be on its receiving end. Hers took his usual discomfort to new levels.

She nodded, accepting that he wanted none of it, dived into her purse for her phone.

In moments, with her eyes fixed on him, she said, "Rose..." She paused as the woman on the other side burst out talking. Realizing he must hear the woman, Gwen shot him an apologetic, even...shy glance. "Yes, I did. Get Ryan here ASAP."

He barely stopped himself at a touch of her forearm. "Tell her to take her time. I'll wait."

The look she gave him then, the beauty of her tremulous smile, twisted another red-hot poker in his gut. He had to get away from her before he did something they'd both regret.

He turned away, headed back to the desk and blindly started gathering the files he'd scattered.

When she ended her phone call, without looking up he asked the question burning a hole in his chest, trying to sound nonchalant, "Isn't your husband coming? Or is he back home?"

He *needed* to see her with her husband. He had to have that image of her with her man burned into his mind, to erase the one he had of her with *him*.

She didn't answer him for what felt like an eternity. His perception sharpened and time warped with her near.

He forced himself to keep rearranging the desk, didn't raise his eyes to read on her face the proof of her involvement with another. He should, to sever his own inexplicable and ongoing one. He couldn't. It would be bad enough to hear it in her voice as she mentioned her husband, the father of her child.

When her answer finally came, it was subdued, almost inaudible. He almost missed it. Almost.

His heart kicked his ribs so hard that he felt both would be bruised. His eyes jerked up to her.

She'd said, "I don't have a husband."

He didn't know when or how he'd crossed the distance back to her. He found himself standing before her again, the revelation reverberating in his head, in his whole being.

He heard himself rasp, "You're divorced?"

She escaped his eyes, the slanting rays of sunset turning hers into bottomless aquamarines. "I was never married."

He could only stare at her.

A long moment later, he voiced his bewilderment. "I thought you were engaged when I saw you at that conference."

He thought, indeed. He'd thought of nothing else until he'd forced himself into self-inflicted amnesia.

Color rushed back into her cheeks, making his lips itch to taste that tide of peach. "I was. We...split up soon afterward." She snatched a look back at him, her lips lifting with a faint twist of humor. "Sort of on the grounds of irreconcilable scientific differences."

Suddenly he felt like putting his fist through the nearest wall.

B'haggej' jaheem…in the name of *hell!* He'd walked away because he'd believed she would marry that Kyle Langstrom. And she *hadn't.*

Frustration charred his blood as realizations swamped him, of what he'd wasted when he hadn't pursued her, hadn't at least followed up on her news. He would have found out she hadn't married that…that *person.* But that didn't necessarily mean that…

"He's not the father of your child?"

She ended that suspicion with a simple, "No."

Before delight overtook him, another realization quashed it.

She might not have married Langstrom, but she had a man in her life. He *had* to know. "Then who is your child's father?"

She shrugged, unease thickening her voice. "Is this about Ryan's condition? Do you think knowing his father is important for managing it or for his prognosis?"

He was tempted to say yes, to make it imperative for her to answer him. The temptation passed, and integrity, damn it to hell, took over. He exhaled his frustration with the code he could never break. "No, knowing the source of a congenital malformation has no bearing on the course of treatment or prognosis."

"Then I don't see how bringing up his father is relevant."

She didn't want to talk about this. She was right not to. He'd never dreamed of pursuing private information from anyone, let alone the parent of a prospective patient. But this was *her,* the one woman he had to know everything about.

He already knew everything that was relevant to him. From her work, he'd formed a thorough knowledge of her intellect and capabilities. Instinct provided the rest, about her nature and character and their compatibility to his. What remained was the status of any personal relationship she might have.

And yet, there *was* a legitimate reason for him to ask about the father. "It's relevant because the father of your child should be here, especially if your child's condition is as serious as you believe. As his father, he has equal right to decide his course of treatment, if there is any, and an equal stake in his future."

Concession crept in her eyes. It was still a long moment later when she spoke, making him feel as if the words caused her internal damage on their way out. "Ryan... doesn't have a father."

And all he could ask himself now was when? When would that woman stop slamming him with shocks? When would she stop giving him fragments of answers that only raise more maddening questions?

"You mean he's not a part of your lives? Is he gone? Dead?"

What? the shout rang inside his head. *Just tell me.*

Her eyes shot up to his. She must be as attuned to him as he was to her. He'd kept his tone even, his demeanor neutral. But she must have sensed the vehemence of his frustration.

She finally exhaled. "I had Ryan from a donor."

This time he did stagger back a step.

There *was* no end to her surprises.

But he was beyond surprised. He was flabbergasted. He would have never even considered this a possibility.

Even though he knew this would mean something huge when he let it sink in, and he couldn't understand why she'd been so averse to disclosing this fact, it only raised more questions. "Why would someone so young resort to a sperm donor?"

She kept her eyes anywhere but at him, her color now dangerous. "Age is just one factor why women go the donor route. And it's been a while since I left the designation 'so young' behind. Thirty-two is hardly spring chick territory."

His lips twitched at this, yet another trace of wit. "With forty being the new thirty even where child bearing is concerned, you are firmly in that territory. If I'd just met you, I wouldn't give you more than twenty-two."

Her shoulders jerked on a disbelieving huff as she gave him one of those glances that made his blood pressure shoot up. "I've looked in a mirror lately, you know. You yourself said I look terrible. But anyway, thanks for the... chivalry."

"I only ever say what I mean. You have proof of that from my unsweetened interrogation." One corner of her lips lifted. "And my exact word was *depleted*. It's clear you're neglecting yourself in your anxiety over your child. It doesn't make you any less...breathtaking."

It was her own breath that stalled now. The sound it made catching in her throat made him dizzy with desire.

He intended to hear that sound, and many, many others, as he compromised her breathing with too much pleasure. For now he pressed on. "And I'll keep it up until you tell me the whole story, so how about you volunteer it?"

Her shoulders rose and dropped helplessly. "Maybe you should keep it up and I'll answer what I can because I don't know what constitutes a whole story to you."

"I want to know why a woman like you, who will be

pursued by men when you're *seventy*-two, chose to have a child without one. Was it because of your ex-fiancé? Was there more to your breakup than you let on? What did he do to put you off relationships?"

The hesitant humor playing on her lips reached her eyes. He couldn't wait until he could see it fully unleashed. "I did ask for it. But you can't be further from the truth in Kyle's case. I'm the villain of the piece in that story. It was because of me that even working together became counterproductive."

Zain. That was succinct and unequivocal. And still deficient.

He persisted, "Then why?"

She looked away again. "Not everything has to have a huge or complex reason. I just wanted a baby."

He knew she was hiding something. The conviction burned in his gut with its intensity. "And you couldn't wait to have one the usual way? When another suitable man came along?"

"I wasn't interested in having another man, suitable or not."

She fell silent. He knew she'd say no more on that issue.

He had more to say, to ask, to think, and everything to feel. It all roiled inside him, old frustrations and new questions. But one thing crystallized until it outshone everything else.

Not only didn't she have a man in her life, but she also hadn't wanted one. After she'd seen him. He *knew* it. Just like he hadn't wanted another woman after he'd seen her.

Elation swept him. Changed the face of his existence.

He didn't know how he stopped from doing what he'd wanted to do since that first moment—sweep her in his arms and kiss her until she begged for him. But he couldn't do it now.

Not having her now was still torment, only sweet instead of bitter, and the wait would only make having her in time that much more transfiguring.

For now, she needed his expertise, not his passion. He would give her everything she needed.

Her eyes were focused on him in such appeal that he could swear he felt his bones liquefying. "Won't you look at the investigations anyway, just to get an idea, while we wait?"

Eyes like these, influence like this, should be outlawed. He'd tell her that. Soon.

He smiled at her, took her elbow, guided her back to the couch. "I'd rather form an uninfluenced opinion."

She slid him a sideways glance, and the tinge of teasing there almost made him send everything to hell and unleash four years' worth of hunger on her. "Is anyone even capable of influencing your opinion?"

He laughed. For the first time…since he didn't remember when. After endless months of gloom, with her here, with her free, he felt a weight had lifted. If it weren't for Hesham, for his unfound woman and child, he would have said he was on the verge of experiencing joy.

"All this because of my interrogation?" He gently prodded her to sit down, got out his cell phone, called Emad and asked him to bring in a meal. When she insisted she'd settle for a hot drink, he overrode her with a gentle "Doctor's orders."

He came down beside her, close enough to feel imbued by the fragrant warmth of her body, but leaving enough space for her attempt to observe a semblance of formality.

She looked at him now, not enraged or wary or imploring, but with fascination, unable to stop studying him as he studied her, and the openness of her face, the clarity of her spirit…amazing.

He sighed his pleasure. "I would be a very poor scientist and a terrible surgeon if I wasn't open to new influences. I should be making the crack about you. After half an hour of my premium persistence all I got out of you was a half-dozen sentences."

She looked away, making him want to kick himself for whatever he'd done to make her deprive him of her gaze. "Your judgment *has* served you, and endless others, unbelievably well. You're one surgeon who deserves to have omnipotent notions."

"You mean my rare detractors aren't right and I'm not just a highborn lowlife suffering from advanced narcissistic sadism laced with a terminal god complex?"

She buried her face in her hands as he paraphrased her opening salvo, before looking back up at him, embarrassment and humor a heady mix in her eyes. "Do you think there's any chance you can pretend I never said that?"

He quirked his lips, reveling in taking her in degrees from desperation to ease. "Why would I? Because you were wrong? Are you sure you were? Maybe I behaved because you handed me my head."

A chuckle cracked out of her. "I doubt anyone can do that."

"You'd be really, really surprised what you can do."

He let *to me* go unspoken, yet understood.

Before he could analyze the effect this declaration had on her, Emad entered with the waitstaff.

Fareed saw the question, the hope in his eyes as Emad took in the situation. Fareed gave a slight headshake letting him know she wasn't the woman they'd been looking for.

But she was the woman *he'd* been looking for.

After preparing the table in front of them, and with disappointment and curiosity filling his eyes, Emad left.

For the next hour Fareed discovered new pleasures. Coddling Gwen—to her chagrin, before she succumbed, ate and drank what he served her, delighting in her re-surfacing steadiness, in the banter that flowed between them, the fluency of appreciation.

Then Emad knocked again. This time he ushered in a woman carrying a child. Gwen's child.

Fareed couldn't focus on either. He only had eyes for Gwen as she sprung to her feet, her face gripped with emotions, their range breathtaking in scope and depth. Anxiety, relief, welcome, love, protection and so much more, every one fierce, total.

He heard the child squeal as he threw himself into her eager embrace. He registered the elegant, classically pretty redhead in her late forties, who Gwen introduced as Rose Maher, a distant maternal relative and Ryan's nanny. He welcomed her with all the cordiality he could access, filed everything about her for later analysis. Then he turned to Gwen's child.

And the world stopped in its tracks.

Four

Fareed hadn't thought about Gwen's child until this moment. Not in any terms other than his being hers.

He hadn't had the presence of mind to formulate expectations, of the child, of his own reactions when he saw him. Had he had any mental faculties to devote to either, he would have thought he'd feel what he felt for any sick child in his care.

Now he knew anything he could have imagined would have been way off base.

She'd said Ryan didn't have a father. He could almost believe that declaration literally now. It was as if he was hers, and hers alone. Even the discrepancy in age and gender, the almost-bald head, did nothing to dilute the reality that he was a pure part of her, body and soul.

But that absolute kinship and similarity between child and mother wasn't why the sight of Ryan shook him to his core. Ryan, even though no more than nine or ten months

old, was his own person. His effect wasn't an echo of his
mother's, but all his own.

Ryan looked at him with eyes that were the same heav-
enly blue as his mother's but reflecting his own nature
and character, inquisitive, intrepid, enthusiastic. His dewy
lips were rounded on his same breath-bating fascination
as he probed him as if asking if he was a friend. Then he
seemed to decide he was, his eyes crinkling and his lips
spreading.

"Say hello to Dr. Aal Zaafer, Ryan."

Fareed blinked as Gwen's indulgent tone cascaded over
his nerves, such a different melody from any he'd heard
from her.

It had an equal effect on Ryan, who smiled delightedly
up at her. Next moment, his every synapse fired as the
child turned back to him, encompassed him in the same
unbridled smile. Then he extended his arms to him.

He stared at the chubby hands closing and opening,
beckoning for him to hurry and pick him up.

Gwen moved Ryan out of reach. "Darling, the adorable
act works only on me and Rose." Fareed's eyes moved
from Ryan's crestfallen face to her apologetic one. "I didn't
think he would ask you for a ride. He doesn't like to be
held much, even by me. Too independent."

She thought his hesitation meant he didn't want to hold
Ryan? She didn't realize he was just…paralyzed? Everything inside him wanted to reach back for Ryan, but the
urge was so strong, so…unknown that it overwhelmed
him.

He had to correct that assumption. He couldn't bear that
she thought she'd imposed on him, couldn't stand seeing
Ryan's chin quiver at being apparently rebuffed.

"I'm—" he cleared his throat "—I'm honored he thinks

I'm worthy of being his ride. He probably fancies one from a higher altitude."

A chuckle came from his left. His gaze moved with great effort from the captivating sight mother and son made to Rose.

She was still eyeing him with that almost-awed expression in her green eyes, but humor and shrewdness were taking over. "Ryan is a genius, and he knows a good proposition when he sees it. And you're as good as it gets."

A strangled gasp issued from Gwen. He didn't need to look at her to know that her eyes were shooting daggers at Rose.

His lips spread in his widest smile in years. "Ms. Maher, I knew you were a discerning woman the moment I saw you."

Rose let out a tinkling laugh. "Call me Rose, please. And oh, yes, I've been around long enough to know premium stuff when I see it, too."

He almost felt the heat of mortification blasting off Gwen. And he loved it. Rose was saying the exact things to dissolve the tension, to set him free of the immobility that had struck him.

"I am honored you think I belong on the premium shelf, Rose, almost as much as I was to be considered a desirable ride by Ryan." He shared another smile with the woman he already felt would be his ally, before he turned to Gwen and held out his arms.

His heart revved at what flared in her eyes. Momentary belief that his arms where inviting *her* into their depths. And a stifled urge to rush into them.

He let her know he'd seen it with a lingering glance before he transferred his smile to the baby who was already bobbing in her arms, demanding to be released. "Shall we, young sir?"

Ryan squealed his eagerness, reached back to him. Fareed noted his movements, already assessing his condition. He received him with as much care as he would a priceless statue that might shatter if he breathed hard. He looked down on the angelic face that was regarding him in such open wonder and something fierce again shuddered behind his breastbone.

Ya Ullah. That baby boy wielded magic as potent as his mother, and both their brands of spells had his name on them.

"You won't dent him, you know?" Rose said.

He swept his gaze to her, his lips twisting. "It's that clear I'm scared witless of holding him?"

Rose let out another good-natured laugh. "Your petrified expression did give me a clue or two that your experience in handling tiny humans *is* nonexistent."

"You don't have kids?"

Gwen's soft question swept his gaze back to her. She looked…horrified that she'd asked it.

Satisfaction surged inside him. She needed to know his private details as much as he'd needed to know hers. Even though she was clearly kicking herself for asking, she *was* dying to know. If he had children, and therefore, a wife.

He'd thought his life wasn't conducive to raising a family, that he didn't have that innate drive to become a father. Now he knew the real reason why he'd never thought of having children. Because he'd never found a woman he wanted to have them with.

Now looking at her, holding her child in his arms, he did.

He looked down at Ryan, who was industriously trying to undo his shirt's top buttons, before he looked back at her, giving her a glimpse of what he felt, if not too much of it. She wasn't ready for the full power of his intentions.

Then he murmured, "I don't."

Her lashes fluttered down. But he felt it. Her relief.

Elation spread through him. "But I am an uncle many times over, through two of my sisters and many first cousins, to an assortment of boys and girls from ages one to fifteen."

Gwen raised her eyes back to his, and...*ya Ullah*. Although still guarded and trying to obscure her feelings, the change that had come over them since she'd walked in here, the warmth she couldn't fully neutralize, singed him. "I bet you're their favorite uncle."

He grinned at her. "You honor me with your willingness to waste money betting on me. But a waste it would be. 'Favorite Uncle' is a title unquestioningly reserved for Jawad, my second-eldest brother. We call him the Child Whisperer. All I can lay claim to is that I think they don't detest me. I've been too preoccupied for the span of their lives to develop any real relationship with them. I would have liked to, but I have to admit, when I'm around them, I wonder how their parents put up with their demands and distraction and still function. I wonder how they made the decision to have them in the first place."

Wisps of mischief sparked in her eyes. "So that's why you kept asking me why I had Ryan? Because you think your nephews and nieces are a noisy, messy time-suck, and that an otherwise sane adult can have a child only by throwing away logic and disregarding all cautionary tales?"

He raised one eyebrow at her. "You know you've just called me Uncle Scrooge, don't you?"

Rose burst out chuckling. "Busted."

Gwen spluttered qualifications, shooting reproach at Rose, and he aborted her protests with a smile, showing her he was offense-proof, especially by anything coming from her. "Don't take it back when you're probably right. Interacting with children has never been one of my skills."

The only child he'd loved having around and taking care of had been Hesham. But he'd been only eight years older. He hadn't had any relevant experience with children outside his professional sphere.

She made an eloquent gesture indicating how he was holding Ryan with growing confidence, picking up various articles for his inspection. "If it has never been, then you're capable of acquiring new skills on the fly."

He'd always been uncomfortable receiving compliments, feeling the element of self-serving exaggeration in each. But her good opinion felt free of ulterior motives, *and* was clearly expressed against the dictates of her good sense. To *him* it felt…necessary.

He transferred his smile from her to Ryan. "It's this little man who's making me look like a quick study. He's the one doing the driving here."

Rose nodded. "Ryan does that. Just one look and a smile and the world is his to command. Very much like his mother."

Gwen's eyes darkened on something that gripped his heart in a tight fist. Something like…anguish. *Ya Ullah,* why?

Next second, he wanted to kick himself. How could he have forgotten the reason she was here? Ryan's condition.

But he had forgotten, during the lifetime since she'd walked in and turned his life upside down all over again. But from holding Ryan, he had a firm idea what his condition was. It was time he did everything he could to put her mind to rest about it.

He adjusted his grip on Ryan, feeling as if he'd always held him, turned his face up with a finger beneath the dimpled chin that was a replica of Gwen's. "Just so I don't look like a total marionette, Ryan, how about we pretend I have a say here? How about you let me examine you now?"

"How about I leave you to your new game and go find me some food?" Rose said, clearly to give them privacy.

Fareed produced his cell phone, called Emad back. Emad appeared in under ten seconds, as if he'd been standing behind the door, which he probably had been. Eavesdropping?

He was resigned that Emad would go to any lengths to ascertain his safety. But what was there to worry about here? Getting ambushed by lethal doses of charisma and cuteness?

He gave him a mocking glance that Emad refused to rise to. "Will you please escort Rose to an early dinner, Emad? And do make it somewhere where they serve something better than the food simulations you got us from the hospital's restaurant."

He expected Emad to obey with his usual decorum, which never showed if he appreciated the chore or not. But wonder of wonders, after nodding to him with that maddening deference, he turned to Rose with interest—almost eagerness—sparking in his eyes. Fareed hadn't seen anything like that in the man's eyes since his late wife.

The gregarious Rose eyed him back with open appreciation and murmured to Gwen for all to hear, "So incredible things *do* come to those who wait, eh, sweetie?" She didn't wait for Gwen's reaction and turned to Fareed. "It's been a treat meeting you, Sheikh Aal Zaafer. Take care of my lovelies, hmm?"

He bowed his head. "Fareed, please. And we'll be meeting again. *And* you can count on it."

She grinned at him, gave Gwen's hand a bolstering squeeze, caressed Ryan's cheek then gave *his* an affectionate pat before turning to Emad. "Shall we, Mr. Dark Knight?"

Emad gaped at her, clearly unable to believe this woman had just petted his prince. And that she'd called *him* that.

Then his eyes narrowed on a flare of challenge and approval as he gave her his arm. "By all means, Ms. Maher."

"Can't come up with a slogan for me, huh?" Rose beamed up at Emad. "But we have time. You'll think of something."

Before the door closed behind them, he heard Emad saying, "I don't need time, Ms. Wild Rose."

Fareed shook his head as the door closed behind them. He looked at Ryan, who was testing his stubble. "Can you believe this, Ryan? Emad teasing? Seems the power to change the laws of nature runs in your family."

Ryan squeaked as if in agreement and Fareed turned his gaze to Gwen, offered her his hand.

She stared at it for moments, her lower lip caught in her teeth, the very sight of conflicted temptation.

Before he gave in and reached for her hand, she gave it to him. He almost groaned and barely kept from bringing her nestling into him. He would make her give in, fully, irreversibly. In good time.

First, he would see to her peace of mind.

He made it a pledge. "Now I'll see to Ryan, Gwen."

Gwen's heart gave another boom before resuming its gallop.

But it wasn't only hearing her name on his lips that caused this latest disturbance. It was that he pronounced it *Gwaihn,* the breathy sound as he prolonged it a scorching sigh, making an intimacy of it, a promise...of so many things she couldn't even contemplate.

As if having her hand engulfed in his wasn't enough.

But she had herself to blame for this. She'd given her hand to him when she should have shown him she'd allow only formal interaction.

But she hadn't been able to withhold it. He was offering her what she'd been starving for. Support, strength other than her own to draw on, an infinite well of it. And whatever the consequences, she hadn't been able to stop from reaching for it.

He took them to the other end of the room, behind an opaque glass partition, to what turned out to be a fully fitted exam room.

"Gwen..." She started again. He cocked his head at her. "May I call you Gwen?"

She almost cried out, *No, you may not. Please, don't.*

Out loud she reluctantly said, "If you like, Dr. Aal Zaafer."

"I like, very much. And it's Fareed."

This was getting worse by the second. "Er...all right, Dr. Fareed...or, uh, do you prefer Sheikh?"

"Just Fareed."

And wasn't that the truth. He *was* unique, as his name proclaimed him to be. She'd looked up its meaning long before...

She shook her head, trying not to let the memories deluge her. "I can't call you just...that."

"Rose did, without a second's hesitation."

"Rose, as you noticed, is...is..."

"Blessedly unreserved. You should follow her example because I won't be called anything else by you. We're not only colleagues—" before she could contest *that,* he pressed on "—working in complementary fields, but I owe a lot of my most positive results to your breakthrough. The drug you developed has been my most reliable postoperative adjuvant therapy for years."

She gaped at him, her heart flapping inside her chest with a mixture of disbelief and pride. "I didn't realize... didn't know..."

He gave her one of those earth-shaking smiles of his. "Now you do. And even though I'm getting impatient with your slowness in developing the other drug that should shrink tumors before surgery, I'll forgive you on the strength of the first one. So we have far more than enough grounds for at least a first-name basis."

His lips listed those acceptable reasons, but his eyes told her the truth. He *wanted* this intimacy, would have it.

But she *needed* formality to hide behind, to keep things in perspective. Otherwise...

No. No otherwise. If anyone was off-limits to her, it was Fareed Aal Zaafer. She'd better never forget that.

"How about that game? It's super-easy and a lot of fun."

The indulgent drawl, which he only produced while talking to Ryan, snatched her out of her latest plunge into turmoil.

She watched him lay Ryan down on the exam bed and hand him a reflex hammer and penlight to play with. He moved around, turning on machines, gathering instruments, all the time explaining what he was doing and naming everything and what they were for.

He was talking to Ryan because he must know she knew all that. And that he was explaining to a ten-month-old, without the least condescension, as if he believed it was never too early for Ryan to learn, as if he hoped Ryan would at least understand the consideration in his attitude, choked her up again.

When he returned to Ryan's side, she asked, "Won't you call your assistants?"

He cocked one eyebrow at her, teasing sparking the

fiery brown of his eyes. "You think I can't handle examining one highly cooperative tyke on my own?"

"Actually, I'm worried this is the calm before the storm. In previous visits, Ryan acted as if the doctors were torturing him."

His eyebrows shot up before he looked at Ryan. "But you won't do that to your obedient ride, will you? And I won't make it such a cheerless endeavor that you'll be driven to tears. You can even assist me, hold instruments, test and taste them to your heart's content. Between us, we'll make this a great game, Ryan."

His thoughtfulness, then the way he said *Rye-aan,* Ryan's similar-sounding Arabic name, lanced through her.

After receiving Ryan's gleeful endorsement, he moved to start prepping him. She moved, too, bumped into him.

Feeling his steadying hands on her shoulders made her jump back. "I—I'll just undress him."

He gave her a tiny squeeze before setting her free and turning to Ryan. "As Ryan's designated driver this afternoon, I think he'd want me to do the honors, right, Ryan?"

Sure enough, Ryan let out a squeal of agreement.

She stood back, every nerve buzzing as he undid Ryan's snap-button jumpsuit with great care and dexterity, although it was clear he'd never performed the task before. Instead of fidgeting as he usually did, Ryan stunned her by chewing on a chart and offering Fareed every cooperation in stripping him down to his diapers.

"You're an extremely well-cared-for little prince, eh, Ryan?"

Her heart gave another painful thud, which was stupid. It was just a figure of speech.

"Now, let's start the game."

She stood mesmerized, watching Fareed's beautiful hands probe Ryan's muscles for power, pushing and pulling on his feet and legs, making Ryan an eager participant. He turned to sensation, walking his fingers along nerve paths, before pouncing with tickles and eliciting Ryan's shrieking giggles.

Next came recording muscle contraction and nerve conduction and he made Ryan help him fit in plugs and place leads over his body, all the time explaining everything. Ryan hung on his every word, his eyes rapt as he watched this larger-than-life entity who'd entered and filled his limited world. Fareed warned him that the tests were a bit uncomfortable, but would be over in no time, and Gwen braced herself for the end of the honeymoon.

But as he started the tests, instead of the dreaded wails, Ryan seemed to only notice Fareed's banter, awarded him with a steady stream of corroborating gurgles.

She shouldn't be surprised. Fareed's darkest silk voice made *her* forget a world outside existed, or a past or a future....

What was she *thinking?* She should only be thinking of running away once this exam ended, forgetting she'd ever seen him again.

She'd only sought him as a last resort, had hoped to slip in among his appointments undistinguished. But she'd ended up having his attention in its most undiluted form. Then it had gotten worse and he'd remembered her, had been treating her since as if he...

Her thoughts piled up as he dressed Ryan then caught her eye. "I'll see those investigations now."

She pounced on the briefcase, but he gently stopped her fumbling, took over. He studied the X-rays and MRIs briefly, set aside the reports without reading them before putting everything back in the briefcase. Then he turned to Ryan, who was demanding to be picked up—by him.

He complied at once. "So how was that? Fun as I promised, eh?" Ryan whooped an agreement. "But you know what? We had all this fun together, and I haven't even introduced myself. My name is Fareed." He pointed to himself, said his name a few time.

Ryan's eyes twinkled before he echoed triumphantly, "Aa-eed."

"Ma azkaak men subbi!" Fareed exclaimed. "What a clever boy you are." Ryan seemed delighted by Fareed's approval, and continued to say Aa-eed over and over. Fareed guffawed. "We'll work on the *F* and *R* later. I bet you'll get it right in a couple of months, being a genius, like Rose said—" he turned to her "—and like your mother is."

Gwen felt about to faint again.

It's dreading his still-unvoiced verdict, she told herself.

But it wasn't. She *was* terrified of having her worst fears validated, but that lightheadedness, as if she'd been hungry all her life, was the effect he had on her. Anything he did, every move and look and breath induced pure emotional and erotic tumult. . . .

What was happening to her? What was it about him that made her someone she didn't know? Someone who couldn't complete a thought without it turning into something. . .licentious?

He was guiding her back into the room, stopping by the desk for a computer tablet. At the sitting area, he set Ryan on the ground, gave him every safe article around to play with. Ryan instead made it clear he wanted to nap. She produced a blanket from the bag Rose had left behind and Fareed spread it in front of the couch, where Ryan crawled and promptly feel asleep facedown.

Once they sat down, Fareed said, "Tell me about Ryan, Gwen."

Don't call me that, she wanted to cry out. She needed to

regain her balance and there was no hope she would when he kept calling her *Gwaihn* in that lion's purr of his.

Instead she nodded her shaky assent. Over the next minutes, he obtained an exhaustive history of Ryan's pre- and postnatal periods and developmental milestones, his fingers flying over the glossy tablet's surface documenting it all.

Finally, he put the tablet down, turned to face her. "You do know he has *spina bifida occulta?*"

His question/declaration felt like a direct blow to her heart. She'd known, but had still been hoping against hope....

Tears surged again as she nodded. "As a researcher of drugs targeting the nervous system, I knew the basics of the condition." Incomplete closure of vertebrae around the spinal cord, which instead of hanging loose in the spinal canal was tethered to the bone, potentially causing varying degrees of nerve damage and disability. "I studied it extensively because I suspected Ryan of having it. But every pediatrician and neurologist told me not to worry, that ten percent of people have it and are asymptomatic, something they discover as adults during X-rays for unrelated complaints. I persisted, and a couple conceded that he has minor neurological deficits, which might or might not mean future disability but that there was no treatment anyway. But I couldn't just wait until Ryan grew up and couldn't walk or never developed bowel or urinary continence. I had to know for sure that there was nothing to be done, and only you...only your opinion will do..."

The sobs that had been banked broke loose.

He was down on his haunches in front of her in a blink, his hands squeezing her shoulders. "It was amazing that you noticed the mild weakness in his legs and clawing in his toes. He's sitting and crawling, and with him far away from being toilet-trained and without previous experience with children, I'm beyond impressed that you discerned his condition even after the repeated dismissal of your worries. But I can excuse the doctors who examined him. It would take someone as extensively versed in the rare as I am to form an opinion on so irregular a condition."

Her sobs had been subsiding gradually, at his soothing and under the urge to swamp him with questions.

The paramount one burst from her. "And you've formed one?"

He nodded. "You were absolutely right. Without surgery, he may develop increasing disability in lower limb motor function and bowel and urinary control."

She sank her fingers into his sinew and muscle. "So there is a surgery? To prevent further damage? What about any that already exists? *Is* there damage? What about bowel and urinary problems? My sources say even when surgery successfully closes the defect and releases the cord, those usually never go away…." She faltered on the last question, what she of all people knew was a long shot. "And if there's a residual handicap, would my drug help?"

He rose, came down beside her. This time, she sank into his solicitude gratefully, only the last vestiges of her willpower stopping her from physically seeking it.

"Most, if not all, surgeons wouldn't touch a case like Ryan's. They'd say their findings are too ephemeral to warrant a surgery that wouldn't offer much, if any, improvement. But I say different."

Hope surged so hard inside her that she choked with its agonizing expansion. "You—you mean you're not telling me to give up?"

He shook his head. "Of course, any surgery comes with risks." The world darkened again. He caught her hand, squeezed it. "I have to mention risks because it's unethical to promise you a risk-free procedure, not because I expect problems. But I can and do promise you and Ryan the best result possible."

Her tears faltered. "Y-you mean *you* want to operate on him?"

He nodded. "He'll be safe with me, Gwen."

She stifled another heart-wrenching sob. Fareed's arm slid around her. "And yes, your drug will regenerate the nerve damage. I know it's not approved for use on children, but because I believed the delay in approval was built on bureaucracy and not medical facts, I have obtained permission from the region's drug administration under my personal responsibility and have used it on even younger patients than Ryan with adjusted doses and certain precautions to astonishing results. Together, we'll cure Ryan, Gwen."

And she had to ask the rest, everything, now, before this turned out to be a deranged dream, before she fainted again. "How long will it take? The surgery? The recuperation? How soon can he have it? How much will it all cost?"

"The surgery itself is from four to six hours, and the recuperation is from four to six weeks. He can have it as soon as I prepare everything. And it won't cost a thing."

That stopped the churning world. Her tears. Her heart.

"You must have misunderstood," she finally whispered. "I'm not here seeking charity. I didn't even think of asking you to perform the surgery, only hoped you'd write me a report stating that it's a surgical case, so no surgeon could tell me it isn't."

He pursed his lips. "First, there's no charity involved—"

She struggled to detach herself from the circle of his support. "Of course there is. You're here performing pro bono surgeries. But I can pay. Just tell me how much, and I will."

"*You* will pay? Not that it's an issue here, but why wouldn't your insurance cover your child's medical expenses?"

She should be more careful what she said. He noticed everything. Now she had to satisfy him with an explanation or he'd corner her with demands for more information she couldn't give. "I insisted on costly investigations the doctors said weren't needed, moving me to an unfavorable insurance category, so the coverage would be only partial now. But that doesn't matter. I'm very well paid and I have a lot of money."

He leveled patient eyes on her. "Of course you are and you do. And there is *still* no cost involved."

She shook her head. "I can't accept a waiver of your fee. And then there are many other expenses besides that."

His lips quirked, teasing, indulgent. "First, I'm a big boy, if you haven't noticed, and I can waive my fee if I want to, which I mostly do. My 'reputation' isn't *totally* hype, you know. Second, there won't be any other expenses back home."

She gaped at him. For a full minute.

She finally heard a strangled echo. "Back home?"

He rose to his feet with a smile. "Yes. You, Ryan and Rose are coming with me to Jizaan."

Five

Gwen stared at the overwhelming force that was Fareed Aal Zaafer, and was certain of one of two things.

Either she'd finally lost her mind, or he was out of his.

She squeezed her eyes shut, as if that would stop the disintegration of this situation, set it back in the land of the acceptable. She opened her eyes again hoping she'd see on his face what should have been there from the start, polite forbearance with a patient's hysterical mother.

But he was looking at her with that indulgent intensity that singed her. Worse, a new excitement was entering his gaze, as if he was realizing more benefits to his decision by the second.

"As soon as Rose and Emad return, we'll go to your hotel and collect your luggage on our way to the airport. We'll be in Jizaan in under twenty-four hours."

He'd said it again. This Jizaan thing. She hadn't imagined it the first time. This was real. He meant it.

But he *couldn't* mean it. He had to be joking. He did have a wicked sense of humor....

No. His humor, while unpredictable and lightning-fast, was not in any way mean, at least, not in any of the lectures and interviews she'd seen. It would be beyond cruel to joke now and he was the very opposite of that: magnanimous, compassionate, protective.

But he was also single-minded and autocratic and she had to stop him before this crazy idea became a solid intention.

He detailed said intention. "We'll go to dinner first, or we can have it on board the jet." He got out his cell phone, cocked his head at her. "What would you like to have? Real food this time, I promise. I can either reserve seats in a restaurant, or have your choice ready on the jet."

"I can't go to your kingdom!"

The shaky statement managed to do the job. It stopped him short.

For about a second. Then he smiled. "Of course, you can."

She raised her hands. "Please, let's not start another 'I can't' 'No, you can' match. We just finished one about payment."

"Yes, let's not. You do remember how you fared in that last match? No point in repeating the same method and expecting different results, hmm?"

The definition of insanity, which also described this situation. She did feel her sanity slipping another notch. "You know what you're proposing is impossible."

"I know no such thing."

She shook her head, disbelief deepening, dread taking root. "You're asking me to just haul everyone halfway across the world...."

"I'll do the 'hauling,' so cross that out on your no-doubt

alphabetized list of worries. I'm sure you have your affairs sorted out for as long as you thought would see Ryan's medical situation resolved. But in case you're not fully covered, and fear repercussions for prolonged or unexcused absence from work, one phone call from me should get you an open-ended leave, with pay."

Her breathing had gone awry by the time he finished. "It's not just my work, it's…*everything.*"

He crossed his arms over his chest, someone who would not be denied, who had an answer to everything. "Like what?"

She groped for something, anything, latched on the first logical thing that occurred to her. "Like passports. We didn't bring them on a trip we couldn't have dreamed would take us outside the States."

His daunting shoulder rose and fell. "You won't need them to enter my kingdom."

"But we'd need visas…."

He intercepted that, too. "Not when you're entering the kingdom with me, you don't. And I'll bring you back with me, so you won't need more than your American IDs to re-enter the States."

Her eyes darted around, as if looking for a way out. There was none. He kept neutralizing possible objections in advance. "And anyway, to make you feel better, once in Jizaan, I'll have the American embassy there issue new passports for you and I'll have visas stamped on them."

She knew he could do that with a flick of a finger. Any country would bend over backward to accommodate him.

"And if you're worried about your family, I'll call them right now, give them all my contact info, so they'd be in touch with you at all times. I can even take any of them who wish to come along, too."

Her heart emptied at his mention of her family. A subject she had to close before he probed it open. "Rose is my closest relative."

And probe he did. "You said she was a maternal relative. So what happened to your mother?"

She could feel the familiar pain and loss expanding all over inside her. She had to get this over with, dissuade him from broaching the subject ever again. "She died from surgical complications just after I entered college. I have no one else."

He looked thoughtful. "And that must have factored in your decision to have Ryan after your engagement fell through, so you'd form your own family."

She let her silence convince him his deduction was right, when it was anything but.

"I'm very sorry to hear you were all alone in the world for so long. Coming from such an extensive family, I can't imagine how it must have been for you."

"I'm no longer alone."

"Yes." After a long moment when sympathy seemed to radiate off him, he smiled. "So we checked off passports, visas, fees and responsibility to family as reasons to resist my plans."

"But these are not the only…" She stopped, panting now as if she'd been trying to outrun an out-of-control car. She *was* trying to escape his inexorable intentions. "What am I saying? I'm not debating the feasibility of something that's not even an option. And the only thing that will make me feel better is that you drop this and…and…" She stopped again, feeling herself being backed into a trap her own capitulation would close shut. And he was standing there, waiting for her to succumb, knowing that she would. She groaned with helplessness, "Why even suggest this? Why not perform the surgery here? If it's because you're worried I'd be saddled with hospital expenses…"

He waved that majestic hand of his. "I could have had the hospital waive them by adding Ryan to the cases I was here for."

"Then why?" That came out a desperate moan.

He gave her such a look, that of someone willing to spend days cajoling and happy to do it. "You want reasons in descending or ascending order of importance?"

"Oh, please!" She tried to rise, failed to inject any co-ordination in her jellified legs. "Just…just…"

He sat down, put a soothing hand on her shoulder. "Breathe, Gwen. Everything will be fine, I promise. As for why, one main reason is that I can't stay away from my medical center any longer. And I certainly won't operate on Ryan, then leave him to someone else's follow-up. The other major reason is that I can only guarantee my results in a case as delicate when I'm in my medium, among the medical team I put together and the system I constructed."

Those *were* major reasons. "But still…"

"No 'but stills.' You're coming with me and…"

She interrupted him this time. "Even if we have to come, we don't have to right away. We can go back home, prepare ourselves, and when you have a surgery date arranged, we'd fly over."

He was the epitome of accommodation, yet of determination. "Why go to the trouble and expense when you have a free and convenient ride now? At absolutely no extra cost or effort on my part? And there's nothing to arrange. Once in Jizaan, I'll take Ryan for the mandatory pre-op tests, then do the surgery at once."

Her heart punched her ribs. "Th-that fast?"

"There's every reason to do it as soon as possible. But don't worry about a thing, I'll take care of everything."

"But I *can't* just let you do everything, pay for everything. If we have to go to Jizaan, then I'll at least pay our way."

He leaned back, folded his arms across his expansive chest. "So what do you propose to do? Give my pilot and cabin crew your credit card? Or will you want to stop by an ATM to get cash?"

"Please, don't joke! The most I can consent to not paying is your own fee. *If* you really waive it on a regular basis."

His face lost any lightness. "After all the things you implied I was, are you now calling me a liar?"

"Oh, God, *no!*" she blurted out. "I meant…"

His serious expression dissolved on a smile that could have powered a small city. She must be in even worse condition than she'd thought if she hadn't realized he *had* been joking.

"I know what you meant." His fingers gently probed her pulse. "Your heart is in hyperdrive. It's physically distressing thinking you'd be in someone's debt, isn't it?" *It's more your nearness, your touch,* she almost confessed. "But rest easy, Gwen, there's no debt. I will always owe many surgical successes to your expertise. Let me try to repay it with mine. As for me, on a professional level, adding the success of Ryan's surgery to my achievements will be more than payment enough for me." Suddenly the eyes that had become serious for real, crinkled on bedeviling. "But if you have money you can't bear having, I'll give you a list of causes in Jizaan and you can donate it in lieu of payment."

She had no answer now but more tears.

They welled up, filling her whole being. It was beyond incredible. To have his incomparable skills and support. It was also beyond terrible. To have to go with him, be near him, for weeks, be exposed to his influence and subjected to her weakness.

Beyond the tragedies that had sheared through her life and heart, that was the worst thing that could have happened to her. She would have gone to hell and wouldn't have bothered coming back to see Ryan healthy and happy. Now she would go to the one place she considered worse than hell. And she could never explain her feelings to Fareed.

She finally whispered, "I—I don't know what to say."

He sat back, his imposing frame sprawling in the contentment of someone who'd fulfilled his purpose. "You do. A three-letter word. Beginning with a *Y* and ending with an *S*."

A thousand fears screeched in the darkness of her mind. And she closed her eyes and prayed. That when she said it, it would only mean Ryan's salvation, and not her damnation.

She opened her eyes, stepped off the bleak, yet familiar, cliff of resignation into the abyss of the unknown.

And whispered the dreaded, "Yes."

The trip to Jizaan passed in a blur of distress.

Fareed, with Emad and the flight crew, orchestrated a symphony of such lavish luxury that it almost snapped her frayed nerves. She was so unused to being waited on, so uncomfortable at being on the receiving end of such indulgence, when she was unable to repay it, too, that it exhausted her.

After the first three hours, she'd escaped by sleeping the remaining eight hours to their refueling layover in London. She'd taken refuge in sleep again in the second leg of the journey, leaving Rose and Ryan to plumb the jet's inhabitants' ceaseless desire to spoil them.

She was floating somewhere gray and oppressive when she felt a caress on her hand.

She jerked out of the coma-like sleep knowing it was Fareed. Only his touch had ever felt like a thousand volts of disruption.

"I apologize for disturbing your slumber, but we're about to land." His eyes glowed like embers even in the jet's atrocious lighting, his magnificent voice soaked in gentle teasing. "I hope fourteen hours of sleep managed to provide a measure of rest."

She would have told him they sure hadn't if her throat didn't feel lined with sandpaper. She rose from the comfort of the plane bed, returning it to its upright position, feeling as if she'd been in a knock-down drag-out fight.

Apart from everything that disturbed her past, present and future, she knew why she felt wrecked. She might have been hiding in unawareness, but she'd felt him as she'd slept, and his thoughts, the demand, the promise in them and her struggle against them, had worn her out.

Rose waited until he left to approach her with Ryan, eyeing her in sarcastic censure. "That was sure record-breaking."

"You mean you and Ryan staying awake for that long?"

Rose huffed. "Oh, we slept, around an hour on each leg. *We* were savvy enough to take advantage of that once-in-a-lifetime experience. While *you* are either stupid, or stupid not to grab at all that…God offers."

From the proof of undeniable experience, Gwen knew that Rose, the only "aunt" she'd ever had, had only her best interest at heart. She'd always counted on her outspokenness to make her face the truth when she shied away from it. But now that smack of reality only made her sink deeper into despair.

Rose had no idea how…impossible everything was.

She was almost thankful when Fareed returned, bringing with him another dose of disturbance. She wasn't up to more evasive maneuvers with the other unstoppable force in her life.

She was unequivocally thankful when Rose engaged Fareed in conversation during landing. It left her able to pretend to look outside her window when she saw nothing but her internal turmoil.

They were really in Jizaan.

After touchdown, Fareed got up and took Ryan from Rose.

Gwen jumped up, tried to take him. Fareed looked down at Ryan. "Which ride do you want, *ya sugheeri?*"

Thorns sprouted in her stomach at the loving way Fareed called Ryan his little one.

Ryan, who seemingly understood anything Fareed said in either English or Arabic, looked back at her with dimples at full blast. Then he bobbed in his arms, spurring him to move.

There. She'd gotten her answer.

As Rose preceded them out of the plane with Emad, Fareed kept a step behind her.

His bass purr hit her back. "I'm not competing with you for his favor."

She slanted him a glance over her shoulder, almost winced at the incredible sight of him, as immaculate and fresh as if he hadn't been up for the past twenty-four hours, after a month of grueling surgeries, too. He towered over her, his shoulders broad enough to blot out the whole world, virility and gorgeousness radiating off him in shock waves.

Looking ahead before she stumbled, she murmured, "It never occurred to me that you were."

"And he's not choosing me over you."

A mocking huff broke from her. "Could have fooled me."

His deep chuckle resonated in her bones. "He's not. I'm just the new toy."

She would have chuckled, too, if she'd been able to draw more air than that which kept her on her feet and conscious.

And that was before he took her elbow, offered the support he must have felt she needed, smiled down at her. "You really should be happy we're enjoying each other's company so much." Her knees almost lost their solidity as seriousness tinged his gaze. "But I can't be more relieved that he likes and seeks me. The coming time isn't going to be easy, and trusting me is going to make everything so much better for him."

He was *that* thoughtful? She'd only ever known one other person with that kindness....

Memories lodged into her heart like an ax. She clamped down on the pain. She couldn't afford to let those overwhelm her now. She needed to be at her strongest, her most resolute. For Ryan. And for her own struggle.

She passed by a time zones clock, blinked at its verdict. Four-thirty in the afternoon in L.A., 5:30 a.m. in Jizaan. Exactly twenty-four hours from the moment she'd staggered into his orbit.

She felt as if her life before those hours had been someone else's, someone whose memories were sloughing off to be replaced by this new reality that had no rhyme or reason.

Then she stepped out of the jet and into another realm.

Her career had taken her all over the world, other desert kingdoms included, but Jizaan felt...alien, unprecedented.

The least of it was the airport itself, what she'd caught glimpses of from the air, what had the design, ambition and otherworldliness of a horizon-dominating space colony.

Everything else was painted with a brush of hyperreality. The star-sprinkled sky midway between the blue of eternity and the indigo of dawn had the vibrancy of another dimension, the stars the sharpness and abundance of another galaxy. The desert winter breeze that kissed her face and ran insistent fingers through her hair, even when jets' exhaust should have tainted it, felt cleansing, resuscitating. The whole atmosphere was permeated by echoes of a history rife with towering passions, unquenchable feuds and undying honor. She felt it all tug at her through her awareness of Fareed, whose blood ran thick with this land's legacy.

She stole a look at him, found him looking down at Ryan, his expression laced with fondness. Ryan, secure in Fareed's powerful grasp, was looking around, his face rapt as he inhaled deep, as if to breathe in the new place, make it a part of him.

Her heart constricted. If only...

"Ahlann wa sahlann bekom fi daari-wa daarakom."

Fareed's deep tones caressed every one of her nerves—until she translated what he'd said.

He was welcoming them to his home. And theirs.

She knew this was simply the ultragenerosity the region was known for, where they offered guests their homes as theirs. She still felt as if a wrecking ball had swung into her. She swayed with the force of the phantom sensation.

Fareed grabbed her tight against his side.

He'd probably saved her, this time from a plunge down a flight of steel stairs. But being ensconced in his heat and hardness, his concern was unendurable.

She groped for the railing, quickened her descent, pretending steadiness. The moment she touched ground, her legs wobbled again.

He caught her, exhaled. "I should have woken you earlier. You're still drowsy. Or you're hypoglycemic again. You barely ate anything since we started this journey."

She didn't refute his explanations. Better to let him think it was all physical. She wouldn't tell him the truth. She couldn't. Not the general truth. Or the one behind her latest bout of chaos. That as soon as her feet touched the ground, she could almost swear the land pulled at her. And yelled at her.

Leave, the moment you can. Before you sustain an injury you won't survive this time.

They'd reached the limo awaiting them a dozen feet from the jet's stairs, where Emad had taken the driver's seat with Rose beside him, when she heard Fareed say, "We're going to my place, Ryan."

The words meant for Ryan skimmed her mind, leaving no impression. Then they slowly sank. And detonated.

She swung to him as he held the door open for her. *"What?"*

He frowned his confusion. "What do you mean 'what'?"

"What do you mean *your* place?"

He smiled, a smile drenched in that overriding sensuality that was as integral to him as his DNA. "My place is the place where I live. And where you'll stay."

"We're going to stay in your center!"

He gave an adamant headshake as he prodded her to enter the limo, making her slide across the backseat by entering after her. "Only during the immediate pre- and postoperative period. And don't contest this again."

"I never contested it a first time...."

"Which was much appreciated, so don't suddenly change—"

She cut him off in return, feeling her brain overheating. "Because this is the first time I've heard of this."

"Not true. I told you during the flight."

"Was I awake when you told me?"

He gave her a thoughtful glance, then his smile scalded her with its amusement. "Come to think of it, that you didn't contest it should have clued me in that you were sleep talking."

"And now that I'm awake…"

"You'll be my esteemed guest."

Before she could utter another protest, Ryan, who'd been getting louder demanding his attention, grabbed his face and tugged. Fareed turned to him and at once they got engaged in another game of fetch-and-explain.

Even though he had been paying Ryan every attention, she knew he relished that timely excuse to end their conversation. She knew there was no use trying to continue it. He had this infallible way of getting his way, of making his unilateral decisions the only ones that made sense. But his place?

She felt she was sinking in quicksand and any move was making her sink faster.

And there was nothing she could do about it.

She exhaled, sought distraction, looked outside the window, her eyes finally registering the splendor of Jizaan's sparkling capital rushing by.

In the first slivers of dawn, the magnificence of Al Zaaferah, or The Victorious, named after the centuries-old ruling house, seeped into her awareness. It felt as if it had been erected today to the most lavish standards. It also looked constantly evolving with extreme-concept projects rising among the soaring mirrored buildings—

everything felt futuristic yet with pervasive cultural influences making it feel steeped in history.

She was lost in recording every detail when she noticed they'd gotten off the main roads and were now driving through automatic, thirty-feet-high, wrought-iron gates. Fareed's "place," no doubt.

The limo winded through ingeniously landscaped grounds, approaching a sprawling stone mansion crouching in the distance. Painted in sweeps of shadow and mysticism, it had the feel of a fortress from a Middle Eastern fable, the abode of someone who craved solitude, yet in having to house those his rank dictated, expanded his domain to give them space, and himself distance.

She hadn't thought what his place would be like. If she had, she would have imagined he lived in either the royal palace, or as imposing an edifice. But even though this place spoke of affluence, it didn't reek of excess. It was amazing how everything was permeated with the privileges of the prince, yet possessed the austerity of the surgeon.

All through their journey to the main door, she felt invisible eyes monitoring their progress, relaying it to forward stations. Even though she'd experienced many aspects of Fareed's status, that seamlessly orchestrated surveillance solidified everything in her mind. Who Fareed was. Where she was now.

He handed her out of the limo feet from stone steps leading to the patio. Footmen appeared as if from nowhere and rushed to open the massive brass-work doors.

She entered beside him with trepidation expanding in her heart into a columned hall that spread under a thirty-foot mosaic dome. The doors closed with a soft click. To Gwen, it felt as if iron prison doors were slammed shut behind her.

Her gaze darted around the indirectly lit space, got impressions of a sweeping floor plan extending on both sides, understated colors, a male influence in decor—his virile influence permeating the place. Her inspection ended where thirty-foot-wide stairs climbed to a spacious platform before winding away to each side of the upper floor.

Fareed led them up one side to a guest apartment triple the size of her condo, faithfully displaying the amalgam of modernity and Arabian Nights feel of the rest of the mansion. If she were in a condition to appreciate anything, she would have found it amazing to walk through doors that looked like they'd been transported through millennia intact only to swing open soundlessly with a proximity sensor. She was sure even Scheherazade's imagination couldn't have created anything like this place.

"Let me take him."

Gwen stirred from her reverie at Rose's words. She found her taking a now sound-asleep Ryan from Fareed.

"We're both done for." Rose stifled a yawn as she gave Gwen a kiss on the cheek. She grinned at Emad as she took Ryan's bag from him. "I'll find us the nearest beds and it might be night when you see either of us again."

In a minute everyone had left her alone with Fareed.

She turned blindly, pretending to inspect the sitting area. She ran a hand along the perfect smoothness of a hand-carved chair before turning to a spherical, fenestrated brass lantern hanging from the ceiling with spectacular chains. She made the mistake of transferring her gaze to him and the hypnotic play of light and shadows over his face and figure only deepened his influence.

He stared back at her for long, long moments, winding up the coil of tension inside her tighter until she felt she'd shatter.

Before she begged him to just stop, he finally exhaled.

"I apologize for not staying to show you around, but I have to go to work, catch up on everything I hadn't been able to attend to long-distance. Use the place as you would your own—and *don't* argue. Just explore, relax, rest. Then tomorrow we go the center."

Her heart almost knocked her off her feet. "You—you'll operate tomorrow?"

He simply said, "Yes."

After losing all of her family, one after the other, Gwen had thought she'd known all kinds of anguish and desperation. All forms of loss.

But now she knew there was more. There was worse. And there was one injury, one loss, she wouldn't survive.

If anything happened to Ryan…

"Everything will be fine."

She chafed at Rose's reassurance. What she'd reiterated over and over since Fareed had taken Ryan and disappeared into the depths of his staggeringly advanced medical center.

It didn't work now as it hadn't worked before. Fareed had come out once, fourteen hours ago, telling them Ryan had been prepared and was already in the O.R. He'd said he'd come out to reassure them as soon as he was done with the surgery.

That had lasted *eight* hours. Two hours longer than his longest estimate. Every second of the extra time, she'd known a worse hell than any she'd known before.

Guilt had consumed her. She'd sought inferior help initially, hoping it would suffice, save her from making contact with Fareed. What if she'd left it too late? What if she'd be punished for considering anything, no matter how momentous, ahead of Ryan's health?

Rose hugged her, sensing her thoughts. "Stop it, Gwen. Everything is fine. Fareed's assistant assured us it is."

"But *he* didn't."

Fareed hadn't come out to reassure her as he'd promised! What if that meant he couldn't face her with what had happened yet?

Rose tsked. "You did see the mass casualty situation that hit the center like a tornado, didn't you? With his being the chief around here and with God knows how many lives to save, I'm sure putting your mind to rest personally plunged to the bottom of his priorities."

Logic droned that Rose was right. But hysteria was drowning it out. They wouldn't let her see Ryan in Recovery or ICU. Fareed's orders. That was six mutilating hours ago.

Suddenly, Fareed appeared at the other end of the expansive waiting area.

She rose, could barely stand erect as his long strides ate the maddening distance between them. Then out of the blue, he was swamped by people. Other patients' frantic families.

He stopped his advance, turned to them with calm, patient and what must have been very detailed reassurance because it defused their tension. By the time he at last excused himself with utmost courteousness and resumed his path to her, she was at screaming pitch.

As he stopped before her, those fiery eyes piercing her, she felt he'd trodden on the heart that had crashed at his feet.

"It all went wrong."

Six

Gwen's lifeless statement barely scratched the surface of the terror in her heart.

Fareed hadn't smiled at her. He'd smiled at the others. She could only interpret his intensity as bad news. The worst...

He smiled. Her knees buckled.

"*Nothing* went wrong." His smile broadened as he caught her by the waist, stopped her from folding to the ground. "I *already* told you that—well, I sent Akram to tell you that everything went perfectly right."

"Oh, you magnificent man, thank you!" Rose charged him, made him relinquish his hold on Gwen and squeezed him in an exuberant hug.

Gwen felt the life force that had felt extracted from her slowly begin to reenter her body. Then he put Rose at arm's length, smiled down at her. "But I can't take much credit. Ryan did most of the work. From the pre-op preps to what my team told me felt like ordering his very tissues to assist me, he was the most interactive patient I ever had. I've never had a surgery go so smoothly."

Rose laughed her delight. "That's our Ryan! But we'll just pretend that you did have an equal role in this, and you'll accept our thanks like a good sport."

"As long as you realize the extent of my contribution, I'm happy to accept."

Their elation hammered at Gwen, demanding to breach her numbness. But the tidal wave hovered at the periphery of her mind, scared to crash and sweep her fears away.

"So why won't you let me see him?"

He turned to her, eyes flaring with sympathy. "Because children look heartrending when they're in ICU and I wanted to spare you the sight."

"*That* was why you left me to go insane out here for six hours? Didn't you realize I'd prefer having my heart rent by seeing him over going mad by not seeing him?"

His eyes widened with her every word, before they narrowed again with self-derision. "My concern was evidently misplaced. Guess I can't put myself in a mother's shoes after all."

Her frustration turned inward, a flame that burned her blood with mortification. "God, no…I didn't mean to imply that…"

"Don't apologize for loving Ryan too much. But even after you blasted me for being so blithely insensitive to your needs, I am still unable to meet them. I have to be this infuriating professional and insist on my position. For now. I promise you he's in perfect condition and that you'll see him in a few hours."

"Please, let me see him now. A look is all I want!"

"What you *don't* want is the image of him sedated and inert and hooked to tubes and monitors burned into your memory. You may know what you'll see, but seeing it for real is something totally different. And I refuse to let you inflict another mental scar on yourself. I've seen parents suffer debilitating anxiety long after their children are cured, and you've suffered enough of that. So even though you probably want to kill me right now, you might want to thank me later."

"But I don't want…" She paused, groaned. "Are—are you doing this on purpose?"

He chuckled, winked at Rose who joined him in chuckling. "Of course, I am. One of my PhDs is in distraction. But while it must feel like eternity now, the hours will pass, then I'll transfer him to a private suite and you'll be with him from then on." His logic was putting out the fires of dread and desperation. But the clamoring of her heart wouldn't subside. He silenced her turmoil. "Until then, how about you ladies join me for a meal? I've long passed starving, and knowing you, Gwen, I'm sure we were on that same path together."

Rose waved her hand. "Oh, you two go ahead. Emad told me to call him as soon as you made an appearance, and to meet him in the center's restaurant. He promised a meal to top the Cordon Bleu he treated me to in L.A., and I sure want to see how this can be achieved." Rose hugged her. "See? You should always listen to me. Now listen to me and take care of yourself. You won't do Ryan any good if you collapse. You're even allowed to smile without sinning against motherhood."

"I'll take care of her." Fareed took Gwen's elbow. "I'll even brave the impossible chore of making her smile." He tilted his head at her from his prodigious height. "Shall we?"

Gwen didn't even nod. She could do nothing but stare

after Rose, as she walked away with her phone at her ear, and let Fareed steer her wherever he wished.

She registered glimpses of their journey down the halls and corridors spread in reflective granite. She barely noticed the people whose eyes held deference for Fareed and curiosity for her on their way to an elevator straight out of a sci-fi movie. She didn't feel it move, but when its brushed-steel doors slid open moments later, it was into a room the size of a tennis court, with twenty-foot, floor-to-ceiling windows spanning its arched side.

It was like looking out of a plane, with Al Zaaferah and its skyscrapers sprawling below and into the horizon, lighting up the clear night sky like a network of blazing jewels. She dimly realized they must be in the top floors of the steel-and-glass tower that formed the main portion of the center.

She'd barely recovered from the breathtaking elevation when the opulence and austerity of the place hit her. This must be his office.

His hand burned its mark into her arm as he escorted her across a gleaming hardwood floor covered in what felt like acres of Persian silk carpet to a deepest-green leather couch ensemble around a unique worked-wood centerpiece table.

When she remained standing, he gave her the gentlest of tugs. She collapsed where he indicated. He stood before her for a long moment, his gaze storming through her. Then his lips spread.

Her heart tried its best to leap out of her throat.

"Even though I know asking your preference in food is an exercise of futility, it seems I like butting my head against a wall. So, again, any favorite cuisine?"

"Anything…with calories."

She was stunned she'd produced the words. She was only sure she had when he laughed.

Her hand pressed the painful, thudding lump that had replaced her heart. There should be a law against such hazardous behavior.

He phoned in his order of food before he turned his attention back to her. Beside that watchfulness that made her feel he was listening to her thoughts, and that supreme assurance that was integral to him, she saw satisfaction.

From what she knew of him from years of following his career, this was a man who knew his handiwork, never exaggerated his results. He really believed Ryan's surgery had been successful beyond even what he'd promised her.

And the floodgates of relief finally burst.

She shook under its enormity, and this time when he reached for her, she surrendered to the potent comfort he offered.

Fareed stroked Gwen's shining head, absorbed her softness and ebbing fear, inhaled her freshness and dissipating distress and told his burning hands that that was as far as it went—for now.

When he'd come out of the O.R., he'd seen no one but her. She'd looked so lost, those eyes that wreaked havoc with his control pleading for reassurance. He'd forced himself to answer the other families first or he would have crushed her in his arms. As it were, he'd been aware of the curious glances when he'd taken her to his private elevator.

Not that he cared. He did his absolute best for all his patients. If he chose to give his personal time and attention afterward to her, it was no one's business.

But holding her like that, having her burrow into him like a kitten seeking protection, was wrecking his reason.

His body had hardened beyond arousal, and that was with her wrapped in those shapeless clothes and only seeking comfort. What effect would she have if she sought him with hunger in her touch and eyes?

He shuddered with expectation. What he'd give to carry her to bed *now* and to hell with his professional code.

But he'd already strained that code for her. All he could do now was keep his passion under a tight leash until Ryan was no longer in his care. Afterward...

Afterward, he expected an even fiercer impediment than the dictates of his professional honor. His father.

He knew he'd wage a more ferocious war with him than when he'd chosen to go into medicine and not into politics or business.

Not that it mattered. He wasn't Hesham, young and vulnerable. He would fight anything and anyone, starting with his father, to have her. He'd face the whole world for her.

And he knew that, beyond a doubt, she wanted him as fiercely. That was what fueled her struggle to keep her distance, what she believed the circumstances dictated. But when her worry for her son and his obligations ended, he would plumb the depth of her answering need.

Feeling he was peeling off a layer of skin, he let her go as soon as her tremors subsided. She pulled away at the same instant.

Embarrassment blazed on her cheeks as she slid to the end of the couch. "You must be so sick of soothing frantic relatives."

"It's part of the job description."

He nearly laughed at his exaggeration. She'd seen how he'd dealt with his patients' relatives. While he'd been courteous and accommodating, he hadn't dissolved their fears in his embrace.

A knock on the door roused him. "Our calories are here." A smile wobbled on her lips. He sighed. "Next time, I'll manage to make that smile last longer than a nanosecond."

He went to the door, returned with a trolley laden with food and beverages. Everything smelled mouth-watering. But the hunger that rose inside him was for her. He could almost taste the grace and femininity in her every line. His body tightened even more.

He should be exhausted. He was. It made no difference when she was around. He remained alert, unable to waste one moment when he could…experience her. Even when she'd slept on the plane, he'd stayed awake to check on her. She aroused not only his passion but his protectiveness, too, to unreasoning levels.

Bowled over. That was what he was. And to think that before he'd seen her, he'd sighed in pity at those who used that expression. Reveling in his condition, he sat down beside her, started uncovering hot plates.

He whistled. "Seems they got us *everything* with calories. Are you up to the challenge?"

Fareed's question distracted her from drooling at the distressing scent. Not the food's. His.

She could only murmur, "No promises."

His fire-tinged eyes turned more enigmatic before he turned to serve the food. Her senses reeled with his closeness, her thoughts tangling at his inconsistencies.

Even though he was known to be most accessible professionally, on a personal level, he was considered inapproachable. Yet from her own experience, he was only too approachable, and she…

She *had* to stop fantasizing about him. He was the one

man she should never want, the one man who was off-limits.

But what if he is the one man you can *want?*

She crushed the insidious voice as she accepted a steaming plate piled with mouth-watering grilled salmon and vegetables, careful not to touch him again. Touching him had infused a dangerous narcotic into her bloodstream. She should be careful not to end up addicted. Or was she already?

Was this how it happened? Inadvertent exposure, moments of surrender to temptation and suddenly you were irrevocably lost....

"Eat, Gwen, and I'll reward you. I'll discuss Ryan's postoperative period and rehabilitation."

This brought her back to earth with a thud.

"Yes, please."

His eyes ignited. She shied away from their heat and her interpretation of it. It had to be her feverish mind superimposing her preposterous cravings on his glances and actions.

She cleared her throat. "Wh-what do you expect?"

"How about a deal?" he countered. "One mouthful a sentence."

"Oh, all right." She loaded a fork, forced it into her mouth.

He tutted. "A bigger mouthful won't get you a longer sentence, and I won't talk any faster if you choke."

She swallowed the lump and almost did just that.

"For God's sake, just tell me!" she spluttered.

"I expect a full recovery." At her evident frustration with his brevity, his eyebrows rose. "You expected more for that forkful? I already had Akram tell you everything. You just want me to repeat myself to see if I'll slip up."

Heat surged to her head. "I realize I'm being obsessive…"

"And I'm totally ribbing you, as you say in the States." His eyes laughed at her, coaxing her to ease up. "But as a scientist, too, I realize you won't be satisfied until you have all the details. So let's start with my findings during surgery."

Her heart jumped. He understood. That she needed to know what he'd seen with his own eyes, fixed with his own hands. That only specifics would make it all real.

"The defect was long and the tethering was more than I'd hoped. The meninges were also prolapsed. But I corrected it all with a procedure I have been developing. It takes double the time of any other procedure—yes, that's why I took longer than projected—but it ensures no scarring and no future retethering. The nerve roots were minimally damaged, but with Ryan's fast growth, and the sites of the tethering, progressive damage would have occurred within the next months. So your persistence couldn't have been more warranted, and the timing of the surgery couldn't have proved more critical. Now, with physiotherapy and a four-month course of your drug, Ryan should regain his legs' full power and sensation, and I don't expect there to be any problems with toilet training."

Tears welled up again as the certainty she'd needed seeped into her bones. "I—I can't find words to thank you."

He grimaced. "Then don't go in search of any." He tapped her plate with his fork. "Now eat. You need to be stocked up on as many calories as you can to be there for Ryan in the coming time."

She ended up finishing a three-course meal.

But taking a leaf from his repertoire, she specified

a reward in return. Letting her see Ryan as soon as she was done.

He'd finally succumbed, telling her she drove a hard bargain.

She'd been standing for what felt like hours behind the glass partition in pediatric ICU, gowned for the sterile zone, watching Ryan sleeping in a cot that looked like a space pod, her tears streaming. Ones of pure relief.

Even though it drove a hot lance through her heart to see Ryan's little body hooked to leads and invaded by drips and tubes, she knew one thing beyond a doubt: he was all right.

Fareed had been sharing the poignant vigil in silence.

He finally inhaled. "And Ryan invalidates my worries again. He looks as if he's sleeping in complete contentment."

"H-he probably is," she whispered. "He must feel how much care he's receiving, must have felt how much you've done for him. He might be relieved for the first time in his life now you've corrected h-his problem."

"Everything's possible, especially with a child as sensitive as Ryan." He turned her to him, wiped a tear that was trembling on her chin. "Now go say welcome back to your baby."

She gasped. "Oh, God…really?"

He nodded, his smile a ray of delight illuminating her world.

She streaked into the ICU. He followed at a slower pace.

He stood back patiently, let her fondle and coo to the sedated Ryan until she turned to him with tears mixing with unbridled smiles. Then he checked Ryan, discussed his management with his ICU staff, before escorting her out.

He took her to a suite on the same level as his office.

The sitting room overlooked the same view that had stunned her from his windows, from a different viewpoint, with the magic of the capital now shrouded in another dawn. She could barely believe it had been just a day since she'd set foot in Jizaan.

He took her by the shoulders. "I recommend another fourteen-hour sleep marathon. Or at least eight. Don't wake up sooner on Ryan's account. I'm keeping him in ICU for twelve more hours."

"But you said you'd let him out in a few hours!"

"And the concrete numerical value of 'a few' is?"

He was teasing her again. But now she knew in her bones Ryan would be all right, she found herself attempting to tease back.

"The world doesn't know how lucky it is that you decided to use your inexorableness for good. But even though you've benevolently steam-rolled me on every decision and I'm now forever in your debt, this—" her gesture encompassed the superbly decorated, all-amenities, expansive suite "—is going too far. Between here and the guest apartment at your place, you'll spoil Ryan and Rose so much that I might have to find us a new place when we return home."

Interest flared in his eyes. "Where *is* home? We never got around to talking about that."

She almost kicked herself. She'd just given him an opening to delve deeper into her life and everything she wanted kept hidden at all costs.

Panic surged. If she told the truth, he'd put things together sooner rather than later. If she lied, rather than omitted the truth, as she had done so far, apart from when she'd had to lie about Ryan's father, those same powers of observation would see through her. But she had no choice.

A lie was potentially less catastrophic than the truth.

Feeling it would corrode her on the way out, she opened her mouth to deliver it…and his pager went off.

She almost sagged when he released her from his focus. Then her breath caught. He was frowning at his pager. "Is it Ryan?"

He raised his eyes at her question, gave a lock of her hair a playful tug. "*No,* Gwen. Ryan is fine and will remain fine. It's just another emergency. Now have mercy on me and sleep. I'm exhausted already and it'll be a while before I get any rest. Don't add to my burdens. I'll *know* if you're not sleeping."

Without waiting for an answer, he turned away.

The door closed behind him in seconds. But she still felt his presence surrounding her, making her world secure, and life no longer a setting for anguish and struggles.

She could offer him nothing in return for the gifts he'd showered on her and her own. A chunk of her life wouldn't suffice. But he'd asked her to make his easier by taking herself off his endless list of worries. Complying with his request was all she had to offer for now.

She found the bedroom, and with a moan, sank into the bed's luxury, into the depths of thankfulness. For him, for Ryan's cure. And for being saved by the pager.

She prayed she'd never be forced to lie to him outright again, until he discharged Ryan.

Once he did, she'd run, disappear, and he'd never know. And she'd never see him again.

The joy that had begun to take root inside her drained. Tears flowed again as she prayed.

Let his obligations keep him away for as long as she had to remain in Jizaan. Let his loss start now.

Only that would save her from sustaining further injuries.

Seven

She should have known.

That anything she hoped for would happen in reverse. With the record of the past years, how had she hoped otherwise?

Apart from Ryan's healing at a breathtaking rate, blossoming under Fareed's comprehensive care, everything else was going wrong. Terribly wrong.

For the week they stayed in the center, Fareed was constantly present. She knew this wasn't true, that he disappeared for hours but he came back so often, in her amplified awareness of him, it felt like he was always there, giving her no respite.

After dreading being in his place, where everything echoed with his feel and was soaked in his presence, she couldn't wait to go back there. She hoped that with him at work during the day, and hopefully returning home exhausted, she'd see less of him. But for the following four weeks, the opposite again happened. He came home too often, too unpredictably, so she couldn't brace for his appearance, worsening her condition at every exposure.

Everyone in the center had told her he made them feel he *was* omnipresent. She could well believe it. After the endless hours in the O.R., consultations, follow-ups and administrative chores, not to mention his duties as a prince, which he said he'd lately limited to steering the kingdom's health system, as if that wasn't huge enough, she couldn't figure out how he had time for her. Not to mention had a life. A private life…

Her throat tightened as it did each time that thought forced its reality on her. It was ridiculous to feel that way, but still…contemplating the horde of glamorous women who no doubt pursued him, of whom he took the most voluptuous and beautiful to bed…

Peals of laughter, masculine and childish, wrenched her mind away from the images, only for different ones to superimpose themselves. The images that would be engraved in her mind, seared into her soul forever. The sight of Fareed and Ryan together, bonding, reveling in each other.

But as painful as the sight was, it was also incredible. And worth any future suffering to live through.

Fareed was sitting with Ryan on the floor, in the middle of his mansion's family room, wrapped up in their game, caressed by the warm, golden lights of polished brass sconces that illuminated the expansive space. The French doors leading to the massive terrace were wide open and the gauzy cream curtains were billowing in the desert's cool evening breeze. The unpolished sand-colored marble floor was spread in hand-woven kilims and scattered in huge cushions covered with the same designs and vivid hues. Fareed had said those were the Aal Zaafers' tribal patterns and colors, intricate combinations of stripes and rhomboids, in vibrant crimsons, gold and greens. He'd also said the room had never been used. Until them.

As if she needed more heartache, to know he'd been welcoming them in the place reserved for his future family.

Before they'd settled down for the evening here, they'd finished another physiotherapy session with Ryan. He'd turned another of the mansion's rooms into a rehabilitation center, and had turned those uncomfortable, exhausting and sometimes painful sessions into Ryan's most antici-pated playtime.

Now he was playing catch with Ryan. After giving Ryan easy catches to get him excited and motivated, he'd throw one out of reach and have him eagerly crawling to fetch.

He was always thinking of another exercise for Ryan, another method to gauge his improvement. He'd made an art of helping Ryan enjoy it, participate wholeheartedly, and subsequently heal faster, develop more power and better coordination.

He now threw the soft red ball on the huge square table that paralleled the couch she sat on. Ryan hurtled after it, reached the table, then stopped, an absorbed expression painting his face as he contemplated his dilemma.

She transferred her gaze to Fareed. "Seems you've given him a challenge he's not up to…yet."

Fareed shrugged, his face spread in the warmth that messed her up inside. "He hasn't given up yet. Let's see what he'll do."

She nodded even as her heart constricted. Every cell in her longed to end Ryan's frustration, give him the ball. But Fareed had been teaching her not to coddle him, to drive him to achieve his potential, and be as loving or even more so while at it.

Ryan finally approached one of the table's corners. Then after some internal debate, pulled himself up in degrees until he unfolded to his feet, stood braced at its edge. Her heart boomed.

It was the first time he'd ever stood up!

Her eyes flew to Fareed. He looked as moved, his smile as proud as hers. But when she moved to get the ball for Ryan, he gave her an imperative "wait" gesture.

She waited. And under her disbelieving, delighted eyes, Ryan hooked his right leg, the one that had always been weaker, over the edge of the table and pulled himself on top of it.

Once there, he weaved through worked-silver plates, gleaming copper candleholders and glass planters like a cat, knocking nothing over. Once he reached his quarry, he grabbed it, waved it at her in delighted victory.

"You did it, darling," she said, forcing back tears, her smile so wide that it hurt. "You got the ball because you're brilliant and strong and determined and the most wonderful boy on earth."

After a satisfactory dose of adulation, he remembered his playmate, the one he wanted to impress most.

Ryan reversed his way across the table, backed off its edge carefully. Once his feet touched ground, he plopped back down, catching his breath after the unprecedented endeavor.

Then he turned to Fareed, shrieking his triumph and throwing his trophy back to him.

He caught it, stuffed it beneath his arm and treated Ryan to a boisterous round of applause. Ryan zoomed to him, sought the haven of his arms. After having enough of

Fareed's validation, Ryan wriggled off and crawled away as if eager to resume their game.

Before following, Fareed spared her a glance, eyes twinkling with pride. "See? Nothing is beyond him. He's creative and problem-solving and ambitious and he'll always surpass your expectations."

She barely stifled the cry. *Stop surpassing mine! Stop making me want you more when I can't even dream of you.*

But it was already too late.

She'd come to depend on him when it was the worst thing she could have done. She couldn't think of a time when he wouldn't be in her life, their lives, when it was inevitable.

She'd fallen in love with him when it would mean destruction.

Yes, she loved him.

And she would have preferred it if he didn't realize she was alive. But she could no longer escape what she'd known from the moment he'd captured her gaze at that conference. He'd made it clear, in a hundred nuances, what he wanted from her, that he was only waiting until any doctor/patient's parent trace of their relationship had faded, to act on his desire.

His desire to have her in his bed.

And even though guilt and dread haunted her, this was the only place she wanted to be.

But it didn't matter what she wanted. She couldn't act on her desire. She wouldn't.

"I'm surprised he hasn't melted yet."

Rose. Sitting right beside her and she hadn't even noticed her come in.

Rose elaborated, "I've seen hunger blazing in eyes before, but the solar flares in yours…yowza!"

Her gaze moved nervously to Fareed, who was far

enough away not to catch Rose's comments. Thank goodness. If Rose had seen it, had he...?

Who was she kidding? He had. He knew he had her on the brink of mindlessness. And he'd been letting her know, subtly, inexorably, how he'd leave her no place to run when he made his move, how earth-shattering it would be when he claimed her.

She let out a resigned exhalation. "Don't start, Rose."

Rose repaid her with a fed up look. "Then why don't *you* stop? Jumping away as if he scalds you each time he comes near?"

"What do you expect? The man has a magnetic field that could upset a planet's orbit." After a moment's hesitation, she admitted, "He does scald me."

Rose nudged her. "Then help yourself to his inferno, girl."

She squeezed her eyes. "I can't, and you know it."

"So you've been mourning. Now enough." Rose turned fully to her, scowling. "Let the dead rest and get on with your life."

Gwen bit her lip, memories a shard embedded in her heart. "It's not only mourning."

"What else is it? Can't be Ryan because Fareed is the best thing that has ever happened to him, present company included."

"You're talking as if Fareed is in Ryan's life in anything more than a temporary way, when you know he's just his surgeon...."

"He's not just his surgeon, and *you* know it."

For a heart-wrenching moment, Gwen thought Rose knew. Who Fareed really was to Ryan.

But there was no way that she did. She hadn't been in her life for the past five years, had missed all the developments and upheavals that had ripped through her life.

Rose knew only what she'd told her once everything had been over. She didn't know about Ryan's parentage. And she must never know.

Rose turned her eyes to the man and baby who possessed Gwen's heart. "I mean…just look at them." Gwen didn't *want* to look. It hurt too much. "Look at *you*. You're burning for him." Gwen averted her eyes, damned being so transparent. "Then look at *him*. He would devour you whole if you didn't flit around like a hummingbird on speed."

A chuckle burst out of Gwen. Only Rose could cut to the truth, yet make it somehow bearable, even light-hearted. "And you recognize the symptoms because you and Emad are suffering from the same condition?"

Rose wouldn't be distracted. "Emad and I have *nothing* like the same condition. *I* don't have melodramatic tendencies and I'm not letting self-perpetuated worries stop me from taking whatever happiness I can now. We're free grown-ups with nothing to stop us from having whatever we want together. Apart from your baffling reluctance, I can say the same about you and Fareed."

Gwen exhaled dejectedly. "I'm not free."

"Because you're a single mother? And I can't fathom your position because I'm not? So enlighten me, what are women in your situation supposed to do? Sacrifice your personal lives at the altar of your children's upbringing?"

Gwen stared sightlessly at the mansion's gardens. She wished with all her heart that she could share her burden with Rose, that everything wasn't so complicated, so impossible.

Why had Fareed of all men turned out to be the one who awakened the woman in her? And so completely, so violently?

To add to her heartache, Rose added, "And anyway,

don't knock temporary. You of all people know that nothing, starting with life itself, is permanent. Think about that and make up your mind."

She swallowed a lump at another impending and permanent loss. "My mind is made up, Rose."

Before Rose could counterattack, Fareed's rich baritone curled around Gwen's sensitized nerves, filling her with regret for what would never be.

He was walking toward them, with Ryan in his arms. He'd said, "I have an announcement to make."

Her heart pounded so fast that she felt the beats merging like the wings of the hummingbird Rose had compared her to.

Fareed stopped before them, so beautiful and vital that a fist of longing squeezed her heart, stilled it into its grip.

"I've done and redone every test there is. And the verdict is in. This magnificent boy is on his way to a full recovery. I expect he'll walk in a few months' time."

Gwen's hands shot to her lips, stifled her soundless cry.

She'd been monitoring Ryan's every notch of improvement obsessively, and from her experience with neurological progress, she'd been hoping for the best. But to have Fareed spell out such concrete conviction, put a time frame on it, made it all real.

Ryan *would* walk!

She raced with Rose to Fareed to drown him in thanks, to pluck Ryan from his arms, then from each other's to deluge him in kisses. Ryan thought this was a new game and threw himself from one set of arms to another, giggling his delight.

But as Emad joined them and dinner followed, Gwen's euphoria drained gradually.

She'd known the day when Fareed would announce the completion of his role in Ryan's care was fast-approaching.

She couldn't have hoped for a better outcome. There *was* no better outcome. For Ryan.

For her…

It was clear from everything Fareed said and did that he thought this day would mark the beginning of that temporary inferno Rose had urged her to hurtle into. *She* knew it would only herald the end. She'd thought she'd be ready for it. She wasn't.

As their "family" evening continued, Fareed's nearness only made it harder. She couldn't stop herself from feasting on his presence like it was her last meal.

And he made it worse still by no longer tempering the desire in his eyes, by barely touching his food, too, showing her that the only thing he hungered for was her.

For the rest of the evening, as she escaped his unspoken intentions, she struggled to convince herself that walking away would be survivable.

Gwen was suffocating.

Tentacles were tightening around her throat, cutting off air and blood, holding her back. Her arms reached out, but the tentacles jerked her tighter, immobilized her. The shadow she was reaching for tumbled in macabre slow-motion down the abyss….

"No!"

She heard the shout ring out even as she felt it tear out of her depths…and her eyes shot open.

She jerked up, her hands tearing at the nonexistent noose.

It had been another nightmare.

Knowing that didn't help. She still gasped, trembled, feeling like the day of the accident all over again. Crushed, torn, strangled by panic and helplessness.

In the months since, night terrors had plagued whatever

sleep she'd succumbed to. During the day, anxiety attacks had dismantled her psyche. It hadn't helped that she knew there had been nothing she could have done.

She stumbled out of the bed. It was 2:00 a.m. She'd barely slept an hour. No use thinking she'd sleep again tonight. She was afraid to, anyway.

She went to Ryan's room, checked on him even though she'd heard his steady breathing over the baby monitor. She found him on his back, which he hadn't done since the surgery, his arms flung over his head in abandon. She kissed him and he murmured something satisfied, melting her heart with thankfulness.

She went downstairs, roamed the seemingly deserted mansion, her steps as restless as her mind.

She felt Fareed all over, his scent clinging to her lungs, caressing her senses. And it wasn't because this was his domain. She'd feel him across the world. And she would, for the rest of her life.

And now, it was over. There was no more reason to stay here. She'd take her tiny family and leave Jizaan in the morning.

And he'd never know how she really felt. But that mattered nothing. What mattered was that he never knew who she really was....

"Do you know what you are?"

Fareed's hypnotic tones hit her with the force of a quake.

She jerked around, her gaze slamming to the top of the stairs, the side leading to his quarters.

He wasn't there. Had she imagined hearing him? Were her dread and guilt playing tricks on her?

Then his voice hit her again. "What I thought when I first saw you? A magical being from another realm."

She almost sagged. He was here. And he hadn't meant what she'd feared.

"And do you have any idea about the extent of my craving for you? How long it has gone unfulfilled? How much it has cost me to suppress it, to stay away from you?"

Each beat of her heart rocked her as a shadow detached itself from the depth of darkness engulfing the upper floor, taking his form. His body solidified, his influence intensified with every step. Then his face emerged from the shadows and she gasped.

Even from this distance, there was no mistake.

The ultra-efficient surgeon, the indulgent benefactor, the teasing, patient playmate was gone. A man of tempestuous passion had emerged in his place.

Making it worse was seeing him for the first time in what he'd been born to wear, an *abaya* that looked tailored of Jizaan's moonless skies themselves.

And she had no right to his passion. She'd lose even the bittersweet torment of his nearness tomorrow. She'd never again feel as alive.

"You sensed me." His voice reverberated inside her as he descended the stairs. "You knew I was coming to you, came to meet me halfway. You knew that I would no longer wait."

Something snapped inside her. Her paralysis shattered.

She needed to tell him…something, anything of the truth, if only that of her feelings, her needs. To have something, anything of him. Just this once.

He quickened his descent as she moved toward him, the *abaya* billowing around him like a shroud of darkest magic. Her feet felt as if they were gaining momentum from his power, his purpose, that force that had entered her life to change the face of her world forever.

Then he stopped. At the platform where the stairs diverged, as if giving her a last chance to retreat.

She stopped, too, three steps beneath him, momentum lost, confessions fled. She looked up at him, overwhelmed. He was even more than she'd ever dreamed.

The obsidian silk *abaya* draped over his endless shoulders, pleated for miles to his bare feet, falling open over the perfection of his chiseled, raven hair-dusted chest and abdomen. The low-riding drawstring pants of the same color and material hugged his thighs, hiding none of the power of his muscles, or that of his arousal.

He seemed as if he'd stepped out from another time, a force of nature and of the supernatural, poured into solid form. But it was the fever radiating from him, the same one that raged through her, that shook her most—setting free the one confession she could make.

"I don't want you to wait."

Eight

Something unbridled flared in Fareed's eyes.

Gwen's breathing stopped. She stood mesmerized by the ferocity that ate her up, finished her. Now...now he'd descend the last steps separating them, sweep her up in his arms....

But what he did stopped her heart. With shock.

She would have never expected that he would...*laugh*.

But he did. Peal after peal of pure male amusement.

His laughter mortified her even as it inflamed her.

What had she said or done that he found so funny?

Maybe it was her braid, mommy robe and fluffy slippers? And the cartoon character pajamas beneath?

God, *of course* it was. He must have gotten a good look at her and rethought his intentions. No wonder he was laughing.

All thoughts scattered as he moved, still laughing, until he was on the same step, bearing down on her with his heat and virility. Then he leaned down, put his lips to her ear.

"I just have one question—" each syllable, each feathering of his lips shot arousal right to her core "—will you ever stop surprising me?"

She raised confused eyes up to his, found fire simmering just below the mirth.

"You exhausted me at every turn," he whispered, intimate, maddening, "contesting my every declaration, my every decision, the minor before the major. Then I tell you I'm taking you to my bed and you just…agree?"

Her gaze wavered as his eyes lost their lightness, flames rising higher. She shivered as her own fever spiked in answer.

Then to her amazement, she heard her voice, husky with hunger and provocation. "I didn't exactly say I agree."

He caught her around the waist, slammed her against his hard length. Her breath and heartbeats emptied against his chest.

Twisting her braid around his wrist, harnessing her by it, ferocity barely leashed with gentleness, he tilted up her face, his eyes now a predator's excited by his mate's unexpected challenge.

His next words poured almost in her gasping mouth. "You said better. You commanded me not to wait. Now I'll obey you, *ya fatenati*. No more waiting, ever again."

Then he bent and swept her feet from beneath her, cut her every tie to gravity and sanity.

She went limp in his hold, becoming weightless, timeless, directionless, as she lay ensconced in his arms. She burrowed into him as the world moved in hard, hurried thuds, each one hitting her with vertigo, the pressure of emotion almost snuffing out her consciousness, like that day lifetimes ago.

And that was before he pressed his lips to her forehead

in a branding kiss. "Never stop surprising me, *ya sahe-rati*."

She almost blurted out that *he* was the enchanter, the sorcerer. She choked on the words. She hadn't let on that she knew Arabic, couldn't bear lying if he asked why she did.

Every anxiety vanished as he relinquished his hold on her and she sank in the depths of soft dark beddings, was shrouded by the golden warmth of gaslight and the intoxication of incense and craving.

Then he came down over her.

She moaned with the blast of stimulation, emotional and sensual, of her first exposure to the reality of him, his weight and bulk and hunger, the physicality of his passion.

He rose off her, slid her robe off. She felt a blush creeping up from her toes to her hairline as he exposed her pajamas.

"Bugs Bunny." He shook his head in disbelief. "And if I find you arousing beyond endurance in this, I might not survive seeing you in something made to worship your beauty."

She crossed her hands over her chest, burning with self-consciousness. "I know how I look in this thing. I picked it to match one of Ryan's…"

"Answer me this other question, Gwen." His hand unlocked hers, before imprisoning them over her head in one of his. "Will I always have to say something over and over before you consider believing me? Will you ever believe I only ever say what I mean?"

She felt her flush deepening. "It's not you I'm doubting."

"Then how can you doubt your own beauty, your effect on me? If anything, I'm holding back, not telling you what you really make me feel, what I really want to do to you."

His eyes flared with mock-threat and too-real lust. "I don't want to scare you."

She shook her head against the sheets. "You won't ever scare me. Show me everything you feel."

Her ragged words elicited a smile that was sheer male triumph and assurance. "*Amrek, ya rohi*—command me."

Yet his hands trembled in her hair as they undid her braid, spread its thickness around her. Then he buried his face in it, breathed her in hard, let her hear in his ragged groans that he was at the mercy of his need for her as she was for him.

"I've wanted you, I've needed this…" He bore down on her harder, pressed all of him into all of her. "Your flesh and desire, you scent and feel, since the first moment I saw you all those years ago. I craved you until I was hollow. Now you're here and you'll be mine, at last, Gwen…*at last.*"

She whimpered her agreement, her eagerness. He swooped up to capture the sound, his lips taking hers in a hot, moist seal, enveloping, dissolving, his tongue thrusting into her recesses, in total tasting, in thorough possession.

She'd imagined this until she'd felt *she'd* be forever empty, too, if she never experienced it. But this far surpassed the imaginings that had tormented her. The power and profundity of his kiss, his feel and scent, and his taste…his *taste*…

He bit into her lower lip, stilled its tremors in a nip so leashed, so carnal that it had her opening wider, deepening his invasion.

Just as she felt she'd come apart, he severed their meld, groaned, "Gwen, *habibati, hayaati, abghaaki, ahtaajek.*"

She sobbed again as she pulled him back. He'd called her his love, his life, said he coveted her, *needed* her.

She knew those were the exaggerated endearments his culture indulged in. They didn't have to be literally meant, and in those moments, were likely driven by arousal.

It didn't matter. Just hearing him say those things was enough. And if it were possible to give him of her life to fill his needs, she would have surrendered it.

She surrendered what she could now, all of herself.

He swept her pajama top over her head, his arm beneath her melting her into his length, circling her waist, raising her against the headboard to bury his face into her confined breasts.

She moaned at seeing the dark majesty of his head against her, let her hands fulfill what she'd thought would remain a fantasy, burying them in the luxury of his silken, raven mane, pressing his head harder to her aching flesh.

He groaned something deep and driven, the sound spearing from his lips into her heart as his hands went to her back. She arched, helping him release breasts now peaked with arousal, throbbing for his ownership.

He gathered her hands again above her head, drew back to gaze at her. Naked to the waist, the image of abandon, on wanton offer. She turned her face into the sheets, unable to withstand his burning scrutiny.

"Look at me, *ya galbi*." His demand overrode her will, drew her eyes to his. "See what your sight does to me." He let one of her hands go, took it to his heart, let her feel the power of its thundering, then to his erection. "Feel it."

Her hand trembled as it fulfilled the ultimate privilege of feeling his potency. She stroked his daunting length and hardness through the heavy silk of his pants.

He undid the drawstring, slowly, maddeningly, holding her eyes as he guided her hand underneath. Her hand shook at touching him without barriers, couldn't close around him. But even with the nip of awe and alarm, knowing all this would soon dominate her, she reveled in his amazing heat, his satin over steel, the edge of anxiety making her readiness flow heavier, soaking her panties.

He came down over her again, thrust his tongue inside her mouth to her stroking rhythm, groaned inside her, "Your touch is a far better heaven than any I imagined."

She was lost in his feel when he suddenly drew back, spread her again, closed trembling hands on her breasts. She arched off the bed, in a shock of pleasure, making a fuller offering of her flesh. He kneaded her, pinched her nipples, had her writhing, begging, before he coaxed and caressed the rest of her clothes off her burning flesh.

The spike of ferocity in his eyes as they touched her full nakedness should have been alarming. It only sent her heart almost racing to a standstill with shyness, with anticipation. With pride that her sight affected him that intensely.

He tore his *abaya* off, finally exposing the body she'd known would make the gods of old fade into nothing. *"Ya Ullah ya Gwen, koll shai ma'ak afdal menn ahlami. Anti ajmal shai ra'aytoh fi hayati...anti rao'ah."*

Her awed hands shook over his burnished, sculpted perfection, barely biting back the protest that everything with *him* was better than *her* dreams, that it was he who was the most beautiful thing she'd ever seen in her life, he who was the wonder.

"Habibati..." His groan roughened to a growl as he rubbed his chest against her breasts until she thrashed beneath him. He bent, opened his mouth over her breasts as if he'd devour her.

Pleasure jackknifed through her with each nip of his teeth, each long, hard draw of his lips, had her shuddering all over.

"Fareed, just take me...all of me..."

He told her he wanted exactly that. All of her now. *Now.*

"Bareedek kollek, daheenah, habibati. Daheenah."

She lay powerless under the avalanche of need, her moans becoming keens as his surgeon's hand glided over her, taking every liberty and creating erogenous zones wherever they fondled and owned, before settling between her thighs. His strong, sensitive fingers slid up to her intimate flesh, now molten, throbbing its demand for his touch, his invasion. They opened the lips of her femininity, slid between her folds, soaked in her readiness.

It took only a few strokes of those virtuoso fingers to spill her over the edge. She convulsed with pleasure, hazy with it, failing to imagine what union with him would bring if just a few touches unraveled her body and mind.

Among her stifled cries of release she heard something primal rumble in his gut, knew it was the sound of his control snapping.

He came over her and her hands fumbled with his to remove his pants, the last barrier between them. She went nerveless as his lips spilled worship into hers, proclaiming her soul of his heart, his need to be inside her.

"Roh galbi, mehtaj akoon jow'waaki."

She couldn't bear not having him filling her, couldn't bear the emptiness he'd created inside her, couldn't... couldn't...

She *couldn't* let him take her when she hadn't told him...

No. She *couldn't* tell him. And she couldn't not have him. Just this once. She needed this once. It wasn't too much to ask, to take. She'd live in deprivation for the rest of her life.

And she sobbed her need, her desperation. "Come inside me, Fareed, now. Don't wait...just take me."

*"Aih, ya hayat galbi...*take me inside you, take all of me."

He bore down into her, as blinded, as lost. She cried out, in relief, in anguish, spread her legs wider for his demand, contained him, her heels digging into his buttocks, her nails into his back, demanding him, urging him.

His pained chuckle detailed his enjoyment of her frenzy as his muscled hips flexed, positioning himself at her entrance, prostrating her for his domination. Then in one burning plunge, he was there, inside her. Flesh in flesh.

The shock to her system was total.

Paralyzed, mute, she stared up at him, everything swollen and invaded and complete. He rested deep within her, stretching her beyond capacity, as incapacitated. Blackness frothed from the periphery of her vision, a storm front of pleasure advancing from her core. Fareed...at last.

It was he who broke the panting silence, his voice a feral growl now. "Gwen, the pleasure of you...*ya Ullah...*"

He rose on his palms, started to withdraw from her depths. She clung blindly, crazed for his branding pain and pleasure.

He withdrew all the way out, dragged a shriek of stimulation and loss from her. Before she cried out again for his return, he drove all the way back inside her.

On his next withdrawal, she lost what was left of her mind. She thrust her hips up, seeking his impalement. He bunched her hair in his fist, tugged her down to the bed, exposing her throat, latching his teeth into her flesh as if he'd consume her.

Then he plowed back into her, showed her that those first plunges had just been preparations. He fed her core more, then more of him with every thrust, causing an unknown, unbelievably pleasurable expansion within her, until she felt him hit the epicenter of her very essence.

She was destroyed, blind, mad, screaming, clinging to

him, biting him, convulsing, the ecstasy rending in intensity.

He withdrew, and she saw his magnificent face seize with ferocity, with his greed for every sensation he plumbed her body for, had ripping through her. Tension shot up in his eyes, as if he was judging when to let go.

She begged him, for him. "Give me—give me…"

And he gave. She felt each surge of his jetting climax inside her. It hit her at her peak, had her thrashing, weeping, unable to endure the spike in pleasure. Everything dimmed, faded…

She had no idea when awareness started trickling between the numb layers of satisfaction. She was still lying beneath Fareed. Then she realized what had roused her. He was leaving her body.

Before she could whimper with his loss, he pressed back over her, his weight sublime pleasure. She moaned her contentment. More bliss settled into her bones as he swept her around, draped her over his expansive body, mingling their sweat and satisfaction.

She closed her eyes, let his feel and those precious moments integrate into her cells. She'd need the memories to tide her through the rest of her life.

But this wasn't over yet. She had hours with him still. She wouldn't waste a second.

"And I thought it would be unprecedented with you."

Everything inside her stilled.

Would his next words elaborate on the disappointment of his expectations? Had he given her her life's most transfiguring experience, but she'd proved no more than a barely adequate one?

Suddenly, she wanted to bolt. She wanted to hold on

to what she'd experienced. It would be all she had of him. And if it turned out to be a one-sided illusion…

"If I'd known how it would be between us, that it would far exceed even my perfectionist fantasies, I would have carried you off to my bed weeks ago."

She raised a wobbling head, trembling with relief. She marveled anew at his beauty, and at how magical their bodies looked entwined.

And she wanted more of him. Of them. All she could get.

She bent to taste the powerful pulse in his neck, dragging her teeth down his shoulder and chest to his nipple, nipping it before she moved her head up, stroking his flesh with her hair.

"I hope you know what you're inviting with this act of extreme provocation."

Feeling all-powerful with his desire, reckless with having nothing to lose and everything to win, before it was too late, she squeezed his steel buttock even as she slid her leg between his muscled, hair-roughened ones, her knee pressing an erection that felt even harder and more daunting than before.

"Which act are you referring to?" she purred, nipping his lips, adding more fuel to his reignited passion.

He grabbed her around the waist, brought her straddling him, menacing lust flaring in his eyes, filling his lips. "I have a list now. Each with a consequence all its own."

Her hunger, now she knew what ecstasy awaited her in his possession, was a hundred-fold that of her previous ignorance.

She rocked against him, bathing him in her arousal and their pleasure. "Terrible consequences all, I hope."

"Unspeakable." His hands convulsed in her flesh, raised her to scale his length. He dragged her down at the same moment he thrust upward, impaling her.

She screamed his name, body and mind unraveling at the unbearable expansion, the excruciating pleasure.

She melted into him, felt the world receding with only him left in existence. Along with one thought.

She'd had him. She'd been his.

Tomorrow, when she lost him, nothing could erase the experience from her body and soul.

Gwen had returned to her bedroom in the guest apartment as soon as Fareed had left her in bed. She'd hoped he'd stay away all day until she'd made her escape.

He hadn't stayed away an hour.

He'd just entered the bedroom, was walking to her in strides laden with urgency, something fierce blasting off him.

Before she could say anything, he hauled her into his arms and drowned her in the deepest kiss he'd claimed yet.

She felt his turmoil collide with hers, until she couldn't bear it, think of nothing but easing him.

She tugged at his hair gently, bringing his head up. And what she saw in his eyes almost brought tears to hers.

She'd seen this in his eyes off and on since they'd come here. This despair. Every time, being with her and Ryan had managed to erase the darkness that seemed to grip him heart and soul.

She'd never asked about the reason behind his anguish. Not only because she didn't feel she had the right to, but also because she thought she knew the answer. But what if she was wrong and there was some other reason? Some-

thing she could help with, at least by lending a sympa-
thetic ear and heart?

"What is it, Fareed?"

He pulled her back, hugged her tighter, pressing her
head to his chest, which heaved on a shuddering exhalation.

He spoke. And she wished she hadn't asked. For he told
her, in mutilating detail, about his dead brother and the
depth of futility and frustration he'd been suffering in his
ongoing, fruitless quest to find his family.

"Then, a week after you came here, Emad found a lead
that looked the most promising we've had yet. He's just
told me it turned out to be another false hope."

Even had she had anything to say, the pain clamping
her throat would have made it impossible to speak.

This was all her fault. And no fault of her own. She
wished she could tell him to stop looking, to have mercy
on himself, that he had nothing to blame himself for, had
already done more than anyone would have dreamed. But
she couldn't.

She could only leave and pray that in time, he'd end his
search, come to terms with his failure, so that it would stop
tearing at him.

Now all she could hope was that he'd go away again,
give her a chance to leave without further heartache.

Before she pushed away, his hands were all over her,
over himself, ridding them of their clothes. She knew the
moment her flesh touched his, all would be lost. She had
to act now.

She struggled out of his arms, hating herself and the
whole world for having to say this, now of all times.

"I'm leaving Jizaan today."

He froze in mid-motion as he'd reached back for her,
stared at her for a long, long moment.

Then his lips spread. In another moment a chuckle escaped him and intensified until he was laughing outright.

He at last wiped a tear of mirth. "Ah, Gwen, I needed that." He caught her back to him. "I love it when you let your wicked humor show, loved it when you teased me in bed. Teasing me out of it—if not for long—is even better."

He thought she was joking! And who could blame him, after the nightlong marathon of passion and abandonment?

He pulled her back into his arms and she gasped, "I'm serious, Fareed."

That made him loosen his arms enough so he could pull back, look at her, the humor in his eyes wavering.

She tried to maximize on her advantage, injected her expression and voice with all the firmness and finality she could muster. "With your follow-up of Ryan over, there's no reason to stay in Jizaan anymore. In fact, we should have left long before now. We've taken advantage of your generosity for far too long."

Devilry and desire ignited his eyes. "If last night has been your taking advantage of my...generosity, as you can *feel*—" he pulled her back against his hard length, his arousal living steel pressing into her abdomen "—I am in dire need for your exploitation to continue."

"What happened between us doesn't change a thing."

"Not *a* thing, no. *Every*thing."

She tried to turn her face away. "No! Nothing has changed or will ever change. We have to leave, Fareed. Please, don't make this hard. I have to—"

"I have to, too." He latched his lips on the frantic pulse in her neck, suckled her until she felt her heart pouring its beats and love into him. "I have to take you again, Gwen. I have to pleasure you again and again."

Then as she struggled to hold on to her sanity and re-solve, he defeated her, practiced every spell of seduction on her viciously awakened body and starving heart.

She found herself naked, delirious with arousal and pleasure, straddling his powerful hips, her palms anchored on his chest as he dug his hands in her buttocks.

He held her by them, had her riding up and down his shaft, showing her the exact force and speed and angle to drive them both beyond insanity, egging her on.

"Ride me, Gwen, ride me."

Lost, mad, she obeyed him, rising and falling in a fever, milking his potency with her inner muscles, mines of plea-sure detonating in her every cell.

It built and built. She rode and rode, faster, harder, her hands bunching in his muscles, her eyes feverish on his, her mouth open on harsh inhalations vented in frenzied cries.

When it became too much, she wailed, *"Fareed!"*

"Aih ya galbi, take your pleasure all over me. Take it." He crashed her down on him, forged to her womb.

She imploded around him for long, still moments, shaking uncontrollably as the tidal wave hovered. Then it crashed, splintered and reformed her around him, over and over.

He took over when she lost her rhythm, a convulsing mess of sensation, changed the angle of his thrusts, hit-ting a bundle of nerves that triggered a fiercer explosion. It wracked her, drained her to her last nerve ending.

Yet she needed more, him, joining her in ecstasy, begged for it.

This time when the world vanished and nothing but him remained, around her, inside her, she promised herself.

This *would* be the last time.

Or maybe another time when next they woke up. Or maybe just one more day. Yes, one more day wouldn't hurt. But after that, there would be no more. Never again…

Nine

Fareed gazed down on Gwen and thought this was what sunlight would be like made flesh, made woman.

Her hair gleamed and her skin glowed in the flickering light of a dozen oil lamps. He'd placed them around this bedroom with only her in mind. This bedroom that wasn't his.

After all the time he'd fantasized about having her in his bed, he'd picked her up that first night, and his feet had taken him here. A guest suite that had never been used before. He'd wanted them to have a place all their own, a place he hadn't been before, where all the memories would be of her, of them.

He leaned over her, his heart in a constant state of expansion. Her lips, slightly parted in sleep, were crimson and swollen from his possession. Just their sight scorched him with the memories of the past days. He bent and took them, unable to have enough. She moaned, opening for him, her tongue first accepting the caress of his own, then dueling with it, in that never-ending quest for tasting, taking, surrendering. Even in the depth of sleep, she couldn't have enough either.

He'd lost track of how many times he'd possessed her, how many times she'd claimed him back.

He pulled back, filled his sight and senses and memory with her, beyond his fantasies, lush and vital and glittering in the dimness, naked and vulnerable and the most overwhelming power he'd ever known. Her hold over him was absolute.

His love for her was as infinite.

He groaned as emotions welled inside him, debilitating and empowering, even as his body hardened beyond agony. He needed to plunge into her depths again, mingle with her body and soul.

His hand glided over her, absorbing her softness and resilience, the pleasure that hummed inside her at his touch, the craving echoing his. He caressed her from breast to the concavity of her waist, over the swell of her hips and the curve of her thigh. His hand hooked beneath her knee, opening her over him.

He savored her every jerk betraying her enjoyment, her torment, even as she still dreamed. He bent and took more suckles of the breasts that had rewhetted his appetite for life. She moaned as she spread her thighs for him, cradled him in the only place he'd ever call home, where the fluid heat of her welcome was unraveling his sanity all over again.

Her eyes half opened, heavy with sleep and lust, endless, insatiable skies. "Come inside me, Fareed...*now*."

He felt he now lived to hear her say this, to know how much she needed him, to join them in unbridled intimacy and abandon, to take every liberty and give every ecstasy.

He pressed into her, reveling in the music of her gasps, the intoxication of her undulations, the urgency of the hands that clamped his head to her engorged-with-need flesh, begging him to devour her. The scent of her arousal sent blood crashing in his head, thundering in his loins.

He raised his head to take her vocal confessions, poured his own. "Every moment with you, *ya roh galbi* is magic. I want everything with you, every contradiction. Right now, I want to be giving and tender and I want to be greedy and ferocious, all at once."

She clung to him, wrapped her legs around him, her lips feverish over his face and shoulders and chest. "You almost wrecked my sanity with your last session of giving tenderness. Give me greedy and ferocious, please. Please, Fareed, please!"

He'd never known there was such pride, such pleasure, as that her desire could engender. Now her urgency hit a chord of blind lust inside him, reverberated it until it snapped.

He snatched her beneath him, rose above her, his senses ricocheting within a body that felt hollowed. Every breath electrocuted him. Every heartbeat felt like a wrecking ball inside his chest. He wanted to tear into her, pound her until there were no more barriers between their bodies. And she wanted him to do it, to plunder her, was shaking apart for his domination.

But he'd give her even better. He'd give it all to her.

He unlocked her convulsive limbs from around his body, ignored her cries of protest, swept her around on her stomach.

She whimpered as he held her down, captured her mound. His fingers delved between her soaking folds to her trigger. She climaxed with the first strokes, bucking and shuddering beneath him.

He showed her no mercy, fingers gliding, spreading the moistness from her core, made her shred her body and throat on pleasure.

He kept stroking her, raggedly encouraging her to have her fill of pleasure, until she slumped beneath him. Then he plunged his fingers inside her, his thumb echoing the action on the outside. She writhed under the renewed stimulation; the need for release a rising crest of incoherence. She thrust against his hand until his *"Marrah kaman, ya galbi"* hurled her convulsing into another orgasm.

She subsided beneath him, a mute mass of tremors. His fingers remained deep inside her, started preparing her for the next peak.

"I swear, Fareed, if you don't take me now…I won't let you take me for…for…" She stopped, panting.

"Not finding a suitable length of deprivation?" He chuckled, removing his hand. "Because you'll also be depriving yourself?"

She threw him a smoldering glance over her shoulder, one that almost caused his already-overheated system to vapor lock. Then she purred, "Maybe there is another way out of this predicament."

She thrust the perfection of her smooth, slick bottom back into his erection. Sensation ripped through him on a beast's growl, making him lunge over her, snap his teeth into her shoulder, making her grind harder into him.

He ground back, whispered hotly in her ear, "I'm finding demonstrations far more effective than threats. Go on, give me examples of what you need me to do."

The look she gave him this time, the sight of her as she trembled up to her knees, her waterfall of sunshine and ripe golden breasts swaying gently, blanked his sanity, almost made him slam into her. But the need to have her seek him, relinquish yet another notch of inhibition, over-powered even the insanity.

She lowered her head and upper body to the mattress. The total submission in her position, the devouring in her gaze as she rested her face against the dark sheets and silently demanded his domination, sent his breath hissing in his throat like steam, his erection filling with what felt like molten lead.

He still needed more. "A superlative demonstration. Now I need accompanying directions of what's required of me."

And she gave him what he needed. "I want you to bury yourself all the way inside me, holding nothing back, until you finish me, send us both into oblivion."

The last tether of his restraint snapped so hard, he rammed into her with all the violence of its recoil, bottoming out in one thrust. A shout burned its way from both their depths.

"Nothing ever felt like this, Gwen," he growled as he thrust deeper, harder into her, feeling as if he'd delved into an inferno of pure ecstasy. "Being inside you, this fit, this intensity, this perfection. Nothing could possibly be this pleasurable. But it is, you are, more pleasure than is possible. You sate me and craze me with insatiability. You burn me, Gwen, body and reason."

She sobbed with every thrust. "You *burn* me, too…you fill me beyond my ability to withstand…or my ability to have enough. Oh, Fareed…the pain and pleasure of you… do it all to me…*do* it."

Feeling his body hurtling into the danger zone, he put all his power behind each plunge. She writhed beneath him, thrusting back, letting him forge new depths inside her, panting more confessions, more proddings. Pressure built in his loins with each slide and thrust, each word, spread from the point inside her he was hitting deepest.

He rode her ever harder, insane for her release, for his.

Then like shock waves heralding a detonation too far to be felt yet, it started. Ripples spread from the outside in, pushing everything to his center, compacting where he was buried in her. He took her, in one more perfect fusion, and it came. The spike of shearing pleasure, his body all but charring with its intensity, slam after slam after slam of spreading satisfaction.

He pitched her forward, filled her with his white-hot release as they melted into one being, replete, complete.

An eternity passed before his senses rebooted. He heard a hum, felt it, pure contentment rising from her as she received his full weight over her back. It made him wish he could remain like this forever, containing her, covering her.

It was beyond incredible, what they shared. Every time had the exhilaration, the voracity, the surprise of a first time, yet had the practiced certainty of a long-established relationship.

After moments, with utmost regret, he had to obey the fact that he was twice her size and weight, and that no matter how much she insisted she craved feeling his weight, practical issues like blood circulation and breathing still existed.

He slid off her slippery, satin flesh, turned her limp, sated body around, gathered her into the curve of his body, locked her into his limbs. She burrowed into him, opened her lips on his pulse, her breathing settling back from chaos to serenity as she sank back into contented sleep.

He sighed in bone-deep bliss. Having her pressed to his side, having her in his life was nirvana.

He couldn't believe it had been only a week since

they'd first made love. It felt as if he'd always gone to sleep wrapped around her and woken up to her filling his arms.

Yet one thing marred the perfection.

Even though he felt their connection deepening, she was only vocal, only demonstrative when it came to physical passion. And only when he aroused her beyond inhibition.

When he'd thought he'd resolved her withdrawal the day after their first magical night, he hadn't.

She'd woken up the next day with renewed desire to leave. He'd had to use every trick in the book of unrepentant seduction to make her relinquish her intentions.

He had, but only until the next day had dawned. She'd pulled back every morning, forcing him to recapture her each night. Then today, he'd come home running when Emad had informed him she'd been trying to arrange her departure from Jizaan.

That had driven it home that something serious was behind her persistence. But chiding her for trying to depart behind his back hadn't shed any light on that motivation, or obtained a promise that she wouldn't repeat her efforts. He'd given up trying, taken her in his arms, and everything had been burned away in their mutual abandon.

He still knew passion-induced amnesia would lift and she'd wake up pinched and troubled, and it would be déjà vu all over again.

But he wasn't worried anymore.

He'd finally figured out why she tried to limit their involvement to a passion with a daily-extended expiration date.

His lifelong experience had been with women who'd wanted him for his status and wealth. But for Gwen, the reverse was true. Even though she appreciated everything that he was, the man and the surgeon, the very things that attracted other women repelled her. She'd made it clear how vital to her equality in a relationship was. How deeply disturbed she must be at what she perceived as the imbalance of power between them.

But now that he knew the source of her agitation and aversion, he had the perfect solution in mind.

Feeling secure next morning would break the cycle of her daily withdrawal, he snuggled with her and closed his eyes, contentment blanketing him.

"You can't mean that!"

Fareed watched Gwen bolt up in bed, sighed. "Here we go again."

Gwen groaned. "Don't *you* start again, you know what I mean. But you still *can't* mean that!"

He stroked the gleaming tresses that rained over the peaked perfection of her breasts. "I can and I do."

She moaned as she caught his hands. "Don't, Fareed. This is out of the question."

"No, it's not. You're ideal, to say the least."

Exasperation rose in her eyes again. "You're just saying that because…"

And he turned serious. "Because I'm lucky beyond measure that the woman who blinds me with lust also arouses my utmost professional respect and satisfies my most demanding scientific standards."

She gaped at him, then groaned, "Don't exaggerate, please."

He sighed again. "Do credit me with *some* professional integrity, *ya roh galbi*."

"Don't tell me you can't find anyone better to be the head of R & D in your new multibillion-dollar pharmaceutical department. A job that seems to have just become available now."

He shrugged. "It's been available for a while and no one satisfied all my criteria. You do. Your narrow field of expertise, your body of work and future research plans, all which made me attend your presentation those years ago, fit the closest with my own practice's best interests, and the center's overall focus." He ran a finger down her neck, between her breasts and lower. "What would you have me do? Look for someone less well-suited because you happen to be my specific libido trigger, too?"

She fidgeted in response to his words and touch. "Many would consider that a conflict of interest."

"I'd consider it a *conflagration* of interest. Beside this…" He caught her against his chest, groaned his delight as her lush breasts flattened against him, as her breath caught and her body heated again. "*I'd* get the most innovative and intrepid researcher in the field I'm interested in, while *you* fulfill your professional aspirations. Think what you can achieve, for your own career, for me and the center, for the world, with all the resources I'll put at your fingertips."

She still shook her head. "I—I can't stay here, Fareed."

He chalked one point up to his cause. She was no longer contesting the position itself, was down to the next worry.

"I know some aspects of the kingdom and culture are alien to you, maybe even disturbing. But many aspects delight you, too, and you've assimilated into much of your surroundings. And then I will never let anything negative affect you, or Ryan or Rose, in any way."

She bit her lip. He restrained his desire to replace them with his—he had to let her air her doubts so he could pulverize them.

She finally exhaled. "Nothing is really negative as much as it's different. But you and your family… I just can't get my head around how much power you wield here."

He'd been right. She was disturbed by the extent of his and his family's influence. She had seen the evidence of their almost absolute power in every aspect of life in the kingdom. "No one, including me and my family, will ever wield any power over you. You'll always be free to make your own decisions, personally and professionally."

"As evidenced by how I ended up doing everything you unilaterally thought was the only thing to be done?"

He cocked one eyebrow at her. "You're saying I coerced you?"

"I'm saying free will and you are mutually exclusive."

"I had to take charge of Ryan's care. Then I had to make you act on our shared desire. But if I ever feel that being with me is no longer your priority or good for Ryan, if you ever have a better offer professionally, I won't try to make you stay. This I promise you. On my honor."

She looked as if she'd burst into tears.

Before he rushed to add something, anything, she choked out, "Oh, God, Fareed…you're being so unfair. You're…deluging me with so much. But I have to say no. I never dreamed it would go this far, but if you're too blinded to care about your best interest, and ours, to end it *now,* I have to do it."

He wanted to kick himself. He hadn't considered those reasons for her reticence. That she believed he was compromising himself, and her, for something that would end. She was calculating the damages, to him, to her and Ryan, after such a finite, even if prolonged and powerful, interlude ended.

But he couldn't make it clear he had no intention of ending this. Before he discussed permanence, he had to first resolve all her issues, about her and Ryan's future here, give her more than offers and promises, show her how it would work in practice.

His cell phone rang. He ignored it, began, "Gwen, *galbi*..."

She grabbed his forearm. "Won't you answer?"

"No." He glared his annoyance at the phone on the dresser, tugged her nearer. "Now, Gwen..."

Her grip tightened. "That's Emad's ringtone."

He shrugged. "He'll call later. Gwen..."

"But he's not hanging up," she persisted. "It might be Ryan or Rose and my own phone is dead or something."

She scrambled to get out of bed, and he stopped her, resigned that the moment was ruined.

"I'll answer him." He jumped out of bed, reveling in her hungry eyes on his aroused nakedness, despite her alarm. "And it's *not* about Ryan or Rose, I'm sure, so you stay right there. I'm coming back as soon as I blast Emad to the farthest kingdom in the region."

He felt steam rising from his skin as he snatched up the phone and put it to his ear.

Emad preempted his frustration. "I need to speak to you."

"You couldn't have picked a worse time," he hissed.

Emad's exhalation was weary. "That's true, if not for the reason you mean. I am waiting downstairs in your office."

"I'll come down in an hour. Maybe two."

"No, *Somow'wak*." Emad sounded like never before. Blunt, brooking no arguments. "You'll come down *now*."

"Now" turned out to be twenty minutes later, the shortest time it took Fareed to dress and to take his leave of Gwen.

He strode into his office, displeasure roiling inside him.

"You'd better have some unprecedented reason for this, Emad…"

Suddenly, Fareed's blood froze in his arteries. The look on Emad's face. This was momentous.

This was about Hesham's family.

A lead had finally led somewhere. He could think of nothing else that would make Emad ask his presence so imperatively, or look so…so…

"You found them?" he rasped.

Emad gave a difficult nod.

Fareed's heart crashed. "Something happened to them?"

Emad leveled grim eyes on him. "No, but it's not much less terrible than if something had."

"*B'Ellahi,* Emad, just tell me," he roared.

Emad winced at his loss of control.

Then with regret heavy in his voice, he said, "I've found proof that Hesham's woman is…Gwen."

Ten

"You're insane."

That was all Fareed could say, could think. That was the only explanation for what Emad had just uttered.

"Her given name was Gwendo*lyn*. She changed it to Gwen in official documents since her college days."

A dizzying mixture of relief and rage churned inside Fareed's chest. "*That's* your 'proof'?"

Regret deepened in Emad's eyes. "That's just the tip of the iceberg. The doubts that made me investigate Gwen began when I became convinced she knew Arabic. She responded appropriately to things said in Arabic too many times, if only in that inimitable glint of understanding in her eyes, that I thought it strange she wouldn't mention it. So I tested my theory by speaking Arabic on purpose when she was within earshot and observing her reaction. She was careful not to show that she understood, but I could see that she did. I became absolutely certain when

I once calmly told a servant to walk out of the room naturally, then run like the wind to investigate the silent alarm I received from the southern guard post. Her alarm was unmistakable, and she tried to indirectly find out if anything was wrong. Because I spoke fast and idiomatically, I became certain she has knowledge of not only Arabic but our specific dialect."

Fareed rejected Emad's words as they exited his lips.

But another voice rose inside his mind, borne of the observations he'd never heeded. How she'd never asked what the things he said in Arabic meant, especially the endearments he deluged her in, how she seemed to respond appropriately.:.

No. She'd only understood his tone. He wasn't letting Emad poison his mind with his crazy theory.

Emad continued. "I couldn't find a reason why she'd hide her knowledge, but because I don't believe in inexplicable, yet innocent, behavior, I tried to get more information from Rose."

"*That's* what you've been doing with Rose?" Fareed growled. "Leading her on so she'd supply you with possible dirt on Gwen? You went too far in your efforts to 'protect' me this time, Emad."

"I was getting close to Rose for real, and I hope to get closer. Although I don't know how I will, with the truth revealed…"

"This is *not* the truth. All you have to support this insane theory is circumstantial evidence."

Pain etched deeper on Emad's face. "I have new evidence that the places where Gwen lived are also where Hesham lived, at the same time, that she now lives in the same town he did when he died. She seemed to be living alone in all these places, but then so did Hesham. They must have kept separate residences in Hesham's obsession to keep their relationship a secret. She became a free-lance researcher for the past four years so she wouldn't have a base. Then she left the job scene around the time she would have been in her last months of pregnancy and during Ryan's first months. She went back to work only when Rose became Ryan's nanny.

"And I didn't get any of that from Rose. She might be shockingly open, but only with her own opinions. She wouldn't have shared anything about Gwen. But she doesn't know much anyway because she lived across the continent with her late ex-husband for the last five years. They divorced years ago, but when he had a stroke that paralyzed him, Rose went back to take care of him. He died two months before Gwen contacted her and asked her to become Ryan's live-in nanny. Two weeks after Hesham died."

Fareed shook his head, repeated what looped in his mind under the barrage of information. "Circumstantial evidence, all of it."

Emad closed yet another escape route. "The one thing Rose mentioned was that a tragedy befell Gwen around the same time her ex-husband died. She wouldn't elaborate and I couldn't probe more than I did and have her suspect my motives."

"Good thing you couldn't afford to alienate the first woman to move your heart since your late wife."

"I couldn't afford to alert her to my suspicions and have her relay them to Gwen. If Gwen felt danger, we might lose Ryan."

"Now I *know* you're insane."

"I would give anything to be wrong, but with you being who you are, with what's at stake, I have to consider the worst possible explanation for her actions, until proven otherwise."

Fareed gritted his teeth. "Just to see what kind of twisted ideas you can come up with, what would said explanation be?"

"The ideas I have are courtesy of the twisted fortune hunters who've pursued you since you turned eighteen."

Outrage, on Gwen's behalf, boiled his blood. "And you somehow suspect Gwen is one of those, among everything else?"

"It's a theory, but it answers every question. She met Hesham in that conference…" At Fareed's stunned glance, Emad grunted. "Yes, I realized why I felt inclined to give her a chance. Seemed I recognized her but failed to place her. Until I remembered that you spent a whole evening staring at her across that ballroom."

So Emad had seen Gwen's effect on him that day. And Hesham *had* come to see him during the end-of-conference party.

He still refused to sanction any of the accumulating evidence. "So they were in the same place once…"

"And my theory goes that she realized you were related. Once you left, she might have approached him to ask about you and their relationship began."

Fareed groped for air. "That's preposterous."

"If you have a better explanation to fill the spaces in Hesham's story, I'd be the first to grab at it. But we can't afford to blind ourselves to what might be the truth. But if you find Gwen irresistible, Hesham, your closest brother in nature, would have found her so, too. It might have developed naturally between them, with the reason they met, you, unknown by him, and forgotten by her. Then everything went wrong and the king made his ultimatum, and Hesham went into hiding with her. Then he died and she walked away from the accident unscathed. Everything till that point could have been innocent and aboveboard. But

I hit a wall trying to find any good reason why she didn't come forward when you searched for her.

"With Hesham dead, from her perspective, the king's threat to her was no more. Without a legal marriage, or the possibility of one, making her and Ryan legitimate heirs of a member of the royal family, she must have realized she'd be beneath his notice, therefore safe. *But* she was also in no position to demand anything from the Aal Zaafers, apart from your own voluntary support. As lavish as that would have been had she gotten it, she might have wanted more. And she had the perfect plan to get it.

"She must have known how she affected you all those years ago, so she approached you incognito through Ryan's crisis. She could have used Hesham's knowledge of you to make you fall under her spell, to have not only all you can provide, for Hesham's and Ryan's sake, but all that you *are,* for hers. And she succeeded, didn't she?"

Fareed pulled at his hair, trying to counteract the pressure building inside his skull. "You're sick, Emad. I thought you liked her, thought…thought…" He stopped, suffocating. "You're *wrong,* about everything. She's not Hesham's woman."

Emad eyed him bleakly. "And if she is? Will you consider the rest of my explanations?"

"No," Fareed shouted. "Even if she is—and she *isn't*—she'd have a reason, a good, even noble reason for hiding the truth."

"You haven't asked her to marry you yet, have you?"

Fareed blinked. "What does that have to do with anything?"

"It explains her sudden persistence to leave. I know you've become…intimate, and she might have feared you might cool down. Threatening you with leaving might have been to push you to offer her what would make her stay forever."

"No. *No way.* She doesn't have one exploitative cell in her body. I don't need to know facts. I know *her.* And I reject your evidence." He bunched his fists, tried to bring his turmoil under control. "That will be all, Emad."

"Forgive me, *Somow'wak,* but I *have* to voice my worst fears."

Fareed barely contained his fury. "And you have. I will ask her. She will refute it all. I will believe her and *that* will be that."

"But we can't afford for you to confront her, *Somow'wak.*"

"Why wouldn't you want her to defend herself against your delusional deductions, except if you suspect they are just that?"

"Because if I'm right, confronting her would cost us Ryan."

"There you go again with this...*absurdity.*"

"It's anything but absurd, *Somow'wak.* I've marveled at the bond you forge deeper by the hour. Now I know you've both recognized the same blood running through your veins, the legacy of your most beloved sibling and his father. I'm certain part of your desire to have her is to have him, too. But she has full rights to him, and if any of the intentions I assigned to her were true, if she's exposed you might enter an ugly fight over him. One you're certain to lose."

Fareed felt he was watching an explosion, played in reverse.

Emad's revelations were the shrapnel hurtling back into place to re-form the bomb. Which might be the truth.

Not his macabre rationalization of Gwen's motives and methods. But that she could be…be…

He couldn't even think it. It would be beyond endurance.

But it would explain so much. Her wariness and resistance from the first moment, her distress when he'd asked her about Ryan's father, his reaction to Ryan—which had the texture of what he'd felt for Hesham, the many similarities that *did* exist between the child Hesham had been and Ryan.

Then came Gwen's continued emotional reticence, her persistent efforts to stop their intimacies, to leave…

The doubt Emad had sown felt like a virus replicating at cancerous speed, infecting his every cell and thought.

He couldn't survive knowing. He wouldn't survive not knowing.

He stopped again. He didn't want his steps to take him back to her. He'd always rushed to her as if every step separating him from her dimmed his life force. Now…now…

Now those remaining steps were his last refuge. They could be what separated him from finding out that he couldn't love her.

Emad had tried his best to dissuade him from taking those steps. His parting advice still cut into his mind, paring away every belief in anything good and pure, painting his world with the ugliness of manipulation and deceit.

Marry her. Without confronting her. Make her give you all rights to Ryan, secure Hesham's son. Then *deal with her, according to her innocence or guilt.*

His steps ran out. They'd taken him where he'd experienced his life's first true happiness, the consummation of his most profound bond. Where he might now end it all.

He opened the door, stepped inside. She wasn't there.

He'd have the respite of ignorance, of hope, a bit longer.

A vase swayed as he bumped into it. It crashed, broke into countless, useless shards. Just like his heart might moments from now.

A door slammed and footsteps spilled onto the hardwood floor.

She emerged from the chamber leading to the bathroom, half-running, the face of all his hopes and dreams, alarmed, concerned, sublime in beauty. "Fareed, what…"

She faltered as she saw the ruins at his feet, took in his frozen stance.

Then it was there in her eyes. The realization. The desperation. The fear. Of exposure.

Certainty flooded him, drowned anything else inside him.

She *was* Hesham's woman.

Gwen stared at the stranger who looked back at her out of Fareed's eyes, desperation detonating in her heart.

He'd somehow found out.

"Laish?"

"Fareed, please…"

They'd spoken at the same moment. But he'd finished even as she stumbled to find words to implore him with.

He'd said all he was going to say.

He'd only asked, *"Why?"*

Why she'd lied. Why she'd kept lying.

She could only ask her own burning question, "How?"

The stranger who now inhabited Fareed's body said, "Emad."

She had no idea how Emad had found out, where she'd gone wrong. He couldn't have gotten it out of Rose. She didn't know.

"This is why you kept pushing me away, insisting on leaving."

Statements. She could do nothing but nod.

She'd trapped herself the day she'd withheld the truth from him. And only sealed her fate when she'd grabbed at that one night with him and hadn't left right afterward, when she'd kept telling herself, just one more night.

"Ryan lahmi w'dammi. Laish khabbaiti?"

Ryan is my flesh and blood. Why did you hide it?

The way he said that, that haunted look in his eyes crushed her. She'd seen him in that videotaped request for her to come forward. He'd looked and sounded wrecked over his brother's death. He looked like that again, as if he'd lost him all over again.

She still couldn't tell him why.

But his eyes weren't only deadened with that grief she'd experienced for as long and as intensely. In them still lay his inexorableness. He'd have an answer.

She gave him all she could. "I was abiding by Hesham's will."

The moment she uttered Hesham's name, Fareed swayed like a building in a massive earthquake.

And if she'd thought his eyes had gone dead before, she knew how wrong she'd been. He now looked at her as someone would at his own murderer.

She couldn't survive his pain and disillusion. She had to try to alleviate them, with what she could reveal.

"I had to keep on doing what he did. You know the lengths he went to to hide his family's whereabouts and identity."

In that same deep-as-death voice, he asked, *"Gallek laish?"*

He'd always spoken Arabic unintentionally, to express his hunger and appreciation with the spontaneity and accuracy he could only achieve in his mother tongue. He'd usually been too submerged in passion to explain.

Now he spoke Arabic as if he was convinced she understood, wanted more proof of the depth of her deception.

Her heart twisted until it felt it would tear out its tethers. "He—he was convinced it would ruin his family to have...*your* family know of...our existence. This is why he hid. This is why I did, too. I—I only sought you out because of Ryan's problem, thought I'd get your opinion and leave. But things kept snowballing, then things between us...ignited, turning my position from difficult to impossible and I kept wanting to leave, to disappear, so you'd never know, never feel like this..."

"Too late now."

Silence crashed after his monotone statement.

She waited for him to add something, to restart her heart or still it forever.

He only said, "Tell me everything about the last years since I lost my brother. Tell me about your life with Hesham."

Gwen looked as if he'd asked her to take a scalpel to her own neck.

Fareed felt he'd be doing the same. Worse. That he'd be cutting out his heart. But he had to know. Even if it killed him.

He no longer recognized that dreadful drone that issued from him. "You met him in that conference?"

She cast her eyes downward. It was an unbearable moment before she nodded.

He felt as if a bullet had ripped through his heart, stilling its last jerking attempts at a beat.

He'd thought she'd recognized him that day, had ended her engagement because she couldn't be with anyone else.

All that time, it had been Hesham.

"Did you love him?"

She collapsed on the bed, dropped her face in her hands.

She *had* loved him. The grief he felt from her now was the same he'd felt at first. Her anguish for Ryan seemed an insufficient explanation, if that could be said. It had been due to the loss of Hesham, the father of her son.

And even though it shredded his heart, he had to tell her. "He loved you. He lived for you, and when he was dying, his only thoughts were of you. Even though he gave up his name and family and whole life to be with you, he thought you deserved more. His dying words were that he was sorry he couldn't give it to you."

Tears came then. Hers. He wished he could shed any.

He bled instead, dark torrents of loss.

Two things had been sustaining him. The hope of finding Hesham's family. And finding her and Ryan.

But they were one and the same, and his hopes for a blissful future for all were doomed to be forever tainted by the past.

It wasn't because he believed the ulterior motives Emad had assigned her secrecy. He wished he could. It would have been a far lesser blow to believe her a self-serving manipulator. He would have been relieved Hesham had died clinging to his false belief in her and at peace. As for his agony at losing his faith in her, it would have been ameliorated if he could have coveted her knowing what she truly was.

But she was everything he could love and respect, the answer to all his fantasies and needs. And that she'd been the same to his brother, had been his in such an abiding love that she'd become a fugitive to be with him...*that* was despair.

For even if he could survive the guilt—and may Ullah forgive him, the jealousy—how could he survive knowing she might never feel the same for him? What *did* she feel for him? Beyond physical hunger? Had he been unable to fathom her emotions because they didn't exist? Had she been unable to deny her body's needs, while her heart remained buried with Hesham?

If it had, had everything she'd had with *him* been an attempt to resurrect what she'd had with Hesham? Had she found solace in their minor resemblances, taken comfort in sensing the love he had for him?

Had she ever felt anything that was purely for him?

He had to get away from her before whatever held him together disintegrated.

He found himself at the door, heard himself saying, "I'll be at the center. Don't try to leave."

He couldn't make this a request. It could no longer be one.

Even if it would kill him, she was staying. Forever.

Gwen raised swollen eyes to the door that had closed behind Fareed. Heartbeats fractured inside her chest as she expected him to walk back, take her with him where he could keep an eye on her.

After moments of frozen dread, she tried to rise.

She sagged back to the bed. The bed she'd never share with Fareed again. In the apartment she'd realized wasn't his.

He hadn't taken her to his private domain, had kept her in what was to him, for all its wonders, an impersonal space.

Relief had trumped the pain of knowing he hadn't thought her worthy of sharing his own bed. She didn't wish the depth of her involvement on him, wished him only the mildness of fond memories when she left his life, not the harshness of unquenchable longing she'd live with.

But as he'd said, it was too late. Whatever he'd felt for her had now been forever soiled and soured.

It wasn't too late to escape. This time, she wouldn't let anything stop her. She'd at least spirit Ryan and Rose away.

Panic finally got her legs working. At the door, her hand slipped on the handle...then she stumbled back.

The door was opening. Fareed. He'd come back as she'd feared....

Next moment, she stood gaping at the stranger...*strangers* on the other side of the door.

The dark, imposing man who looked like the highest-ranking among them, advanced on her, said without preamble, "You will come with us. The king has summoned you."

The ride to the royal palace passed in harrowing silence.

Her escorts wouldn't answer her questions. They'd said the king had summoned her, but in reality, she was being abducted.

Even if she hadn't heard enough from Hesham about his father, this act of blatant disregard for her most basic rights made her expect the worst.

She'd long dreaded this man. Her fear only deepened with every step through his palace's impossible opulence and extravagance.

Then she was ushered into his state room.

As the door closed behind her, she felt engulfed by malice.

It didn't matter. She'd fight him, king or not....

"Harlots always had the intelligence and self-preservation to try to entrap my sons outside my domain."

The voice was pure wrath and mercilessness, short-circuiting her resolve. It issued from the deep shadows at the far end of the gigantic room.

The owner of the voice rose from a throne-like seat and advanced to the relatively illuminated part where she stood. She almost cringed. Almost. She wouldn't give him the satisfaction.

"But you're here to steal Fareed under my very nose. You're either recklessly stupid or unbelievably cunning. I'd go with the second interpretation because you managed to have my most-level-headed son eating out of your hand."

This was about Fareed? He didn't know who she was?

Relief almost burst out of her, but she couldn't give any outward sign of it. She stood staring ahead, face blank.

This provoked him even more. She felt his rage encompassing her as he stormed toward her. Then she saw him clearly for the first time. It took all that remained of her tattered control not to recoil.

The man was an older version of Fareed, as tall but bulkier, must have been as blessed by nature once upon a time, but ruthlessness had degraded his looks, turning him forbidding, almost sinister. And he was incensed.

"You think I'll lose another son to another American hussy? One who wants to foist her bastard child on him, too?" He snatched at her. Her heart hit her throat as she stumbled out of reach. He brought himself under control. "But I'll give you the choice I would have given the trash who deprived me of my youngest son. Leave, disappear, and I'll leave you alone. If you don't, what happens to you and yours will be your fault."

And she knew. That the lengths Hesham had gone to, to hide from that man, what she'd always suspected had been at least a little exaggerated, had been warranted, and then some.

But ironically, because of the king's ignorance of her

true identity, he was giving her a way out of this horrific mess. He'd even provided the means for her to leave against Fareed's will, what she might have never secured on her own.

"What will it be?" the king rumbled, a predator about to pounce and to hell with giving his opponent a running chance.

She looked him in the eyes, made her answer a solemn pledge. "I'll leave. And I'll disappear. Fareed will never find me again."

The king had believed her.

But knowing that Fareed wouldn't just let her go, he'd said he would give her every assistance in her disappearance efforts.

His men had delivered her to Fareed's mansion to collect Rose and Ryan on her way to the king's private airstrip. She'd phoned Rose ahead, told her to be ready, wouldn't answer her confusion.

She now ran into the mansion, had reached the bottom of the stairs when his voice came out of nowhere.

"If you're still trying to leave, Gwen, don't bother."

She stumbled with the force of the déjà vu.

Fareed was separating from the shadows at the top of the stairs like that first night he'd made her his.

God, *no*. Now this wouldn't be the clean surgical amputation she'd hoped it would be.

He was coming down the stairs now, as deliberate, as determined as that other night. But instead of the passion that had buffeted her then, the void emanating from him did now.

"I'm not letting you and Ryan go, Gwen. And that's final."

She took one step back for each he took closer. But

nothing stopped his advance. He was now mere feet away....

Then two things happened at once.

Rose appeared at the top of the stairs with Ryan. And the king's men, all six of them, who'd been waiting for her outside, entered the mansion in force.

Fareed swerved to advance on them in steps loaded with danger, putting himself between her and them, his expression thunderous.

"What's the meaning of this, Zayed?"

The man who'd led the task force that had taken her to the king gave him a curt bow.

"Forgive me for the intrusion, Prince Fareed, but the king has changed our orders. Only this woman and her female companion will leave the kingdom. The child, Prince Hesham's son, will remain—will be taken to him."

Eleven

"This woman and her child are in my protection."

At Fareed's arctic outrage, her gaze slammed from Rose and Ryan—frozen like her at the top of the stairs—back to him.

"My father is never coming near either of them. As for all of you, you will leave my house, right now, or suffer the consequences."

She'd never dreamed Fareed could look so lethal. And she knew. He would fulfill his threat without a second's hesitation. He was ready to fight, go to any lengths, inflict or sustain any injury, in their defense.

A chill of dread ran down her spine. She'd tried everything she could so that it would never come to that. But— No, she could have left sooner, prevented this. Now it was too late.

The king had discovered Ryan's identity.

The man called Zayed, what Gwen imagined desert

raiders must have looked like, harsh and weathered and unbending, stood his ground. "*Somow'wak,* by the authority vested in me by the king, I order you to stand aside."

Fareed barked a laugh that must have sent every hair in the place standing on end like it did hers. "Or what? You'll tell my father on me? Do so, and take this message back to that uncompromising fossil while you're at it, word for word. I'm not Hesham, and not only won't he intimidate me, but he also wouldn't want to make me his enemy. I will be if he even thinks of Gwen or Ryan again. And that's his first and final warning."

Zayed's face clenched in a conflict of reluctance and determination. It was apparent he liked and respected his prince, wouldn't want to fight him. But his allegiance, even if he didn't appear to relish it, was to the king, and it was unswerving.

He finally said, "My orders were clear, *Somow'wak.* I can't back down. *Arjook,* I beg of you, don't force a confrontation."

"That's exactly what I'll do, with anyone who dares threaten Gwen or Ryan." Fareed advanced on Zayed, a warrior who had the same steel-nerved precision and efficiency of the surgeon. "I'll go to war for them. Will you? Will he?"

She could feel Zayed hesitating as her mind churned, trying to work out how to exploit this standoff, take Ryan and Rose and escape them all.

But there was no way out. Either the king won, and she was thrown out of the country, or Fareed won, and he kept her here.

Either way, Ryan would end up being lost to her.

Suddenly, the simmering scene fractured.

Zayed made up his mind and gestured to his men. They advanced instantaneously, a highly organized strike force.

Two men ran past her and Fareed, targeting the stairs. She heard Rose's shouted protests and Ryan's alarmed crying as they advanced. Fareed intercepted Zayed and three of his men as they made a grab for her. She gaped in horror as violence erupted.

She cried out as a fist connected with Fareed's face, as she heard the sickening impact of knuckles with flesh and bone. And she threw herself into the fight, blind now but to one thing: defending him, preventing any injury to him at any cost.

Fareed took the man who'd hit him down with one blow to the throat and Zayed with another to the solar plexus. The third man he took down with one roundhouse kick to the temple. He was fighting with the economy of the surgeon who knew the anatomy of incapacitation. She hit and kicked the man she'd attacked, but he finally managed to restrain her.

Fareed turned on him, rumbling like an enraged tiger. "Take your hands off her, Mohsen, or have them torn off."

"*Assef, Somow'wak*—sorry, but you will stand aside now and let me complete my mission." Mohsen produced his gun from his holster.

She drove her elbow into his gut with all her strength.

He gasped, staggered, but he tightened his hold on her neck. She choked, the world wavered and receded. She heard Fareed's roar as if from a distance, saw his contorted face as he charged toward her and her captor, saw a gun pointing at him, from a hand beside her face. Dread for him swelled as she fought to sink her teeth into that hand...

"That's enough!"

A roar reverberated in her bones, then she was snatched from the vise imprisoning her, and swept into the arms she'd thought she'd never feel again in this life. Fareed's.

Her wavering gaze panned around. Emad was at the top of the stairs standing between Rose and Ryan and the men who'd gone after them, protecting them with his own body, like Fareed had done for her minutes ago. Fareed's guards were cordoning the scene, four or five to each of Zayed's men, pinning them at gunpoint.

"Took you long enough, Emad," Fareed snarled as he took her deeper into his embrace, beckoned to Emad to get Rose and Ryan down and into his protection.

"My apologies, *Somow'wak*." Emad led the shaken Rose who was clutching the bawling Ryan in a feverish embrace down the stairs, encompassing her by his side. Gwen bolted from Fareed's arms, reaching out to Ryan who threw himself in her trembling ones.

Fareed's footsteps almost overlapped hers, and the moment Ryan filled her arms, he took them both back into his own.

Ryan's sobs subsided as soon as he found himself nestled between their bodies, his arms around her neck but his face buried into Fareed's chest, recognizing him as their protector.

Emad went on. "I was on the road when I got your emergency signal. I had to investigate the situation and organize enough men and the plan to end this farce with minimum fuss."

"With *no* further fuss." Fareed turned his wrathful glance to Zayed. "Isn't that right, Zayed?"

Zayed, still trying to recover from the vicious blow Fareed had dealt him, looked at him with grudging consent, acknowledging that he'd outmaneuvered him, had won. This round. He gestured for his men to stand down, retreat.

In minutes, all armed men, the king's and Fareed's, had left the mansion.

Rose was the first one to break the silence that expanded after their departure. "Holy James Bond! What was all that about? And what do they mean Ryan is some prince's son?" Rose put her hand on Gwen's arm. "Is this true?"

Gwen gave a difficult nod, unable to meet anyone's eyes, hugging Ryan tighter, the fright still cascading through her in intensifying shudders.

Fareed tightened his arm around her, as if to absorb her chaos, squeezing the restless Ryan between them, crooning to him, "It's over, *ya sugheeri,* you're safe. I'm here and I'll always be here. No one is ever coming near you again."

A whimper caught in Gwen's throat at the protectiveness and promise in Fareed's voice, at the way Ryan responded. As if he understood and totally believed him, he transferred his arms from her neck to Fareed's, burrowing deep into him, his whimpers silenced.

She almost snatched him back into her arms, cried to Fareed not to promise Ryan what he wouldn't be able to deliver.

Before she could say anything, Fareed turned his eyes to her. "I'm sorry about what happened. My father will pay for this."

She shook her head. "It doesn't matter."

"Of course, it does. And it's partially my fault, *our* fault, my siblings' and mine. We've long become too involved in our lives and projects, we've left his council to work unopposed. He's always been old-school, and has grown more rigid with age. That had once proven effective in matters of state, but when his inflexibility started causing problems, we just fixed them, instead of fixing his views and policies. And we've been paying bigger prices for treating the symptoms instead of the disease. His last unforgivable action was what he'd done to Hesham. But today he's gone too far."

Her headshake was more despondent this time. "I meant it doesn't matter what you, or I, do now. He's found out about Ryan, and everything that Hesham feared has come to pass."

Fareed frowned down at her, the intense pain that seemed to assail him when she mentioned Hesham gripping his face.

He turned to Emad, his frown deepening. "What I want to know is how my father found out about Ryan." The accusation was there in Fareed's voice. But when the confession surfaced with equal clarity on Emad's face, it still seemed to shock Fareed to his core. "*B'Ellahi,* why?"

Emad exhaled heavily. "I had no idea he'd react that way, but…I'd do it again, *Somow'wak.*"

Fury overcame confusion in Fareed's eyes as he ground out, "And you have a sane reason for this?"

Emad held his eyes, his grim but unwavering. "Because I've known the king longer than you have, have seen different sides to him than what he shows his children. But you are pragmatic and emotional at once and have never given your status or its dictates precedence over your decisions, so you never try to understand his position. There are worlds between being a prince who's not in line to the throne and being a king. That is the loneliest place to be."

"And is this analysis of my father's character and position and your view of both supposed to make any difference to me right now?" Fareed growled.

Emad shook his head. "I'm not asking that you forgive, just that you try to understand."

Sarcastic disgust coated Fareed's voice. "*Shukran,* Emad. I can't fault my father for playing true to type, but

I have *you* to thank for this impasse. You're a sentimental fool and you romanticized that heartless relic."

Emad cast his eyes downward, as if realizing anything he said now would incense Fareed further.

But Fareed wasn't done. "Because you've run to him with your discovery almost the moment you made it, have you also been keeping him updated on my efforts to find Gwen and Ryan?" Emad just nodded. Fareed snorted. "I can't tell you how great it is to find out that my most trusted ally is also a double agent. And for what? The most misguided sentimental *crap* for someone who's never shown anyone the least sympathy." He stopped, his fingers digging into Gwen's shoulder, his arm tightening over Ryan, as if he was intensifying his protection. "And among all those fond memories of my father, didn't you store the one when he forced Hesham into exile? Apart from the vile threats to the woman he loved, you do remember what he thought of the 'inferior union' that would soil our venerable line? So, because you're the expert on my father's deepest emotions and motives, *b'haggej' jaheem*—what by hell's name does he suddenly want with Hesham's son, the child he disowned before he came into being?"

Emad looked as if he wouldn't answer that, at the risk of enraging Fareed even more.

Then he did, his eyes heavy, solemn. "I know you think the king cared nothing about Hesham, and I might never be able to convince you otherwise. But he cared too much. He never stopped looking for him either, and in the last year or so, I believe it was to call him home, find a resolution that Hesham would accept. Then Hesham died and remorse and agony almost drove him to the brink of insanity. Only knowing Hesham had a son, and the hope of finding him, has been holding him together. Once I found out who that son was, I couldn't hide Ryan's existence and presence in Jizaan from him."

Fareed looked at Emad as if he was seeing him for the first time, his eyes gone totally cold for the first time since she'd seen him. "And I hope you're happy with the results of your catastrophic misjudgment."

And even though Emad had caused irreparable damage, she couldn't help squirming, as she felt Rose did, too, at the intensity of Fareed's disappointment in him, at Emad's mortification.

After a moment of heavy silence, without looking at Emad anymore, Fareed said a curt, "Ready the helicopter."

Emad only gave one of his deferential nods and strode out of the mansion. Rose ran out in his wake.

Gwen clutched Fareed's forearm. "Where are we going?"

"Where my father can't find us."

She clung harder, implored, "He will find us, sooner or later, Fareed. If you want to help me, help Ryan, you'll help us disappear. If you don't, your father will take Ryan away from me."

His face turned to stone. "No, he won't."

Her desperation mounted as she felt his finality trapping her, dooming Ryan. "If I don't disappear, he will."

His eyes bore into her as he put Ryan down on the floor, gave him a few things to play with. "So you're proposing to do what Hesham did? But Hesham could only do that because he gave up his Jizaanian nationality, changed his name and was a freelancer who could continue to be an artist wherever he lived. You won't be able to do any of that and remain yourself or sustain your career. *You* won't be able to wipe out your existence. Now that Emad has enlightened me about my father's obsession with finding Ryan, I know he would only trace you and kidnap him.

I also realize that was why Hesham begged me with his dying breaths to protect you. He must have known our father was still looking for him, was afraid he would find you and take Ryan from you. But it doesn't matter that he has now. I *will* protect you, but I can't do that long distance. You have to stay with me."

She was shaking all over now, feeling her world slip through her fingers like water, and there was nothing she could do to hang on to it.

"But you won't always be around," she pleaded. "You can't. I stand a better chance of keeping Ryan from him if I'm on the other side of the world, not here, where he rules absolute. You didn't see how he treated me. I wouldn't be surprised if he had me…"

Fareed's dug his fingers into her shoulder, stopping her projection in its track. "Gwen, you have nothing to fear, I swear it. I will fulfill my oath to Hesham. I will protect you, with my life. As for my father, he won't even think of coming near you once you're my wife."

Twelve

Gwen didn't know what happened after Fareed declared that she'd be his wife.

Everything blurred before her as he led her to a helipad behind the mansion where a sleek metal monster awaited them with Rose and Emad already inside. He buckled her in the passenger seat and took the pilot seat after securing Ryan in the back with Rose.

She barely noticed that he flew them over the desert, then out to sea. It could have been minutes or hours later when they came upon an island. He landed in front of a house in the same style as his mansion, only much smaller, steps away from darkening emerald waters and a golden beach glowing with the last rays of sunset.

Emad took Rose and a sound-asleep Ryan upstairs, leaving her and Fareed alone. Fareed gestured for her to wait for him as he walked away to get engaged in a marathon of phone calls.

He now walked back to her, tall and broad and indescribable, everything she could love, his fists clenched in the depths of his tailored pants pockets, his eyes cast downward, his brow knotted, his face cast in the harshness of dark thoughts.

Had she imagined hearing him say she'd be his wife? Or was this why he looked so troubled? Because he was regretting it, was preparing to tell her that he hadn't meant it?

He raised his eyes. Her heart clenched at what filled them. Nothing she could understand. He'd been always near, clear. Now he was as far, as unfathomable as the stars that twinkled in the sky framing him through the open veranda doors.

He exhaled. "I've arranged everything. The cleric and the lawyers will be here in a couple of hours."

Her heart stumbled through many false starts as she waited for him to elaborate. He just kept his heavy gaze fixed on her, as if he expected her to be the one with something to contribute. An answer. An opinion. An acceptance.

But of what?

She finally asked, "What...what do you intend to do?"

His jaw muscles bunched. "Whatever will keep my father at bay. Now I know his true inclinations, we will need every weapon to stop him. In our culture, a paternal grandfather's claim to a child, especially if he's an elder or a man of status and wealth, can trump even a mother's. My father's claim as king would be absolute without any foul play. I now understand that when Hesham begged me to find you, he hoped I'd find you *first,* so I would do this."

"This? You mean..."

"Marry you," he completed when she couldn't. "A mother can only gain power against a grandfather's claim if she's married to a man of equal status and wealth. My status might not be as lofty as his here, but my international status and assets are weightier. When I adopt Ryan, we'll have enough rights among us to outweigh my father's claim to him."

This was a dream come true.

And the worst nightmare she could have imagined.

Fareed was offering her marriage. But only because he thought Hesham had meant him to, to keep his child out of their father's clutches.

She'd already known she'd been just a lover to him. As intense as it had been, had she stayed at his insistence, he would have ended it sooner or later. He would have never offered her anything permanent. He would have never loved her.

She'd been grateful for that. She should be grateful now. For this proposal that would secure Ryan's future.

Even if it destroyed hers.

Fareed had thought he'd already hit rock bottom.

He'd thought he'd never know deeper misery than when he'd found out Gwen had been Hesham's worshipped lover, the mother of his child. Now he knew there were more depths to sink to. It seemed as long as Gwen was in his life, and that was now going to be forever, he'd never stop spiraling down.

He hadn't expected her to jump for joy when he'd mentioned marriage. But he'd thought even if her emotions weren't involved, that she wanted him, might welcome the idea of marrying him, at least see the benefit to her and to Ryan.

But it seemed nothing worse could have happened to her.

It seemed she'd suspended her grief in her gratitude

for him and relief over Ryan's cure. She'd plunged into sexual intimacies with him, but must have thought she'd been betraying Hesham's memory, and with his brother of all people. To ameliorate her guilt, she'd been promising herself she'd leave, and he'd never know. She might have thought that by disappearing and putting up with any subsequent hardship to protect her child and Hesham's, she'd atone for succumbing to her need to feel alive and desired again. It had all been bearable, as long as it remained temporary.

But now she'd found out it would turn permanent. She'd realized that the only way to protect Ryan was to marry him, Hesham's brother, when she'd been unable to marry Hesham himself. This looked as welcome to her as a dull knife through her heart.

He had to stop her punishing herself, assure her that he wouldn't be compounding her guilt.

His voice was as dead as he felt inside as he said, "I want you to know that I will never ask anything of you again. This is to give Ryan, and you as his mother, the Aal Zaafer name, what Hesham should have been able to give you, with all the privileges that you're both entitled to. This is also to give Ryan the father he needs, the only man on earth who'll love him like a true son."

He'd thought he'd seen her distraught before. But now, she looked as if her heart were fracturing, as if his every word crushed it.

He knew this pact would sentence him to a lifetime of deprivation, but he had to finish detailing it. "I'll give you the *essmuh*. In our culture, this means that you'll control the marriage. You'd be able to end it, if you so wish, without my consent. I'll also give you full power of attorney, giving you control of my assets. In case anything happens to me, I'll make a provision to circumvent our inheritance laws, so you'd inherit everything. If we're both gone, everything will be Ryan's. If he's not of age, anyone you choose would be his guardian until he is. This will make you as powerful as I am, will give my father no way to attack you even if I'm gone. As for our daily life, I'll be in Ryan's life however you choose me to be."

And he was done. Finished. She looked as annihilated.

He watched her sag to the couch, then turned around.

He heard a helicopter.

It was time to make this terrible pact securing Gwen and Ryan forever binding.

"Zawaj'toka nafsi."
I give you myself in marriage.

Gwen droned the words, her eyes glued to the pristine white handkerchief. Her hand was clasped with Fareed's beneath it. The cleric had his hand on top of theirs as he recited the Jizaanian marriage vows and prompted their repetition.

Emad and a guard were their witnesses. Rose and Ryan were present, one crying rivers, the other giggling a storm.

Soon the brief ritual was concluded and the cleric documented their marriage. She watched him drawing intricate script that looked as if he was casting spells, in a huge, ancient edition, the royal book of matrimony. Then he invited them to sign their vows and the details of the holy bargain they'd struck.

Fareed looked as if he was signing away his life.

Sinking deeper in misery, she signed, wishing she could sign her own. If only he'd take it, she would have.

One of the female servants let out a *zaghrootah,* a shrill, festive ululation. Rose—who thought this was all real in spite of the irregular circumstances she was just beginning to understand—was highly intrigued and tried to replicate the sound. Ryan was delighted and did his own ear-piercing imitations. Gwen felt her head might split open at any moment.

Fareed looked as pained at the unbridled mood as *sharbaat ward*—rose essence nectar—was distributed to those present in celebration of the happy marriage. But he endured it all with a stiff smile. He was the one who'd organized it after all.

She wondered why? It couldn't be because he was treating this as a real marriage. He'd told her in mutilating detail not to expect anything from him. Except everything she didn't want, that was. His status, his name, his wealth, in life and death. His heart had never been on offer. His passion, his ease and humor were things of the past. She wouldn't even have his companionship. She could only expect his presence where Ryan was involved.

She would have preferred it if he'd been enraged and outraged that she'd lied to him all this time. At least those would have been emotions, something to make her hope anything he'd felt for her survived, even if wounded. But he'd just turned off, as if he'd never felt a thing, not even on a physical level.

He hadn't even suspected her motives for hiding the truth. Didn't doubt she could be hiding even more. He'd just accepted her announced reasons, then proceeded to trust her with the sum total of his life and achievements.

But that wasn't for her, as he kept pointing out. That was for Hesham's woman, for Ryan's mother.

He was now probably putting on a show for those present, so they'd spread news of their marriage's authenticity. All for Hesham's memory, for Ryan's future.

None of it was for her.

And if he knew the whole truth, she'd lose even the crumbs he'd been forced to give her.

* * *

Tranquil waves frothed on the shore, erasing the names Fareed kept inscribing in the sand.

Gwen. Ryan. Gwen. Ryan.

He felt as if his world had emptied of anything but them.

It had been a week since they'd come here. He'd been away only to go the center for a few hours a day. When he returned, he hadn't been able to stay away from either of them all their waking hours. He had nothing but those. Longing for her kept him up nights, his mind and body on fire. He'd only slake it inside her, in her passion. And that was forever gone, too.

He might have survived it if he hadn't known what it was like with her, the pleasures that had enslaved his brother before him....

His thoughts convulsed on a torrent of regret. Jealousy and guilt were slowly poisoning him. And he could do nothing but let the emotions corrode him.

But at least his objective had been secured. He'd called every favor he was owed worldwide, had thrown money and influence at every obstacle in his path, and he'd gotten Ryan's adoption finalized. Gwen had been stunned when he'd told her in the morning.

Then this afternoon, she'd come out of the villa for the first time with Ryan, followed him as he'd paced the beach.

What had followed had been an unexpected torment, a simulation of the times they'd spent together as the family he'd thought they'd been forging. A glimpse of what might never, probably *would never* be. But then, whatever spontaneity and warmth he'd thought they'd shared had had probably been both of them responding to Ryan's delighted discovery of his surroundings, his tireless demand that they join him in frolicking in the sand and sea. Left to her own devices, she'd probably avoid him for life.

She would have.

Suddenly her scent carried to him even over the tanginess of the open sea. He braced himself, hating his weakness, the molten steel of ever-present desire that poured into his heart and loins.

"Ryan is finally sand-free."

He turned at her breathless declaration. She seemed to be floating to him in a full-length dress the sunlit color of her hair. It molded to her, accentuating her willowy splendor as if made for her. Seemed he *could* translate his obsessive knowledge of her every dip and curve and swell to ultra-precise fit. It was one of the dresses he'd had delivered for her because she'd left her belongings in his mansion. He'd never thought he could buy a woman clothes. Visualizing, fitting and buying them for *her* could turn into an addiction. As everything concerning her had.

She stopped before him, her skin and hair reflecting the radiance of the setting sun, her eyes the endlessness of the sky. Her warmth enveloped him, her hesitant smile pierced his vitals.

Then she reached out, almost touched him.

He wouldn't be able to resist such a brutal test. If she touched him, he'd drag her to the sand and take her. And she'd beg him to do everything to her. Then after the mindlessness of abandon, she'd sink into that misery that had so baffled him, that he now understood. He couldn't survive that of all things.

He caught her hand in midair, his jaw, his whole being rigid fighting the need to drag her by that supple hand, crush her beneath his aching flesh, ride her.

He hurt. Inside and out.

She pulled her hand away, her smile as shaky. "You have sand in your hair. Ryan bathed us both in it."

He gestured to her glowing cleanliness. "You're sand-free."

"Took a lot of heavy-duty scrubbing. The sand here is incredibly fine, like powdered gold."

He bit back a groan as the images and sensation bombarded him. He could almost feel his hands running down the smoothness of her slippery body as he lathered her, kneaded her under a steady jet of warm wetness, as he drove inside her tight, fluid heat, over and over until she climaxed around him, singed him with her pleasure. Then he would rinse her, caress and fondle her, whisper to her how she felt around him, what more he'd do to her as he brought her down from the pinnacle of pleasure, had her simmering for the next ride....

He exhaled forcibly, trying to expel the encroaching madness. "I'm glad Ryan enjoys the beach. Activities on the sand and in the sea are the best natural form of physiotherapy for him."

She bit her lower lip, made him feel she'd sunk those white teeth in his own, in his heart. "I never even took him to the pool. I was afraid to expose him to physical stress because I had no way of knowing if I'd be harming him. So it was his first exposure to the sea, and as you saw, he went berserk with delight."

He had been as thrilled as he could be in his condition with Ryan's joy. "We'll come here as often as possible, then."

She gave him such a look, hesitant, anxious, as if asking him what was to become of them, what kind of life they'd have.

What *did* she expect? They'd come here, they'd be together everywhere, where he'd be Ryan's father and her parenting partner, but never again her lover. They'd never be a real husband and wife and just a simulation of a family.

B'Ellahi, why was she here? Trying to smile and make small talk and shake sand out of his hair? Did she think he could be her easy companion now as he shared Ryan's upbringing?

Or *was* she considering resuming their intimacies because they were now married, for worse or worst?

Would he want this, if this were what she was after?

No. He'd either have all or none of her, couldn't share…

"Fareed, there's something I need…I *have* to confess to you."

His focus sharpened on her. Her incandescent beauty was now gilded by the lights emanating from the villa. The spasm of sheer love he felt for her, the enormity of it, suddenly crystallized one irrefutable fact.

He was wrong. He had been wrong. About everything he'd felt or thought since he'd found out she'd been Hesham's woman.

What she had been didn't matter. What she was did.

She was the woman he'd loved on sight, the only one who'd ever aroused his unadulterated desire, possessed his unqualified trust and admiration. She had been a selfless lover to his brother, then as sacrificing a mother to Ryan. She'd been the best thing that had ever happened to him, too, his life's first absolute intimacy. And he had been willing to give up anything, risk anything for her. His assets, his peace of mind, his hopes, his life. He now realized he could give up even more. He would.

He'd give up his jealousy, that Hesham had loved her first. His guilt over loving her when Hesham no longer could. His anguish over surviving when Hesham was no longer there.

But maybe she was already meeting him halfway. With this confession she wanted to make. He gestured for her to go ahead.

"You didn't question the reasons I stated for hiding Ryan's paternity…" She stopped, her agitation mounting.

He had to spare her. "There was nothing to question. You were doing what Hesham would have wanted you to do. He lived in fear of our father finding him and spoiling his life and yours. He clearly knew what Emad did, that our father *was* looking for him, not in the way I thought, out of anger. When he knew he'd die, he knew if he ever found you, you could lose Ryan to the man who almost destroyed him. My siblings and I were lucky because we had our mothers, whom everyone called the lioness, the Amazon and the harpy, to fend for us. But Hesham didn't. His mother died giving birth to him."

Her gaze wavered. "Hesham said your father never let anyone mention her to him as he grew up."

Fareed exhaled another of his frustrations with his father. "It *was* whispered around the kingdom that she couldn't withstand him, being this artistic, ethereal creature. It did seem that our father was so furious with her for being different from what he'd wanted, then for dying, that he banned any mention of her. When he realized Hesham was turning out like her, he did everything to force him into the mold he thought acceptable for a son of his. Hesham was right to fear our father and to instill that fear in you. If Ryan had fallen into his hands, he would have suffered an even worse fate because Hesham at least had us, older siblings who'd done all we could to temper his autocratic upbringing. So I understand that you had to hide the truth with all you had. I only wish you'd trusted me. At least, trusted Hesham's decision to entrust your and Ryan's futures to me."

She grabbed his forearm, urgency emanating from her. "I trusted you with Ryan's *life,* with *both* our lives when I came to the land I feared most on the strength of nothing but my belief in you. But it's more complicated than you think. And when we…we…"

"Became lovers?" He placed his hand on top of hers before she could retract it. "I *can* see how this made you feel more trapped. But after I was furious with Emad when he revealed the truth, then told my father, I can't be more thankful to him now. Like we say here, *assa an takraho shai wa hwa khayronn lakom*."

She nodded. *"You may hate something and it's for your best."*

He smiled. "I'll never stop being impressed by how good your Arabic is. Hesham taught you well."

She blushed. *Blushed.* With pleasure at his praise. And at the ease with which he now referred to Hesham, and the beauty of the relationship she'd shared with him?

Then her color deepened to distress again. "But Emad didn't find out the full truth. And when you know it, you won't find acceptable excuses for my half truths."

He took her by the shoulders. "No, Gwen, whatever you hid, I'm on your side, and only on your side, always."

The tears gathered in her eyes slipped down the velvet of her cheeks as she nodded. "Hesham said your father told him his life story when he was fifteen. He said he married three women, one after the other for political and tribal obligations, had children from each, sometimes almost simultaneously." Fareed knew well the story of his father and his four wives and ten children. He had a feeling she'd tell him things he didn't know. "But he didn't love any of them."

"It was mutual, I assure you."

Gwen winced. "Yes. Then he met Hesham's mother and

they fell in love on sight." Fareed's jaw dropped. *That* he surely didn't know. He believed his father was love-proof, let alone to the on-sight variety. "But even if his marriages were to serve the kingdom, she wouldn't be a fourth wife. So he divorced his wives wholesale, and dealt with the catastrophic political fallout."

He was only six when this happened. He still remembered the upheavals. "My mother and the other two women say it was the best day of their lives when they finally got rid of him."

She nodded. "It was how he convinced Hesham's mother to marry him. She feared if he could divorce the mothers of his children so easily, that she couldn't trust him. So he let her interview them and they told her it was what they longed for, how they, like him, had felt trapped in the marriages, that he'd never loved anyone but her in his life. He pledged only death would part *them*.

"Their marriage was deliriously happy, and when she got pregnant, he told her he'd love her child the most of his children. But she died, and he almost went insane. He at first hated the son he blamed for killing his love. Then as Hesham grew up and he saw her in him, he transferred all his love and expectations and obsessions to him. He ordered no one to mention her because it made him crazy with grief."

Fareed felt more disoriented than when his father's guard had struck him. "And it seems I will keep finding that I know nothing about those I considered my closest people."

She shut her eyes. "Th-there's more. Much more."

"Then *arjooki,* please, tell me everything."

She drew in a shaky breath. "What nobody knew is that a few years after Hesham's mother's death, her tribe, the royal family of Durrah, invoked an ancient Jizaanian law.

That if a king married more than one woman, the sons of his highest-ranking wife would succeed him to the throne, with no respect to age. Since Hesham's mother was a pure-blood princess, that made Hesham the crown prince."

He stared at her, beyond flabbergasted.

This…this…explained so much. Yet was totally inexplicable.

Not that he considered disbelieving her for a second.

But he had to ask. "*Kaif?* How could my father hide something like this? How is that not common knowledge?"

"Your father pledged to Hesham's maternal relatives that Hesham would be his crown prince. On one condition—that they reveal this to no one until he prepared his kingdom and his other sons, especially the one who lived his life believing he was his heir, for the change in succession. But most important, until he prepared Hesham for the role he'd be required to fill. They agreed, in a binding blood oath. The king told Hesham when he turned fifteen and your oldest brother, although still in confidence. Hesham said Abbas was sorry for him, if relieved for himself. He didn't relish being crown prince."

Fareed could believe that. Abbas was a swashbuckling, extreme-sport-loving, corporate-raiding daredevil. He dreaded the day he'd have to give up the wildness and freedom of his existence to step into their father's shoes. He always said, only half-jokingly, that the day of his *joloos* on the throne he'd turn the kingdom into a democracy and be on his way.

But it was making more sense by the second, explaining the infuriating enigma of his father.

"So this was why Father pressured Hesham to that extent. He was trying to turn him into the crown prince he knew he wasn't equipped to become."

"Yes, and this was why he so objected to…to…"

"To his choosing you. He must have had some pure-blood royal bride lined up for him, too. This does explain why he reacted so viciously to Hesham's news that he was marrying you."

"But even with Hesham gone, Ryan…"

"Wait, Hesham meant Ryan's name the way I pronounce it, the Arabic version, didn't he? But he picked it because it worked in your culture, too, with a different meaning."

She nodded, her urgency heightening at what she considered unimportant now. "What I was saying is that Ryan might still be considered the king's first-in-line heir. And this is why he might never give up trying to get custody of him."

He ran his hands down his face. "*Ya Ullah.* I see how your fear of our father is a thousand times what I believed it should be. But you no longer have to worry. Even a king's claim to his rightful heir wouldn't trump our combined custody."

"You might be wrong…"

His raised hand silenced her. Ominous thunder was approaching from the darkness that had engulfed the sea.

A helicopter. He would bet his center it was carrying his father. This had to be Emad's doing.

His fury crested as he turned to Gwen. "Go inside, please. I'll deal with this."

"Fareed, let me tell you first…"

But he was already running to meet the helicopter as it landed, needing to end this before it started. And to end Gwen's worries once and for all.

The moment his father stepped out of the helicopter that, to Fareed's fury, Emad was piloting, Fareed blocked his way.

"Father, go back where you came from. Gwen told me

everything. And it's over. Ryan will never be in your custody."

Challenge flared in his father's eyes. "I'm surprised you even think your 'adoption' is a deterrent. Our laws don't sanction adoption, just fostering, and adopting him according to another culture's laws means nothing."

"The deterrent is not only that Ryan has the Aal Zaafer name through me, not Hesham. It is that I'll give up my Jizaanian nationality if it will make my adoption binding anywhere in the world, starting with here. But most of all it is that I, a man of equal status to you and superior wealth, am married to Ryan's mother."

The king only transferred his gaze behind him. Gwen had followed him, was almost plastered to his back.

Then, without taking his eyes off her, his father said, "That is not your greatest weapon but your greatest weakness, Fareed. Gwen isn't Ryan's mother. She's his aunt."

Thirteen

Fareed heard his father's declaration. He understood the words. He couldn't make any sense of them.

Still looking at Gwen, his father addressed her this time, "It was your sister, Marilyn, who was Hesham's woman."

After all these months, Fareed had a full name for Hesham's Lyn. Marilyn. Not Gwendolyn.

He turned, no longer of his own volition, but under her agitation's compulsion.

She was looking at him, and only at him, her eyes flooded with imploring. Certainty was instantaneous, absolute.

She wasn't Hesham's woman. Wasn't Ryan's mother.

They would register. The import and impact of this knowledge. They would crash on him and rewrite his existence. But not now.

Now only one thing mattered.

He turned to his father. "It makes no difference. Ryan is Gwen's and you're not getting him."

His father's expression was one he well knew. A "you dare?" and a "dream on" rolled into one eyebrow raise.

Before he did something irretrievable, his father said, "I won't continue this discussion standing by a helicopter on a beach. Anyone would get the impression I'm not welcome."

"You're not," Fareed growled, aborting his father's stride. "And this discussion is over. There is nothing to discuss. And don't try to pull rank. You're not king here. I am."

His father ignored him, looked at Gwen. "And you're queen here. You won't invite your father-in-law into your home, even if your husband is rude enough not to?"

"Leave Gwen out of this, Father. I'm warning you…"

Gwen's hand on his arm stopped his tirade.

Then she stepped in front of him. "It would be an honor and a pleasure to receive you in o-our home, Your Majesty."

Fareed wanted to hug the breath right out of her, emotions colliding inside him. Pride and delight, at how she held herself, addressed his father, the effect her graciousness and classiness had on the old goat. Delight that she'd said *our* home. Oppression that she'd hesitated while saying it. But mostly, dread of letting his father deeper into their lives under any pretext.

He watched his father take Gwen's elbow as she led the way back into the villa. He walked a step behind, felt Emad fall into step with him. He only spared him a gritted "Later."

His father tossed him a glance. "Later, I might take him off your hands. It appears I've been remiss in estimating his worth."

"I'll make you a gift of him. It appears I've overestimated it."

Emad grunted something, the very sound of politeness.
To Fareed's versed-in-his-noises ears, it sounded like a
grown-up groaning at the posturing antics of two juvenile
charges.

Once inside the villa, Gwen turned to his father. "We
were about to have dinner. I hope you'll be able to join us.
If you don't like seafood, I'll get something else prepared
right away."

"The only time we met, I insulted and threatened you."
The king's regard turned thoughtful. "Even if I abhorred
seafood, it would still be better than crow."

Fareed blinked. Had his father just cracked a joke?

He could think of only one explanation for this aberra-
tion. He got his confirmation in Gwen's crimson discom-
fiture.

"Oh, no, you don't, Father. I'm damned if I let you play
on Gwen's sympathies. You're not some kind, bereaved old
man, so you can quit trying to blindside us into lowering
our guard right now. We're not letting you get your hands
on Ryan."

His father gave him a considering glance. "What have
you told her I'd do when this comes to pass?"

"No 'when' here. And it was Hesham who told her—"
he tried again to adjust to the fact that it hadn't been her
Hesham had told, had loved "—told her *sister* that you
almost loved him to death, pressuring and coercing and
hounding him into becoming the heir you would find acceptable." Suddenly he couldn't stand not knowing. He
swung his gaze to Gwen. "What happened to your sister?"

He knew the answer. If not from the fact that she had
Ryan, then from the grief that he'd felt dimming her spirit.
She'd been mourning her sister. How had she died?

He hated to resurrect her pain, her loss. But he needed knowledge to stop his father's incursion, especially now that he was using unexpected weapons.

He still almost retracted his question when mention of her sister reopened her wounds right before his eyes.

But she was already answering. "After the accident, they gave her only a preliminary exam. M-Marilyn was told she was fine. They discharged her to make room for those with obvious injuries. Hesham had already…" Her tears ran faster. "By the time I got to her she was deteriorating. I rushed her to another hospital, but she hung on only long enough to start my adoption of Ryan and give me her and Hesham's last will. I knew everything already because I more or less shared their lives, moving everywhere when they did. I stayed even closer after I realized something was wrong with Ryan…"

"So you *were* the one who diagnosed him."

A tear splashed on his hand, burning him through to his soul. "When he was four months old. But Hesham feared seeking you out."

He rounded on his father, snarling, "*That's* why you're not coming near Ryan, Father. Because Hesham feared you so much he wouldn't seek my help for his son, his own brother, the best-equipped to offer that help, until he was on his deathbed."

His father ignored his wrath, addressing Gwen directly. "But your adoption of Ryan hasn't been concluded yet."

Fareed felt his head about to explode.

It almost did when Gwen said, "It's still pending." That imploring that compromised his sanity intensified. "That's what I was trying to tell you. I expected you to find out when your legal team discovered I'm not the birth mother, and my adoption hasn't been finalized. But they somehow got *your* adoption approved without this coming to light."

His daze deepened. "I told them not to bother me with details, to just do *anything* to get my adoption through."

His father tsked. "Seems *anything* included falsifying data. Once a discrepancy is found, the adoption might be invalidated."

He erupted. "No, it won't. Go ahead. Do your worst, Father. I'm getting this fixed, and Ryan will be Gwen's and mine, legally, anywhere in the world, no matter what you do. I'll fight you, I'll fight Jizaan and Durrah and the whole world for him, for Gwen's right to be his mother. And I'll win. Ryan will never be anyone's but Gwen's, the one who loves him, who sacrificed all for him."

His father only sighed. "Have I ever told you how much I wish *you* were my heir?"

"You know better than to try to appeal to my ego, Father."

"No, you're right. What I wish is irrelevant. In matters of state, it always is. I hope Abbas will come around when it's time for him to take my place. He might not think so, but he'd make a formidable king. While you are more ben-eficial to Jizaan and the world being who you are, where you are."

"We're not talking matters of state here. I mean it, Father. I won't let you near Ryan."

"But it's not up to you." He turned to Gwen. "I would see my grandson now, *ya marat ebni.*"

At hearing his father calling her "my son's wife," Gwen's eyes filled.

Fareed stopped her as she moved. "You don't have to."

Those eyes that were his world glittered with too much that they took his breath away. "He has more right to Ryan than I do."

"That's not true," he gritted. "You *are* his mother."

Twin tears slithered down her face as she tore her gaze away and hurried out of the room.

He stood glaring at his father as they waited for her to come back. She did in minutes, hugging a flushed-with-sleep Ryan.

At the sight of him, Ryan perked up with the smiles and sounds he bestowed on no one else. He was endlessly thankful for that, for he did love Ryan as if he were his own.

Then Ryan realized Gwen was taking him elsewhere and turned to investigate his new destination.

Ryan blinked and looked back at Fareed as if to make sure he hadn't teleported.

Fareed's jaw bunched. Surely Ryan didn't think he resembled his father *that* much? And even if they did share much of their looks, he couldn't possibly feel the same vibes from him!

Next moment, Ryan buried his face into Gwen's bosom. *That* was more like it.

Before satisfaction seethed inside Fareed's chest, he saw Ryan peeking shyly, inquisitively, *interestedly* at his father from the depths of Gwen's chest, and his tension roared back.

His father spoke, his voice rough with emotion, "*Ya Ullah,* this is Hesham as an infant all over again."

"That's not true," Fareed hissed. "Ryan is a replica of Gwen…of her sister, his mother."

His father turned to him with dazed eyes shimmering with what suspiciously looked like tears. "His coloring is throwing you off and that dimpled chin. But I am the one who hung on Hesham's every detail from birth. He has his same bone structure, the shape of his features. And wait until his hair grows out. It will be the exact color and curl as Hesham's. He'll also be like his father in many other ways. Isn't that right, *ya ebni?*"

Ryan squirmed excitedly in Gwen's arms as if he understood what the king was saying, and that he'd called him "my son." Then the king reached out to him, and with one last look at Gwen and Fareed, as if he was asking their permission, Ryan reached back.

Fareed's mind almost snapped when a tiny whimper escaped Gwen as she let Ryan go. He was about to snatch him back when her hand on his arm stopped him. He wouldn't have stopped if he'd seen dread filling her eyes. But what he saw there…it was something truly feminine, knowing, almost…serene.

He stood beside her, confounded, watched his father caress Ryan, murmur things for his ears only, what Ryan clearly liked.

When the introduction between child and grandfather seemed concluded, and they seemed to have come to an understanding, Ryan made his wish to be held by Fareed clear.

Fareed took him, feeling as if he was returning his own heart to his chest.

Silence reigned for endless moments.

His father finally let out a shuddering exhalation. "I have been more than half-mad since I lost my Kareemah." He looked at Fareed. "You might now realize how it was for me."

Fareed grudgingly had to concede that. If he lost Gwen…

He couldn't even think of it.

"Is that your excuse for what you did to her son and yours?"

"I thought I was honoring her memory, making her son my heir. But I wasn't sane most of the time. Not when it came to Hesham. He had too much of her, inspired in me the same overwhelming emotions." Suddenly his father seemed to let go of the invincibility he cloaked himself in, seemed to age twenty years over his sixty-five. "Now it's too late to right my wrongs. I'm the reason he's lost."

Gwen took an urgent step toward him, her eyes anxious, adamant. "You may be the reason for many things, but not that, Your Majesty. *Never* blame yourself for that. The accident that cost you your son, cost Fareed his brother and me my sister, was an act of blind fate. But I want you to know Hesham and Lyn *didn't* live in fear. While Hesham took hiding to unbelievable lengths, he and Lyn soon approached it all as an adventure, one they included me in. I never saw anyone more in love or delighted with every second they had together. The shadow of separation only made them appreciate every breath they had of each other. So in a way, you were to thank for the extraordinary relationship they had."

His father swayed and reached for the nearest chair, only to collapse in it, dropping his head into his hands.

Fareed stood frozen, watching this unprecedented sign that his father was human.

He finally raised reddened eyes, looking at Gwen. "I wish I could have met your mother, *ya bnayti*." Gwen started at hearing him call her "my daughter." "She must have been a remarkable woman to raise not only you, a woman who possesses such generosity, you'd offer me this absolution, this solace, after the injustices I dealt you and yours, but to raise *two* women who had my most fastidious sons think their lives are a small price to pay to have them. That was the kind of woman my Kareemah was. I hope she had a man worship her as she deserved, as I worshiped my Kareemah."

Gwen shook her head, her eyes as red. "Regretfully,

no. Our father took off while she was still pregnant with Marilyn. She raised us alone until an accident in the factory she worked in left her paralyzed from the waist down. She died from the complications of a spinal surgery years later, with only me and Marilyn with her. We changed our names to McNeal, her maiden name, because she was our only parent, our whole family."

Those were more shocking revelations to Fareed. More insights illuminating Gwen's life and character and choices.

"Your father had better be dead, too, or I will avenge her," his father rumbled as he rose.

Gwen started in alarm. "Oh, no. He's not worth it." Then she gave him a tremulous smile. "And then Mom always said it was the best thing that happened to all of us that he walked. She was happy without him. We were happy together. What happened afterward...blind fate was again to blame."

Fareed hugged her into him, unable to bear her losses, the gratitude that she'd survived it all, that he'd found her.

His father approached, his steps not completely steady. "I was only stating facts when I mentioned your pending adoption...."

Fareed cut him off. "Adoption or not, I will fight you, and I will win."

His father looked at Gwen. "Will you hold your dragon of a husband back?"

Gwen stared at him. Fareed did, too. A shaken king was unbelievable enough. An indulgent one had to be a hallucination.

His father exhaled. "I came here to negotiate, and that's why Emad let me come. But I won't now. Not because I believe you would triumph over me in any fight, Fareed. And not because I've learned a lesson I'll never recover from with Hesham. It's because seeing you together, talking to Gwen and meeting Ryan has changed everything. Gwen has given me a reason to live again with her forgiveness, on her own behalf and that of Hesham and her sister. I'm not losing this reason or more of my flesh and blood to the demands of duty and pride." He placed a hand on each of their shoulders. "You are Ryan's mother, Gwen. I will swear to that to the world, starting with the Aal Durrah. Ryan will be your heir, Fareed. While I only want to remain part of your lives, if you would have me."

Fareed gaped at him. He'd never...ever...

His stupefaction was interrupted by another surprise.

Gwen threw herself at his father, clung around his neck, reiterating, "Thank you, thank you."

His father was as taken aback. It took him long moments before he brought his shock under control and hugged her back.

At last he put her at arm's length, looked down at her. "You are all heart, aren't you? But you don't have to accept me. Your husband *can* get me off your backs permanently if he so wishes."

Her smile trembled up at him. "I don't want him to. And Ryan doesn't either. He wants his grandfather. He... recognized you, like he recognized Fareed."

"He was *far* more eager with me," Fareed protested.

His father *dared* placate him. "Of course he was. He knows his priorities, recognized you'd be the one who would be constantly present in his life and therefore in need of more intensive...humoring."

Fareed harrumphed. "With all due respect, Father..."

His father suddenly laughed. "I think you left it too late to even mention respect where I'm concerned, Fareed."

"Fine, we won't mention it. But even though I am thankful for your change of heart—make that flabbergasted by it, not to mention distressed that I have to revise my opinion of you, and of my whole life, and we do have to discuss the past, present and future down to the last detail later—please, *go away now.*"

The king went away. Eventually. After the dinner Gwen had invited him to.

She was sorry she had. Not because it didn't turn out to be beyond her wildest expectations. It was because Fareed constantly looked about to explode with wanting him gone.

He didn't, thankfully, but he kept prodding him with demands to eat faster. He even cut up his food so he'd finish it sooner.

Now everyone was gone. She was alone with Fareed.

She wanted to do one thing. Beg. His forgiveness.

Before she found the words, he said, "Tell me. Everything."

Everything was made of one simple statement. "Lyn was with me during that conference party."

He looked at her as if he was revisualizing the past. It was as intense a gaze as what had mesmerized her during that conference. And changed her life forever.

"And Hesham was with me. I walked out, but he stayed behind, approached her."

She nodded. "I didn't notice much that night, but she told me later it was love at first sight."

"And the rest is history."

She had nothing to add. Not about this. But she had so much to say about everything else.

Words rushed under pressure. "I never dreamed your father could be this way. Hesham and Lyn made me dread him so much I…"

He waved away her explanations. "You had every right to expect the worst. I myself can't believe what happened still, am wondering if he's biding his time until he can pull something."

"I *know* he won't. But I wanted to be the one to tell you the whole truth, and…I left it too late."

The weight of his gaze increased. "Why *didn't* you tell me?"

She'd probably lose everything answering him. She probably had already. But whatever happened, she owed him a full confession. "I believed I'd just pass through your life, and I'd be risking losing Ryan by revealing my weaker claim to him, weaker than yours, let alone your father's. I *did* trust you, but I thought if you knew, your father eventually would. But I should have told you. You married me because I didn't. I was still hoping that my adoption would come through and the marriage would serve its purpose. But we now know Ryan will be safe, so the marriage no longer serves any purpose. Now you can…end it."

His eyes had been flaring and subsiding like fanned coals. Now they went almost black. "I gave you the *essmuh*."

"Then…take it back."

"It doesn't work that way. Only you can end it now."

So this was it. Moment of truth. He would have never chosen to be her husband. But he would remain in this non-marriage for Ryan's sake or if she didn't release him.

"H-how do I do that?"

"You just tell me. The rest is just paperwork. It's the words, the intention, that are binding."

She looked at him. The only man she'd ever or would ever love. She'd be forever empty when he left her life. But she'd be destroyed if she clung to him when he didn't reciprocate.

And she let go. "I…end it."

* * *

Gwen closed Ryan's nursery door lost in dark musings.

Would he miss her if she left? Did he even need her anymore? Now that he had Fareed, his grandfather and an extensive family to love and cherish him? Or was she the one who needed him? He who was everything she had left to live for?

Fareed was probably realizing this now. That her role in Ryan's life had been as temporary as it had been in his. She'd protected him until she'd delivered him into the hands of those capable of giving him the love and life he deserved.

But knowing Fareed, out of kindness, he wouldn't say anything. He hadn't said anything as she'd given him back his freedom. But he must have welcomed it. Chivalry and honor aside, he'd probably welcome her disappearance from his life completely, would prefer not to have her in it through their connection to Ryan.

She approached the bedroom he'd given her. The one farthest from his. She'd hoped he'd cut her off from his passion because he'd thought she was his brother's woman, that when she confessed, his desire would be reignited.

But it had just been extinguished. The bad taste of her duplicity, however he mentally rationalized and accepted it, must have put out the lust that would have burned itself out sooner rather than later.

God, what was she still doing here? He no longer wanted her. Ryan no longer needed her. She had to go away now. She'd solve all their problems this way. She'd unburden Fareed of her presence, and Ryan was too young, he'd forget her in a month.

As for her, she might be less miserable without them, than with them and unwanted and unneeded. She might even survive.

She wouldn't if she stayed.

She opened the door, hesitated on the threshold.

What was she doing here anyway? She didn't need to gather her stuff. It wasn't hers in the first place. Nothing here had ever been hers.

She'd leave like she'd come, with nothing.

And this time, Fareed wouldn't come running to stop her. He'd stand by and would be relieved to see her go. He might even help…

"Do you know what I wanted to do when I saw you standing on that podium?"

Goose bumps stormed through her. The deep purr, like a coiled predator's, issued from the bed.

Fareed.

She grabbed at the light switch, her hand hitting and missing it many times before soft, indirect light illuminated him.

He was wearing an *abaya* again, both it and the loose pants beneath, white and gold trimmed this time. His hair gleamed wet and sooty from a shower, his skin glowed with the same bronze of the headboard he was propped against, with his legs stretched out almost to the end of the bed, crossed at the ankles.

He hurt her with his beauty.

What was he doing here? What did he mean when he asked…

His voice drowned everything again, answering his own question. "I wanted to walk up to you, gather your papers, tell you that you didn't need to solicit the world's approval or endorsement anymore, that you have mine, that I would put everything that I have at your disposal. Then I wanted to haul you over my shoulder and take you where I can ravish you."

She'd walked up to the bed. Was looking down at him. Was she dreaming this?

But he was saying things she hadn't even dreamed he'd say.

And he was saying more, infinitely better than any dream. "Then I discovered you were engaged. I was enraged, stunned. How could you not wait for me? I was also noble, *stupid* and I walked away. Four years of stoic deprivation later, you tell me you walked out of that conference and on that fiancé I fantasized about exiling to some undiscovered island."

His hand clasped hers, tugged her down. She fell over him, disbelief and debilitating relief racing through her. He melted her softness and longing into his hardness and demand. She shook, gasped, resuscitation surging from his every word and touch.

"Then instead of our siblings paving the way for our being together, everything they did kept us apart and it took a string of tragedies to unite us as we should have been from that first day."

He dissolved clothes that felt like thorns off her inflamed flesh as he spoke. She writhed in his arms, a flame igniting higher as he tore off his own clothes, the feel of his flesh her fuel.

He crushed her lips under his, breached her in a tongue-thrusting kiss that had her begging for his invasion now, no buildup, just total, instant possession.

He rolled her over, pressed his flesh onto her every exposed inch, driving her into the bed. "Then you were mine, then you were not, then you were my wife, but not really, then you set me free, when my freedom lies in making you mine, in being yours."

"You mean...you really wanted...this?" she gasped.

"Want is a flimsy, insubstantial emotion. Does it feel

like this to you?" He pressed the red-hot length of his erection, of every cabled muscle and sinew into her. Nothing flimsy or insubstantial there; everything invincible, enduring.

"I meant...you told me the marriage was only for Ryan, and to fulfill Hesham's last request."

"What would *you* tell the woman you were disintegrating for, if she looked like she was breaking up inside with grief and guilt, if you thought it was over your dead brother, and that she was hating you and herself for succumbing to your seduction and her needs? And when you're buried under misconceptions, would you tell her, and yourself, to get over that trivial matter of a beloved dead lover and brother, demand she be your wife for real?"

She gaped at him. And gaped some more. What he was saying...

Everything she hadn't been creative enough, daring enough, to hope for. His own version of her own misconceptions.

But one thing she couldn't get her head around yet. "You mean...you would have asked me to marry you... anyway?"

"Why so disbelieving? You wanted me from the moment you saw me, too. And you wanted me forever because it was how I wanted you. But I wasn't going to propose yet because I thought I first had to battle your issues with my family's clout and your fear of being a kept woman. Little did I know that, although those might have been considerations under other circumstances, you were only bound on sacrificing your heart for Ryan's safety."

She shook a head spinning with the revelations and re-alizations. "Fareed...I—I...can't..."

"Yes, you can, Gwen. Like you let me go, to be noble and self-sacrificing again, you can take me back. I'm giving you all that I am again, this time when you know it's all for you. Because I fell in love with you from that first moment, thought I'd be alone forever if I didn't have you."

"Fareed, oh, my love..."

He captured her hot gasp. "Say this again."

"I might never say anything else ever again. I've loved you from that first moment, too, knew that if I can't have you, I'd never want anyone else. Then..."

"Then everything happened. But we found each other again, and this, what we share, is worth every heartache we endured getting here, earning it. And even though Hesham and Lyn are gone, they left us Ryan, the most beautiful part of them. We'll continue to love them both in him, and he'll have us both to love."

"He...uh...might soon have more...people to love," she mumbled.

He stared at her. "You mean..."

She felt a flush spreading over her. "Too early to be sure, but...most probably." She hid her face into his chest, burning. "That's why I never mentioned protection. I wanted to have your baby, thought it would be all I had of you."

He turned her face up to his, his smile delight itself. "Same here." Then whimsy quirked his lips. "I shudder to think what more complications we could have had if we weren't already on the same wavelength."

She pulled his head down to hers, took his lips in a kiss that pledged him everything, melded them for life. "I'll tell you all I can think of. You. All of you. Your flesh in mine, your pleasure, your happiness, your existence."

And he joined them, took her, gave her, pledged back, "Then take all of me, for life, *ya hayati*. For you *are* my life."

* * * * *

The World of Mills & Boon

There's a Mills & Boon® series that's perfect for you. There are ten different series to choose from and new titles every month, so whether you're looking for glamorous seduction, Regency rakes, homespun heroes or sizzling erotica, we'll give you plenty of inspiration for your next read.

By Request
Relive the romance with the best of the best
12 stories every month

Cherish™
Experience the ultimate rush of falling in love.
12 new stories every month

INTRIGUE...
A seductive combination of danger and desire...
7 new stories every month

Desire™
Passionate and dramatic love stories
6 new stories every month

nocturne™
An exhilarating underworld of dark desires
3 new stories every month

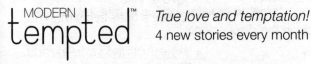

MILLS & BOON®

Why shop at millsandboon.co.uk?

Each year, thousands of romance readers find their perfect read at millsandboon.co.uk. That's because we're passionate about bringing you the very best romantic fiction. Here are some of the advantages of shopping at www.millsandboon.co.uk:

* **Get new books first**—you'll be able to buy your favourite books one month before they hit the shops

* **Get exclusive discounts**—you'll also be able to buy our specially created monthly collections, with up to 50% off the RRP

* **Find your favourite authors**—latest news, interviews and new releases for all your favourite authors and series on our website, plus ideas for what to try next

* **Join in**—once you've bought your favourite books, don't forget to register with us to rate, review and join in the discussions

Visit **www.millsandboon.co.uk**
for all this and more today!

MILLS_WEB